OUT OF NIGIRO

(nee-JHEE-row)

A novel

PATRICIA HOPKINS

OUT OF NIGIRO

Visit my website at http://www.patriciarhopkins.com

Published in the United States by Wanderlust Books

Cover art photo by fellow artist Anthony C. Kaczka

ISBN-13: 978-0-9914491-3-2 (Paperback)

THIS NOVEL IS DEDICATED TO ALL THE MISSING
AND EXPLOITED CHILDREN WHO NEVER MADE IT
HOME.

MAY THE ALMIGHTY GOD PROTECT AND KEEP
YOU.

...I AM YOU

YOU ARE ME

WE ARE ONE

BY PATRICIA HOPKINS

~~~NOVELS~~~

LOST IN THE OFFBEAT

LOVING IN THE OFFBEAT

LIVING IN THE OFFBEAT

MORE THAN A NOTION

~~~SHORT STORIES COLLECTION~~~

I AM THE SHADOWMAN (AND OTHER
SUPERNATURAL TALES)

OLD GRACIOLA YOUNG

INVASION OF THE GLOBOTS

~ ~ ~ Dedications~ ~ ~

Zander, Noni, Dayvion, LaNiyah, Sunny, Lavon, Alex, Joey, Hollybear, Korina

Working to leave the world a better place than I found it.

For you.

***

To all my loved ones who received their angel wings in 2020;

Soar high... Be free!

OUT OF NIGIRO

Prologue

The three countries my parents named me after are Kenya, Mali, and Zambia. When I was younger, I asked what was so special about those particular African countries. Was this the land of our ancestors? Had they ever visited Africa? The responses were not what I expected. My dad simply shrugged and told me to go ask my mother. My mom's response was slightly more interesting on why she chose my name.

She told me that several relatives on my father's side had discovered their people originated in Mali long before the Transatlantic slave trade, purported to have begun in the 15th century, ever happened. When my parents learned that 'Mali' was known as "the place where the king lives", they considered it an appropriate name for their baby girl. By naming me 'Zambia', one day we all might be lucky enough to travel to the country to actually see the magnificent Victoria Falls in person. And my mom chose 'Kenya' because it is a beautiful country, and well... she finally admitted, the word Kenya sounded *pretty*. Confessing that her knowledge about Africa was basically non-existent, she wanted me to have a connection to the Motherland. And by naming me after those three countries, I would never forget my ancestral roots.

Because I was named after those magnificent African nations, I made it my goal to learn as much as I could about each country. Well, as much as possible for a young child. Thus, for every birthday thereafter, I asked my parents if we were any closer to visiting Africa. Every year, they gave me the same answer, *'We don't have the money for a family trip to Africa. Maybe next year...'*. You would think that after years of receiving the same response, I would have given up. But I never did. I persistently tended to that little seed of hope presented to me when I first learned the origins of my name; refusing to give up until the branches of that tree, laden heavy with the weight of my parents unfulfilled wishes, bore ripened fruit enough to nourish all our souls.

Due to my parent's unconventional method of selecting my name, it was not a coincidence that I ended up being their most inquisitive child. My father often remarked that I asked too many questions about subjects I had no business questioning. My mom thought I was trying to get attention because I was the only girl, as well as the middle child. My response was, I came by my curiosity honestly because I was from the 'Show Me' state. No one took exception to that explanation. From the moment I learned to put together my first sentence, I was the child who needed to know the why's and the how's. Visiting relatives noticed how 'smart' I was for my age when to my parent's chagrin, I often interrupted their adult conversations with comments and challenging questions.

My brothers, Malcolm and Stokely, and I grew up watching reruns of *The Outer Limits, Twilight Zone, Night Gallery, X-Files, Star Trek, Star Wars* and any other television show that expanded the limits of our youthful imagination to seek the possibilities existing in the unknown. As we grew older, my brothers' fascination with space and aliens was replaced by girls and sports. My curiosity never went away. Every free moment was spent on the internet searching for information about planets, stars, the Sun and the Moon.

I'm sure my obsession with extraterrestrial life can't totally be attributed to watching television, because I've had recurring dreams about aliens arriving in magnificent spaceships and coming down to sweep me away, for as long as I can remember. The notion of beings existing in another time, place, or dimension was firmly planted in my young impressionable mind. The thought of actually seeing an ET was more cool than terrifying to me.

Studying celestial bodies eventually became my hobby. I tried to get my family interested, but nothing ever stuck. In fact, my brothers used to tease me because I welcomed the sunrise with a proclamation of *'Good Morning Sunshine!'* and at night I whispered, *'Goodnight Moonlight!'* In my mind, acknowledging the sun and moon was like greeting loved ones I hadn't seen for days.

Although my family didn't join in my interests, I participated in theirs. I often watched the evening news with my dad. He'd get so upset! Screaming at politicians who made promise after promise to black folks but never delivered. It did not matter if they were local, state, or national. All politicians—Republican, Democrat, Independent—were all the same in his eyes regardless of their party affiliation. He then told me that black people are the most faithful people in this country. When I asked what he meant, he explained, 'for decades black people have wholeheartedly supported the Democrats, no matter how often those jokers failed to deliver on their campaign promises, yet we kept voting them back into office'.

He was angry because those elected officials didn't return to our community until it was re-election time. The media called it 'pandering', but my daddy called it 'shucking and jiving' when they pulled out bottles of hot sauce from their purse, claimed they smoked weed and listened to hip-hop, knew how to 'do the dougie', played the saxophone, and could sing a few bars of a gospel song. In his mind, ambitious politicians lied to the voters and made empty promises they had no intention of keeping to get elected into office at the local level. Then to reach the state level, they made more promises. To reach the national level, more promises were made to cover the ones they lied about before. He posed the question, 'At what point in their ambitious careers do they think they can stop lying?'.

Though I did not understand his frustrations, that did not stop him from assuming I did. One day, he straight up asked me, *'at what point will we, as a people, stop supporting a party that takes our vote for granted with no intention of ever making our lives better?'* The biggest lesson I learned watching the evening news was that those in positions of power don't always play fair.

From the moment I had the ability to string two thoughts together, I knew something was not quite right in this world. Things didn't add up. I simply could not understand why our country was involved in so many never-ending wars. Why the level of poverty in the most powerful country in the world continued to increase? It didn't make sense that so many of the people around me struggled while others seemed to have it so easy. The older I became, the more I questioned everything.

My dear sisters and brothers, I have provided these details of my childhood to help explain why I am sharing my story. Some will read through to the end and consider this as only as an unbelievable fantastical tale. I caution those doubters to take heed; this is an account of what happened to me and a warning of what is yet to come for you.

Chapter One

My family and I lived north of St. Louis, Missouri, in an area of the city where up to a few years ago, was known as 'the hood'. It was not yet considered a desirable place to live. My hometown never made the top one hundred on any list except 'cities with the highest crime rate'. The local news bombarded us with stories backing up that statistic, providing confirmation to all that the north side was still the ghetto and should never truly be considered as safe. But that declaration did not stop greedy real estate investors from beating down the doors and offering cash-strapped residents only pennies on the dollar to buy up their family homes. Despite what the news articles said, *they* considered our neighborhood to be a hot market in an 'up and coming area'. For those of us who actually lived on the north side, we didn't want to reside anywhere else.

The once crime infested, low-income neighborhood that used to have more stray animals than people, where previously burnt out shells of houses dominated the landscape, was gradually being replaced by a thriving ethnically diverse community. Before the neighborhood began its shift with its new round of residents pouring in, my greatest fear had been getting accidently hit by a stray bullet as I walked home from school. The biggest threat now seemed to be stepping into a steaming pile of doggy poop carelessly left behind by someone's pet. In other words, my neighborhood was in the throes of gentrification.

The date was October 17—I remember it well because it was my sixteenth birthday—the day my life would forever be changed in an incredible way.

It was Friday evening. The public city bus I used for transportation to my suburban school had just dropped me off at the bus top. I was hurrying home because the temperature had dropped over thirty degrees from the morning's warmth catching everyone off guard. As the sun dipped below the skyline of historical buildings with 'For Sale' signs posted in windows darkened by years of dirt and city grime, a brisk wind whipped in from the north like a hawk chasing down its last meal. It felt like an early winter was on its way.

I turned my jacket collar up and walked with my face down, not only to ward off the frigid wind, but because my focus was on my phone. I was checking my friends posts on how they thought track practice went, adding my comments underneath theirs. When I walked past someone coming in the opposite direction, I looked up briefly before averting my eyes. Not making eye contact was a survival tactic I learned from being in one too many fights over the years. In this part of town, getting caught staring at someone, intentionally or not, was enough to get your butt kicked. It wasn't the smartest way to live, but this was simply how we rolled.

As I finished a text to my mom letting her know I was on the way home, I heard a car trailing closely behind. But I was not alarmed. Slow moving cars weren't unusual. This time of day the streets were busy with adults rushing home from work and children from their afterschool activities. A rash of automobiles came and went without much fanfare. Plus, since I was on the sidewalk minding my own business, I figured no one would bother me.

Thanks to my brother's text from earlier today, reminding me to not eat anything after practice, I guessed my family had planned a surprise birthday party which most likely would include dinner at my favorite Thai restaurant. I prayed the surprise would also include a car. And not just any car, but the new hybrid electric solar car, because it was compact and had built-in wi-fi, plus all the cool kids in my school drove E-cars. Though I was turning sixteen, I sensibly considered the financial situation of my parent's lower middle-class status in my desires. An E-car was inexpensive, yet extremely dope.

The cell phone I held in my cold hands buzzed with a text from my girlfriend asking about my plans for the weekend. I poised my thumbs to tell her after I got my new car, I would be right over to pick her up. On second thought, just in case I didn't get a car for my birthday, I decided a witty response of emojis would be better. No sense in jinxing myself. I sent the text and stuffed the phone in the back pocket of my jeans, then shoved my cold hands inside my jacket pocket.

By the sound of the idling engine, the vehicle had slowed way down, but I still wasn't worried. After all, I was on a busy street. My mother made it a point to scold me about paying more attention to my phone than my surroundings. She warned that one day I would be snatched right off the street like all those other missing children if I wasn't careful. And my dad constantly preached to me and my brothers the importance of being aware of our surroundings because the city was dangerous for black children. Instead of dismissing their valid concerns all those years, I wished I had taken both their words to heart that day.

The thing is, I noticed the reflection of the men in a store window a couple of blocks back. I paid them no mind. Until a year or so ago, it was strange seeing folks of various ethnicities out for a casual stroll in this neighborhood. Nowadays, since this area had become gentrified, just as many whites lived here as did blacks. And more were moving in with each passing month.

Unfortunately for me, I did not notice I was being followed until it was too late. They were so close I smelled stale coffee on their breath with each exhale. In the very moment I turned around to tell them to back off, I felt a strong grip on my arm. Then another hand grabbed my other arm. Before I knew what was happening—even before I could catch my breath to scream—I was quickly forced inside a van. The doors slammed shut behind us.

Once inside the van, one of the men pointed a large gun to my head and warned if I screamed or tried to getaway, he would shoot me in the face and toss my mangled body on the street in front of my house for my family to find.

"Where is your cellphone?!" he shouted.

"I don't have a cellphone!" I lied.

"Where is your phone?!" he repeated.

"I-I-I don't have one." I knew that once my connection to the outside world was lost, so was I.

The man shoved me against the wall of the van and thrust his hand first in my jacket, then the pockets of my jeans until he found what he was looking for. He pushed me down to the bench.

"Lying bitch!" He grinned.

I opened my mouth to speak, but no words came out. I watched helplessly as he threw my phone to the floor and stomped it to pieces.

"My parents just gave me that phone! Why did you have to break it?!"

"When your parents finally notice you're gone, we can't have them tracking us by a damn cell phone, now can we?" He passed the broken pieces to the driver who unceremoniously tossed it out the window.

I was so scared I peed my pants. Right then and there. Without any embarrassment or shame. I felt the hot liquid warm the seat underneath me and pool on the floor at my feet. It smelled bad. Like how fear smells if it had an odor. It didn't matter. The man kept the gun to my head without flinching.

Thoughts of my mother popped into my mind. She watched a lot of television in the evenings, mostly crime shows like *Law and Order, Luther, True Detective, CSI...* whatever was popular at the moment. I recalled the TV police always asked the victim to describe their abductor. Most times, the victims were so traumatized, their descriptions were useless. Mom used those scenes as teaching moments on what to do if someone tried to take us. She always told me and my brothers to be careful because we lived in a city where black lives were less important than others, despite what the mayor spouted out during her campaign. Seemed like every day another child from an urban area was reported missing, raped, or killed.

It dawned on me that I was being kidnapped. Or more probably 'abducted', I thought, because my family did not have any money to pay a ransom. Either way, I had been snatched off the street in the same manner a dogcatcher traps a stray dog. In that moment, I realized my picture would soon be added to the tens of thousands of other children never to be seen, nor heard from again. Just as my mother warned. She used to say that unless the missing child was Caucasian, wealthy, or both, families should not expect an all-out search party.

I used to complain about the amber alerts on my cellphone that awakened me in the middle of the night. My daddy believed those amber alerts were mostly due to non-custodial parents, usually the father, taking their child from the mother because that was the only way he could see them. Too often those poor kids were used as pawns to piss off the other, usually for their own selfish reasons. But I digress... My Uncle Ricky provided even more horrendous explanations for the abductions of all those black children. He said that kids were being either 'human trafficked'—he described it as slavery rebranded and given another name—or would be killed and their melanated organs sold on the black market. If any of what my uncle said was true, I was in deep trouble.

I didn't plan on being one of those girls who couldn't remember anything so I took notice. Both men had blue eyes. Not a pretty shade of blue like the sky appears after it rains, but were translucent. Like a glacier. They wore skull caps pulled low over their ears with no visible hair showing. Their skin was very pale like they avoided the sun. When they threw me inside the van it took some effort so it is fair to say they weren't the most muscular of men. I glanced down at their feet. Most of the boys I know, including both my brothers, complained about how difficult it was to find shoes in their size. I noticed that neither of these men, who wore military styled boots, had big feet. In fact, at a size eleven, mine were probably larger than either of theirs. The dirty blonde five o'clock shadow, sprouting on each of their pale faces, made me question whether these guys were actually brothers who'd coordinated their decision that morning not to shave. I also wondered with growing terror, what these monstrous devils had in store for me.

To make myself less afraid, I imagined that I was being pranked by my parents as part of a birthday surprise. That they had hired a couple of actors to kidnap and take me to a wonderful celebration. In just a few minutes, we would pull up to a magnificent birthday party where everyone would jump from behind parked cars and shout, 'Surprise!' But deep down, within my heart, I knew they would never ever pull a stunt such as this. This was much too cruel.

For the record, I am tall and big-boned, as my girls like to say. I'm not fat, but I'm not skinny either. I am athletic with curves in all the right places. I wear my hair in microbraids so I don't have to waste time getting ready in the morning or worry about looking crazy after track practice. I don't have a boyfriend yet but I have a crush on my best friend, Rashawn. I maintain a 4.2 GPA and I plan on going to college to become an astronomer. But my mom wants me to be a doctor, lawyer, or any other safe traditional profession with a high earning potential. She said only Caucasian and Asian men studied astronomy and they would never accept me as an equal. My daddy simply wants me to be happy.

My eyes scanned the contents of the spotless van. I didn't have a chance to see what color it was, but the inside was steel gray. The windows were tinted so dark, I could barely see out. A metal divider with a small slot separated the driver from the cargo department. Hard metal benches lined either wall. The man with the gun sat next to me; the other man, directly across. My warm breath was visible in the cold air. I wasn't able to get a glimpse of the driver, but I heard him speaking into a radio. Or maybe it was a cell phone. Either way I couldn't hear what he said, but it sounded like instructions. One thing was for certain, from the sound of his accent, I could tell he wasn't from St. Louis.

The van slowed to a crawl. I caught sight of two young black men, similarly dressed as my captors, closely following a little girl crossing through the parking lot of a recently opened strip mall. She was alone, but couldn't have been more than ten years old. The girl had her head down talking into her cell phone. The van was so close I noticed that one of the orange barrettes securing the end of her pigtails threatened to come loose.

Both men wore hoodies, dark pants, and the same style military issue boots as my abductors. Sunglasses covered their eyes and nicely groomed millennial beards sprouted from the lower half of their faces. I couldn't believe what I was witnessing! There were so many people in that parking lot, either entering stores or returning to their vehicles. There were at least a dozen folks, including several single women, a couple in deep conversation, even a group of young men standing in front of a clothing store. Practically everybody's heads were down with eyes focused on their damn phone!

I prayed that someone would look up. Take notice of two men stalking a little girl walking alone. Sadly, she was invisible. Just like me.

A car playing music so loud the bass notes reverberated within my chest, swerved in front of the girl causing her to jump back. She shouted something at the driver and the men following the girl, temporarily stopped and pretended to check out a window display advertising protective face masks. I mentally pleaded for the young driver sporting long dreadlocks, as he exited his car, to see the child before going into the convenience store. He did not.

I watched helplessly as the men resumed their hunt. The little girl was an innocent lamb who had no clue how badly her day was about to turn. I wanted to give warning on the two wolves stalking her, so I raised up from my seat. The man sitting next to me pressed the gun's barrel to my head. The feel of the cold metal was very sobering.

He whispered harshly, "One word and I'll blow your fuckin' head off."

I lowered my wet behind down to the cold bench and watched on in horror.

The men continued to follow the little girl. She turned the corner. That's when the van sped up. The man opposite me quickly opened the door. I felt a blast of the cold air hit my face. One man pushed the little girl inside the van and jumped in after her. The other man continued walking down the street as if nothing had ever happened. I looked at the child. She was crying. Her backpack with the smiling 'Frozen' characters belied the terror in her eyes.

"Help!" she shouted struggling against the man's grip. "Let me go!"

"Quiet!" The man pushed her unto the floor. He snatched the phone from her hands and tossed it out through the slot to the front seat.

"I want to go home!" she cried. "Mommy! Help!"

"Shut up!" the man yelled.

"Please! Let me go!"

"I said to shut the fuck up!" He raised his hand and slapped the girl's face.

"Why did you have to hit her?!" I yelled. "She's scared! She's just a little girl!"

"If you don't shut that little bitch up right now, I'll shut her up for you!" shouted the man with dreadlocks, staring at me with his dead eyes.

I whispered to the girl, "Stop crying. It's going to be all right."

"I want my mommy," she said, voice quivering.

"It's going to be okay," I reassured her. "What's your name?"

"Samaria," she replied.

"Hi Samaria, my name is Kenya."

She stared at me with those big brown frightened eyes. Her dark chocolate unblemished skin shimmered with beads of perspiration. I hoped she couldn't see that I was just as scared.

"Don't worry. The police will send someone out to look for us..."

One of the men laughed out loud.

"What's so funny?" I asked, sounding braver than I felt.

"The police are not coming to look for you. In fact, no one will be looking for you," replied the man with the gun.

"How do you know that?" I asked.

"Because you're *black*. Nobody cares if you go missing," he replied matter-of-factly with a smirk plastered across his face. "Now shut the fuck up or I'll tape both your mouths."

I looked through the window, both horrified and dismayed to find no one calling out the alarm. Someone must have seen something on this busy street. Somebody had to have heard the commotion and called the police.

The driver did not speed, nor did he drive erratically, nor make any sudden moves that would cause undue attention. When the van stopped for a red traffic light, I grew hopeful when an elderly black woman stared intensely at the van. Her rheumy eyes focused on the dark windows as if she were looking directly into mine. She raised an ancient hand and pointed towards the van, tugging at the jacket of the younger woman by her side. The younger woman followed the old woman's gaze, shook her head and said something that caused her to avert her eyes. But before they continued on their way, the old woman balled up her fist and pointed her index finger up to the sky. I felt a tear slide down my cheek, as hope faded with each tottering step of the old woman as she then turned and slowly walked away.

The young man with the dreadlocks leaned forward, held his nose and said to the driver. "Man, pull over and let me out. It smells like piss back here!"

The driver pulled to the side of the road. The young black man sneered at us before quickly exiting through the door, said, "Y'all be good little bitches and those white boys won't mess with you."

My heart sank when I realized there were no men, women, or even other children shouting out that the little girl had been taken. People continued on with their lives—parking their cars, catching the bus, shopping from store to store, walking their dogs—going on with their lives as if nothing had ever happened. Maybe the man was right. We were black. Nobody cared.

Just as I had disappeared without a trace, so had she. The truth of the matter was a difficult pill to swallow. We were both abducted from a busy city street and no one gave a damn. And if anyone had noticed, they hadn't tried to stop it. Unfortunately, it would be hours before we were missed by our families. Even longer before the police would take our families seriously enough to send out a missing child alert. By then, we could both be dead. Or worse...

Chapter Two

Samaria carefully crept across the van to sit beside me. She snuggled close resting her head against my shoulder. I let her, surprised neither man tried to stop her. I think the man with the gun was tired of sitting in urine, so he changed seats across from me. The menacing weapon rested heavily on his thigh with the barrel aimed squarely at my crotch. His finger remained close to the trigger as if we, two scared young girls, would suddenly spring forth to overpower two adult men.

It was now dark. Headlights from oncoming cars bounced through the small slit in the driver's compartment illuminating the men's faces. They looked bored, but alert. Samaria and I also remained vigilant for we had no idea what the men had in store for either of us. The first chance I got, I planned to grab Samaria's hand and make a run for it. But that moment never arrived.

We must have ridden for hundreds of miles and at least eight hours without stopping. I watched the landscape of the gritty city streets give way to vanilla suburbia and then change to rural farmland. After awhile, the skyline of an unfamiliar city shone brightly in the distance. Once the tall buildings of the cityscape rolled out of view, we ended up taking hairpin turns up a mountainous road through a dense forest of pine trees. I had no idea where we were or where we were headed. What I did know however, was there were no mountains this high in Missouri, not even in the boot hills of the Ozarks. The tires of the van slipped and slid as we ascended into an eerie darkness I imagined existed only in a nightmare.

After what seemed like an eternity, the van abruptly stopped. The driver parked and killed the engine. The view through the windows offered no clue as to the location. It was pitch black as far as the eye could see.

The doors of the van flung open, bringing in a frigid gust of wind and a flurry of snow to replace the funky stale air inside the van. I inhaled sharply, the cold air taking me by surprise. Yet I was grateful to be breathing fresh air again. I peered outside and pulled Samaria close to keep her calm. I saw we were in a clearing and considered if we should make a run for it. But if we did, where would we go?

The man with the gun jumped out first. "Get out of the van!" he ordered.

"Where are we?" I asked.

"I said to get out of the fuckin' van!"

We stepped down onto the ground. I heard the crunching sound of old snow underneath my shoes. Not having moved since I was thrown in the van, my legs almost gave out underneath me. I slipped but managed to catch myself before landing in the snow, accidentally grabbing the closest man's arm to steady myself.

"Watch where you're going you clumsy bitch!" the driver shouted, quickly moving out of reach.

"Is that language really necessary?" came the calm voice of a woman.

"That bitch peed on me! I had to smell her piss the entire trip," said the armed man.

"I'll bet this wasn't the first time a woman has urinated on you." She raised her eyebrows knowingly, "and I'm sure it won't be the last."

I turned to see from where the voice came. A woman dressed in a parka held a flashlight on all five of us. I couldn't make out her features as the fur lining of the parka's hood practically covered her entire face. Only her reddish nose was visible.

"Well... You can never be too careful with these people," the man retorted. "Never know what kind of tricks they've got up their sleeves."

"*These people* are a young girl and a child. If three adult men can't take them on without the use of a gun, then God help us all. Now put those things away."

The men did as they were told and holstered their weapons.

Everything felt surreal; like I was trying my best to awaken from a horrendous nightmare. I felt Samaria shivering, her teeth chattered noisily together. I pulled her closer to share what little warmth I had to offer as I took in the surroundings. In my mind, I laid out a strategy of where we would go if we made a run for it; and more importantly, how we would survive. The light of the full moon revealed we were in a forested valley with snow-capped mountain peaks surrounding us in every direction. In the distance, mountain ranges that seemed to touch the glorious star-filled sky appeared to go on forever. The calls of wild animals pierced the silence of the night, quickly changing my mind about trying to escape. Neither of us were properly dressed for these conditions, not to mention I didn't know the first thing about camping or hiking, nor did I have any outdoor survival skills.

The woman pulled the men out of earshot to talk, turning her back to Samaria and I apparently confident we would not run.

"Are you okay?" I quietly asked Samaria in the few moments we had alone.

"I'm cold. And scared."

"How old are you?"

"Eight. But I'll be nine next month."

"You're very brave for an eight-year old," I told her, hoping to make her less frightened. "Much braver than I was at your age."

She managed a quick smile before shrinking back into herself.

A non-descript concrete building protected by a barbed wire fence seemed to be the main source of activity. It reminded me of military bunkers or a prison. Several vans similar to the one we just got out of were carefully parked side-by-side in a clearing. Brilliant florescent lamps lit the perimeter of the camp. Armed guards patrolled by foot and vehicle.

"Where are we?" I asked the woman.

"On paper this is an Immigration and Customs Enforcement detention center. ICE for short."

"I heard about these detention centers on the news. I thought they were built to house illegals. For migrant workers and their families who snuck across the southern border."

The woman chuckled at my obvious naivety. "You at least seem to be semi-informed. Those camps were officially built to house undocumented immigrants supposedly to stop terrorism and discourage illegal crossings at the Mexican border. Unofficially, they are being used to house children separated from their parents."

"Miss, I am an American citizen. We both are!" I pointed to Samaria who tried her best to put on a courageous front. "We're not illegals! We're from St. Louis, Missouri."

She ignored my outburst, and instead raised two gloved fingers signaling for Samaria and me to follow. The men trailed behind us grumbling among themselves. Samaria and I tromped through the snow, no longer fearing the men. Instinctively, we both understood they were merely following orders. Not in charge at all. It was the woman in the parka we should be worried about.

"Why are we here?" I asked. "I don't understand why we're in a detention camp."

"This way," she replied, once again ignoring my questions.

"Miss, we were abducted by those men. That is against the law. You know you can get into serious trouble for taking us against our will, right?"

"You seem to be quite the curious one." She smiled, amused.

We followed the woman through a heavy double metal door which led to a large corridor with a series of progressive locked gates. Each gate locked securely behind us while we waited in the narrow gap for the next one to open. At least it was warmer inside. I no longer saw the condensation of my breath, nor did I her the chatter from Samaria's teeth. The men peeled off at the first gate towards another section of the building. I can't say I was sorry to see them go.

"We take security very seriously here." She lowered the parka hood revealing a mass of curly hair tinted an unnatural shade of fire engine red. Cheeks were ruddy from the cold weather. Eyes were a gorgeous shade of emerald green. She waved her access card over an electronic reader. "If you ever consider trying to escape, the nearest town is at least 100 miles away. The altitude is over a mile high and we are completely surrounded by mountains. If hiking over rugged terrain in sub-zero temperatures doesn't kill you, the wolves will."

Samaria clutched my hand tightly. By default, she had nominated me as her big sister. Her best friend. Her protector. But I mostly felt like a horrible babysitter who accidentally locked the baby in the car. I couldn't help her, much less myself. Neither of us knew where we were. Or why. But from the look of things, we both understood we would never see our families again. The shock of this revelation thankfully prevented me from crying. I held her hand just a tad bit tighter for reassurance.

We trailed two steps behind the woman until she stopped before an entrance with a split-door. Two armed female guards simultaneously monitored several computer screens with rapidly changing scenes of indoor activity.

I heard the rumbling of young excited voices before we saw from where they originated. I braced myself to see a sea of brown and black Spanish-speaking migrants, whom the government determined to be 'illegal'.

For months, the headline story in the news cycle had focused on the Department of Homeland Security's ICE detention centers and the imprisonment of thousands of non-citizens from other countries. Apparently, children were being ripped from the loving arms of their immigrant and refugee parents and then scattered throughout the United States in various DHS centers. The really awful part of the story was that hardly any of those children had papers to document their names or country of origin. Most of those kids didn't even know the names of their parents; as children up to a certain age only know their parents as mommy and daddy. Sadly, the children who didn't speak any English were destined to forever be lost in a convoluted bureaucracy of a poorly managed government program. It would take years for those distraught parents to locate their children. If, at all.

We are not those children. Samaria and I are American citizens. We don't belong here, I thought.

"How are they behaving today?" the redhaired woman asked the guards.

"Not much better than yesterday. But at least we haven't had to break up any fights."

"Not yet," the other guard stated flatly.

"Excuse me, miss. Can you please tell me why we're here?" I said to the woman for the second time. "We're not illegal aliens."

For only the first time since Samaria got in the van, she spoke, "I don't like this place. I want to go home."

The guards looked at one another before turning to the woman for confirmation on how to proceed. One woman was much older than the other, although they closely resembled each other to the point they may have been related.

"They don't know?" asked the older one. Her expression was not only disinterested, it was robotic. Without feeling. No empathy displayed at all for children who had been taken from their homes and forced to live in what amounted to a jail.

"Know what?" I asked becoming more frightened by the moment. It was obvious none of these people would help us get out of there.

"The others will fill them in soon enough," the red-haired woman replied. "Now open the door."

"Where do you want 'em?" asked the younger one.

"The Delta section for now."

"Yes, ma'am."

The younger guard pushed a button. Immediately, the heavy double doors swung slowly open to a cavernous room. A burst of barely warm air was forced downwards through a maze of air ducts on the ceiling. Not a trace of color graced the dull concrete walls.

The arrival of myself, Samaria and the guards created a lull in the noise. Conversations ceased as everyone stared at the newbies. While the occupants checked us out, I did the same to them. The scene was eerily similar to the images I'd seen on TV. Armed guards carrying assault weapons roamed the crowded space filled with dozens of cages. I blinked several times to ensure my vision was not betraying my mind because there was one huge difference in this camp. The people in those cages were not Mexican. Or Guatemalan. Nor were they from Ecuador, San Salvador, or any other Central American country. The hundreds of faces I saw were familiar. Like mine. Like Samaria's. Like the two brothers I had left behind. And like every other black child's picture on those post cards that come in the mail addressed to *Resident*. Those postcards listed missing children—on one side was a photo at the age when the child went missing, next to a computer-generated version of what they were supposed to look like at their current age—and advertisements on the other. How many times had I tossed those thin pieces of cardstock straight from the mailbox into the garbage with no more than a passing thought?

An awful feeling of dread overtook me as I scanned over the occupants in the warehouse. This ICE detention center was not a place to detain illegal immigrants or their children. This center was being used to imprison hundreds of *African-American* children.

Chapter Three

The redhaired woman motioned for the nearest guard to open the door to the cage. Three other girls stared silently, standing behind a line on the floor made from red duct tape. I gripped Samaria's small hand tightly for reassurance.

"Not her. Just you," said the guard, pushing me along with the butt of her weapon.

"I'm not leaving Samaria. She stays with me." I replied bravely.

"You people don't make the rules in here. We do," she replied smugly. "This section is for ages thirteen through eighteen. Twelve and under are in another area."

A different guard grabbed Samaria's hand and ripped it from mine. I struggled to get back to her. I knew nothing more about the little girl than I did when she was first tossed inside that van, but I now felt responsible for her safety.

"Kenya!" shouted Samaria. "I'm scared! Don't let them take me!"

I pleaded with the redhaired woman, "Please let her stay with me. Just for tonight. Just until we understand what this place is. Why we are here."

The woman seemed impressed with my bravery. Either that or she would want this favor repaid at a later date. She waved the guard off and said, "Tonight only. Tomorrow the little one gets moved to her proper place."

"Thank you," I replied, grateful for the small victory.

"I'll be seeing you shortly," she addressed me before exiting the cage.

Samaria visibly relaxed as she threw her arms around my waist. Though she was barely nine, by her behavior she had reverted to half that age. I guess being traumatized does that to a child.

"Why don't you go lie down. Try to get some rest," I said gently.

"If I'm good, do you think they'll let me go home?"

"I don't know. But try to get some sleep, anyway."

"I'll try. But promise you won't leave me."

"Go on. I'll be here when you wake up."

"Dang! You stink!" said a short girl holding her nose. She was probably fourteen—fifteen at the most.

"Yeah? Well, you would stink too if someone held a gun to your head and threatened to blow your brains out."

The rude girl shrugged and returned to the opposite side of the cage. She faced the wall instead of the others and held an intense conversation with a reflection of herself on the metal post.

"Don't mind her. She is half crazy. Been here longer than any of us. Almost a year," explained an older girl who sat cross legged on the floor. Shoulder-length locs framed her square shaped face and those alert brown eyes seemed to take everything in at once. She spoke with a beautiful lilting sing-song accent of a Jamaican, so in my mind, that became her nickname.

"A year?" I asked.

"Yeah," the girl continued. "From what I can tell, most of us are here for about six months before they take us some other place. We call that chick CraCra. I advise you to leave her alone."

"Why do you say that?"

"I think they must have done something to her. Every time she returns from wherever those guards have taken her, she comes back with some crazy batshit stories. That girl is not right in the mind..."

My eyes scanned the massive warehouse space filled with row after row of cages constructed of chain linked fencing. Each cage was about 10 x 20 feet and held four sets of bunk beds covered by thin metallic blankets, the kind I had only seen on television shows. The floor was concrete. Hard, cold, and grey. On one side of the room, a large sign hanging from the ceiling pointed to the community bathroom.

The Jamaican's gaze fell on Samaria. "She your sister?"

"No. We just met. They made me watch while they snatched her off the street." Thinking about how those men treated us reignited my anger, but I remained helpless to do anything about it. "I was already inside the van. With a damn gun pointed at me."

"Dang! She's so young. I'll bet she is scared to death."

I nodded in agreement. "By the way, my name is Kenya. What's yours?"

"Shhh... We are not allowed to use our real names. They forbid it."

"Are you kidding me?!"

"Nope. They get us with those tazers if they hear us using our birth names."

"Who are these people?! What the hell is this place?!" I asked keeping an eye on Samaria. She had found an empty bunk and laid there sucking her thumb. An older teen lied on the upper bunk, probably asleep.

"The guards call it a camp. But this don't feel like camp to me."

"Feels like jail," I said glancing over the small space. "Even looks like one."

The girl smacked her plump lips together, shaking her head from side to side. She sighed wearily, "Girl, no matter what they call it, this place is not for illegals. I have only seen black kids like us since the time I arrived. And I've heard this isn't the only location they use."

"How long have you been here?"

"A few months. Maybe more. I lost track of time." She picked at a scab crusting over her elbow. "Time doesn't matter here. The days all seem to blend together."

"How did it happen to you?"

She shrugged matter-of-factly. A blank expression overshadowed her face as she replied in that wonderful island accent, "I was on the street. Homeless. A woman offered to take me to a shelter. Said she wanted to help me. I ended up here."

I shook my head in disbelief. "Why us?"

"Who knows? Everyone I've met has been abducted. Snatched off the street and thrown into a van against their will. Most of the girls are between nine and eighteen. The males are as young as six with the oldest I've seen probably in their early twenties. Most are healthy. Athletic. They don't seem to like the fat ones much."

"I can't believe I'm actually imprisoned. This feels like a dream I can't wake up from."

"Sorry to burst your bubble. This is not a dream, but it is a nightmare. One that has no end in sight."

"Has anyone ever tried to escape?" I asked, hopefully.

"I don't think so," the girl said. "They dress us in these bright red uniforms because it's supposed to increase our energy flow. I remember hearing about this girl who requested pink scrubs instead of red, but they flat out told her, no. Supposedly our energy flow slows way down when the color pink is introduced."

"Really?! I never heard that about the color pink. Now it makes sense why it was reserved for females. It makes us weak? Wow!"

"And we have these flimsy sneakers that are only good for walking indoors. None of us have coats so we would freeze to death if we did try to escape, especially since its always snowing up here." The Jamaican fingered the thin blanket. "This is supposed to keep us warm, but all it does is piss me off."

"Where are we?"

"They won't tell us, but most of us guess we're either in Colorado or Utah because of the mountains, the snow, and because of how long the drive took getting us here."

"Where are you from?" I asked the Jamaican, expecting her to say New York or some other major city.

"Used to live in L.A. But it doesn't matter because we're from all over," she replied, apparently picking up my train-of-thought.

"I still don't get it. What are they planning to do with us?"

"Don't know that either. They call this a camp but treat us like we're prisoners. Always got guns pointed at us. Tell us when to wake up. When to sleep. Feed us tasteless crap they call healthy food. Barely turn up the temperature to above freezing." She nodded towards the guards at the door. "I don't know where they got them bitches from, but they are mean as some hungry-ass dogs. Treat us worse than dirt. Like we personally did something bad to them."

I pushed down the wave of emotions that tried to overtake me once I understood the enormity of my situation. I was a prisoner held against my will with no understanding of why I was there. No idea of where I was, nor did I know if I would ever see my family again.

"My mother used to tell me to pay attention to my surroundings. She was obsessed with those reports of missing children. Used to comment about how heartbroken those families on television were when the pleaded with the public to come forward with info on their kids. Most of the people on the news crying over their lost kids was white. Unless your parents were rich or famous, black kids didn't even rate a mention unless they were shot dead. Dang... Never in my wildest imagination would I have thought that I'd be one of the missing."

Chapter Four

A homely overweight guard with a bad case of acne, who looked like she survived on a diet of Twinkies and Doritos, came for me. The guard did not know my name but I knew who she meant when she referred to me as 'Braveheart'. Her cheeks, ruddy from the exertion of merely walking, reminded me of the Petunia pig character from the Porky Pig cartoons my parents used to watch as children.

I approached the front of the cell. I decided to call this place a cell because calling it a cage made me seem like I was an animal. At least if it was a cell, I was a prisoner. A human being.

"Time for you to take a shower, Braveheart. You smell like a goddamn outhouse."

"What about her?" I asked pointing to Samaria.

The fat guard laughed. "Did she piss her pants too?"

"It's okay," said the Jamaican. "I'll keep an eye on her."

"Finally!" CraCra shouted. "I was going to puke if I had to smell that disgusting stench for one more minute."

I followed the guard to the bathroom. Two other girls were showering in what I imagined was barely lukewarm water by their hurried movements. She tossed a threadbare towel and a small bar of soap at me, pointed to an open shower stall and ordered me to strip.

"Can I use the bathroom first?"

"Why?" she giggled. "You can save time by pissing in the shower like everyone else."

"You want me to shit in the shower, too?"

Her laughter was replaced by that wheezing sound fat people make when struggling to breathe. "You got five minutes to do both. I suggest you be quick about it."

Teetering on the edge of the filthy toilet seat in the open stall was not only difficult, it was also embarrassing. Defecating under the watchful eyes of a guard who despised my very being was almost impossible so I stared back until she looked away. I discovered the need to rid myself of this afternoon's burrito lunch was more powerful than the expression of disgust registering on the guard's face. I was grateful for the chance to shower as the toilet paper was insufficient to do the job it was intended to do. I stripped, trying to maintain what little bit of dignity I could after what amounted to a public display of my bodily functions. Just as I suspected, the shower was barely warm. I hurried before my time ran out, as the guard didn't seem the generous type. I dried off as much as possible with the rough towel.

"Do you have any lotion?" I asked the guard.

"Lotion? Now why the fuck would *I* have lotion?"

"Never mind."

"Get dressed," she instructed, handing me a pair of oversized underwear, an old-fashioned pointy bra, and a set of bright red scrubs that were much too big.

"Do you have to watch?" I asked, feeling her lustful eyes roaming over my body. I tried to cover my breasts as I wasn't used to being exposed. Even in the locker room at school with a bunch of immature teens, none of the girls stared at one another like the guard did with me.

"Give me a break! I have seen hundreds of bodies just like yours. There is nothing you have that I haven't seen before. Now hurry up and get dressed!"

"What's the rush? It's not like I'm going anywhere. This is a prison after all."

"This is a DHS ICE facility. But we like to call it camp or a detention center. Kinda takes the sting away. This is not a prison," she smugly retorted, as if she believed what she said was true.

"Then why are we locked in cages? Why do you carry a taser and a gun? And why can't I leave if I want?"

"You ask way too many questions. Let's go."

On my way from the bathroom, a young male guard, with a shock of stringy blonde hair covering one eye, approached us, carrying a pair of socks and canvas sneakers in his hands. He interrupted, "The lady told me to bring the one with the big mouth to her after she's cleaned up."

"Perfect timing. She's all yours."

"Follow me," he instructed.

I trailed the guard through a maze of hallways, each one cordoned off by securely guarded steel doors. We finally entered a corridor with at least a dozen doors. Some constructed of metal, others were glass.

"Where are we going?" I asked.

He ignored my question, continuing to walk ahead towards a sign marked exit. As we left that corridor and entered another, I captured a glimpse of several guards gathered outside in a courtyard speaking loudly. I relaxed a bit. At least this particular guard didn't threaten to shoot, taze, or punch me in the face like the female guards. In fact, this guard treated me like I was no threat at all. He never looked over his shoulder to see if I was still following. He just assumed I was.

"Fine," I said, "Don't answer."

We approached a large unguarded glass door. I waited to hear the loud buzzer, followed by the clicking sound of the steel disengaging, before moving forward. Surprisingly, this door wasn't locked. He merely pushed the door open and walked in. Three sides of the large room were painted in vibrant shades of orange, yellow and red with beautiful exotic plants scattered about. One side of the room was comprised of a ceiling to floor glass window that allowed views of the scenery outside. The furniture was modern, yet appeared comfortable. Soft ethereal music played in the background.

I was surprised to see dozens of young men and women of all ages, shapes, sizes, and various shades of melanin gathered together in small groups. The females wore colorful flouncy gowns, unlike the red scrubs provided for me. The young men wore long white shirts and matching pants. I saw no signs of fright. None seemed like they would try to escape the first chance they got. In fact, they were talking and laughing as if they were enjoying themselves immensely.

"Sistah girl, you are working that hairstyle!" I complimented one usually tall young lady sporting afro puffs. "That outfit is fabulous too!!!"

With the look she gave me, I was a piece of nasty toilet paper stuck to the bottom of her overpriced red bottom *Louboutin* shoes.

"Do not speak to the clients," the guard warned.

"Clients? What the…"

We walked to an area away from the group. He pointed to a chair outside an office. "Wait here."

The girl's response upset me way more than it should. If I were in my right frame of mind, I would have told her what I thought of her stank ass attitude, especially on the heels of me offering a compliment. I pinched the thin patch of skin under my wrist until it turned beet red. My track coach taught us girls the technique to keep our emotions in check when we lost a race. I usually did this to help maintain my control and keep from crying. Yet still, I was confused by what I'd just seen with the disparity between the two groups. What could have happened to change the sullen girls in those cages into those happy females? Were they brainwashed? Would the same happen to me?

I recognized the type of ethereal music streaming softly through the hidden speakers. It was supposed to calm your mind, in preparation for meditation, yoga, or relaxation. My mother played similar music for my little brother to help him fall asleep. My eyelids became heavy. It obviously worked.

"She's ready for you," the male guard said when he returned.

I slowly rose from the chair, noting the plush rug under my feet. It was much warmer in here. A comfortable temperature for how sparsely I was dressed.

A painting composed of interlocked circles with rainbow colors within the connected spaces, caught my attention. I imagined the picture was of what one might see when brilliant rays of sunlight bounced off the surface of a swimming pool and reflected beneath the surface on the bottom tiles. I was mesmerized by the fluidity and vibrancy of the painting. The artist had masterfully captured the images causing the observer to question if the painting was in perpetual motion.

"You wanted to see me?" I said, still admiring the painting.

"Come in," the redhaired woman replied. She no longer wore the heavy parka but was now dressed in a full-length dress made from sheer white flowing material with golden threads throughout. "Sit. Stand. Your choice."

Her eyes followed mine. "You like?"

"It's... beautiful. Makes me want to touch it; check to see if it's water instead of paint."

"It was given to me by a dear friend of mine many, many years ago. It is titled The *Flower of Life*. The geometrical design is said to be old as time. He told me it represents the beginning of creation and symbolizes how we are all connected."

My eyes narrowed at the woman. I wasn't about to be lulled into a false sense of security, bonding with her over a painting, no matter how beautiful. I had a feeling I wouldn't be permitted to make my own decisions within the next few days so I decided to exercise my will now by standing.

"Is this the part where you explain why I was abducted and what your diabolical plans are for me?"

She smiled revealing perfect teeth. "I have no diabolical plans for you."

"Then what do you want? Why am I here? And who are you?"

"All will be revealed to you in due time." She ran her hand along the desk in the movement one does when checking for dust. Satisfied there was none, she clasped her hands together.

"Why did you have those men abduct me?!"

"There are so many people in this country... In this world... who have no idea about the horrendous state of this planet. It is absolutely disgraceful how we treat this place we all call home. Planet Earth. But even more disgraceful is how we treat one another."

"What are you talking about?!" I asked in disbelief listening to her nonsensical rant. I had more important things on my mind like what was going to happen to me. To all of us. "Those men terrorized a little girl and stole her from her family! That is what I call disgraceful!"

"My intent is to make life better for as many of you as possible. Unfortunately, some of you cannot be helped. They are too far gone. But you... I believe you can be saved."

"Lady, I don't know who you think I am, but you have got the wrong person!" I shouted.

The male guard stepped inside the office when he heard shouting. The woman waved him off.

"I'm cool." I inhaled to calm myself but felt my hands shaking uncontrollably with rage. Or maybe, fright. "How are you supposed to be helping when you're holding me against my will?"

"Kenya, you are safe here. Try to relax."

She poured a cool glass of water and offered it to me.

I accepted the glass in my trembling hand, spilling almost half on my shirt. I hadn't realized how thirsty I was. After I downed the freshest and cleanest water I had ever tasted, I felt much better. I asked, "Do you meet everyone like this on a one-to-one basis?"

"I usually provide a mass briefing to the new clients..."

"Client?!" I snorted. "Now that is funny because being your client is the last thing I feel I am."

"As I was saying, every now and then, we find children who have a little bit more of something than the others. They have unique innate abilities that make them very special. I think you fall into that category."

"There is nothing special about me. I'm just me..."

"We shall see."

My thoughts were all over the place. I was scared, intrigued, excited, frightened, curious, angry—all at the same time. This woman summoned me like I was her servant. Told me they kidnapped me because I was special. My parents taught me to respect my elders, but this wench looked like she was barely out of her thirties.

"I'm going to tell you a bit about my background to help you understand who I am and why I want to help."

I couldn't wait to hear what she had to say to shed some light on this awful situation.

"I majored in pharmaceutical engineering. Even got my PhD. The things they taught me in university would blow your young mind. After I graduated, I began to question my career choice. I worked for a major pharmaceutical company whose primary focus was developing designer drugs for non-existent illnesses."

"That doesn't sound like anything I'd ever want to do. Actually, it sounds awful," I replied.

"My colleagues and I were bored developing drugs for the same routine illnesses. To make our lives more interesting, we began placing bets on who could create the most ridiculous disease, invent a drug to treat it, and then make the most money within the first year of release. Sometimes we conducted experimental trial runs on patients who could least afford their medication. I was very, very successful."

"What does that have to do with me? Are you using us for drug testing? If you are, I wouldn't be surprised. Black people have been this country's guinea pigs ever since the first enslaved Africans were brought here to build this country." I stared at the woman. "Are you even listening to me?"

"Getting FDA approval was easy. The heads of those agencies were deeply connected to our industry. We would run a few trial tests, request approval, wait a few months...a year at most, advertise heavily, and then watch the money roll in. Other times we just fudged the numbers by dispersing the medication to our pharma reps who pushed it to the doctors in the field. We relied on feedback from their patients to determine success. If the side effects weren't serious, we went full force with production. On the other hand, if too many people died, we went back to the drawing board."

As the woman spoke, she stared outside the massive window into the darkness on the other side. To me, because it was pitch black out there, it looked like she was staring into an abyss. I listened, taking in the soothing décor. The beige color scheme with aqua green highlights reminded me of summer at the beach, which was in stark contrast to the wintry landscape surrounding the camp. The piped in mystical music only emphasized my current surreal situation. The woman continued to speak as if she were alone but voicing her thoughts aloud.

"I was bored with making money. One day I withdrew twenty thousand dollars from the bank. Twenties, fifties, and one hundred-dollar bills. I went home, tossed the money in the fire pit, soaked it in lighter fluid, and then burned it all just to see how it felt."

"You must be crazy!" I thought about how that much money could have made a huge difference in my families' life. Here she was talking about burning money because she was bored. Give me a break!

"No, I wasn't crazy. In fact, I had never been saner. Money lost all meaning to the point that I wasn't fazed by any amount. I could make ten times what I burned in that fire pit by developing the next drug."

"Where I come from, twenty thousand dollars is a lot of money. I could have bought food, clothes and shoes for my entire family with that much money. And had enough left over to pay a bunch of bills."

"Money is just fancy paper with pictures of dead presidents. It's really not worth the paper it is printed on if you think about it. Money is an IOU for the Federal Reserve Bank. Nothing more. Nothing less."

"Easy for you to say when you have a lot of it." I rolled my eyes, not that she noticed. "Lady, I really don't care about your privileged existence or how much money you made. Tell me why I'm here!"

"Patience. I'm getting there," she said before continuing. "A coworker and good friend invited me to go on a thirty-day excursion through Africa. We visited over a dozen countries. Took in all the exotic sights. Met with native businessmen interested in doing business with us. Even though there are numerous European and Asian countries in Africa and already poised to make huge profits from their pharmaceutical industries, we quickly discovered the potential to make millions by getting our drugs in those countries where the market remains untapped."

"Colonize much?" I replied since she wasn't paying attention to anything I had to say anyway.

"When we returned from Africa, I imagined hundreds of diseases that could be developed in the laboratory. The money to be made from creating the cure for those diseases was infinite! My company was thrilled to be one of the first American companies gaining foothold there. All those African countries with little to no government oversight. We were like children in a candy store."

"You're actually telling me your people intentionally created viruses like AIDS? Ebola? SARs? What about Zika? Or that damn coronavirus that continues to mutate?"

She shook her head. "With the exception of the coronavirus, all those other viruses were courtesy of our competitors."

"What the...? Are you serious?!" I didn't know whether to believe her or not. Maybe she had been up in this thin air too long and it had affected her brain cells. "You were responsible for a pandemic that killed millions of people?!"

"One of my colleagues accidently created a new virus when he began working on a cure for the virus that causes the common cold. When we first began studying effects of the virus that got its name because under a microscope it resembled the corona around the sun, I had no idea what we were embarking upon. The coronavirus was supposed to be tested on animals to learn how quickly new viruses can mutate if left unchecked. The effects were devastating. The government got wind of the new coronavirus and wanted to use it for a biological weapon. When the money started rolling in, fewer questions were asked. Besides, that coronavirus wasn't the worst one. There are others in the pipeline that are even more deadly. We believed we were discovering cures for viruses, not creating them."

"A million people worldwide perished! Hundreds of thousands of Americans died!" I shut my eyes tightly to block the tears threatening to fall. "All that death was because of your little experiment?!"

"Don't be so naive. The United States has conducted experiments on its people from the very start. For instance, I know you are aware of the Tuskegee experiment. For decades, researchers studied hundreds of black men in Alabama who had syphilis but didn't know they had it. The researchers convinced those men for decades that they were being treated for their bad blood. In actuality, the men were not being treated, but were being studied for the long-term effects of syphilis left unchecked. Without their voluntary participation, those scientists would have never discovered a cure for that disease."

I screamed at her to make sure she heard me. "You must be out of your mind! Those men would never have agreed to participate if they knew what the government was doing to them! And the part you're conveniently forgetting is even when they discovered penicillin was the cure, they didn't offer it to those men because they wanted to continue studying the devastating effects of the disease! And even when those poor men finally did die, those damned people still couldn't let them rest. They removed their brains and continued to study the effects long after they were long gone. To those so-called doctors, those brave men were nothing more than lab rats or guinea pigs. Do you think any of those men volunteered for that?!"

Signs of frustration were written all over the woman's face because she was obviously not getting through. Her intent was to express how she felt about the country that had afforded her with luxurious opportunities at the expense of others. Like most of her fellow researchers, her initial desire to work in the biomedical field was focused on the betterment of humanity, but also like so many others who started out with good intentions, once the money started flowing, she slowly got sucked into the corrupt system.

The redhaired woman stated, "The novel coronavirus was supposed to be a biological virus targeted specifically towards Asia to destroy their growing economy. Slow them down because they were becoming too powerful. Our government thought they had it under control... The plan was to release the virus and provide a vaccine shortly thereafter. We never planned for it to spread throughout the world so quickly."

"I was too young to remember what happened, but my parents told me everyone was ordered to remain inside their homes for over a year before it was safe to mingle with other people. It took years before life went back to normal."

"What I eventually learned was the development of viruses was part of a larger plan to depopulate the world's population. Get rid of the elderly, the poor, and most black and brown people who they consider a drain on societal resources. Those few very powerful women in charge..."

"Women? I thought men ruled the world."

She chuckled and replied, "When you get older, you will reach the same conclusion that most women eventually do and realize that they are the ones running things. Behind every powerful man is a woman telling him what to do. Mothers, wives, sisters, daughters, even girlfriends."

"Women rule the world? I thought all wives did was stand next to their husbands and look pretty."

"That is because that's what they want you to believe. Although men dominate the boardrooms of the most successful companies, hold high political offices, are heads of states, and the rulers of the most powerful countries in the world, make no mistake about it, the women behind the men are really the ones who hold all the power. Don't worry, one day you'll understand." She sighed and continued, "...as I was saying, those powerful people who are intent on world domination, won't stop developing biological agents until they get the results they want."

"Why are you telling me all this?"

"One Saturday morning, I was up here—in these breathtakingly gorgeous mountains—taking a hike when it suddenly occurred to me that what I was doing was wrong. I no longer cared about humanity. The world's population had morphed into one humongous test subject for my experimental purposes."

"That is a cold-blooded way to think about people. Something must be missing in your soul."

She lowered her eyes as if a moment of shame had silently crept within. But just as quickly she regained her composure. "A week or so prior, I was in New York for a conference. To get a more authentic flavor of the city, I decided to take the subway since it's now a fairly safe way to get around. When I was on that train, I studied those people and wondered how their bodies would react to a particular drug I was in the process of developing. I began to plan how I would introduce the drug to certain communities. Blacks, Latinos, Asians, Jewish, the elderly..."

"Damn, lady! Who are you?!" I asked, rhetorically.

"That particular morning, on top of the mountain, in the midst of nature and all its glory, that is the moment I made up my mind to quit. I walked away. Because you are correct. Something was missing from my soul and I wanted to rectify that as quickly as possible."

In my shocked state, I didn't know what to say. I blurted out, "Lady, I don't know if I'm looking at a monster or just another pale-faced woman who thinks this world, and everything in it, is yours to do with as you please."

"You must understand. I am not your enemy. *White people* are not your enemy. *Your* enemy is the system that oppresses your people."

"I know all white people aren't my enemy, but there are enough of y'all who hate me and everyone who looks like me to believe otherwise."

"Your feelings are valid. Racism is intentional. And our government has deliberately sown division to keep us separate. To keep us fighting among ourselves. It is all part of their plan."

The skepticism I felt churning in my gut was clearly displayed on my face. All my life I had been taught whites were not to be trusted. They wanted nothing more than to remain on top. To them, the proper place for blacks was the bottom. And in my short life's experience, that's just the way the cards fell in this society.

She bristled at my fatalistic attitude, despite it being warranted. Clearly, she recognized she wasn't getting through. "Look, I started this institution to help save humanity. To help make the lives of everyone around me better, especially the disenfranchised."

"If you want to make life better, why imprison us? Couldn't you just start a school or provide free college tuition? Do you have any idea how expensive a college degree is these days?"

"Education in this country..." She released another sigh of frustration. "...the current system, which is supposed to facilitate higher learning, actually does more harm than good. Furthermore, the United States has done reprehensible damage to your people. To pay colleges a skyrocketing tuition, which is by the way intentionally designed to discourage poor people from participating, or to saddle them with huge debt upon graduation, would not help one bit. It would only encourage the corrupt education system to continue."

"By *your people*, are you referring to black Americans." I was getting tired of this conversation. My temples throbbed trying to follow her logic. "The best way for *my* people to get out of poverty is to get a college degree. Or have you been out in this wilderness so long that you no longer understand how life works?"

"So, we're back to color again. I'm surprised you haven't figured out labeling citizens as black, brown, white, yellow, and red are social constructs put in place by powerful elites to establish a pecking order between the races. It's a mind game! Look at the color of my skin. It is no more white than yours is black."

"You don't think skin color matters because you are white. Have you looked around lately before you holed yourself up in this isolated bunker? Being white gives you advantages no one else has..."

"White is not a race! And neither is black!" she screamed so loudly, a tiny vein on her forehead appeared.

"Don't get angry with me! I'm not the one who started this white against black mess. Blame *your* ancestors!"

"Before this country was even established, the British ruling class was determined to find a way to divide its subjects. First it was religion and country of origin. No one seems to remember that the Irish, Italians, Spaniards, and Greeks—though European—were the first undesirables because they practiced Catholicism. But when those groups arrived in America, they became so-called 'white' people because of their pale skin. And when other ethnic groups arrived from Europe, they too were designated as white in the eyes of the U.S government. Consequently, because the color of one's skin was so easily identifiable, unlike defining nationality or determining one's religion, it was the perfect method for division."

"And I'll bet not a one of those groups complained because they were given privileges based on their pale complexion. White privilege!" I rolled my eyes.

"I hope in time you will understand this isn't about the color of one's skin. It never was."

"You could have fooled me because everything in America is about color and race. White over black, brown, red and yellow. That's how it's been all my life and for as long as anyone I know can remember. Why do you think there are so many dumb people who believe in White Supremacy?"

"You do realize you have named colors that only exist in a box of crayons? My point is, until we made defined efforts to combat racism, it will continue to thrive. In actuality, the only place white supremacy truly exists is in the mind of racists. Ignorant people who bought into that theory because they refuse to compete on a level playing field." She then added, "Unfortunately, the entire system of the U.S. government was systematically constructed under the premise of white superiority."

I remained skeptical of her position because I'd never heard a white person admit they weren't better than everyone else. She was frustrated by my skepticism. But I didn't care. This woman had never walked in the shoes of any of my ancestors. She had no clue the trials and tribulations my people lived through.

"Poor innocent misguided child," she replied condescendingly. "You are so convinced you are right about this thing called race. But have you ever considered the so-called *white people* have been lied to as well?"

I shrugged. Since she seemed to know everything about everything, I let her go on.

"You want to know the real truth?" she asked, crossing her arms over her heart

"Sure. Why not. Lay it on me since you seem to be comfortable in your whitesplaining."

"Pale skin like mine is relatively new and only came into existence about 7,000 years ago when the 'Africans' left the continent and migrated north. Before then, hundreds of thousands of years earlier—and quite possibly, millions of years according do some records—all human beings were dark-skinned melanated people. At a certain point in history, pale-skin began to be classified as 'white'. Race is more of a social construct than a truism. The intent is to keep the people fighting amongst ourselves instead of focusing on who designed this system in the first place! White, black, brown, yellow, or red doesn't amount to a hill of beans. It all boils down to varying degrees of melanin in the skin and where your ancestors eventually migrated to."

I remained skeptical because all my life, I was referred to as black or African-American. And more recently, 'people of color', which annoyed my grandfather to no end.

"You still don't get it, do you?" she asked.

I watched her retrieve a large globe of the earth from a closet behind her desk. She set it down and gave it a spin. Barely able to keep her voice above shouting, she said, "Where is the country called 'Black'? For that matter, where is the country called 'White'?!"

I stared at the crazy woman, smacked my lips together, and said with confidence, "There isn't a country named Black or White that I'm aware of."

"Exactly! When you ask people about their origins, they say their ancestors are from England, Italy, Spain, Mexico, Canada. Even the dark hued Africans say they are from Ghana, Kenya, Ivory Coast. Or whatever country they were born in. Nobody in this world claims to be from the country of 'Black', except your people."

"We can't claim a country because we don't know where our ancestors are from."

"And that is the true tragedy of America. An entire group of people have no connection to any one country and no way of ever knowing who they truly are. That fact alone made it easy for this government to label you 'black' and your oppressors 'white'."

Now that she mentioned it, I had never entertained the possibility whites were just as ignorant about the real world as everybody else. I sat up in my chair at this tidbit of information that could change the world had it been shared.

"Do you know what happens when a so-called white person learns they've also been lied to their entire life? That they are not the smartest, most intelligent, hardest working, most deserving, privileged beings on earth? I'll tell you... They are devasted when the truth is revealed that there is absolutely nothing special about them. And they could not have gotten to where they are in life without the government's affirmative action working for them. Why do you think the opioid addiction and suicide rates are so high? Those people are the ones who have woken up from the American dream only to discover it is actually a nightmare. Their spirits are so fragile they cannot fathom a life of not being number one."

I exhaled loudly, "Listen lady. I don't know what problems you are working through but I don't want to be here! Let me go and I won't say anything to anyone. I promise."

"Where will you go? Back to St. Louis?" She shook her head. A sad smile teased the corners of her mouth. "You want to return to a city that is rapidly collapsing upon itself due to the unimaginable levels of violence and crime? Maybe I misjudged you. I thought you were smarter than that."

"My family lives in St. Louis. My mother. My father. My brothers... It's my home!" I felt the tears stream out of my eyes which made me even more angry. "Everyone I know and love is there!"

"Your home? Really? When you walk the streets of your city... Do you feel safe? How about your brothers? Are they safe? Or do they continually watch their backs to avoid becoming involved in the next shooting, stabbing, rape, or robbery? How often does your mother pray that no one in her family becomes the next victim?"

"We've had our share of incidents, like years ago when that asshole cop murdered Michael Brown in Ferguson, but it's not like St. Louis is a third world country or anything... They're not randomly shooting us in the streets like they used to."

"One could argue that you are wrong about that." She smirked. "I challenge you to research the number of police shootings over just the last decade not only in St. Louis, but your entire state. Moreover, if you considered the entire United States, you'd be shocked!"

"Okay, I get your point. But the fact that we all have cell phone cameras the shootings should slow down. Right?"

She released yet another weary sigh, but this time fury blazed in her eyes as she shouted, "Are you aware of the rampant lynching and castration of black men from the time of colonization up to as late as the 1950's? Or what really happened during the 60's civil rights movement? Integration ruined the black community instead of helping. In the 1980's, black communities in every city all over the country were flooded with crack and guns. Do you know why the welfare system was so enthusiastically offered to minority women?! It was to keep fathers out of the home! Factories that used to pay decent wages were removed from your neighborhood and moved overseas. Local policies were established to ensure that the buses poor people needed to reach those good paying jobs did not run where you live. Fast food establishments proliferated low income areas without offering healthy food options. Predatory payday loans were offered like candy, sucking those who couldn't make ends meet on a normal day into a horrible web of high interest rates and astronomical fees. There are other ways to destroy you without firing a single shot."

"I appreciate the history lesson, but things are much different now. I live in a good part of St. Louis that's getting better all the time. For instance, my mother used to have to drive to the grocery store, but now I can walk to one they built around the corner."

She managed to recover her poise lost from the last outburst to explain, "You are proving my point! Your revitalized neighborhood is slowly being gentrified to the degree it will soon become unaffordable to the people who currently live there. Was there not a community before wealthy young white hipsters started moving in and claimed it as their own? You think this was all an unfortunate coincidence? This is part of the plan. Gentrification is happening all over America! Don't you see?!"

I shrugged because I didn't see how anything had changed for the worse. All I knew was ever since the hipsters started moving in, the cops patrolled more which decreased the drive-by shootings. Churches, liquor stores, check cashing places, Chinese takeout, beauty supply stores, and pawn shops still dominated the landscape, but had significantly decreased in number over the years.

The woman faced me toe-to-toe peering deeply into my eyes as if searching for something hidden deep within. I took a step back. Her barely contained fury was like electricity jumping from one pole to another.

"Who protects you? Who protects your family? The police? Of course not! For the most part they see you as subhuman. They shoot you because of their ignorance and fear. Or worse, because of their hatred. The people in your community do not watch out for each other anymore because they are as terrified of the police as they are of criminals and drug dealers. Think about it. You and the little girl you came here with were snatched off a busy city street. You actually want me to believe that no one saw or heard anything?! That is not the case! They won't say anything because they are filled with fear of retribution by members of their own community!"

I wanted to cover my ears and scream at her to 'shut up!' I was annoyed, angry, tired, and sick of listening to her rant. Yet she continued as if she were speaking to someone other than me.

"Politicians are corrupt. They make promises and provide people with false hope that their situation will improve. They make catchy proclamations such as, 'Keep Hope Alive!' 'Change We Need!' 'Yes We Can!' 'Make America Great Again!'. Give me a break... Democrat. Republican. Independent. It doesn't matter. All politicians are in the pockets of the few powerful families that run the United States. Every four years they tell you to be a good citizen. Take off from your 9 to 5, go stand in line and cast your vote, as if it will make a difference. And like obedient little sheep, you all turn out in droves to vote for the person you believe is less corrupt than the other. Make a selection from the lesser of two evils. The U.S. is a corporation and you, my dear, are nothing but a pawn in the game."

"Not everyone in the community is out for themselves. I know lots of people who help each other out," I provided a weak defense.

"Only when it benefits them," she countered.

"Even if everything you say is true, how is *this* helping?"

"Change begins with taking the first step."

No one had broken it down to me like she had. I mean, I knew life was hard for black people, but I had no idea it was all planned to be so. If history was any indication of the future, my life as a young black woman in the United States of America didn't amount to much. On the scale of importance of its citizens, I had unfortunately been relegated to the lowest rung on the societal ladder.

"Since you're so full of information... Tell me this. Are you responsible for all the thousands of black and brown children who go missing each year?!"

"I wish we were the only group responsible for the missing children. Unfortunately, there many individuals, corporations, and even foreign governments that fund abductions for nefarious purposes. Don't get me wrong, there are many children and quite a few adults who are runaways trying to escape from their current life situations. Some children are kidnapped by family members due to custody disputes. Many are sold as slaves to men in foreign countries who don't give a damn because slavery is a tradition deeply embedded within their cultures. They place those unfortunate children into life-long bondage to pay off family debts. Others are sold as sex slaves to sick and perverted men. And even some women!"

"Damn.... I had no idea there were so many sick people in this world! They're raping young boys and girls?!"

"Unfortunately, yes. Those pedophiles have got it in their sick minds that having sex with children is a glorious thing. There are entire groups dedicated to providing child pornography for the gratification of perverts. This has always been the case with the Catholic church and their priesthood." She shook her head to clear the images.

"Those poor, poor kids..." I didn't know what more to say.

"The children we focus on rescuing are the ones most desired by researchers, scientists, and the very wealthy elite. These children have highly developed and evolved brains that provide the children with extraordinary abilities. They are used for experimental purposes, drug trials and such."

"Is that why I am here? Is that why all the kids here in this camp are melanated? You guys think we're special?"

"For the most part." She nodded. "Children born around the turn of the century, and subsequently their offspring, are thought to be of superior intelligence and more highly evolved than previous generations. Because these children's brains are highly evolved, very wealthy and powerful individuals are buying and then murdering these poor babies for their brain stem cells. They then inject those cells into their own bodies in an attempt to prolong the aging process. It is a very profitable, but also a dangerous cut-throat business," she explained. "Unfortunately, those people who participate go unpunished because this system was intentionally designed for no one to care whether those missing children live or die."

"I can't believe this! You're telling me that kids are being traded like stocks and bonds in the stock market?!"

"Yes, on the black market..."

"Black market?! What the...?!" I interrupted. "Is that why it's called that? Because they are still buying black people and enslaving them like they did back in the 1800's?"

"Slavery never ended." She nodded and continued, "There is a black market on the dark web where slavery continues to this day. Children are purchased, murdered and then sold off for body parts; to allow those who have enough money to purchase organs, cells, and blood they need to survive."

"This is insane! It sounds like you're talking about vampires and parasites, instead of people! How can anybody get away with this?!" She explained all this much too calmly, which made me feel a certain kind of way when I considered how easy it was for me to be snatched. It occurred to me numerous times during this conversation that I could have ended up in much worse circumstances.

She glanced at a folder bursting with yellowed paper resting on her desk, and nonchalantly stated, "Some children are also selected to participate in space trials because they possess extraterrestrial DNA. Building a future for mankind to survive in outer space."

My eyes trailed hers to the folder. Apparently, whatever was inside held critical information. I wanted nothing more than to grab it and run. But where would I go? Who would I take the papers to? I felt trapped.

"Not all of us are in this for your bodies. We want your minds before you become corrupted. One lesson we took from this nation's military leaders, what they learned during their perfection of making war is, once you control the minds of a people, you control everything about them."

"What is this place?! Who the fuck are you?!"

"Kenya... please do not swear. The use of foul language is a reflection of poor upbringing." She continued, "...as I was saying, this will be the very last time I speak your name because names do not matter here. But I need for you to open your eyes to see the world around you."

"I don't care about all that! Tell me why am I here!" I shouted.

"You are here because you are different than the others."

"What are you talking about?!"

"Your family. Friends. Total strangers. People who are dead in their minds and set on paths of self-destruction to their bodies. They might as well be zombies. You are not of that ilk. You see the injustices playing out when it concerns your people. You know there is something not quite right with the world. You pose important philosophical questions that even your teachers cannot answer. School is not an indicator of intelligence, but your grades are off the chart. Yet, you don't seem to be impressed with the accolades for high achievement. You possess a drive to fix what's broken in this system if you only knew what it was. Deep down, you understand that you are much more than this society permits you to be. You know you are destined for something much bigger than yourself."

I sank down in the chair to allow her musings to sink in. Everything she said, I had heard many times before from my Uncle Ricky, my mother's youngest brother. The sibling my mother said was crazy because he had smoked too much weed. Whenever he started talking like that, we all laughed, called him the Conspiracy King. He was nothing but a joke to us. Easily dismissed. But now, as I listened to this woman basically saying verbatim what my uncle had proclaimed for as long as I could remember, left me devastatingly numb.

"What does any of this have to do with me?"

"This has everything to do with you. This facility, this program... it is all for you. And those who are like you."

"I was told this is an ICE camp. But from what I've seen so far, a prison or a correctional facility is a more accurate description."

"You are not a prisoner."

"You could have fooled me."

"Let me explain. After my epiphany, I started a non-profit corporation. And with approval of the U.S. Park Service, of course, I purchased this land with the money I received from selling my company. Thousands of acres, as far as the eye can see, belong to my private corporation. I negotiated with the government to build within the boundary of the National Park. Told them I wanted to help rid the country of its 'problems'. It was all very clandestine. Top Secret at the highest level that there are no records of our existence. Thanks to the feds, no one has access to this area of the park, nor to my land."

"See. That's exactly what I'm talking about. This is what white privilege gets you. A secretive deal with the government."

"The fact of the matter is, I was able to purchase this land and can do whatever I want as long as they believed I was helping rid the country of illegal immigrants."

"The government lets you do whatever you want with us since you promised to deport Mexicans?" I asked, though not surprised because the non-completion of the southern border wall had been in the news for years.

"The President is primarily concerned on those immigrating from central and south America, but yes, you are correct. We told them we would help eliminate the tide of undocumented immigrants crossing the southern border. Including those from Mexico."

"That's interesting considering part of this country belonged to Mexico before it was stolen. Funny they never mention building a wall with Canada," I remarked, staring through the window at the dark night. "You mentioned the public parks. I didn't realize that land was available for sale to the public."

She grinned and replied, "You are correct. It's not."

"Don't lots of people go missing in these parks?" I recalled several stories of the missing never being found or their bodies were later discovered mauled by wild animals. Those were only a couple of reasons I never wanted to go camping out in the wild.

"You are correct. Hundreds go missing every year in the backwoods of this nation. And not all reasons are innocent. Or accidental." Her eyes widened as if she harbored some deep secrets. "There are reasons why the government has designated wide swaths of wilderness, restricting land to national parks, controlling access. Reasons the general public will never know."

"Now you want me to believe the U.S. government is also involved with missing persons? C'mon, lady..."

She didn't directly answer, but her cryptic response spoke volumes. She picked up the folder, rifling through loose pages marked Top Secret and Confidential. "I have witnessed some very strange occurrences while living in the mountains. Things that made me question my sanity.

There are secrets concealed within the confines of these national parks that have a direct correlation to your people. The purpose of the restricted land is not what you think."

"You talk like every other conspiracy theory nut job I've ever read about. Why would the government hide the truth about national parks from its citizens?" I replied skeptically. "What's out there besides forests and wild animals?"

"It doesn't matter..." Her fingers pulled out a weathered sheet of paper that looked like it had been through many other hands. She pushed it towards me. "This is documentation of visitation from extraterrestrial beings going back to the 1920's. Proof that the government knows we are not alone in the universe."

I held the fragile paper from the United States Army Air Corp, dated September 11, 1925. The typed written transcript described numerous visual sightings of strange aircraft in Britain, France, Germany, and the United States of America over a two-year period. It also included details of an encounter in the USSR where a spaceship had actually landed and several dark-skinned aliens resembling the American Negro had made contact with their government. I handed the paper back, not knowing what to make of what I had just read.

"In exchange for my secrecy for any unexplained, strange phenomena I may happen to observe, I offered up one major stipulation before signing the non-disclosure agreement."

"What's that?"

"That I be left to my own devices and given the latitude to personally select all my clients for the camp. No one comes here without my say so. Not even the feds."

"All that is very interesting, but who gave you the right to decide my fate? Or the fate of all those hundreds of kids out there?! Why didn't you just blow the damn whistle?! Start telling others what was happening instead of hiding up here in these mountains?!"

"Because of fear."

"What could you possibly be afraid of? You're a wealthy white woman in America. It's not like they're killing your kind in the streets."

"Not my fear. The fear that would engulf the masses. If the public ever discovers what their government is truly capable of, or the secrets it holds about what is really happening in this world... That their government experiments on them using drugs that should have never seen the light of day. That we have been visited by extraterrestrials on numerous occasions... If any of those things were made public, there would be chaos in the streets. The system would break down overnight."

"Yeah, I understand. My parents told me when the coronavirus first became a pandemic, people all over the world panicked. They raided the stores and stocked up on toilet paper of all things. People lost jobs, couldn't pay bills, started buying guns. They said it was pretty scary."

"The fear of scarcity and the unknown spread more quickly than any virus ever will. But you must realize it is all part of the one world agenda. Create chaos, cause fear, and then provide a solution. The public willingly gives up its freedoms as it becomes grateful for its government's protection."

"What I don't understand is, with all that you've just told me, why you are focusing on abducting black children? Why aren't you trying to save your own people since you guys will probably go extinct before we do?"

"You're asking the wrong questions."

"So, tell me this... You've explained what you're doing to help us, but not why. How did you become involved?"

"The morning on the top of the mountain, the day I had my epiphany and walked away, I was contacted by a strange looking man who seemingly materialized out of nowhere. He asked me if I wanted to help change the world."

I looked at her as if she had truly lost her mind, but I played along to see where this was going. "Just like that? Weren't you scared?"

"Of course, I was taken aback by his sudden appearance. And how he looked. At first, I believed I was suffering from altitude sickness and having hallucinations, or that he was some government experiment gone awry. But when he read my mind, notifying me how many people I had hurt or even killed with drugs I was responsible for developing, I knew he was not a figment of my imagination. He gave me a brief lesson on what was happening in this world, in particular how African-Americans were being treated in this country by those in positions of power. People like me. He said if I helped him, all the horrors I inflicted on innocent people with drug trials would be forgiven. When I asked him who he was, he simply told me he was 'The Teacher', sent here to help his people out of an imminent demise. He informed me that I would never know anything more about him or the process other than what he permitted. And he would know before I did if I even thought about lying to him."

"That's interesting. So what made you want to help him?" I squinted, suspiciously. "Nobody ever wants to help black Americans."

"Because I had already made up my mind to quit the pharmaceutical industry, I figured doing some good would make up for all the bad I'd done. Besides, The Teacher was a very convincing individual."

"Don't expect me to say, thank you," I murmured, wondering if she was crazy. "I just hope you're not like all the other white people who say they want to help black people, then turn around and stab us in the back."

She waved off my concerns, took her seat, interlaced her fingers, turned her back to me and asked, "Did you see those young people on your way in?"

"Yes, I saw them."

"Did you happen to notice how relaxed those children were?"

I nodded.

"The doors at this level are not locked. With the exception of Section D, which is basically the detoxification section and where you were placed when you first arrived, the children are free to roam the entire site."

"Detoxification section? What's that for?"

"It normally takes months—or in some cases years—to rid your body not only of toxic food, personal care products, household and environmental chemicals, vaccinations, and the cocktail of drugs you've been exposed to during your brief existence. But it also takes time and training to rid you of the poison that has infiltrated your mind courtesy of the media, the educational system, all religion, and certain misguided ones who think they are 'woke'."

"I'm sure parents would understand your intent is to help the children live better lives. But, why put us in cages if that's your vision? Cages are for animals, not people."

"I agree. But when you have lived your entire life in an invisible cage, it is dangerous, for you as well as the others, to not take matters slowly. In spite of what the world has told you and what you have been led to believe, you are not free and have never been free. Melanated people in America are used to being treated a certain way and whites have been indoctrinated to naturally consider themselves to be superior over all others. That is why I chose white guards."

"You intentionally recreated a prison-like system because we're used to being treated like second-class citizens? Wow!"

"Blacks learn from birth to fear and respect every group except their own. And the United States has manipulated its 'white' citizens to believe that the color of their skin makes them superior. But if either group ever took a moment to stop and consider that the strongest things in nature are full of wondrous color, we would realize how false that notion of white superiority is. But to acknowledge the fact would mean giving up the power."

"I am only sixteen and I know what you say is true. My question is, why don't they?"

"The system dictates our reality. He who has the power, makes the rules. And at this point in history, the white man has all the power."

"Nothing about this feels right."

"Unfortunately, this is the system we're stuck with and being right doesn't mean a thing."

"I still think you are insane."

"Possibly, but my method works. And by the way, what is wrong with being 'in-sane'? To me that is a compliment. Being anything else would mean you are out of your mind. Think about it... Most people who are declared *insane* by society's definition have actually woken up. They see the real world, understand the hopelessness of trying to change it, which also unfortunately causes some to go mad."

"Well, there is nothing wrong with my mind!" I felt the anger returning, rising up through my chest, to my vocal cord and through my mouth. I shouted, "You do realize you've given the guards the power to shoot. To kill! Just like the police do back home."

"That has never been the case in all the years of operation. I personally screen each and every guard. They all must undergo psychological testing to weed out the criminals and racists. This is not a prison and I do not hire police. Or thugs. Of course, although they can shout, call you names, and otherwise behave in the manner of which they were raised, the one stipulation I make with the guards is they are not allowed to injure clients unless there is a real and certain threat of danger. There is a brilliant parallel to how we treat you here with how it is out there. Don't you agree?"

"You must have let one slip through. That asshole in the van hit Samaria because she was crying."

I watched the woman's expression barely register any change in emotion. Until she spoke, I wondered if she heard what I told her about the man.

"Wait here," she said and went into the hallway to speak with the guard. In less than 30 seconds she returned and continued with her spiel.

She continued, "After you are free from the toxic waste fed to you through every point of entry in your body, next comes the most difficult aspect. The purpose of the mental detox unit is to clear your mind until you no longer are a threat to yourself or others. The length of time it takes to clear your system depends upon how indoctrinated you are. The younger children usually take much less time. Once they enter the public education system, the process becomes much more difficult."

I thought back to all the junk food I'd eaten over the years. Fried chicken, pizza, doughnuts, potato chips, French fries, cookies, ice cream and cake. Thinking about all that delicious food reminded me the last meal I had eaten lunch because I hadn't wanted to spoil my birthday dinner.

"There is nothing you could have done differently because the system is setup to encourage unhealthy eating and addictive habits." She sighed wearily shaking her head. "The United States is a business and unfortunately, as with all businesses, the goal is to makes lots of money. Even to the detriment of its own citizens."

I could not count the number of hours spent watching mindless television or totally dumb movies every single day. I wondered why all the things that were bad for us were so readily available.

"My point is, when your body and your mind are clear and functioning properly, you are no longer captive. You are free. With discipline, like the others, you too will get there."

"Why don't they just leave if they are so free?"

"They now have options as never before. They choose not to leave because they have a mission. A life's purpose."

"Now I get it..." I uttered in contempt. "You have a savior complex. Trying to save us poor folks from ourselves. Well, I do not need saving, especially from people who look like you. I am not going to allow myself to be brainwashed."

"I like to think we help free young minds from the enslavement of this corrupt system. Those children are well on their way of discovering who they could be."

"This is some bullshit! You people steal us from our families, brainwash us into thinking whatever you want us to believe, and then try to convince us we're better off with you! Here! In this godforsaken hellhole place of wherever we are! Sorry to disappoint you lady, but I am not some poor misguided youth you can rescue from the hood!"

"You are only poor in knowledge of self." She stared at me with those brilliant green eyes. Nonplussed by the outburst, she whispered, "My question to you is, do you know who you are?"

"Of course, I do. I'm Kenya Williams. I'm sixteen years old. I was born and raised in St. Louis, Missouri and I'm a junior in high school. I run track and I'm the fastest sprinter on my team."

"Did you know the name Kenya has no historical basis other than being a resource rich country on the very recently named continent of Africa? The same is true for the country Zambia. And that Victoria Falls you want to go visit so badly was named after a British monarch. What you or your parents don't know is both those two countries offer a rich history that was white-washed hundreds of years ago by European colonization. Ask yourself why Gerald and Carmen gave you those names?"

"How do you know my parents?!"

"I know everything about you." A genuine smile graced her face. "As I was explaining... School is a state sponsored mandatory activity that has mostly corrupted your mind and served to foster your miseducation to keep you enslaved in the United States capitalistic system. The purpose of schooling is for you to be a cog, a tool, a moneymaking asset. A productive citizen. You are much more than you realize."

"If everything I've learned about myself isn't true, then who am I?"

She murmured in a voice barely above a whisper, "That is precisely the question you should be asking yourself, *Who* are you?"

Chapter Five

The greasy haired male guard waited patiently outside the woman's office the entire time. When she gave the signal, he returned to escort me back to the Detoxification Section. As we approached a different group of 'clients', gathered in a discussion circle, I studied them in the few seconds I had, taking note of their dress, mannerisms, and expressions. None of the girls sported weaves, fake nails or eyelashes, nor did they wear a ton of makeup. An authentic beauty radiated from the tops of their natural hair down to the tips of their manicured toes. Some of the young men wore locs and beards, while others sported clean shaven heads and faces. The young women wore colorful dresses. The males were dressed similarly in long-sleeved shirts—white, purple, or black and loose-fitting pants.

The way the young women tilted their heads slightly back when they spoke; the young men who patiently listened without interruption or any sign of disrespect; how they all sat with backs straight and heads held high... The scene brought only one word to mind. Regal. The tone of their conversation was friendly, yet intense. The usual signs of foolishness one normally witnesses when a group of teens are gathered, were nowhere to be found.

The redhaired woman's words reverberated throughout all the corners of my mind. They bounced off the area of common sense, over to conspiracy theories, and rested on the real probability that she had spouted nothing but lies and deception, before finally settling on the possibility everything she said was true. In spite of all she'd told me, the most disturbing phrase she mentioned was firmly planted in my mind and taking root. The question, *Who am I?* continued to resonate in my thoughts.

Once we returned to detox, the male guard peeled off, returning me to the mean-spirited female guards. The older one gave me the once over with a look of contempt. The younger woman's hand instinctively settled on the butt of a riot stick resting on the desk. The air of superiority seeping from the pores of both their pale skins was as palpable as molasses poured from a bottle on a cold winter day. That smug expression on the younger guard's face irked me more now than it had before.

"Hope you had a nice visit with the lady," she smirked, now tapping the riot stick to her palm. "...because for the next few months, your black ass belongs to me."

My first thought was to laugh out loud, tell the chunky guard to go to hell because I was hip to the game. There wasn't anything she could do to me except talk smack. I rolled my eyes at her then entered the cell without her assistance.

The Jamaican girl sat with Samaria on the dirty floor playing tic-tac-toe in the grime. From the amount of build-up, the floor hadn't been cleaned in quite a while. Both looked up at the same time when the guard locked the cell. A case of water that wasn't there when I left sat near the entrance. Someone had graciously placed a couple bottles on each bunk.

"That sure took a long time!" noted the Jamaican.

"Did it? I hadn't noticed," I replied, thinking my visit with that crazy redhead was much better than sitting here in this depressing cell. At least her office was comfortable.

"Where did they take you after your shower?"

"I'm not sure," I responded truthfully.

"Hi Kenya," Samaria said. "I took a long nap..."

"Good for you." I laid down on an empty lower bunk bed. The bare mattress was covered in questionable stains. The pillow smelled like dirty hair and bad breath.

"... then we had dinner and I could eat all I wanted. Sorry you missed it."

"I'm sorry I missed dinner too. I'm so hungry."

"You didn't miss much. I think they are trying to starve us to death. We are served mostly raw fruits and vegetables," explained the Jamaican. "Breakfast, lunch, and dinner. Hardly any food served is ever cooked. They believe raw is better."

"That's okay," I uttered between yawns. Raw food must be the initial start of the detoxification. "I am too tired to eat anyway."

"Did this little girl tell you that she's a champion chess player?"

"No, she didn't." I looked over at Samaria. No longer sullen, she wore a huge grin, returning her persona to the happy child she most likely was. The clothes she arrived in were replaced by a scaled down version of the red scrubs like all the other girls. "That's awesome!"

"She told me she can beat kids twice her age," the Jamaican said proudly. "I kept telling these girls. They don't kidnap any dummies."

The girl nicknamed CraCra ambled over. She took a seat on my bunk bed causing the thin mattress to sink so low I rolled over, touching her backside. I withstood the urge to push her away.

"What's so special about you?" she asked the Jamaican.

"I told you I qualified for the Olympic trials. In the 400- and 800-meter race."

"Oh yeah, I forgot." She sneered. "You can run fast. Big whoop."

"My ability to run fast is much better than being a psycho walking calculator like you. What good is that?"

CraCra then turned to me, obviously trying to figure out what my special ability was. As I searched her chestnut colored face, noticing the subtle slant of her light brown eyes, the short pug nose, and the thickness of her neck, I wondered if she had Down's syndrome.

"You don't stink anymore," she said sporting a huge grin. "Thank you for changing your clothes."

"Whatever. If someone had put a gun to your head and threatened to kill you, you would have peed your pants too."

Her eyes darted to the nearest guard whose focus was on girls in another cell. She whispered, "I heard they took you to see the warden. Be very careful who you trust around here. That green-eyed woman with that funny looking red hair tells nothing but lies. She told me I was special. Said I have something no one else does."

"You special, all right," joked the Jamaican.

"The warden said I can do things like very few others. If only I would apply myself." The girl tilted her head and whispered, "Did she tell you that you can move things with your mind, too?"

"Leave that girl alone. She just got here a couple hours ago. Ain't nobody got time for your foolishness."

"No, she didn't," I replied.

"Humph, I wonder why. She only lets us special girls visit her office. I have been three times already. The green-eyed lady says I need more time in Section D before I can move up. I practice all the time but so far... nothing."

"Anyway, she isn't a warden because this isn't a correctional facility," I explained.

"If it looks like a duck, walks like a duck and quacks like a duck, it's a duck," replied CraCra.

I didn't want to discuss what the woman spoke to me about. I wanted to close my eyes, go to sleep, and wake up from this horrible nightmare at home in my own warm bed. I wanted to hear my brothers bang on my door telling me to wake up so they could get into the bathroom. Even though I refused to eat it, I wanted to smell the delicious scents of bacon and eggs wafting from the kitchen as my mother prepared for a day of shopping in celebration of my birthday. I wanted to get my braids redone because the ends had started to unravel and the roots were all poufy. I wanted to hear the soothing sound of my daddy snoring making all us laugh at how loud it was. I closed my eyes to ward off the ugly images of the chained link cage and the dull gray covering every available inch. I hated sleeping under the crinkly mylar blanket, on an old smelly mattress, on a rickety bunk bed. I wanted privacy when I used the toilet and the ability to go without having to ask permission.

CraCra climbed into the bunk above me, squirming around until she found a comfortable position. I prayed for sleep to arrive quickly as the rumblings of my stomach were almost too much to bear. I took a sip of water from one of the bottles of water left on the mattress.

Over the loudspeaker came the announcement I had waited for since returning to the cell. Now I could rest. Gather my thoughts. Make a plan on not only how I was going to survive but also how to maintain my sanity.

"Lights out, ladies!"

Almost immediately, the rise and fall of voices quieted first to a whisper, then ceased altogether. The chatter was now filled with the soft snores of hundreds of girls dreaming about their families. All yearning to go home.

Chapter Six

When I opened my eyes, to my surprise and delight I discovered I was at home, snuggled under the covers of my own warm bed listening to the familiar sound of my family drifting upstairs from the kitchen below. Turns out that the events of yesterday were just a horrible nightmare! I reached over to the nightstand, my fingers searching for the hard silicon case of my cell phone. I picked it up, feeling the reassuring weight of the phone in my hand. The display indicated it was a little after 7.

The soft light of the morning sun had yet to find its way through the blinds of my bedroom's east facing window. As I laid there taking my time to fully awaken, my thoughts returned to the fantastical dream from the night before. Snippets of the nightmare gradually wafted back like a bad smell. I had been kidnapped, thrown into a dirty van and taken by gunpoint to a strange location; only to be confronted by a crazy redhaired woman with eyes so green they appeared artificial. I pushed the horrific images from my mind.

Shaking off the nightmare, I suddenly remembered that today was my sixteenth birthday! This also meant that since today was my birthday, it was also Friday, and I was running late for school. Didn't matter though because it was going to be a wonderful day. I heard my younger brother's chatter on the other side of the door so at least I wasn't the only one who was late. Excited to get downstairs to find out what gift my parents had gotten for my birthday, I sat up and dangled my legs over the edge of the bed. My vision was slightly clouded from sleep for as I surveyed my surroundings I did not immediately know where I was! The room looked to be triple the size of my bedroom and decorated with unfamiliar furniture. Maybe I was still in that confusing space between sleep and wakefulness, so I pinched myself to fully wake up.

Something was definitely wrong. My feet weren't even touching the floor like they normally did.

Confused was the best word to describe how I felt. Instead of waking in my twin size bed underneath my favorite worn bedspread that was covered in the repeating pattern of the sun, moon, and stars, I was sitting on a huge bed with an expensive champagne-colored satin comforter as the cover. I rubbed my eyes and loudly yawned hoping this would get me going.

I lowered my feet until my toes hit the floor, trying to locate the old house shoes I'd worn for years. The once pink, bunny rabbit slippers with each shoe missing a black button eye, was nowhere to be found. I slowly lowered my body from the bed and sank to my knees to peer underneath the massive four-post bed. An expensive pair of Ugg slippers, that looked like they had never been worn, rested side-by-side on the soft rug partially covering the entire highly polished gleaming wood floor.

"What is going on? Where am I? Whose bed am I sleeping in? Where are my shoes?" The questions shot through my mind one after another as my eyes traveled the length of the large room.

My knees slid on the rug due to the smooth silky fabric covering them. I was not wearing the oversized *Tupac Poetic Justice* t-shirt I normally slept in. This birthday morning, I was dressed in fine silk pajamas, purple with gold trim and gold-colored buttons. "What the...? This is weird. I cannot be fully awake yet."

I stood to my feet, more convinced than ever that I must be sleepwalking. Either that or my parents had pulled one heck of a surprise for my birthday. The rays of the sunlight finally made its way through the windows bathing the room in its brilliant golden light. But there were no blinds covering this window, rather sheer lace curtains that fluttered in the breeze of the partially opened windows. I tentatively made my way to the dresser—the likes of which I had only seen in magazines—noting the intricately detailed carvings in what appeared to be exquisite wood. As I approached the dresser, the delightful sounds of my family comforted me that I was in a safe place.

I stared into the mirror. The reflection of the young woman staring back was me, but not *me*. The long braids I went to bed with were replaced by a short curly natural. All previous traces of acne had cleared up to reveal smooth flawless skin. My reflection was at least twenty pounds lighter in appearance. When I gasped, so did she. When I covered my mouth with my hand, she did the same. The sunlight simultaneously kissed both our faces with the same intensity, highlighting the golden flecks of our brown irises. And when I moved in for a closer look, the surprised expression on her face mirrored my own. I pressed my hands to feel the cool glass pressing back. Satisfied the girl on the other side of the mirror was somehow indeed me, I backed away.

I recalled writing a short story for a Creative Writing class. It was about a girl who lived on the other side of the mirror who I named Aynek. My mirror-image lived a totally different existence than what I experienced in my world. We shared a reflection and were the same age, but that is where the commonality ended. My teacher was intrigued by the story, encouraging me to flesh it out, and then suggested I submit it to a writing contest. But I never did. Because at the time, I feared my delving into matters skirting the supernatural might get me in trouble with my God-fearing, yet no-longer practicing religious parents.

Even with the consideration of my imaginative story in mind, I knew this was not that. I was not the girl inside the mirror, but I was also not the person I once knew myself to be. My curiosity became piqued as to what awaited me on the other side of the intricately carved bedroom door. I turned the knob. It was quite heavy and took some effort to open.

For the record, we did not live in a dump. Both my parents worked full-time so we lived fairly well in a modest home with four bedrooms and two bathrooms. But there was nothing special about our house, it was like all the others on the block. I had friends who lived in nice houses in much fancier neighborhoods, thus living well was not a foreign concept. But I was not prepared for the opulence on the other side.

I was greeted by a long hallway tastefully decorated with exquisite pieces of art hanging from the wall and expensive looking vases atop what appeared to be antique end tables. Several more doors, similar in style to my bedroom's, bordered either side. The color palette was natural, reflecting the interior found on a tropical island, unlike the bland beige walls I was used to at home. The house felt warm, welcoming, and so very familiar. As if walking in slow motion, I opened the door closest to me. It was not occupied. This room was obviously a young girl's as it was painted a subtle shade of tangerine. The neatly made trundle bed was covered with too many stuffed animals to count. A dollhouse populated by tiny brown and black dolls decked out in tiny traditional outfits sat in one corner next to a miniature table covered by a four serving tea set.

A child's burst of laughter came from the next room. I closed the bedroom door and pushed the other one open. Inside sat a boy of around nine who looked nothing like my younger brother, Stokely. He was playing games on a screen that I could not see, and yet he was totally engrossed in it. I was surprised when he turned towards me because I wasn't quite sure I was physically able to be seen. But he smiled and continued playing that virtual game with whomever was on the other end. Though I heard him speak, I did not understand the language.

I continued down the long hallway until I reached a grand staircase made entirely of Mahogany. Beautifully carved wooden posts at the top and bottom added just the right touch of elegance. As I descended the stairs, only then did the opulent décor become apparent. The walls were not painted but were covered in fine luxurious fabric. Massive paintings of what I imagined were African inspired scenery were strategically placed along the walls. As I reached the last step that ended at the foyer, the front door opened.

Through the oversized entrance, in walked an unfamiliar version of a man I knew to be my father. However, this man was much darker than my daddy. He also seemed younger, healthier, and had a full head of dark hair. He looked happy. Instead of his shoulders being slumped from decades of performing manual labor, he stood very tall. Proud and strong. I involuntarily gasped upon seeing him, taken aback by his appearance. He gave me the most beautiful smile, filled with warmth and love like I had never experienced.

My heart pulsed in my throat until a lump of emotion became lodged there. I became filled with so much utter joy that my body responded in kind by levitating a foot in the air. Upon realizing that my feet had actually left the floor, I became frightened as I did not know what had caused this to happen. Without uttering a sound, my father came to me, gently nudged me down and enveloped me in a loving embrace. With his simple touch, I experienced a level of love such as never imagined. He kissed my cheek and led me by the hand to the kitchen.

The woman I believed to be my mother fluttered around the kitchen preparing breakfast. As I studied her, I noted this version was not the same woman I had battled with since turning thirteen, when nothing I did ever seemed good enough. The vibes coming from her were carefree, without stress or worry. She pushed plates piled high with ripe fresh fruit towards versions of my two brothers. A young girl of six sat on the floor playing with a floppy doll. I assumed this was my sister. No one uttered a sound. In my thoughts I 'heard' all their conversations and happy chatter as clearly as if they were speaking aloud.

An older woman wearing a colorful print dress with a matching scarf tied on her head sat at the table sipping fragrant tea. Her smooth skin, the color of café au lait, seemed to glow from within. And when she raised her hands to drink, the numerous stone and crystal bracelets she wore around both wrists rattled with the melodious sound of wind chimes.

My mom's eyes twinkled brightly when she 'communicated' to me, *"Today is the day I gave birth to my beautiful daughter. I thank my husband for planting such a glorious seed. And I thank The Creator for allowing me to bring you into this world. You are truly a special young woman who The Most High has blessed with many gifts. In time you will know the truth about who you really are."* She looked at me as if seeing me for the first time and smiled warmly. Then planted a tender kiss on the apples of both my cheeks.

I was positively flabbergasted! The woman whom I had butted heads with since I turned thirteen, who made it a point to criticize me on a regular basis—lest I get too full of myself—had looked past my flaws to see the beauty that lies within me. This was not the mother I remembered, but it was the mother I felt I needed.

The matronly woman, whom I did not recognize, interlocked her arm in mine. She silently guided me through the kitchen door which opened to a large outdoors space. We strolled through a courtyard garden unrivaled by any I could imagine. Various shades of green foliage graced the numerous trees lining the property. The lush grass grew in such a vivid shade of green, one might have thought it was fake. Tropical flowers of multiple varieties in just as many colors lined the manicured lawn. Older men with garden tools that seemed to require very little effort to operate, expertly tended to the landscaping. They smiled and wished us a good day.

We sat on a stone bench next to a pond filled with brightly colored fish. I turned my face upwards to allow the warmth of the sun to touch my skin. I felt something stir deep inside, akin to the delightful feeling of butterflies in one's stomach. As I glanced around the garden, I could not help but want to remain there. It felt like home. At this point, I understood this was not reality, or at least not any reality I had ever experienced.

"I am not who you think I am," I mentally confessed in a language I could not have possibly known.

The woman turned to me. Telepathically, she relayed, *"Beloved, you is who ya is. The question you should be askin' yo'self is, 'Who am I?' When ya learns the truth 'bout that, then ya will unnerstand that you is 'xactly who I know you is."*

"I don't understand. How will I know what is the truth?"

"You will know the truth, when ya know it." The woman smiled mysteriously.

I felt myself quickly being yanked backwards by an invisible rope tied around my mid-section. I tried to hang on to the woman, but the force was much too strong. The image of the woman sitting on the bench blurred into nothingness as I went through a long tunnel into a dark space where no light reached. I did not want to leave. I was not ready.

When I opened my eyes, I found myself surrounded by chain link fencing, inside a cage with four other girls, tightly clutching the stinky pillow, lying on a gross mattress of the bottom bunkbed, staring straight into the closely set eyes of the girl I now believed was appropriately nicknamed CraCra.

The reality of my horrific situation finally sank in. I allowed the tears kept pent up since my arrival, to now flow freely. I had never felt so alone in all my life.

Chapter Seven

"Don't cry," whispered CraCra, grinning. "It really isn't that bad. You'll get used to being here in no time at all."

"I don't want to get used to this place. I want to go home!" I cried with remnants of the fantastic dream fresh in my mind. An overwhelming sensation of sorrow overtook my emotions threatening to send me into a downward spiral of despair from which I might never recover.

"Might as well get those thoughts of going home out of your head. Once they get you, you're here for good," she explained. "We're your family now for as long as we're in this cage together."

The Jamaican girl eased down from her bunk, pulled a pair of socks on her bare feet, then stuffed a toothbrush and small tube of toothpaste inside her bra. "CraCra is making sense for a change. The only thing you'll accomplish believing you'll get out of here is to make yourself miserable."

"This isn't fair! I shouldn't be here!" I felt a terrifying grip of anxiety tighten around my chest. My breath began to come in short bursts.

"Calm down. You're going to hyperventilate if you keep breathing like that," CraCra whispered. "Hold your hands over your nose and mouth like this."

I took her advice. I inhaled. Exhaled. Inhaled and exhaled deeply, twice more until I felt my breathing return to normal.

"That's better. You had better get up. They will be coming around to take us to the bathroom in a few minutes. If you miss your turn, you will have to wait until after lunch."

"Is it time to get up already?" I asked, rubbing the combination of sleep and tears from my eyes.

"Every morning at six o'clock! Time to rise and shine!" CraCra gathered her personal hygiene items in preparation for the guards coming for them.

"I'm sorry for crying. But I want to go home. Don't you guys miss your family?" I asked the Jamaican, wiping the snot from my nose with the bottom of my shirt.

The Jamaican replied, "Hell yeah I miss my family. My mom, dad, and my brothers and sisters. I miss them all so much it hurts. I miss taking a bath. I miss sitting in front of TV eating a pint of rocky road ice cream all by myself. I miss my dog. I miss my friends. I miss getting my hair done by the Africans who braided my hair so tight I looked Chinese." She laughed at the memories of a life unrealized. "Shoot, I even miss the sound of tires screeching on the street when they drag raced through the hood. I miss my boyfriend... But missing any of those things doesn't make me feel any better or get me out of here. And it won't help you either. So, get yourself together."

"I haven't been here as long as you but I understand." I reminded myself, "Daddy always told me and my brothers don't bother crying unless there is absolutely nothing we can do about our situation. Crying can make you feel sorry for yourself and prevent you from taking action to find a solution. He used to tell us we have two choices. We can either sit there and cry like a baby or get up and do something about it." I wiped the tears away and pushed myself up to a seating position. "I'm going to do something about it."

"Your daddy sounds like a smart man," replied CraCra.

"Hmph! I'd sure like to know what you intend to do. We all been sitting here for months trying to figure out a way out of here," muttered the Jamaican.

CraCra went to Samaria's bed to gently nudge her awake. The little girl woke with a start. You could see the terror she felt waking up in a strange place, slowly be replaced with recollection of where she was now. She yawned, stretched, and then calmly reached underneath her mattress to retrieve a compact toothbrush. Considering the fragile state of mind, she was in when we first arrived, a180-degree turn in her attitude would be welcomed.

"Where did you all get toothbrushes?" I asked running my tongue over teeth that needed a good cleaning.

"The guard was supposed to bring toiletries for you last night. Guess they forgot," replied a girl who hadn't uttered a word the entire time. She looked much older than the rest of us. Her dark chocolate skin was flawlessly beautiful.

"Thanks for letting me know," I replied.

"I have a couple extra ones. You can have one until you get your own," she said reaching inside a toiletries bag stashed in the corner near a bookcase filled with dozens of dog-eared books.

"Thank you." I accepted a toothbrush that was less than half the size of mine at home. It was actually smaller than those given out by dentists after an annual exam.

"I've seen chicks like you before. You probably won't be here very long."

"What do you mean?"

"You are already natural," she said standing with her back propped against the wall.

"Natural?"

"Most chicks come here with relaxed hair, be all weaved up, got hair dyed up in every funky color of the rainbow. Chicks be wearing fake eyelashes looking like fuckin' caterpillars crawlin' across their eyelids! Acrylic nails so long I don't see how they wipe their asses clean. Some still wear color contact lens. We niggas be fake as fuck! Haven't seen nobody here with fake asses or tits yet. But you're not like that. You got braids, but I can see your natural hair underneath. Look like you don't wear makeup. Your fingernails your own. You're natural. All authentic and shit."

"Uh, yeah. I guess I am."

"How old are you?"

"I just turned sixteen. What about you?"

"I turned eighteen a few weeks after they snatched my ass from the backseat of an uber. I was on my way home from a fuckin' concert."

"Does this get any easier for you?"

"Tell you the truth, I don't really miss home." She added as an afterthought, "I'm from Kansas City so there ain't much to miss."

"How can you not miss home?" I asked incredulously. In my mind I filed away her nickname as KC.

"I wasn't doing much of nothin' 'cept working part-time at Whole Foods barely making enough for rent. Everybody I know back there is messed up in the head. Majority of my friends are hooked on some kinda drug. Pretty much all the men I know got criminal records so long they can't even get a real job that pay more than min wage."

"I know what you mean. It's the same story back home in St. Louis." I wondered what was taking the guards so long. I seriously had to use the bathroom. "Most girls my age already have one or two kids."

KC lowered her gaze, inhaling slowly as her hands rubbed against her thighs. "When I got here my hair was relaxed and dyed bright red. I had a weave that messed up my scalp so bad they cut all my hair off. Been three months and it's just now starting to grow in." She rubbed the half inch stubble covering her head. "I had to get rid of them fake nails. Look how messed up my fingers are. It's going to take months for my nails to look right again."

"The last time I got a manicure was for junior prom. That little Vietnamese man messed up my nails so bad that I thought they would never grow back," I chuckled remembering the nail salon my friend dragged me to. My girl had a weekly standing appointment and didn't think twice about spending money she didn't have to keep up the illusion.

"Those damn nail salons are a trap. Once you get your fingernails done, you have to keep going back or else your shit is gonna look all messed up. You wouldn't believe how much money I used to spend on hair and nails." She gazed at her hands. "Half my damn paycheck went to those Asians."

"I would still rather be at home than in here. Wherever we are," I replied, rolling my eyes at the disgusting condition of the cell.

"That's because you probably have a family to go home to. A momma and daddy who care somethin' about your ass. I didn't have that."

I almost couldn't believe what I was hearing. This girl preferred being locked up over having her freedom. I swore I wouldn't let them get to me like that. "There is no way I want to remain locked up like an animal."

"You don't have no right to judge me!"

The Jamaican and CraCra joined us in the corner to listen because there wasn't much else to do while waiting for the guards to come. Samaria sat on the floor drawing designs in the grime.

"I'm sorry. I wasn't trying to judge you."

"You want to know why I hate where I grew up? Why I'm not in no hurry to get my ass back?!"

I nodded.

"As soon as I turned fifteen, I got a little job at a Burger King because that was the only way I'd have money to buy clothes and stuff for school. One Friday night I had to work the late shift. By the time I got off, the buses had already stopped running. I called my brother to come pick me up. He couldn't because the battery in his car had died earlier that day. So, the only way to get home was to walk. I remember being nervous because it was so damn dark out there and it wasn't in the best part of town. I had walked about two miles when this police car pulled beside me."

"Damn..." the Jamaican interrupted, shaking her head. "I know where this is going."

"Muthafuckin' bitch-ass white cop rolled down his window and called me over. He wanted to know where I was going. Asked me if I was trying to pick up men." She guffawed. "I told him I was on my way home from work. He pretended to be all concerned and said it was dangerous for a girl my age to be out walking alone that time of the night. Then he offered me a ride."

"That was nice of him," I replied. "I don't think the cops in St. Louis would have done that."

"Yeah, I thought he was being nice too until his bitch ass raped me."

"You were raped by a police officer?" CraCra asked with eyes as wide as saucers.

"That muthafucka turned off his headlights, drove into a parking lot, and parked behind an abandoned gas station. He told me to get out of the car and said if I screamed or tried to run away, he'd shoot me and hide my body inside that building. I was so damn scared."

All eyes and ears were on KC imagining the terror she experienced. I lowered my head as I felt the pain settle in her voice.

"He told me to pull my pants down and bend over the hood of his car. I thought he was going to kill me so I did everything he told me to do. I cried while he shoved his nasty dick inside of me. Asshole didn't even bother using a rubber..."

"I'm sorry," I said again.

"The hood of that car was so hot. But I placed both hands on it to keep from falling. Then his police scanner buzzed with reports of robberies, car chases, some shit like that. His ass didn't stop until he came inside of me." She wiped her angry tears away with the back of her hand. "Here I was listening to all these muthafuckas dispatching cops to crimes when I was in the middle of being raped. I felt sick to my stomach and started to wretch. He told me I had better not puke on his car because it was just cleaned."

"What did you do?" asked the Jamaican.

"Didn't do nothing 'cept cry like a bitch. He finished his business, pulled up his pants, slapped my ass, and got back inside his car. Then he picked up his radio and reported in. Told the dispatcher he was five minutes out from where ever he needed to be. That bitch-ass muthafucka laughed and told me to be careful walking home because there were a lot of bad people on the streets this time of night. I didn't even know his name. I was too scared to ask. After he left, I tried to clean up-- get his sticky nastiness off me--with a pack of tissues I found in my backpack. I wiped the tears from my face and walked the rest of the way home."

"Did you tell your mother?" I asked.

"Hell yeah, I told her!" she replied sucking her teeth.

"What did she say?" I asked wondering how my parents would react. They didn't have much in the way of money or power, but I know my father would have been down at that police station pressing charges before that asshole knew what was happening. After he tried to kill him...

"We didn't have it like that. My mama told me to go take a shower and go to bed. Told me not to tell nobody what happened because they might kick her out of the Section 8 program. She even warned me not to tell my brother because he would go out looking for that cop and would end up getting shot like so many other young black men. She believed child services would also threaten to take us away from her if I reported it. So I did what she said to do. Nothing. And nine months later, I gave birth to a little boy."

As I listened to KC relay her awful story, I suddenly felt grateful for my mostly uneventful life.

"You don't have anything to be ashamed of. It's not your fault that cop raped you. And it for damn sure ain't your fault your momma couldn't protect you," said the Jamaican.

KC turned her back to Samaria to shield her from the conversation and continued with her story, "I named my son Samson. From the very moment I saw those gray eyes, his delicate little features, the soft curly light brown hair, I knew I couldn't raise him. For two months, I tried to be that baby's momma. I tried my hardest to love him. But I couldn't. Every time I looked at his face, I saw that man raping me. I hated my own child."

"What did you do?" I asked. I couldn't fathom any of what she was describing. The most difficult thing I faced growing up was being bused from my neighborhood school. The really bad stuff always happened to someone else.

"I dropped out of school, moved out of the house, and left him with my mama to raise. I made her promise to never tell him who his biological parents are." Her restless hands found a place on the thin mattress, pulling a thread loose. "For a year, I was homeless. Survived on the street doing whatever I could to make a little money. I even did drugs, but thankfully I didn't get hooked like some of the people I hung out with. When a good friend died of an opioid overdose, I knew I had to make a change. I couldn't go out like that."

"Wow! You have a baby?" Samaria chimed in.

"Yeah, I do."

"I have a little brother. He just turned four. Mommy would sometimes take care of him when she was supposed to be home-schooling me."

"Samaria," I asked, turning my focus off KC to her. "I don't remember seeing you around the neighborhood. Did your family just move there?"

"Yes, after I was adopted, my mommies thought it was best if we lived in a diverse gentrified neighborhood... They wanted to expose me to as many different cultures as possible."

"Wait!" interrupted KC, surprised by the maturity displayed in such a small package. "How old did you say you were?"

"I'll be nine soon. Why?" she asked.

"No reason," KC responded, rolling her eyes a little.

All eyes were now focused on the little girl sitting on the floor. I hadn't even considered her family situation because no one I knew was adopted.

"You have two mothers?" asked CraCra. "How does that work?"

"At first I thought it was kinda weird having two mothers and no daddy. But I got used to it. I call one Mama and the other, Mommy Susie. One is black and the other is white. They said they had always wanted a baby girl and when they saw me, they knew I was their perfect daughter. They adopted me when I was five," she explained, matter-of-fact.

"Guess which one is the black one," the Jamaican replied with a chuckle. "Don't no black women I know allow a child to call them by their first name."

I glanced sideways at the Jamaican's ignorant comment. The others must have been used to her attitude, because no one else said anything.

"We moved in our new house this past summer. I am home-schooled because my parents wanted me to learn about stuff I needed to know about life instead of being brainwashed to become a servant for a capitalistic system bent on destroying the black man," she explained before returning her focus back to drawing in the grime. Although she appeared to be uninterested in the older girl's conversation, her ears were finely tuned to their words.

"Watch this," KC whispered to the older girls. She turned to Samaria and asked, "Do your mothers believe in God?"

"Why are you asking her something like that?" I asked, surprised.

She shrugged and replied, "They're lesbians. I just want to know if they believe in God. And if they do, do they think He is cool with how they're living. That's all."

"It's fine, I don't mind answering," Samaria replied. "Mama believes in a Universal God who loves everybody no matter your color. Or who you choose to love. Mommy Susie says she is agnostic—whatever that means."

"Cool answer," was my response.

"God is always with me. And whenever I ever feel sad to remember I am never alone. Mama told me that when the sun is shining to look for my shadow."

"Your shadow?" I asked. "Why?"

"My shadow is a reminder that the Universal God will never leave me. And when the sun is brightly shining, I can see God when I see my shadow. Because She lives within me. And She also lives in you."

I looked at KC who looked embarrassed and surprised. I had to admit I never heard of God being referred to as *She*.

"That's why when my other mother, Susie, wanted to move to Portland, Oregon, Mama told her no way. She said she needed to live where the sun shines and tropical plants grow wild. We were going to move to Miami, but her job fell through. That's why we stayed in St. Louis. She wasn't too happy about it though."

"I know your mama wasn't thrilled about staying in Missouri. With four seasons, it has some really cold and dreary days. I remember last year we got a foot of snow," I added.

"Mama said when people live where they hardly ever see their shadow, they sometimes get a little nutty and forget all about God. That's why whenever the sun was out, she told me and my brother to go outside in the backyard and play."

"Have you always known you were adopted?" KC asked with thoughts of her son on her mind.

Samaria nodded and explained matter-of-factly, "My biological mother put me up for adoption when I was just a baby because she wasn't able to raise me the way I needed to be raised. Mama told me that every child need someone in their life who tells them they're beautiful and special. A person who believes in and encourages them. A parent who can provide unconditional love. My real mother couldn't give me those things so she gave me up. If it wasn't for Mama and Mommy Susie choosing me to be their daughter, I wouldn't be the person I am today."

"Well, damn!" responded, the Jamaican laughing. "Kudos to the modern family!"

"That's a great story Samaria. Thanks for sharing." I rubbed her arm reassuringly.

"You're welcome," she replied before retreating back into her private thoughts.

While everyone else was caught up in the conversation, CraCra sat Samaria on the floor between her legs and cornrowed her thick hair into a cute style, clipping the orange barrettes to the ends of the braids as a reminder that she was still a little girl.

I turned to KC and naively uttered, "I'm sorry. Sounds like you've both been through a lot."

"Thanks," she replied. "I was definitely going through some changes living on the street so I ended up calling a hotline. They pointed me to a recovery program for homeless and drug addicted teens. Thanks to those kind people, I finished high school and got me a job at Whole Foods. Even found a one-bedroom apartment to rent."

"What about your baby?" asked the Jamaican.

"Girl, I can't even think about Samson. I know he is innocent and had nothing to do with how he got here. But damn...." She shook her head as if that motion would somehow rid her of the memories. "Up 'til the day I was snatched, I sent money to my mother every month to help out. I'm not sure how she's handling things now since she's not getting any money from me."

"Maybe she can get welfare for the baby. I mean, it is her grandchild she's raising," I added trying to be optimistic.

"I can only pray he never finds out how he was conceived." KC leaned back against the wall exhaling loudly, blowing away the awful memories of that horrible night. "That asshole wasn't concerned at all about being reported. He knew it was my word against his. And if I did press charges, the rest of those corrupt muthafuckin' cops would have made my life—and my family's life—a living hell."

"You did the right thing for both you and your baby," added the Jamaican. "I know people who have turned up dead for way less than that."

As I listened to KC and the Jamaican speak, I hadn't realized how privileged or sheltered my life was. My parents had shielded my brothers and I from the worst of the streets. Even though crime was rampant in some sections of the city, we very rarely were exposed to it.

KC continued, "Since I've been here, I can think more clearly. My mind isn't filled with all the bullshit I had to deal with back home. I don't have to worry about where I'm going to sleep or what I'm going to eat. Those guards think they got some power over us because we're locked up in these cages. Be acting like the po-po and shit. For real though, all they really do is keep us on schedule. Every last one of them bitches would fall apart if they had to spend one day in my shoes. I play the game because I know it's just another aspect of this fucked up system."

CraCra added, "I've been in jail many times for minor things like shoplifting. This is nothing like it. Those guards act tough; like they are better than us, but they're not and they know it. If you treat all this like a game, life becomes much easier."

"I hate playing games, especially when it involves my life. I don't know what their plan is for us, but I can't see them ever letting us go," I replied to CraCra.

"Well, if I ever get out of here, maybe one day I will tell Samson that I am his mother." KC pondered the possibility.

"Yeah, I get why you think it's not so bad here. Compared to your previous life, living in a cage might be considered an improvement, but you're still locked up You have no freedom."

"Freedom is only an illusion. Are any of us truly free?" observed the Jamaican.

"Well, I know I don't have any freedom today. But I will eventually when I find out why we are here," I replied to the Jamaican.

CraCra added, "When I get out of here, the first thing I'm going to do is buy a full screen television and watch cartoons all day long. Maybe football games. And cooking shows. I love watching those baking competitions."

The Jamaican sighed and shook her head at CraCra.

KC remarked, "One thing I'm glad we don't have in here is a damn TV. At the end of the day, whenever I finished watching a sitcom, drama, or reality show, I felt like I had just watched some nasty porn. Ya know?"

"I know exactly what you mean. I don't miss television, either," added the Jamaican. "Look over there. You see that? That's where you'll find your freedom." She pointed towards a bookshelf propped against the back wall filled with hardback and paperback books.

"My Uncle Ricky used to say TV was made to tell lies to your vision," I added. "He said that television programs were used to program your mind to what the media wanted you to believe about yourself. But mostly all shows about black people were negative."

"Now that you mention it, new girl," CraCra interrupted, "I think you're right."

"To pass my time here, I have read more books in the last three months than I have in my entire eighteen years. And not just any books, these are written by famous black authors; Frederick Douglass, James Baldwin, Langston Hughes, Zora Neale Hurston, Angela Walker, Toni Morrison, Richard Wright, Octavia Butler, Ta-Nehisi Coates, and so many others," KC stated.

"Wow!" was all I managed to say. I silently wondered why our abductors would provide us with so many books, especially Afrocentric ones likely to piss us off. Maybe to relieve the monotony?

KC said, "My skin has cleared up. I don't know if it's the mountain air, the fresh food, or a combination of both. All I know is, even though I am locked up in a cage, I feel better than ever."

"Me too!" CraCra chimed in.

"As for you," she addressed me. "I watch chicks like you come and go. But they said I can't move up until these damn chemicals are out of my system. Plus, my head is all fucked up from what I been through. Shoot, according to the last test, it could take months—or even a year—before I'm totally clean. And the weight I've lost! Thirty pounds and counting."

"That lady told me that this is the detoxification level," I recalled. "That must be why everyone feels better."

"I believe it. I know I feel a hundred percent better since I stopped relaxing my hair and eating all that fast food. No telling what kinda bullshit they be pumping in that mess they call food. Hell, I used to love me some chicken. Fried, baked, barbecued, roasted. And hot wings! Lawd have mercy! Now, I'm not certain that was even real meat I was eating. Probably some GMO shit," she replied, trying to find some good in a bad situation.

"Let's go ladies!" shouted the guard interrupting our conversation. "You got fifteen minutes to take care of your personal business before breakfast."

"Here ya go, Braveheart!" Another guard tossed a bag of toiletries at my direction. I surveyed the contents. An unscented bar of soap, toothbrush, fluoride-free toothpaste, a tub of whipped shea butter, and a few other personal care products were inside. The bag also contained a large tooth comb I could actually use, not like the ones in hotel rooms suitable only for fine straight hair.

"But you know what, new girl?" KC said.

"What's up?"

"Even though I got lots of work to do before I get myself straight. I know I'm special. I just got to let go of this garbage—hate, bitterness, depression and fear—that I've been holding on to for years. But my heart is slowly becoming filled with joy. I got lots of good inside that is just bursting to get out."

As I glanced around the room, I slowly began to appreciate the small changes the others had undergone. Maybe this process wasn't so bad after all.

"Come on, little one," the Jamaican said to Samaria. "After we clean up, we're going back to that cafeteria you liked so much."

She nodded, wiping the sleepiness from her eyes.

"Don't be scared," I told her. "I don't think they're going to hurt us."

Samaria looked at me with her big bright brown eyes and said, "I'm not scared. I saw my birth mother last night. She told me to be brave. That I'm not in any danger."

CraCra interrupted, "That's impossible. You couldn't have seen your mother last night."

"I spoke to her in my dream. I told her those bad men took me away from my adopted parents. She said I'm going to be okay and that she's going to help me get through this. I told her I miss her. She misses me too."

"You know that it was just a dream," I explained. "Dreams aren't meant to be real. It's just your subconscious mind speaking to you."

She shook her head. With a quiet determination she crossed her arms protectively over her chest and countered, "My dreams are more than images in my mind. I have them all the time and I know things other people don't. Mama says I am special."

"I'm special, too!" CraCra said. "I don't dream like she does, but I can see the future. I can even move objects with my mind just by thinking about it moving."

The Jamaican used her finger to make circular motions against her temple, silently mouthing the word 'cuckoo'.

CraCra crossed her arms and retreated to a corner to sulk. She hated it when the others dismissed her as if she were lying. Or alluded to her being 'crazy'. One day she vowed to show them all that she was neither.

"If your mommy says you're not in danger, then I believe her," I replied reassuringly as I watched the smile return to her young face. No need to remove the modicum of comfort provided by her dreams.

Listening to KC's story, I had almost forgotten about the critical state of my bladder being on the verge of release. Before yesterday, the last time I peed my pants, I was a baby and much too young to remember. I had no intention of setting a new record of wetting myself two days in a row. I hurried to the entrance, got in line with the rest of the girls, and rushed towards the first available toilet.

Chapter Eight

After cleaning up, we headed to breakfast in groups of twenty-four, lining up single file against the wall until it was our turn to enter the cafeteria. My stomach was so empty the rumblings ceased long before I went to sleep. I imagined sometime during the night my own body turned on itself for sustenance. I sniffed the air trying to catch a whiff of what was for breakfast.

"I hope they have those delicious blueberries today," Samaria stated. "Strawberries are good too, especially those big juicy ones. But blueberries are my favorite fruit."

"Fruit does sound delicious, but I need to eat some real food I can sink my teeth into," I said hoping the selection would be more than tasteless gruel. "I can feel myself getting hangry!"

The Jamaican and CraCra burst out in laughter.

"What is so funny?" I asked.

"That's right. You missed dinner yesterday. This is your first meal in the cafe. It's probably not what you're expecting, but you might be pleasantly surprised," CraCra replied with no intended malice.

I turned towards the Jamaican. I felt like slapping that grin off her face. When she noticed I was not amused, she at least had the courtesy to explain.

"Don't be so damn serious. We're laughing because the only food in here is vegan or vegetarian. They don't serve meat or any animal products. You won't find no yogurt, cheese, or butter in this cafeteria."

"That's fine with me. I don't eat that crap anyway," I replied. "I've been a vegetarian for four years."

"What?! You don't eat meat?!" CraCra asked. "What about drinking milk?!"

"Nope, not even milk."

"Well, I guess you can have all the fruits and vegetables you want. Or beans if you don't mind farting the rest of the day," the Jamaican remarked.

"Navy beans for breakfast, navy beans for lunch, and navy beans for dinner. There is always a big pot of juicy navy beans they're ready to serve up with a scoop of wild rice," CraCra added. "It's not bad once you get used to it. I eat 'em once a day."

"Quiet!" shouted the guard at the entrance.

"Why only fruits and vegetables?" I whispered.

"They make beans and ancient grains, too." KC whispered, "It's part of the detoxification process. They say our bodies were never meant to consume animal products. And I know for certain we weren't meant to be drinking no nasty ass cow's milk. Everybody in my family is lactose intolerant."

The Jamaican remarked to KC, "I developed fibroids a few years ago. My periods were so heavy, I thought I was bleeding to death at least once a month. The doctor even suggested a hysterectomy if I were older. I don't miss meat and dairy, or the chemicals they add to all the food. Since coming here and changing my diet, the fibroids shrank so much that my periods have returned to normal."

Samaria said, "I used to drink milk, but I started getting sick from it so now I'm a vegetarian. Once I was adopted, my mothers fed me an abundance of fruits and vegetables. Never any candy, cookies, or sweets. I've never eaten animal flesh, which used to make my foster families very angry, but I did not like the way it felt inside my mouth."

I smiled at Samaria's innocence despite her grown up thoughts.

"Mommy Susie would say, 'if God intended for people to eat meat, he would have given us a different kind of teeth.'"

"That's why this child is so smart," the Jamaican hugged Samaria. "She was raised by two intelligent parents."

The little girl beamed with pride before her bottom lip began to quiver. All that talk about family brought back the realization of her abduction and the slim chance she would see either parent ever again.

"It's okay, little one," said CraCra who ceased sounding crazy a long time ago. "We got you. All of us."

"I'm afraid you won't have me for long," she said.

"What are you talking about?" I asked.

"Yesterday, while you were gone, the guards came and got me. They took me to a room with a very kind lady who took blood from my arm. I was surprised because she wasn't Caucasian like the guards, she was African-American. Anyway, after she tested it, she said I don't need to stay with you guys. That I would be moved to another room later today."

"What a minute?" I asked. "Did you say a black lady took your blood?"

Samaria nodded. "She was really nice."

"You're telling me these people have black women helping them?! What the hell?!" I gasped.

The guard who stood at the entrance headed in our direction. She tapped the nightstick threateningly against her hand. "Didn't I tell you all to be quiet? One more word from any of you and back to your cage you go. Do I make myself clear?!"

We all nodded in unison. What I soon learned was there was only a few times a day we were allowed out of the cell. Thirty minutes each for breakfast, lunch, and dinner. And if the temperature allowed, we had a few minutes outdoors afterwards. No one wanted to mess that up.

I don't know what I was most upset about; the fact that Samaria would be moved up another level and out of my sight, or that a black woman was helping these people with the abduction of all those boys and girls. My uncle warned me about the gatekeepers. During times of slavery, they were more commonly known as 'house niggers'. He told me that the modern-day gatekeepers are black people who are placed in roles of authority by the power establishment. Their sole purpose, of which they are handsomely compensated, is to prevent other blacks from progressing or getting too 'uppity'.

My thoughts swirled with questions about Samaria and why they wanted her so badly. The redhaired woman said the younger kids were more evolved. Samaria was raised vegetarian. Home-schooled which meant her parents were in complete control of what she thought. And she could beat adults at chess which meant she was super intelligent. Her natural hair was unprocessed, thick and healthy. Her mother obviously believed in God but that didn't necessarily mean her family was religious. I knew the little girl was from around my neighborhood, but I had never run into anyone like her before. Mostly I was surprised she was out walking alone, all things considered.

The redhaired woman explained the younger children don't take as long to detoxify as us older kids. Their young minds hadn't been corrupted yet. After meeting Samaria and hearing how she was raised, now it all made sense.

~ ~ ~

The cafeteria was much smaller than I imagined, with seating for only about fifty girls. The overall industrial setting was stark with a scattering of tables and chairs throughout the space. However, the selection of vegetable-based dishes was impressive. From the looks of things, the older inmates or 'clients' as the redhaired woman referred to them, staffed the food stations. What was skimped on in accommodations, was more than made up by the generous selection of food.

My cellmates, the girls I came to refer to as my crew, immediately spread out to the station which offered their favorite dish. From the corner of my eye I saw Samaria at the salad bar piling a bowl full of plump blueberries. She balanced a juicy red strawberry on top before sprinkling what looked like granola or nuts all over. The salad bar was better than any I had seen at some of the restaurants my family frequented.

"I see you found the blueberries," I said.

"They're my favorite." She grinned popping a fat juicy berry into her mouth.

"Find us a table. I'll be over after I get my smoothie. You want one?"

"No, that's okay." She tilted her head with the beginning of a question forming in her young mind. Yet she never asked it.

The hot food line was better than I expected. The trays filling the steam table included oatmeal, an unfamiliar cooked grain, raisins, nuts, and various raw and cooked fruits. "I'll take a bowl of oatmeal with chopped walnuts and dates." I scooted my tray down the line. "A cup of tea and an orange. And a slice of whatever that is that looks like bread..." I pointed to a container filled with a cross between old saltine crackers and pita bread.

At the end of the line was a huge vat of steaming navy beans with a rice cooker conveniently positioned nearby. I smiled when I watched CraCra carefully place a big heaping bowl on her tray.

The smoothie station was plentiful with every variety of tropical fruit imaginable. I stuck to fruit I was familiar with and stuffed a cup with bananas, mangoes, strawberries, kiwi, blueberries, and pineapple before handing it over to the attendant. The girl dumped the fruit in a blender, topped it with chalky liquid, slipped the lid on, and thirty seconds later, I was sipping on the most delicious smoothie I have ever tasted.

The noise level inside the cafeteria was surprising low key, especially considering the small space was filled with girls and young women who in normal situations were full of chatter. I soon learned why. As soon as the girls finished their food, they dropped off their dirty dishes and rushed through the exit doors to the courtyard outside.

This morning, though the temperature was a 'balmy' forty degrees, the sun was out in full force ushering in a beautiful day.

I scanned the room looking for Samaria, but she was nowhere to be seen. Less than five minutes after I began eating, KC and the Jamaican were heading outside. Thus, I assumed Samaria was with CraCra.

I quickly finished my oatmeal, washed it down with what remained of the smoothie, dropped off the dirty dishes at the designated location, and headed for the exit. I trailed the last few girls remaining in the cafeteria outside. Immediately, I spotted the crew huddled together near the far perimeter fence.

"What's the hurry? Why did you all eat your food so fast?" I shouted over the chatter created by dozens of teenage girls.

"We only get thirty minutes and if it's not too cold we can come outside." CraCra pointed to the flagpole. "Not much of a wind chill today ..."

A flagpole centered in the middle of the courtyard proved to be of extreme importance to the girls' daily schedule. This morning, a green flag fluttered lazily with the passing of each gentle breeze. Though the winds were relatively calm, it was frigidly cold, especially since none of us were properly dressed for the weather.

Groups of girls I recognized from the other cages in section D were huddled together tightly taking advantage of each other's warmth; sharing stories of their abductions and placing bets on who would be next to progress upwards.

"...when the flag is green, it's warm enough to be out. Red means the weather is too bad to go outside. And when there is no flag, we have to stay inside, but that usually has nothing to do with temperature."

As it was still early, the sun had just begun to rise, peaking over the majestic mountain range in the distance. The dark blue sky became flooded with brilliant sunshine bouncing off the snow-capped mountains, gradually lifting the shadow of dawn and revealing forested pine trees surrounding a spacious snow- covered valley. The camp was situated on the western side of the valley facing east. I squinted at the horizon hoping to gain a clue to our whereabouts.

"I don't know what you're talking about. Its freezing out here!" My teeth chattered in protest; I crossed my arms over my chest to conserve my precious little body heat. "And don't say it's not. I see you're shivering too."

"Yeah, I'm cold. But we haven't been outside for over a week. At least the sun is shining." KC turned her face to the warmth.

"Come closer, we don't bite," Jamaican added pulling me close to share one another's warmth. "Being outside in the sunshine is worth it even if it is a little chilly. Shoot, I'll take a cold sunny day over being stuffed up inside that smelly cage."

It was a tad warmer clustered in the group, but I wouldn't admit it. "I don't care what y'all have to say. Whoever decided to let us out in this freezing weather must be crazy."

Several professional armed guards patrolled the outside perimeter of the compound. Unlike us girls, they were all appropriately dressed for the weather, donned in thick leather jackets, furry hats, all-weather gloves, and insulated boots. I noticed that although they walked with rifles pointing towards the sky, their posture led me to believe they were prepared to take aim and fire at a moment's notice. In addition to the rifles, each wore handguns holstered at their hips and another strapped to their ankles.

On the other hand, the men guarding us within the courtyard resembled out-of-shape security guards from down at the mall. They wore jackets and carried rifles but didn't appear as threatening as those other guards. I recalled the woman saying the guards could not harm us, but upon seeing the stark contrast in behavior between the guards on the outside with those on the inside, I was not convinced the perimeter guards had received the same briefing as the others.

"Do they actually think we're going to make a run for it dressed like this?" I asked, rhetorically.

We all broke out in laughter as we imagined ourselves tromping through several feet of snow dressed in what amounted to pajamas and flip flops with armed guards on our heels.

"Anybody see Samaria?" I scanned the other groups gathered in the courtyard, but she was nowhere to be seen.

A large flock of geese flew over the trees and headed in our direction. *Must be a lake or pond nearby*, I imagined. One lone goose heading from the same area squawked directions to any stragglers pulling up the rear.

"I thought she was still inside with you." KC closed her eyes and inhaled, thoroughly enjoying the fresh scent of the mountain air. "Last time I saw her she was stuffing berries inside her mouth."

"That little girl sure can eat some blueberries. I wonder if they give her the runs," the Jamaican remarked.

After the noisy geese had passed, a lull in conversation came over all the girls simultaneously. For several moments, the courtyard became eerily quiet. The deafening silence was then interrupted by a large herd of deer rushing across the valley towards the safety of the tree line opposite from where they came. From the sudden appearance of the deer, I imagined a pack of hungry wolves had taken chase.

"That's strange." I watched as one guard raised his binoculars to his eyes, then point at the trees. Another guard followed suit. "Any of you notice how those guards keep watching the forest?"

"Girl, what are you talking about?" asked CraCra, looking towards the clearing.

A plume of snow erupted high above the forest accompanied by a loud rumbling that caused the guards to take immediate action. Something unusual was definitely happening within the forest. Several more guards hurried from their posts and jumped into nearby jeeps. They followed in the tracks of at least six snowmobiles rushing towards the area of the forest from where the deer came.

"Whoa! What the heck is going on?!" I shouted. "Do you guys see that?!"

"See what?" KC turned her focus to the forest where I pointed.

"I don't see anything," added the Jamaican huddling tightly to the others.

"Over there!" I pointed excitedly. "The guards heading into the trees!"

Jamaican laughed out loud and stated, "Girl, we'd better get you back inside. Looks like this cold weather is playing tricks on your mind."

"You guys didn't see all that snow shooting up into the air?!"

They all shook their heads.

"You must have heard that explosion that sounded just like thunder!"

It felt like all the crew had intentionally ignored me. Or possibly they knew more than they were willing to share. I toyed with the idea they had all conspired to gaslight me. Either that or my mind was slowly falling to pieces.

"You had to have seen something!" I pointed to the snow falling back to the tops of the trees. "Look! Right over there at our two o'clock position!"

"What are you talking about new girl?! There is nothing over there except snow, trees, and more snow." The Jamaican shuddered because she was cold, irritated or both. "You must be seeing and hearing things. Pace yourself with the crazy! This is only your first day."

"Okay ladies. Time's up!" shouted the guard nearest us. He stared in my direction as he reached for the door handle.

"Not fair! We still have eleven more minutes," protested a girl just leaving the cafeteria.

"This is not up for discussion," he said pressing his shotgun against his side. "I said time's up. Get your asses inside. Now!"

"C'mon, y'all. You guys know the drill," shouted one of the female guards holding the door open.

Everyone quickly hurried through the door and formed up in lines outside the cafeteria. Being outside was nice, but I welcomed the warmth of the indoors more.

The guards lined all the girls against the wall. The girl at the head of the line starting counting off. She yelled, "One!" And one-by-one, each subsequent girl called out her position in line. Because I was new, when KC who was ahead of me shouted out, "Eleven", I didn't realize they expected me to shout out, "Twelve", until one of the guards stopped by and poked me in the side with her nightstick.

"Thirteen!" CraCra shouted in quick succession.

"Fourteen!" the Jamaican called out.

"What happened out there?" I asked no one in particular. "Why did they rush us inside like that? Was it because of the explosion?"

"Sister, I don't know you, but I advise you to stop asking all these damn questions," an older girl in front of KC whispered loudly. "These crackas don't like to be questioned."

"I still haven't seen Samaria. Anybody know where she is?" I asked ignoring the girl's unsolicited, but probably sound advice. I craned my neck to the side and tried scanning the line.

"She's not here. They probably already came and got her," CraCra answered. "On to the next level."

"Where is that?"

CraCra shrugged. "Dunno. I've never made it past Section D. With the exception of my trips to the warden's office, no one who leaves this section ever returns."

"That's right. Once you leave the detox section, you never come back," the Jamaican added with a blank expression. "Personally, I cannot wait to get out of Section D. Can't nothing be worse than how we live now. Like a bunch of fuckin' lab rats trapped in a damn cage."

"You've both been here for almost a year and have no idea what's next?" I asked KC and CraCra incredulously.

"Nope, I'm not sure where they take you after you pass the blood test," KC whispered. "I've seen the guards come get girls, tell them to pack up their stuff, and off they go. We never see them again."

"Dang! I didn't even get to tell Samaria goodbye. I hope she's all right."

"Braveheart!" came a man's voice from behind.

Immediately all conversation ceased as the man made his way forward, surveying the line. I stopped talking to the crew and faced forward as I was unsure who this authoritative person was. From the corner of my eye, I ascertained he stood at least ten feet tall! I slyly tilted my head to the side to catch a glimpse of his face, seeing beautiful blueish-black skin that appeared to glow in perfection. Thick black hair that covered an oversized head was matted, as if he had just removed a snug fitting hat or some sort of helmet.

I thought, *If this man is one of the guards or helps run things, I might have to rethink this place. Maybe the woman wasn't telling lies about trying to help us, after all. Maybe there's more to this camp than meets the eye.*

"Oh my goodness!" I tried whispering to KC from the corner of my mouth. "Who is that?!"

She did not turn around, instead I watched her shoulders shrug her response.

"Did you not hear me?" he asked. "Are you the one they call Braveheart?" The baritone voice barreling from his chest was strong, confident, and commanded authority.

He was no longer surveying the girls in line. Before I realized he was speaking to me, I felt his magnetic presence at my side, calmly breathing warm minty fresh breath on top of my head. Glancing slyly from the corner of my eye, I tilted my head slightly upward comparing him to a living statue. Or a godlike being from one of the many superhero movies my brothers and I loved. I searched his handsome face; took in the chiseled Ethiopian features. I peered deeply into two large slightly slanted eyes whose pupils were so dominant, the gold-flecked brown of the surrounding cornea was barely visible. Even more strange was the whites of his eyes were almost non-existent. Though some may have considered his appearance to be frightening, I was not afraid. I was mostly intrigued as to why he was dressed in a shimmering emerald green bodysuit. And the gold collar that encircled his neck sparkled with such an intensity one might mistakenly believe it to be alive.

My heart beat wildly in my chest with excitement. I gasped when a vague inkling of recognition upon seeing his face fell upon me. From where or when, I could not say. Yet he was familiar in that unsettling way you remember someone significant from your early childhood. Before you started to forget.

I stammered past the knot in my throat to respond, "Yes, sir. The guards have called me Braveheart. A few times..."

"Shhh!" KC advised in hushed tones. "Stop talking before you get us all in trouble!"

"I'm talking to him!" I explained to the back of her head.

She shook her head from side to side, loudly exhaling her annoyance. As far as she was concerned, the only thing I was about to accomplish was getting them punished.

"You *can* see me," the man remarked, with slight amusement tinging his voice.

I nodded, confused. Of course, I could see him! He was a ten-foot-tall blue-black man wearing a sparkling emerald green flight suit. I was wondering why none of the other girls were as excited as I was. After all, he was truly a sight to behold.

"Come with me," he said lightly resting his hand on my shoulder.

"What did I do?" I asked nervously. "Where are we going?"

The man did not answer. He walked ahead, motioning with his long slender finger for me to follow. I was shocked because the guards made no attempt to quiet or to even stop me. I stepped out of the line.

I took one last glance at KC, CraCra, and the Jamaican who all averted their eyes as I passed by. They made certain the guards knew I was acting alone in my disobedience. Also, gauging by their reactions, none of the girls could see or hear the man. Only I could. So in their minds, I had just lost mine.

Deep within my soul, as I strolled by the now passive guards who stood idly by, behaving like trained toothless dogs under the spell of their master, I instinctively understood I would possibly never see the crew again. Whether this was a good thing or not, I did not know.

Chapter Nine

As we continued down the long corridor away from Section D, the cold gray concrete walls gave way to colorful tiles. We were alone, though he did not once acknowledge my presence. For the first time, I noticed he carried something in his hand. It was about a foot long, metallic, and looked very heavy. It wasn't a purse, briefcase, or anything like that. It was a cross with an oval shape on top and what resembled hieroglyphic symbols etched on it. *Where have I seen that thing?* I wondered, trying my best to remember.

I noticed only my feet made noise on the highly waxed floor. Slap, slap, slap, with an occasional stutter as the toe of the rubber shoe sole caught hold on the slick floor, causing me to constantly stumble. Though the tall man was massive in size, his movement barely made a sound. I have heard the expression of one being light on their feet, but had never truly understood the phenomenon until I witnessed it with the man. He glided more than he walked. I, on the other hand, felt like a klutz padding down the hall.

"Who are you?" I asked bravely. "Where are you taking me?"

Although the man ignored my questions, I continued to follow him like a newborn puppy follows its mother. Blindly. Instinctively trusting that she will lead it away from harm.

We wound up in the redhaired lady's office, arriving through a different entrance than I had the night before. As I entered her private space, I realized less than twelve hours had passed since we last spoke.

She rose from behind her desk adjusting the automatic shade on the windows to block out the direct light of the sun. A hint of a smile teased at the corners of her mouth.

"I expected I would see you soon. But not this quickly," she said to me.

"From what the other girls told me I am surprised I met you at all. Most of the others never made it this far."

"The child sees me," the man replied matter-of-fact, in a calm gentle voice, unexpected from a man of his stature.

"That is impossible. She has only arrived yesterday."

The man stared intensely at the redhaired green-eyed lady before they spoke again. Her eyes twitched involuntarily during those few long seconds.

"I agree she must be more advanced than the others, but we haven't had time to fully screen or detox her yet."

The man's eyes rested on hers, and though he appeared to remain silent, he was communicating.

She appeared to cave in as if someone had released most of the air from an overly inflated balloon. "I understand, but we need more time to make sure she is ready."

He nodded once. Then he raised that object, took two steps backwards and became as transparent as the rays of sunshine streaming through the plate glass window. Then, in the blink of an eye, the man disappeared into thin air.

I imagine it would not have been unexpected for me to faint after witnessing a man disappear right before my eyes. Fainting would have been welcomed at this point. Actually, flabbergasted was the only word that would do justice to what I'd just seen. The woman stepped forward and kindly lifted my chin, returning my mouth to the closed position. She sighed wearily, dropped back in her chair, and cocked her head to the side in silent contemplation.

I opened my mouth to speak but complete words refused to come forth. Only unintelligible sounds of uh, ah, eh made their way through. I blinked several times to make sure my vision hadn't been affected, took several deep breaths to prevent hyperventilating, and then pinched my wrists to convince myself I wasn't losing a grip on reality. It worked. I was fully conscious and what I witnessed was real. Not only had the man communicated with the woman telepathically, but he had also vanished into thin air.

"Congratulations!" she broke the silence. "You have just graduated to being his next 'pupil'. But first we must remove that god-awful synthetic hair from your head. I don't know how you girls fell into that trap of believing this material, made from who knows what, adds to your beauty! It serves only to block your natural ability to receive."

"W-w-what the hell just happened?!" I caressed the faux red hair braided into my own, trying to remain conscious, then sank to the floor in disbelief. Feeling as if my mind had just betrayed me and fled when I needed it most.

"He brought you to me because of your gift."

"What did he do to the guards? They never made a move to prevent my walking off. Why couldn't anyone see him?"

"He blocks their ability to see. None of the guards have ever seen him." She exhaled loudly. "Even I can only see him when he allows it."

"Who is he?"

"*He* is The Teacher."

"The Teacher? Why was he dressed like that? How did he disappear?" I felt my shallow breathing becoming sporadic as I was on the verge of having a panic attack.

"Calm down," she left her desk and sank into the carpet beside me.

I gripped my head with both hands to avoid coming undone. This was too much to handle.

"Take a deep breath. You are fine. You are not losing your mind. This is really happening."

"How do you know what I'm thinking?" I stared in surprise. "Did you read my mind?"

"Yes, I am getting pretty good at hearing highly emotionally charged thoughts. Like yours are right now. But I am not so good with implanting thoughts or transmitting. Still have lots more practice before I learn that part."

"What do you want from me?"

"Your reaction now is exactly why I told him you need more time. You're not ready to receive more."

"Receive more of what?"

"The truth about who you really are."

"I don't understand. I told you I already know who I am."

"Do you have any idea why you could see The Teacher when others could not?"

"I don't know. Maybe I pay better attention that the others."

"Possibly, but that's not the reason."

I waited for some plausible explanation of why none of the other girls, nor any of the guards possessed the ability to see The Teacher.

"You have a gift of sight and discernment. Some are naturally born with it, but others have to work extremely hard to develop theirs."

"How do you know that?"

She sighed long and slow before rising from floor and going to the window. I tried to stand, but she motioned for me to remain sitting. "I want you to recall moments of your life when you experienced strange occurrences. The chance encounters you wrote off as coincidence."

I backed up against the wall, pulling my knees close to rest my weary head. I allowed my thoughts to drift as they may. I had always felt a bit off, like I never truly belonged in my family. In my city. My school. This country. In my own skin. Or sometimes, on this Earth. My parents chalked it up to my uniquely overly active imagination. Told me I wasted too much time daydreaming when I should be doing something constructive.

I often knew things were going to happen before they actually occurred. For instance, a couple years ago, my older brother and I were on the way to school. He was driving. It was early and the streetlights were still on. In my mind, I thought it would be really cool if the lights dimmed, one at a time, as we passed by. And just like that, the lights starting going off in succession. When I pointed this out to my brother, he explained that it was just a coincidence that we happened to be under the lights the moment the sensors clicked off.

Then I recalled when an obscure song looped in my mind for days. I mentioned it to my mother because I couldn't remember the title since it had been years since I last heard it play. The very next day—it was a Saturday because it was housecleaning day—the song came on the radio. It took me by complete surprise! But when I remarked to my mother it was the song that had been stuck in my head all week, she dismissed it as just coincidence.

I recalled another 'coincidence' that occurred during a family outing. My dad was driving and we all were listening to music. During a lull, I randomly asked my dad when was the last time he'd eaten his favorite snack, pork rinds. He explained he had stopped eating them because they were really bad for him; too much fat, salt and preservatives. Anyway, all that talk about food made me hungry, so I suggested we have lunch at a seafood shack that I spotted along the way. Everyone agreed, even my finicky brothers. Lo and behold! As soon as we sat down, the waitress came over and placed a large basket of greasy pork rinds on the table. My mom, dad, and brothers all stared at the basket, then at me. We immediately broke out in laughter, shocked by the weird coincidence.

"Most of what you have experienced are examples of synchronicity. The Universe is trying to contact you. You just haven't realized it yet," she explained.

"Wait a minute… Did you just read my mind again?" I asked, looking up from my seated position.

"Don't get excited. You will eventually learn how to block others from reading your mind."

"That's good to know. Because I don't want all my thoughts out in the open for just anybody to listen to when they want. Since I don't have privacy, I'd least like to keep my thoughts to myself."

She didn't reply. Just smiled.

"So, you really think I have a special gift?"

"Your gifts may be unimaginable to you at the moment, but yes. You have many."

"Is that the reason I was abducted?"

She nodded.

"Is it because we are gifted that you are abducting black children?"

"What we learned through research using DNA samples we obtained—voluntarily, of course—from millions of African-Americans who wanted to know their ancestry…"

I shook my head in disgust. "I told my family to stop sending their DNA to those companies! Why would the very people who participated in stealing our history provide us with the truth about where our ancestors came from?"

"…we discovered that many melanin rich people, especially the younger children, have special abilities. Supernatural abilities. What we do know is, unless these children are rescued from the ills of society, all your gifts will be forever destroyed and you will never know what you are capable of doing. Or who you are intended to be. Once we studied the strands of DNA we were able to establish your uniqueness."

"I knew those commercials for ancestry companies were too good to be true. They not only took our money *but* stole our DNA to use against us! Incredible! We happily paid our hard-earned money to be lied to. Again!"

"Desperation to learn your roots fostered an influx of DNA. We were floored by the responses considering your people are usually very conservative and skeptical about releasing your medical information," she said.

"Well, what happens now? Do I return to Section D for more detoxification?" I asked.

"You will continue with the process of detoxification, but not in that section. However, I will give you a brief overview of how this works. You will be moving up to Level 4, as requested by The Teacher. That is the academic level. For the next several months, you will attend sessions to unlearn what the education system has accomplished during its previous twelve years to mis-educate you."

"If I'm going to Level 4, what are the other levels?"

"Level 0 includes those who suffer from inequalities resulting from the prison industrial complex that takes a young man who should be in school, and due to minor run-ins with the law, eventually lands in jail or prison. The criminal justice system's population is maintained through mass incarceration, years of probation, and never-ending parole. The adults we bring into the fold, usually none over thirty years of age, often come from this group."

"That includes most of the guys in my neighborhood."

"At this level, the adults are typically so disillusioned with society, they are very receptive to what we are teaching. That said, we are very selective with this group and avoid brining in any who are considered to be without redemption."

"But if they're in prison, how do you get to them?"

"We have our ways of reaching the incarcerated despite the locations." She fiddled with a quartz pendant dangling below her neck. "The imprisoned are no longer under an illusion that this system is anything other than what it is. In fact, many ex-cons are the most intelligent people we have met because once their freedom is taken away, they have nothing except time on their hands. The really motivated ones spend their time reading and pursuing higher learning."

"Is that where the term, 'jailhouse lawyer' came from?"

"Yes. Because neither these men nor their families have money to pay for an attorney, many choose to represent themselves. The only problem is, once they do get out most are too jaded to be of any use to us."

"My Uncle Ricky told me the prison is filled with 'woke' people. I used to laugh and tell him if they were so woke they wouldn't be in prison. Now I understand what he was trying to tell me."

"Level 1, from where you were rescued, includes children who are being raised in the typical lower to middle class existence. Socialization is the most challenging level as far as we are concerned due to an incessant bombardment of destructive ideas from the educational system, mass media, socialized religion, and an overall systemic racism that's so tightly woven into the fabric of society that most don't even know it exists."

"I thought I was being a good student by keeping my grades up. I had no idea I was being indoctrinated and mis-educated," I added, listening to her explanation.

"Level 2 is the process you are undergoing now. The entire compound was re-purposed for housing children to undergo detoxification that cleanses the body of as much toxicity as possible. Unfortunately, we cannot get rid of it all. Some of it will remain. Tooth fillings that leak impurities and traces of mercury and other materials remaining from vaccinations will always be present."

"The next level—Level 3—cleanses one's mind of all indoctrination received by living in this capitalistic system. However, it is important to understand Levels 2 and 3 can be achieved on the outside by those in pursuit of a higher level of consciousness. It may take more time detoxifying the mind on one's own, but it is time well spent. Many are awakening by reading books, watching videos, and finding like-minded people for thoughtful discussion. These individuals are the lucky ones who gradually realize the world is not all that it appears to be, so they search to find out why."

"Level 2 and Level 3 are both located in this camp?"

"That's correct."

"You said I'm moving up to Level 4?" I asked.

"That's right. You will be transported to another location to undergo further learning. The Teacher tells me this is the most intensive level for the children, but from what he says, Level 4 is the most enlightening."

"What comes after that?"

"I am not privy to the process past Level 3," she explained.

"I appreciate you breaking down all the different levels and all, but I really don't want to be brain-washed." I frowned and thought aloud, "With all the bad stuff you told me is being done to kids, how do you know they won't mistreat us once we leave your camp?"

"Because I trust The Teacher. And you should too."

"That's it? Just trust that they'll do the right thing with me?"

"I have no reason not to trust him. Or any of the others you'll come into contact with."

"To tell the truth, I have no reason to trust either of you."

"You are safe with us. Besides, look at it this way. Your mind is polluted with misinformation. Your body has been compromised by ingesting unhealthy food and exposure to toxic chemicals. We want you detoxified to allow your mind and body to function the way it was originally intended, at its highest level of performance."

"I think I understand. My body and brain are polluted from all the crap I've been exposed to since birth, so you guys are trying to clean me up."

"Exactly."

"I know you're trying to help, but can you please tell me when'll I'll get to see my family again? I really miss them."

"I cannot say for certain either way. After the children leave my care, I rarely see them again."

"So, what happens now?" I asked, starting to experience the peculiar fluttering of butterfly wings tickling my nervous stomach.

"The Teacher has made a request to transfer you to Level 4. And that is exactly what I intend to do. But first, let's get rid of this... this... whatever this strange material is that's braided in your hair."

"Wait," I stammered. "I just got here. What if I'm not ready to progress to Level 4?" I didn't say it out loud, but she already knew I had reservations about leaving the crew after such a short time.

She turned and faced me. Her green eyes sparkling with delight because not only was I finally beginning to comprehend, but I was willing to accept my situation.

"I do not want to overload you with too much information all at once. Just know that we, *I*, am not your enemy. You might believe our methods are extreme, but the results will more than make up for them. Trust me, you are ready."

She was right, she had provided me with lots to consider. My instincts said to trust the woman. The visions that came to me in the form of dreams, the synchronicity from the universe, and the feelings of not belonging were all finally going to make sense.

Or at least, I hoped.

Chapter Ten

The woman summoned a female guard and provided instructions that I was to be moved to Level 4. But to first escort me to the hair stylist. I followed closely as she navigated our way through another long corridor, passing several locked doors marked 'Restricted', and finally into a large open space with private rooms cordoned off by accordion style doors. The guard obviously did not share the woman's excitement about my departure, for she was about as enthusiastic as if she were delivering a sack of groceries to a homeless shelter. She retrieved a jumpsuit the shade of ocher with a green belt at the waist, a pair of tangerine colored sneakers from a storage bin, and then directed me to one of the rooms to change. After I was dressed, I stood admiring myself in the mirror, feeling like I'd stepped into Vincent Van Gogh's *Sunflower* painting.

Shortly thereafter, a pretty young woman, the hairstylist, knocked on the door and asked in a husky voice, "You ready?"

"Be right there," I replied, staring at my face. I didn't feel, nor did I look any different than I had when I first arrived. But everything had changed. Apparently, there was something very special about me. I should be thrilled, right? After all, everyone wants to feel special. However, my excitement of self-discovery was overshadowed by the fear of the unknown. What if I wasn't special? What if they were wrong? What if my 'special gift' was used for harm instead of good? What would happen to me if I didn't live up to these people's expectations? Would I end up like all those other missing children? Yet as all the scary 'what-if's' bounced around in my thoughts, a sudden feeling of calm overtook me. My inner spirit whispered that I would be alright. I was in good hands. Not to worry. To enjoy the ride. And with those thoughts pushing away the others, I released my fears and prepared myself to embrace wherever this journey would take me.

"You okay in there?" she called out again.

I took a deep breath and opened the door. With confidence I replied, "I'm ready."

The bored guard waited by the door as the stylist carefully unbraided the faux hair from my own. When she had completed that task, we moved on to the wash bowl where she shampooed, conditioned, and massaged my scalp. As she continued working, she didn't fill the air with useless chatter, instead she opted to fill the space by humming a lovely tune. It worked; I was totally relaxed by the time she set me under the hair dryer. In less time than I expected, I was complimenting her on how nicely she had braided my natural hair in a beautiful style.

The guard walked me to an exit where numerous jeeps were parked side-by-side. She whistled loudly and two male guards appeared.

While waiting to get into the vehicle, I watched two older boys lower the green fabric from the flagpole. They did not raise another. I recalled CraCra telling me that 'no flag' meant there was something out there which prevented the girls from being outdoors, but she knew nothing past that. I suspected the danger the guards had reacted to was the arrival of The Teacher.

I felt bad for my crew and all the other kids who remained encaged. In a warped sense of jailhouse etiquette, I should not be leaving so soon after arrival, especially since many of the girls I met had lived in those cages for well over a year.

I was loaded up in a jeep by two armed guards who kept watchful eyes on the road bordered by thick trees. Though the guards resembled the men who abducted me, right down to the dark clothing, bearded faces, and military boots, these particular guards handled me with the same detachment as the female guard. One drove and the other rode in the backseat next to me. Neither bothered to speak to me. Or to each other.

The wind had really picked up since morning, delivering fast-moving ominous storm clouds over the mountain range. Wherever we were headed, I hoped we would arrive at the destination before that storm did.

The air blowing through the jeep's heater did nothing to warm me. I unsuccessfully tried to steady my teeth from chattering. Apparently, in their minds I was not yet at the stage where they trusted me to not run off because I remained without a coat. But they could not have known that escaping was the last thing on my mind.

I pulled both knees to my chest to conserve my precious little body heat. The guard noticed my uncontrollable shivering and perhaps he took pity. He pulled an old army blanket from behind the backseat and tossed it to me. I quickly wrapped myself in the scratchy wool before he changed his mind. As the wind howled in from the north, thankfully the vinyl top covering the jeep was sufficient to keep most of the frigid air out.

The driver sped away from the site that, from this vantage point, resembled nothing more than an abandoned industrial plant. I don't know if it was fortunate or not, but I observed more vans arriving with children who would be dis-indoctrinated from everything they grew up knowing to be true. From what I went through getting kidnapped, I'd bet anything the majority of those kids were more traumatized from being abducted than they had been living in neighborhoods overridden with crime.

As I hung onto the roll bar on the jeep's roof, it was hard to believe only a few days had passed since I was abducted. My mother and father would be worried sick by now, probably placing calls to anyone who knew me, filing a missing child report with the local police, driving the streets in hopes of finding me wandering around lost. Being a very organized person, my mom would form a missing child group and circulate my most recent school picture with hopes that someone would call with information on my whereabouts. My brothers would walk the neighborhood asking all within earshot if they had seen or heard from me. Their grades would suffer and football practices would be skipped.

From watching all those detective shows with my mom, I had an inkling how this would eventually play out. After a respectable amount of time with no reliable leads, the police would place my case on the back-burner with the final ruling of unsolved. My parents would continue their own investigation handing out flyers and printing up t-shirts with my picture and description including height, weight, age and what I was last wearing. My mother would continue the search while my daddy would immerse himself in work to alleviate his pain. I imagined my oldest brother Malcolm would move on with his life and head off to college where he would probably study business, architecture or some other nerdish profession. My youngest brother Stokely would be most affected because we were very close, but I hoped he would successfully complete high school and find his way through the trauma of my disappearance. Unfortunately, he would always be known as the brother of the girl who went missing. And my parents, depending upon how strong their marriage was before I went missing, might even stay together.

I hoped and prayed my family would find peace and not allow my situation to ruin their lives. But from the horror stories I heard on the nightly news when it came to locating missing children, peace for my family would be a difficult thing to achieve.

The further we drove, the gray building which produced terror upon arrival, now seemed wholly insignificant. My thoughts went to the girls who remained locked up in those cages. I prayed they would make it out of Section D with their wits intact. I also thought of little Samaria, immediately regretting not asking the woman about her status.

We bounced along the mountainous road, ascending upwards through harrowing mountain tunnels that were so tight we had almost become trapped at least twice. However, the driver expertly navigated through dense forest passages made more treacherous by snow laden, low-hanging tree branches of which the waning sunlight could not penetrate. Three black bears, possibly a mother with two cubs in tow, ambled across the snowy path ahead which caused the driver to momentarily slow.

Deep in the forest the snow continued to fall creating blizzard-like conditions, limiting visibility in some areas to almost zero. The eerie silence was only pierced by wolves howling in the distance and the revving of the engine as the driver shifted gears to gain better traction. Despite the hazardous weather conditions, the driver expertly handled the jeep without showing hesitation or fear. I, on the other hand, felt nothing but trepidation *and* fear as my life literally depended upon the skill of these men to keep me safe. Whereas the redhaired woman may have totally entrusted these men with my safety, from what I knew about white men dressed in paramilitary clothes, they weren't too fond of blacks. At any moment, had they been so inclined, they could have pushed me out of the jeep and into the forest where I would be at the mercy of weather and wild animals.

After what felt like an eternity, we finally cleared the tree line. I estimated it had taken a nerve-wracking hour just to reach that crest. At this point in my journey, I had released all expectations of normalcy, for there was nothing 'normal' about any of this. Thus, I was not surprised when we stopped at the base of a geodesic dome the size of at least two football stadiums. It was situated on a rocky outcropping surrounded by snow.

"We're here," stated the driver, momentarily waiting for the entrance door of the dome to fully retract. He pulled into a large oval shaped room measuring maybe 75 by 100 feet, cut the engine, and got out of the vehicle.

From my perspective inside the dome, I noticed the structure wasn't actually white, but was constructed of clear interlocked panels which allowed the sun to shine through, giving it a greenhouse effect.

"Follow me," instructed the guard sitting in the backseat next to me. He exited the jeep first with his weapon raised.

At this high altitude, the air had thinned considerably, hence my sudden lightheadedness and difficulty taking a deep breath. I anticipated the temperature within the dome would be brutally cold, so I prepared myself for the shock of frigid air.

I carefully stepped from the jeep into an unexpectedly warm space. My feet touched the ground and sank into lush green grass. The driver roughly tossed the dirty blanket I had used to keep warm at my feet and I watched it fall to the ground, not giving it another thought. My attention was focused on the interior. It was densely packed with varieties of exotic tropical plants and wondrous trees that reached up the height of the cavernous space. The plants were unlike any I'd seen before, even counting the ones from the Missouri Botanical Garden I loved visiting. Considering the altitude, it was a miracle any vegetation grew in the thin mountainous air.

"Wow! It's beautiful!" I whispered loudly, stepping closer to get a better look at a particular flower.

"Hands off the foliage!" he warned, not wanting to be held responsible for a client being harmed under his watch. "These exotic plants might be poisonous!"

In the very moment the guard uttered his warning, two young men who appeared to be in their early 30's, stepped forward as if they had materialized from the air. Neither carried weapons, but their appearance gave the impression they were not to be played with. They were dressed in an interesting combination of traditional Native American and African-esque type clothing. One wore his hair in freestyle locs, while the others was closely cropped to his head. Both wore neatly trimmed beards which covered the lower halves of their face.

"Leave us!" commanded the one with the locs. He raised his hand with a shooing motion, delivering a menacing look at the guards.

Without so much as an utterance, the guards' eyes glazed over as if in a hypnotic trance and they quickly returned to the jeep. The exit door of the dome lifted to allow sufficient space for them to back out. Oddly enough, no cold wind made its way in. Once the door closed, the opening to the entrance became indistinguishable from the circular walls. The vegetation miraculously rearranged itself to camouflage the opening as if it were never there. And just like that, the guards were gone and I remained in the entrance with the two brothers.

"Uh, hello. I'm Kenya," I said trying to sound friendly. "Is this Level 4?"

Neither man responded, rather they ignored my introduction and turned their backs to me.

"Hey!" I watched as they took several steps into the foliage. "Where are you guys going?"

Silence was the response.

"Nice to meet you, too," I replied sarcastically.

With the guard's warning in mind about avoiding poisonous plants, I wandered around the large space, checking out at the foliage but keeping my hands to myself.

The area was warm and humid. Beautiful flowers in all different colors and shapes grew at the bases of exotic palm trees. Brightly colored climbing vines, some with deep purple leaves streaked with yellow, and others so vividly green I thought they were artificial, clung to the trunks of avocado, lemon, and magnolia trees. I spotted what I thought was a banana plant because clusters of green banana shaped fruit hung low towards the ground. Mysterious red, black, and blue succulents sprouted from plants attached to the structure. Groups of dark colored fungi sprang from the moist edges of the room where the sunlight did not reach. Without any further identification of the spores, I instinctively knew the fungus were poisonous.

After several minutes of searching for an entrance into the actual dome, I concluded I had explored the entire area.

"Hello!" I called out. "Is anyone here?"

My question was met with more mind-numbing silence.

"Okayyyyy...." I whispered to myself. "That crazy woman had me dropped off in the middle of nowhere. The two brothas didn't explain anything to me. Now I'm stuck in a greenhouse where I'm afraid to touch anything less I become poisoned."

The sound of something hitting the dome's roof drew my attention. It was sleet. I watched the sky grow darker through the clear ceiling tiles, heavy drops of frozen rain mixed with snow pelted the roof. It was an eerie sensation standing in a warm greenhouse while ice fell from the sky outside. The room darkened with the arrival of nightfall resulting in my imagination going into overdrive. As I tried my best to steady my nerves, I imagined shadowy figures moving in the background. I really did not want to spend another moment in that place.

"Hey, you guys?! Can you please come back and tell me how to get out?! It's getting kind of scary in here!"

No response. Only more silence. My stomach began to rumble as I hadn't had any food since breakfast. I sat down in the grass trying to not think about food or water. Nor the darkness settling all around me.

The gurgling sound of running water drew my attention. I dropped to my hands and knees, pressed my ear to the ground and listened. I began to crawl around, moving plants out of the way, until a familiar looking yellow fruit growing in a low-hanging bunch on a plant with very long green leaves, caught my eye. I found bananas! Disregarding the guards warning, I plucked one from the bunch, peeled it and ate it in four bites. It was the most delicious banana I had ever eaten! I plucked another and ate this one more slowly, savoring the sweetness of the fruit. I'd all but forgotten about the water, however, the source of the gurgling soon became evident. My eyes trailed upwards. Melted snow trickled inside the greenhouse through a pipe and gathered into a container that spread the water in all directions. It was an irrigation system! I scooped up the cool liquid with my hands and drank.

"Well, since I'm here, I'd better make myself comfortable. No telling how long it'll be 'til someone comes for me."

I was grateful for the warmth of the greenhouse as I had only the clothes on my back, which provided minimal protection from the harsh elements outside. If the inside temperature dropped later this evening to match that of outdoors, I'd be in deep trouble.

I did another walk through to determine what I could use to survive until someone came. Against the base of a palm tree was the blanket the guard was thoughtful enough to allow me to keep. Dozens of palm tree fronds had fallen into a heap on the ground, of which I gathered together and assembled into a makeshift bed and tossed the blanket on top. I used a few banana tree leaves for cover, then laid on my back and gazed up through the clear ceiling at the darkening sky. Huge snowflakes continued to fall from the heavy clouds, sliding off the dome's roof to accumulate on the ground below. The grumblings of my stomach were satisfied by the bananas, so I closed my eyes and drifted off to a welcomed, restful sleep.

Chapter Eleven

Early the next morning, I opened my eyes to see the transparent ceiling above me. I felt groggy, like I had slept too long. The warm rays of the rising sun beamed down unto my face awakening me from a dreamless slumber and I shielded my face from its brightness. As I stretched out my aching muscles, the memory of my whereabouts gradually returned, causing me to sit up and take account of my whereabouts. I had to pee really badly and thus, located a depression in the ground behind a grouping of tropical plants. Using broken sticks to dig a fairly deep hole where my urine wouldn't contaminate the other plants, I squatted and relieved myself. After it was fully absorbed, I repacked the dirt into the hole.

Once my eyes had adjusted to the morning light, I spied a small rodent sifting through the decomposed vegetation scattered on the ground. The mouse-like creature stopped in its tracks and stared at me with its beady little eyes, never taking its eyes off mine for what seemed like minutes. Considering that nothing in the last few days had made any sense, I went with my gut instinct and accepted that the rodent was trying to communicate with me. I rolled from my makeshift bed and followed its path as it quickly scurried away leading me to a small clearing. A large wooden door, barely visible due to the overgrown vines covering it, caught my attention. I pulled the vines free.

"Hello?!" I shouted, pounding on the heavy door. I traced my hands on the unfamiliar symbols etched in wood.

Several moments passed with no response. I pounded on the door again calling out, "Hello?! Can anyone hear me?!"

A woman's gentle voice came to my thoughts in the form of a whisper, "I have waited for you, beloved. Turn the handle. Open the door."

I stopped pounding on the door and looked around to confirm I was still in the space alone. With the exception of the rodent, I was. The strange little creature had perched on its hind legs, watching me, continually cleaning its face with its little paws the way squirrels do. I grasped the door handle that I had would have sworn was not there earlier, gave it a turn, and then felt the lock give way. The door swung open.

I wasn't sure what to expect but I entered the massive dome and was greeted by the two young men from the evening before. They stood on either side of a beautiful woman whose ebony skin shimmered under the light of the sun. In stark contrast, thick locs of silver hair trailed down her back. She was entirely regal in appearance, dressed in a floor-length robe made of a velvety gold material. She wore no makeup yet resonated a natural beauty and grace. I felt like curtsying in her presence as if she were a true queen. In my mind, I deemed her the 'Magnificent Queen'.

She whispered, "Follow me."

I followed closely behind the woman, noticing she also appeared to glide instead of walk. The two young men remained at her side as we traversed through a cavernous space populated with thousands of pupils quietly sitting at the feet of hundreds of men and women who resembled 'The Teacher' I met in the woman's office.

I followed the Magnificent Queen to a small sparsely furnished room where the tall black man in the emerald green suit, The Teacher, patiently awaited our arrival. The Teacher motioned for me to take a seat of which I eagerly did.

"Welcome, Miss Kenya Mali Zambia Williams," said the Magnificent Queen in a voice that projected grace and dignity.

"How do you know my name?"

"I know everyone's given name when they initially arrive."

"That is impressive because there must be hundreds of kids out there."

"There are." She stated, "However, I shall refer to you by your given name, Kenya, only sporadically. After a certain point, you will no longer require it. As for everyone here, you may consider them to be your sisters and brothers and address them as such."

I furrowed my brow in confusion. "Ma'am, I only have two brothers and their names are Stokely and Malcolm. They live at home with my parents in St. Louis."

"Beloved, we are all related. Rather than differentiate one another by an arbitrary given colonial name, we refer to one another as 'Brothah' and 'Sistah'. In regards to The Teacher, please refer to him accordingly."

"Okay...," I replied because I could not dispute what she said. "Um, can you please tell me where I am? Is this Level 4?"

"In regards to how this process was previously explained to you, yes, this is considered to be Level 4. But you no longer need to concern yourself with that. Those designations for levels were used to make distinctions between the pupils from where you came."

"That's good to hear. Not having to worry about getting to the next level takes the pressure off, because I am very competitive. And I love to win."

She smiled at the mention of competition, as it was a very American way of thinking. "As far as where you are now, we like to refer to this great structure as the king dome."

"Did you say, 'kingdom'?" I asked, allowing my eyes to take in the extraordinary setting.

"Yes, king-dome, kingdom... Regardless of how you pronounce the word, they are one and the same."

"Um, the only kingdoms I know about are in England or Saudi Arabia where they have Queens and Kings who rule over their lands. They make the rules for their citizens to follow and if they don't... well, it's not pretty." I thought about the many historical stories I read of citizens hands, feet, and even heads being chopped off for disobedience to the throne.

"The meaning of king has been bastardized to be a title reserved for those born into a so-called 'royal family' who possess extraordinary wealth and power. In European traditions, the king rules over the land and all its subjects. In reality, it means 'one who inherits by birth'."

"Oh, I see...."

"The king dome will provide a higher degree of enlightenment. Your natural mind will expand to regain a knowledge of self that will make you wealthy beyond belief. Being a king has nothing to do with material riches, as the only kingdom that truly exists on this planet is right between the ears. While you are in this dome, you will discover what The Most High intended for his children."

I squinted at her with a growing suspicion, and then at the man, who though remained quiet, now studied me intensely. I noted that gold collar around his neck appeared to occasionally brighten like it was being charged by electricity. I pondered what was on his mind. Something about this entire conversation didn't feel right. I was nobody special but they were trying to make me believe otherwise.

The Magnificent Queen continued, "We realize you have not had adequate time to come to the realization of why you were chosen to be here. Or who you truly are. Just know that you belong and very soon you will discover the truth."

"The truth about what?"

"The truth of who you are," she whispered.

"Is that redhaired woman really working for you? Or are you working for people who abduct children for something else?" I spoke bravely narrowing my eyes. I wasn't about to be taken for the okey-doke even if they were black.

"What is this *okey-doke*?" she asked, unfamiliar with the slang of another generation.

"Oh, I guess you can read minds, too?" I sucked my teeth, disappointed that my mind had once again been accessed without my permission. "Well, the *okey-doke* is when someone is trying to make you believe something that isn't true. Like you're lying to me on the sly."

"This child thinks we are being disingenuous!" exclaimed The Teacher with obvious disapproval.

"Why don't you know what okey-doke means?! That is a black thing!" I boldly asked her.

"This child remains under the disillusion from a lifetime of indoctrination. I was wrong for believing she was ready. She should be sent back to rid her body and mind of all remaining toxins," the woman communicated telepathically to The Teacher.

I noted the woman's face barely registered any emotion. And yet, within the quiet confines of my thoughts, I clearly heard her disappointment and warnings of sending me back to detox. "Ma'am, I'm sorry. I know you're trying to help me. I promise I will work extra hard if you keep me here. I don't want to go back to Section D in Level 2," I pleaded with the woman.

Her expression immediately changed to surprise, then amusement. "This child clearly possesses the ability to hear my thoughts. She is ready to proceed forward."

The Teacher acquiesced. "As you wish."

"Beloved one..." The Magnificent Queen raised her slender hand to caress my face. "Pay close attention. Listen carefully for truth, knowledge and understanding. The wisdom will come. You will soon learn that you and all those who have come before you have been taught nothing but lies."

"May I ask you a question?"

"What is it, my beloved?"

"That redhaired lady was able to read some of my thoughts but I couldn't hear any of hers. How was I able to hear yours?"

"The woman you speak of has studied diligently for many, many years to develop her current level of ability. But she does not possess a supernatural ability and never will. Only certain people have and fewer understand the direct connection to source."

"Uh, I think I understand." I studied the Magnificent Queen's face. She seemed familiar, yet unfamiliar at the same time. I think if our paths had truly crossed, I would have remembered someone with her beautifully unique appearance.

"I am familiar to you because our paths have crossed many times. In another time and place. And other dimensions. As it has with the others who have also awakened."

"You read my thoughts again?" I sighed. "Is there any way to prevent it? I don't always have good thoughts and I wouldn't want to offend anyone."

"I take no offense to the inner thoughts I receive from the children. You all lived in an obscene world of which your thoughts are a direct result." She smiled. "In time, you will learn how to block, but for now I don't want you to be concerned."

"That's a relief," I smiled. "Because I wouldn't want to offend you."

"I will now leave you with your Teacher," she said before gliding from the room.

I watched as the two attendants appeared to escort her from the room. I did not see either one during our conversation, yet they quickly materialized at the exact moment when needed.

The Teacher towered over me as I sat at the table. I felt like a new student on the first day of school. I crossed then uncrossed my legs numerous times trying to find a comfortable position, but mostly as an attempt to distract myself from the intensity of his disapproving glare. I snuck a peek at his handsome face. The darkness of his skin contrasted against the shimmery green material of his clothing, reminding me of tender blades of grass springing forth from rich black soil. His large eyes were focused only on mine.

After what felt like eternity had passed with neither of us budging, I finally found the nerve to speak. "What are we waiting for?" I asked.

"Clear your mind," he ordered.

"How do I do that?"

His response was curt, "It is a fairly simple task."

"Mr. Teacher, sir," I replied trying my best to contain my growing frustration. "I know you think I don't deserve to be sitting here at this table. But it isn't my fault. I don't even know what the process is. So please do not be angry with me because I didn't complete whatever it is you thought I should have."

For the briefest of moments, I imagined a flicker of delight had crossed his face. Just as quickly as it appeared, it was gone. Only his stone-face remained. He raised his hand which held that strange heavy object. Before I understood what was happening, we were in a dark space, so void of sound that we might as well have been inside a vacuum.

"Where are we?" I asked, staring into his peculiar eyes.

"Is your mind clear?"

"Except for wondering where we are, it is."

"You will now learn of our beginning..."

"What do you mean, *our*?"

"Observe closely. I will show you."

In the blink of an eye, the darkness of the room morphed into the vastness of the solar system and completely engulfed us in every direction imaginable—up, down, and sideways. A brilliant display of stars, planets, and galaxies far away, literally took my breath away. Asteroids and meteorites soared past us barely making a sound. I reached for the man's arm as I began to levitate!

"Are we in outer space?" I asked, holding on for dear life, afraid I would float away and become space junk orbiting endlessly around the Earth for infinity. "How is this possible?"

"This is a powerful simulation that exists only in your mind."

"Why does it feel so real?"

"The brain is an extremely powerful processor—a computer, if you will. If your mind believes you are in outer space, your body reacts as if it were true."

"You mean we're not really floating?"

"No. We are standing on a solid surface and physically remain in the room."

"This is crazy! I actually experienced the sensation of zero gravity, but as soon as you said we remained on a solid surface, my feet returned to the floor!"

"Pay close attention, Braveheart. This is important." He continued to zero in to sections of space I had no idea existed. "This planet is what I wish to show you."

I relaxed, releasing my grip from his muscular arm. My eyes had finally adjusted to the darkness. With his explanation I was no longer afraid, but more so amazed with the amount of detail the simulation provided to accurately build a realistic model. I watched in utter fascination as The Teacher gripped an area of the solar system with two fingers to bring it closer. The swiping motions he made reminded me of many science fiction movies where the actors magically moved screens around until they got down to the level of detail they searched for.

"This is where our ancestors originate..." he said, proudly pointing his long spindly finger to a bluish planet that was far away from The Milky Way, the only galaxy I could identify. "...this is the planet, Nigiro."

"What the...?! This alien man actually wants me to believe my ancestors are from some planet he probably made up and calls Nigiro?! That's ridiculous!" I thought, snickering.

The Teacher glared at me with such intensity I thought he might fly into an uncontrollable rage at any moment. I slowly backed away from his reach into the path of a simulated meteorite. He grabbed me by the arm and roughly pushed me down into the chair. We were immediately back inside that little room.

"Not until your mind is free can I teach you anything. Leave my presence!" he demanded, turning his back to me.

I wasn't aware that he could also read minds which is what I was afraid of when I expressed my angst to the Magnificent Queen, "I'm sorry, Mr. Teacher. I didn't mean to offend you. Please, don't dismiss me! I really do want to learn about our ancestors."

"I said, leave! Now!"

Gathering what was left of my humility, I slunk away from The Teacher's wrath and into a narrow hallway separating it from the interior of the dome. I had no clue where I was supposed to go. I only knew I wanted to remain in Level 4 to learn. I headed back to the area where I first entered. Neither the woman, nor her two attendants were anywhere to be found.

"Dang! I am so stupid!" I smacked my hand across my forehead. "My first lesson and I act like an idiot."

I knelt down in the thick grass next to the floor-to-ceiling window, staring out at the snow-covered mountains in the middle of nowhere. My hands sank deeply into the soft blades of grass; I marveled how this simple act of gripping a handful took me back to when I was a child. Many years had passed since I had taken the time to enjoy the lawn in our backyard of which my father so lovingly maintained. Many a Saturday morning, he'd spend hours outdoors tending to the landscape, cutting back shrubbery while my mom pulled weeds from the flowerbeds. Everyone always said we had the prettiest yard on the block.

It was beautiful outside, despite layers of heavy snow blanketing every surface. The massive dome blended so well into the scenery that unless you knew exactly where to look, the structure was virtually invisible from the air. Armed guards maintained strict 24/7 surveillance. And no visitors, hikers, or tourists dared to venture this far out into the wilderness. We were literally cutoff from the world.

The inviting interior of the dome was in stark contrast to the wintry landscape outdoors. If I were to take a selfie and post it on any social media platform, you would assume I was vacationing on an island. Tropical plants, flowers, palm and fruit trees gave the impression that I was living it up in paradise. The temperature-controlled environment was warm and humid; perfumed by the sensual fragrances of the tropics. Gurgling streams flowing throughout the space, helped to maintain lush grass and vegetation that flourished. The transparency of the ceiling, separating all from the frigid temperature outside, revealed the bluest of skies with a bright sun peering down.

Hundreds of children sat quietly in the grass, in dozens of tightly clustered groups, listening intently to their respective Teachers, learning their forbidden history. What was most impressive is how those kids gave the Teachers their undivided attention. From the look of the children, they were all in a meditative state, listening with eyes closed. The Teachers, all tall blue-black men and women, similarly dressed in emerald green bodysuits and carrying those odd objects, seemed to be communicating to their pupils telepathically. The Teachers' eyes were open, yet they did not see me.

I pondered the mind-blowing possibilities revealed by The Teacher. He did not give me the impression of being a foolish person. In fact, he was serious to a fault. Thus, if he said we were originally from a planet named Nigiro, there must be a reason. I used my finger to write the word in the frost-covered window. N-I-G-R-O.

"That's interesting..." I whispered to myself, taking a step back to get a better perspective. "That can't be right... Teacher pronounced Nigiro as *nee-JHEE-row*. That spelling, N-I-G-R-O is too close to 'negro' to be a coincidence."

"You're on the right track," said The Magnificent Queen who appeared behind me as if she had been standing there the entire time. She peered over my shoulder at the words I'd written in the frosty window.

"Did someone intentionally misspell Nigro as Negro? Is that how we ended up being known as Negro? Is that why they now call us niggers?"

"Possibly," she went to the window and added an 'I' in the condensation. You missed a letter."

"Huh?" I asked, frowning, watching the letters begin to run.

"The correct spelling is N-I-G-I-R-O."

I rewrote the word again. One letter at a time. N-I-G-I-R-O. "Oh my goodness!" I exclaimed, clamping my hand over my mouth to contain my excitement. "Wait a minute... I noticed something very interesting." I reversed all the letters. O-R-I-G-I-N.

"That's incredible! Nigiro is 'origin' spelled backwards! The definition of origin is, *the source from which all begins* and it's also the root word of 'original'. Was Nigiro intentionally spelled backwards in the English dictionary all those years ago because they knew our people were the original humans?"

She nodded her head slightly to acknowledge the writing on the frosted window was on point. "Often times, the best place to hide something, is to hide it in plain sight."

"Oh, my goodness! Does this mean what I think it means?"

"You are learning quickly, I see."

"Why would they do this?"

"The Trickster purposely spells words differently, and yet the pronunciation remains the same. The English gave it some fancy word. *Heteropalindromes*, words that are also words, but spelled backwards."

"Ma'am, who are you talking about when you say, The Trickster?"

"The Tricksters are employed by a very powerful and wealthy conglomerate of families that are less than .01% of the world's population who own over 99% of the world's wealth. These families rule the world from the shadows, own all the major corporations, run the world's banking system, and ensure leaders of every single country on this planet are in their debt. World leaders, presidents, prime ministers, even religious leaders... The Tricksters, primarily European men, have done the bidding for these families and have infiltrated practically every country on this planet for hundreds of years. But believe me when I tell you they are not what they appear to be..."

"Who are these families? Why haven't I heard about them before?"

"Very few actually know their true origins. Furthermore, religious leaders would have you to believe The Holy Trinity is The Father, The Son, and The Holy Spirit, worshipping a false deity without ever knowing the truth. However, in all actuality, the true meaning of this trinity involves collaboration between The Divided States, Great Britain, and the state of Israel, which only came into existence sixty years ago. This axis of evil has conspired to rule the entire planet," she explained.

"I've never considered the people in charge were corrupt. Why would anyone want that much power?"

"Corrupt is an understatement," explained the Magnificent Queen. "The Tricksters are beholden to these families to assist in their quest of world domination. Those countries choosing not to cooperate with this trinity face the full force of the American military's might."

"That explains why we're always at war with countries unable to defend themselves. The US spends billions of dollars bombing countries of people who defend themselves with basically sticks and stones. Wow...."

"Beloved, the most effective method to maintain chaos is to divide, conquer and sow division among the world's population. And in the process, instill puppet dictators to start wars from within. The Trickster successfully puts in place the U.S. puppet administration to further destroy our people, create more poverty, disease, and an overall miserable existence. The plan is to keep us fighting amongst ourselves without us ever learning who the real enemy is."

I pictured a fat white rat hoarding a huge wheel of cheese and then tossing out a few measly crumbs for millions of starving brown and black rats to fight over.

"They had to establish a pecking order. Religion and skin color were the easiest differences to emphasis. Erase and then replace spiritual beliefs with European religions provides a foothold. Plant the seed of white supremacy with Caucasians at the top, and all hue-mans at the bottom."

"Damn! That is some purely evil shit!" I stated. "Um, sorry, I didn't mean to swear..."

She continued, "When they discovered the true nature of Nigiro and what we are capable of doing, the focus shifted to us. We are the only people with the ability to destroy them. This is one of the reasons these Tricksters have toyed with the language given to the world. To cause confusion."

I recalled words spelled differently with the same pronunciation... Be, bee. But, butt. Hear, here. Hair, hare. Rain, reign. Waist, waste. Right, write. It couldn't be a coincidence that 'blackmail' and 'black male' are pronounced the same. Then there's blacklisted, black sheep of the family, even delicious chocolate cake is called devil's food cake because of its rich color. "Come to think of it, practically everything having to do with the color black has a negative connotation. "

"When we were classified as black, it was deliberate." She closed her eyes, took a deep breath and then opened them widely, as if she were gathering strength to continue. "Beloved, though you may live in this world, understand you are not of it."

"Nana, my great-grandmother, used to say that all the time, but she was quoting scripture from the Bible. I still don't know what she meant by that."

"Our ancestors did not always embrace the stranger's ways. They had their own languages and means of communication, spoken and unspoken."

"If we were of the Nigiro people, why would they switch up and refer to us as Negro, colored, black and now African-American?"

"Removing a peoples' knowledge of self is the fastest way to colonize the mind. After that, you can tell them anything and they will believe it." She gazed dreamily out at the snowy landscape and continued, "Hundreds of years ago, Tricksters instilled plans to enslave the Nigiro to work stolen land. This country, the United States of America, was originally the land of our people. The story perpetuated in their history books is that millions were stolen from Africa, sailed across the ocean in wooden ships, and then enslaved upon reaching the shores of America."

"We didn't come from Africa?"

"Some did originate on the continent known as Africa. But the majority of Nigiro were already here in the Americas."

"Wow..."

She explained, "When those European explorers first arrived on this land, they discovered copper colored people living abundantly on this land rich in resources. The native people were thriving in successfully run cities all up and down the eastern seaboard. Using lies and trickery, they convinced about a dozen or so Nigiro men to accompany them back to England. The brothers were agreeable because they hoped by teaching the Brits about electricity, engineering, and other modern conveniences they would remain in their countries and leave them be. Upon meeting those brilliant men, the Tricksters made immediate plans to overthrow the Nigiro, return to their land to dominate and enslave the people to mine resources. The colonizers presumed that because of their pale skin, they were naturally superior to the copper colored indigenous people. Using the guise of pilgrims escaping religious persecution from England, they gradually inserted themselves in villages throughout the eastern seaboard by proclaiming they were 'spreading the word of God' to the heathens. Before the natives realized what was happening, those evil doers had taken over and insidiously gentrified each and every village they encountered."

I dropped my head to hide the tears building at the corner of my eyes. "Damn... They were gentrifying our cities and displacing us from the very moment the Brits stepped on our land."

"Beloved, you have been lied to your entire life."

I couldn't tell if she was actually speaking words or thoughts. Or both. I wiped the tears from my eyes. This was no time for crying.

"We communicate with you in this strange and vulgar English language as it is the only tongue you understand. With the words you speak, you are not only unwittingly cursing yourself, but each successive generation that follows."

"Is this why English is the universal language?" I thought of conversations I had with students who did not speak English as their first language. They often said how hard it was to learn. The language was filled with inconsistencies and twists and turns.

"They took our beautifully structured written language—what you have learned was so-called Egyptian hieroglyphics—and replaced it with theirs. In the beginning, we also did not speak these guttural languages. We communicated through vibration and telepathy. Unfortunately, once the language was lost, it became a barrier from the motherland and the ancestors."

"Ma'am, you said 'our ancestors'..." I stared at her lovely face. "Are you one of us or one of them?" I asked, referring to The Teachers.

"The Teachers are Nigiro. So am I. As are you. We are their descendants. Beloved, I am you. You are me. We are one. I was liberated just as you. Over seventy years ago. What you are experiencing now, I have already gone through."

"You were abducted too?!"

"Not abducted, liberated. Just as hundreds of thousands of children over the past hundred years were."

She noticed the confused expression cross my face, feeling the need to provide further explanation.

"I was on my way home from the market when a man and woman—I don't recall if they were white folks or black people passing as white, snatched me into the backseat of a motor carriage and drove off. Keep in mind I was only nine or ten at the time, but I was advanced for my age. When those people took me, I understood what was going on. For as long as I could remember, every black person I knew—my parents, the pastor at the church, my teachers—they all warned us about people stealing children and doing God knows what to them. So as I rode in the backseat, I prepared my young mind and body for unthinkable things because I had heard how sadistic these people can be with us. But I ended up here, in the king dome, discovering for the first time who my people were and where I came from."

"This is crazy," I thought, feeling my mind teetering on the verge of insanity. "How is it possible so many of us allowed ourselves to be brainwashed? Were we that naïve and gullible to believe these people actually wanted to help us?"

"This is my mission. I am here to help my people create the world we were destined to live in. What you know of your short existence, is not all there is," she explained. "We believe that you are one of the chosen ones. A child of The Most God, a direct descendant of the original Nigiro bloodline. You are one of the children still capable of being rescued who can help to change the world. But as time goes on, the number of those we can save shrinks each year."

"I don't understand."

"You will soon learn all you need to know." The Magnificent Queen raised her hand to signal for the two young bearded men. "Until you truly understand the horrible condition of our people in this country... how so many of us continue to suffer in ignorance, you will never fully comprehend my explanation."

I nodded, not because I was satisfied with her response, but her body language made it clear she was finished explaining.

Two young men appeared at the Magnificent Queen's side. As I gave the one nearest me the once over from the tips of his thick locs to the discolored nail of his big toe on his left foot, I found him to be extremely handsome. For a moment, I forgot where I was and slid back into my sixteen-year-old way of thinking. If I were a few years older, maybe I would have a chance to get to know him better.

She smiled. I blushed, forgetting she had access to my most inner thoughts.

"Ma'am, please let me apologize to The Teacher. I wasn't very nice. I think I might have offended him."

"You shall have time for that later. For now, follow the brothah. He will show you to your room. Bathe first and then change into clean clothes. You will feel much better after you rest."

I could barely contain my excitement! For the first time in my life, things were finally starting to make sense. The questions that bothered me about the injustices black and brown people faced on a daily basis had nagged me to no end. We truly are extraordinary people and there are those who will do all within their power to keep the truth from being discovered.

"Beloved..." she added.

"Yes," I replied.

"Please do not think of me as your 'Magnificent Queen'. That term is not an accurate description of who I am, especially in the way you have been taught what a queen is."

"Then what shall I call you?"

"I prefer to be called Sistah." She paused, "Also, we do not use our government names because we have elected to not label ourselves with their cursed words."

"But my parents gave me my name," I retorted. "I like being called Kenya."

"Yes, but your parents were also misguided when they named you. Not knowing the ancient original language, they had to use words of the colonizers."

"Then how do you know *who* is who?"

"We have the ability to recognize one another by energy. Their vibration. We all were born with this ability. In time, you will regain yours. Energy and vibrational frequency are unique to all."

"Like recognizing one's face? Or fingerprints?"

"You catch on quickly. Your vibration is your personal energy frequency." She gave a slight nod towards the man of my interest. "Go now. The brothah will show you to your room. Rest. Study. I will see you again soon."

Chapter Twelve

A petite figure sitting cross-legged in the grass with her back pushed up against a boulder looked familiar. Her small hands rested motionless by her sides. I recognized the young girl from the hairstyle created by CraCra back in the cell of Level 2. Her eyes were tightly shut.

"Samaria!" I shouted.

The handsome young brother hushed me instantly. "You must not disturb the children during the lesson. The sistah cannot hear you anyway. The children's bodies are here, but their minds are in the unseen world. Her inner vision is transfixed on her Teacher in another dimension."

"Oh, ok." I reluctantly accepted his explanation. "Maybe I'll see her later."

I trailed closely behind him as he led me from the large open space of the king dome through a set of doors, to the end of the hallway, to wait before the doors of the elevator. He pushed the button with a '3' in the center. Afraid of getting lost in the massive space where no one spoke a word, I didn't want to take a wrong turn and get lost. I studied the young man who couldn't have been that much older than I. He reminded me of the football players in my school. Athletic and slightly arrogant, but not in a bad sort of way. One might say it was confidence rather than arrogance.

I found it difficult to think of the lady as anything other than a Magnificent Queen. The queens I was most familiar with, courtesy of Walt Disney movies and the British monarchy, were to be respected and admired. They ruled over kingdoms and their subjects; sometimes with kindness, but most often cruelty. Come to think of it, I can see why she doesn't want to be called that. The title of 'Queen' was simply another labeled created by the British hierarchy, and I truly had no idea what it actually meant. Therefore, I decided "Auntie Sistah" would be a better way to respectfully address the regal woman who was my elder.

Auntie Sistah said we all have a unique personal vibrational frequency. I wondered if the flutter in the pit of my stomach was caused by the brothah. In spite of my current situation, I thought he was really cute. At the same time, the guilt I felt over having lighthearted thoughts when my family was at home worried sick about me, quickly squashed my developing crush.

"My sistah: Please. Enter," he instructed in a baritone voice that continued to provide me with that tingling sensation.

I was a bit leery about stepping into an elevator that descended into the frozen tundra. When the elevator stopped, the doors opened to a setting that reminded me of a college dormitory I had visited earlier in the summer. The hexagon shaped room included a door on each side with a large common area. All-in-all, the room was pleasantly decorated in soft colors and pictures of happy looking black people in an unrecognizable city. Several built-in nooks provided comfortable places to read. A comfy sofa with huge pillows propped in the corners was an inviting addition to the room.

It was apparent this process was big on reading. Similar to what I saw in the cage when I arrived in Section D, this room contained two floor-to-ceiling built-in bookshelves, each loaded up with books written by great authors—W.E.B. DuBois, James Baldwin, Toni Morrison, Carter G. Woodson, Nikki Giovanni, Richard Wright, Maya Angelou, Alice Walker, Dr. Frances Cress Welsing, Ta-Nehisi Coates and dozens of other authors of which I was not familiar. Biographies on the lives of Nat Turner, Harriet Tubman, Sojourner Truth, Frederick Douglass, Martin Luther King, Stokely Carmichael and Malcolm X were also shelved alongside the others.

I went in for a closer look. At least a dozen versions of different Bibles—The King James authorized version,

New Living Translation, American Standard—and several I had not heard of, including The Complete Jewish Bible, a Catholic Bible, the missing books of the Bible, and most surprisingly The Slave Bible more commonly called 'Parts of the Bible' took up two full shelves. Having only recently learned about the slave bible when the African-American museum in Washington D.C. opened, I couldn't help but to realize how successful the progenitors of this nation were with using education and religion to completely brainwash millions of people. Back then and with subsequent generations!

"Can I ask you something?" I asked, tracing my hand along the wooden shelves. At least a dozen books displayed intricate designs etched in gold-gild on the spines. I selected one, and then held the book in my hand, turning it over gently before flipping through the unlined pages. This wasn't a book. These were writing journals.

"What is it, my sistah?"

"For real... What is this place?" I said, admiring the exotic expensive looking furniture. From the look of things, money was not a factor.

He motioned to a chair. "Please, take a seat."

I did.

"We conduct our rescue missions from the safety of this structure. If you had completed your training, you would know the children provide the intricate details to help create this overall illusion. It's intended to make your arrival less stressful."

"The children created the greenhouse?"

"In a way... You are experiencing their shared reality, but from your perspective."

"I don't understand," I replied, caressing the crushed velvet fabric covering the chair cushion. I slipped the tangerine colored shoes from my feet and pushed them aside.

"What did you see when you first arrived?"

I thought about the long drive up the mountain. "Well, we were in a pretty bad snowstorm during the last few miles. The driver could barely see beyond his highlights. When we finally broke free of the storm, this huge white geodome, larger than a football stadium, seemed to rise up out of nowhere. And then when I entered the dome's foyer, I first considered it was a greenhouse—similar to the St. Louis Botanical Garden back home—because of the beautiful foliage and tropical plants, but then I thought, how was it possible to be inside a massive greenhouse on the top of a mountain in the middle of winter?! And why would it be here in the first place?"

He smiled. "You are fond of nature, my sistah?"

"Yes, I am. And apparently whoever planned the landscaping is too. I've never seen such a pretty place."

"My arrival to begin class was entirely different. There was no greenhouse. No botanical garden. No trees at all."

"Really?!" I exclaimed, waiting to hear more.

"The sistah, whom you met earlier, greeted me in an amusement park setting complete with rides, carnival games, and all the unhealthy food I could ever eat. In my mind's eye, I could very well have been on vacation. The attention to detail, from gobs of pink and blue bubble gum stuck underneath the picnic tables, to the magical music coming from the merry-go-round, there was nothing to cause me to question the park wasn't real. And in every sense of the word, it was real. But then I discovered the images were a creation from my own memories."

"You're telling me that everyone's experience is different?"

"Only upon the initial arrival. After you become accustomed to how things work here, you can easily adapt your vision to coincide with others. And vice versa."

"Sounds like a version of 'I'll show you my reality if you show me yours'."

"Exactly. In your mind, a beautifully landscaped tropical garden paradise is etched in your memory as a wonderful place. It is your happy place."

"If I created that scenery from my private thoughts, how is it possible for you to see it?"

"Everyone creates their own reality but it is possible for it to be shared with others."

"How is that possible?"

"Prior to your arrival to the king dome, the children accessed a pleasant memory from your subconscious and then recreated it for you. Our thoughts become synched based on our common experiences, beliefs, ideas, and proximity."

"Those kids out there accessed my subconscious thoughts? And can do this for everyone?" I asked.

"Yes," he replied.

"It still doesn't make any sense...."

"Let me try to explain..." He cocked his head to one side, both eyes on me. "Do you recall learning about the terrorist attacks that happened in New York City, Washington D.C. and over a field in Pennsylvania on September 11, 2001?"

I nodded.

"You agree that incident, that particular date of 9/11, would be a memorable experience for most Americans?" he asked, "If you were to ask anyone old enough to remember where they were that day, they could rattle off a response off seconds. Americans tuned to their televisions like never before for updates. The news cycle looped scenes of an airplane flying into one of the World Trade Center towers, over and over again, until the image of that sacred financial landmark being destroyed was seared into everyone's mind. Then the news showed the Pentagon, a symbol of this nation's military strength, with a gaping smoldering hole. And finally, we witnessed the second tower come tumbling down, followed by the image of bits and pieces of a fully loaded airplane scattered over a Pennsylvania field. It was considered to be the first attack on American soil since the Japanese attack on Pearl Harbor which justified the United States' involvement WWII."

"Actually 9/11 was way before my time, but my parents remembered it well. And you're right..." I added for his consideration, "It's funny how everyone repeats the scenario almost verbatim, like it was scripted."

He nodded in agreement. "That terror attack became a collective consciousness event not only for Americans, but for the entire world."

"They said it was horrible. Everyone was scared! The entire country was devastated, but for the first time in a long while, everyone pulled together," I remarked.

He smirked as he spoke his thoughts out loud. "To have thousands of Americans perish on that one day was indeed horrific, but thousands of people die in other countries every single day in terrorist attacks. But those tragedies in other countries don't make the news cycle like 9/11 did, because those foreigners are not 'Americans'."

"Now that you mention it, when I used to watch the news with my daddy, very rarely did we see extensive news reports from other countries, unless it was England. Even to this day, for something that happened way before I was born, in our school we still have a moment of silence on 9/11."

"Tell me, sistah. And please take a moment to consider this. What do you think about when you hear the phrase, 'nine-one-one'?"

"I don't need time to think. 911 is the number you dial for emergencies, when you need the police or the fire department because something bad has happened."

"Do you see how quickly you responded? There are no coincidences in this world. That date for the attacks was selected for a specific reason so whenever you hear the reference to 911, you not only associate it with danger, but also terrorist attacks. That number is now part of our collective consciousness because it is a shared reality," he explained.

"You think our government was in the planning?" I frowned. "That sounds like a conspiracy theory."

"Before you dismiss what I've told you, consider that a lesser known definition of conspiracy is, *a combination of persons banded secretly together and resolved to accomplish an evil or unlawful end; or an illegal, treasonable, or treacherous plan to harm or destroy another person, group, or entity.* And the definition of theory is, *a belief, policy, or procedure proposed or followed as the basis of action; or a judgement, conception, proposition, or formula formed by speculation or deduction or by abstraction and generalization from facts.*" He then added as afterthought, "Of course, based on the facts presented to the world, I will leave it up to you and anyone else to reach their own conclusions."

"If those attacks were planned, that would be horrible. Especially since our president declared war on Iraq because of it," I allowed that bit of information to sink in.

"There is one more consideration for you before we move on."

I was beginning to think there was nothing more he could say that could shatter my beliefs about the role our government played in our democracy, than what he had just shared. But I listened anyway.

"My sistah, how many people on those airplanes, inside the Twin Towers, or the Pentagon did your family actually know?"

"None. Except I do remember my father and my uncle saying that all those people who died on 9/11 were innocent victims who were sacrificed to give American a reason to declare war."

"Now tell me, how many young black men in your hometown have died as a result of crime since 2001? And of those who have died, how many does your family know?"

I lowered my head thinking of the number of funerals I had already attended over the past several years. "To tell you the truth, I've experienced death way more than anyone my age should."

"Where is the national sympathy for those young victims? Where are the television cameras? Why are those stories not given national attention in a never-ending news loop showing those grieving parents? Do you see anyone starting a charitable fund for those families who lost children?" he asked rhetorically before calming himself. "I will tell you why... Most Americans simply do not care about black people murdering each other. It has become a way of life. It is normal. With the daily setting of each sun, more of our people shall perish."

"When you put it like that, our entire situation sounds hopeless. What can we do?"

"You are here. So are many of the children. Which means all is not lost." He sighed wearily and then explained, "The reason I used that specific incident as an example was to indicate how one shared reality became a collective consciousness event. The news replayed those images and repeated the description of what happened by calling it a terrorist attack, to the point it became imprinted on the nation's psyche. We subconsciously recall the horrors of that day and the terror we felt, whether or not you were alive at the time to experience it. These days, most people can't even say those numbers without thinking about terrorists. And with every call made to 911, we are automatically triggered to be afraid. But in reality, those three numbers are in reference to bible scriptures."

"Really?! Which ones?"

"Revelation 9 thru 11. I caution all to read those scriptures and to take heed."

"Brothah, you have given me much to consider and I thank you," I stated with much respect.

"In regards to the children, they can do what mass media does, but in reverse. Instead of their creating a horrible memory for you to instill fear, they take what's in your natural mind and recreate pleasant images."

"You're telling me all those children out there possess the ability to read my thoughts?"

"Precisely."

"I don't think I'm comfortable with that." I stood to my feet and paced the floor. My toes sank into the plush rug. "I understand why they did it, and I appreciate them using my good memories to make me feel comfortable. But..."

"What is it, sistah?"

"How can I stop people from reading my mind?"

"With practice, you will learn the ability to put up mental blocks to prevent."

I needed a distraction from the wealth of information downloading into my brain. A flat screen monitor hung from the wall. I found the remote and tried to turn on what I assumed was a television.

"Sistah, please, put down the remote controller. The monitor you see does not pick up television signals from the outside."

I laughed in spite of myself.

"What is so funny?"

As I held up the slender plastic object found in 99% of homes today, I had an epiphany. "I think television shows are used to sedate us from real life. And from watching the news with my daddy all those years, I am starting to think the news was pure propaganda."

He clasped his hands together, joining his fingertips in a gesture unusual for a teen. "When you get most of your information from television, do you not comprehend that you are watching actors playing out roles? From the evening news, to reality shows, drama or comedy sitcoms, whether it be blockbuster movies or Broadway play, it is all scripted. Everything!"

"Ugh! This place is a real downer. It's has been nothing but negativity since I've been here. When am I going to start having some fun?"

He stared at me with disappointment written all over his face at my ignorance. Obviously, I still had lots to learn so I quickly changed the subject.

"How long have you been involved with this?"

"That is a difficult question to answer." He returned his hands to his sides and began to pace the room. "Technically, I was rescued when I was six. About thirty years ago."

What?! This brother is thirty-six?! I gawked in disbelief. *I thought he wasn't a day over seventeen. Eighteen at the most.*

"Time is irrelevant when your existence is outside the world you once knew. When you are in your right mind and a clean body, you will not age like others." He stopped pacing and stood before me. "Take for instance the one you call Auntie Sistah…"

"You can read thoughts, too?" I replied, embarrassed.

"All of Yahweh's children are born with this ability." He took a seat on the sofa and patted the unoccupied space, motioning for me join him. "…as I was saying, the sistah you met earlier is over a century old."

"Really?!!" I sat down beside him. "My mother is forty but Auntie Sistah looks much younger than she does."

"Living in this world ages our people prematurely."

I tried to think of anyone I knew who lived to be a hundred. Matter-of-fact, very few black people actually made it to their seventies. "So, what is your story. How did you end up here?"

"Well… when I was around five years old, my mother needed a dress for a special occasion. I don't remember what the occasion was, and actually it really doesn't matter. She drove us to the mall in the white part of the city because that's where the nicest clothes were. I remember my mom telling me to wait in the chair outside the fitting room while she tried on a few dresses. We had been shopping for a long time and I had to use the bathroom."

Listening to him speak, I was reminded how much my brothers hated going shopping so they convinced my mom to buy all their clothes online.

"Mother was busy trying on clothes so I went to find the restroom myself. I thought I would get back before she noticed me missing."

"How do you remember all those details if you were only five? I can barely remember what I did a month ago"

"I'm getting there." His face came alive with a smile. "Please, be patient."

I zipped my mouth and listened.

"I found the men's restroom by following the signs. You know... the ones with the little white man and woman on a blue background. When I went inside, an older man was at the sink washing his hands. From his view of the mirror he could see me. When I saw him watching me urinate, I got really nervous."

"Damn pervert!" I interjected, wrinkling my nose. "I will never understand how a grown-ass man can become aroused looking at little kids."

"He asked me if I was alone. I didn't know any better so I said 'yes'. When I tried to leave, he blocked the door, unbuttoned his fly, and then partially pulled his pants down to expose himself. He told me my parents had sent him to take me home, but I had to do him a favor first. I kicked him in his leg, managed to open the door, and then ran away because I knew he was lying. I returned to the women's department and tried my best to find the dressing room. But since I was running scared, I got lost."

"That must have been scary," I said, remembering the one time I got separated from my mother in the movie theater. A teenage girl escorted me to lost and found where I waited for my parents to find me.

"I was terrified."

"What did you do?"

"I left the store, located the entrance to the mall, and went outside to the parking lot. I wandered around for about an hour searching for our car before I gave up.

Then I sat on the sidewalk and cried like any young child would. In time, a kind older black woman took pity on me. She asked what was wrong and after I told her I was lost, she offered to help find my mother."

"Thank goodness!" I replied.

"The woman walked me back inside the mall and we returned to the store and searched all the dressing rooms. When we couldn't find my mother, we went to the mall's 'Lost and Found' hoping she would be there waiting. She wasn't, but the man from the restroom was. He told the lady not to worry because he would take good care of me. She started to leave but I ran to her and told her about what happened in the bathroom. She told the man I was leaving with her. He threatened to call the police because technically I should be reported as a lost child."

"Dang! He had a lot of nerve!"

"I didn't know what it meant at the time, but the lady called the man a child molester. She also told him if he stopped her from leaving with me, she would call the police and report him."

"I would think she'd do that anyway. You probably weren't the first child he tried to molest."

"When I was safely in her possession, she did report him to the police." He chuckled at the memory. "On the way home, she asked what my name was. Who were my parents? And if I knew where I lived."

"Did you know?"

"I told her my name and my mom's name, but I didn't know where I lived." His eyes misted over briefly. "You're not going to believe this, but that lady knew my mom! She even showed me an old picture to prove it was true."

"What?!"

"I was shocked! My mother was the daughter she hadn't seen in over six years. This lady turned out to be my grandmother!"

"For real?! That is crazy!"

"My mother was pregnant with me when she ran away from home. She was seventeen, about the same age as you are now. I don't remember much about our life except she tried her best to raise me. But it was hard. She was so young."

"Yeah, but what a wonderful coincidence for your grandmother to have found you!"

"Sistah, what I have come to learn is there is no such thing as coincidence. My Grandmama told me she was destined to find me because for months she had visions of locating her daughter and her missing grandchild. She told me about a bright future awaiting me in a world far away." He stood up to pace the floor, lost in the memory. "She took me home. Fed me. Nourished my mind and soul. Her husband, my grandfather, had passed a year earlier from complications of heart disease so I never had the chance to meet him. But my grandmother shared stories of our greatness, passed down to her through generations. That is when I began to believe I was special."

I shook my head, not because I didn't believe him. I did so because I was astonished by his story. "Did you ever see your mom again?"

"Yes. A few days after she found me, Grandmama happened to come across a social media post with my picture. She called the number and found out it was her daughter. She told my mom I was safe. My mom came to the house and after many hours of tearful arguments, they reconciled. Grandmama asked if she could raise me. My mom only agreed because life was very difficult for a young uneducated single mother. She knew a life with my grandmother would afford me opportunities she was unable to provide. My grandmama taught me to read and write. She instilled me with pride and knowledge of myself. She made me believe that I was destined for a life greater than the one I lived."

"I don't understand. You said you were rescued when you were six. What happened to your grandmother?"

"Grandmama was diagnosed with cancer and died less than a year after I moved in with her. No one had any information on my mother's whereabouts and none of my relatives volunteered to take me in. I eventually wound up in the foster care system where I spent a year with a Caucasian family who was more concerned with receiving a monthly check than raising me. I was miserable in that cookie cutter neighborhood where no one looked like me. One day, a woman came and took me away. I don't know what she told that family that convinced them to let me go, but the next thing I know, I was in a cage similar to the ones you were in when you first arrived."

"You were so young. You must have been scared out of your mind." Then I thought about his poor mother. How she must have tortured herself when she found out her once estranged mother had passed and her son had gone missing.

"I cannot change the past." He watched the scene playout on a movie screen that only he could see. "However, I remember that day as if it happened yesterday. Time is an eternal loop that crosses upon itself. Past, present, and future all occur simultaneously in one's mind."

"Infinite time. That's what the astronomers say about space. It is infinite and eternal." I thought aloud.

"You are correct on both accounts," he replied.

"Well that's a lot for a little boy. How did you handle being separated from your mother and then having your grandmother pass?"

"When a loved one transitions, the memory of them doesn't go away. Their spirit lives on in the minds of their loved ones, which means they will never die. Only the physical body ceases to exist. For example, the spirit of my grandmother lives on within my heart for as long as I have a breath. She was a significant part of my life."

I thought about home. My family. My grandparents. I added, "My great Nana, my mom's mother, was pretty special too. I didn't spend as much time with her as I would have liked to before she passed. Some days if feels like she is right here guiding me."

"That's because your elder's spirit lives on. In the spiritual realm, she never dies." The smile on his face could have lit up the night sky. "The soul, your connection to Yahweh, is infinite and eternal."

"We never die. Our spirit lives on... I can dig that," I responded.

"My mother remains alive in the physical world. I have attempted to communicate with her in ways of which she cannot yet comprehend. I have also reached out to my half-siblings, the ones she birthed later on in life."

"How can you do that?"

"Spiritually; through dreams and visions using a very high vibrational frequency to communicate with their subconscious minds. Occasionally I use what you may recognize as synchronicity, but not too often because many dismiss it as coincidence."

"I think I have might have experienced synchronicity. Were my ancestors reaching out to awaken me?"

"Because you are here. In this place. With us now. Yes, I believe they have started you on a journey to awaken your mind." He closed his eyes in deep concentration as if receiving an incoming telepathic message. "We can only contact those who raise their frequency of mind and body. Because of lifestyle, most people are perpetually trapped in a low vibration. Unreachable throughout their entire lives..."

"I don't want to sound ungrateful, but I'm not sure if this is a good thing. Being awakened. Life was much easier when I was just like everyone else," I explained. "But now that my eyes are open, I don't think I can return to my old life."

"On this journey to reach your highest level of consciousness, you will be grateful for having your eyes opened to see the truth of this world. I have yet to meet anyone who was not."

I exhaled loudly. "I haven't a clue what I'm supposed to be doing with my life."

"Practically no one at the beginning of the journey knows how Yahweh will use their gift as part of His Plan."

"How long did it take for you to discover yours?"

He fiddled with his thick hair, tucking a stray loc into an elastic band. "It took years before I discovered my true calling. It was revealed I have a natural ability comprehending mathematics, all manners of engineering, and artificial intelligence. No formal education was ever involved."

"You never went to school for any of that?!" I asked, surprised by his response.

"No, because those are my gifts."

"Cool!"

"I often enter the outside world to monitor developments in technology by taking specific jobs in the artificial intelligence arena. The Nigiro has eyes and ears in all levels of industry and the government."

"That is so awesome! You're a spy!"

"One might say that..."

"I have always been interested in astronomy. Maybe my calling lies in discovering unknown celestial bodies."

"Possibly," he responded, signaling the conversation was reaching an end. "You have free reign while you are here to explore everywhere except outside the structure. There, you will surely freeze to death."

"You all trust me like that?"

"If you were not trustworthy, you would not be here." He turned away from me, gesturing over the contents of the room. "You must learn to think differently than the world you were raised in, because you are now among your people. You are safe here."

"I'll try..." I wondered what he saw when he viewed the room, or if he regarded it at all. To me, it was homey and nice. A comfortable girly space.

"This is the living quarters for the children." He pointed to two entrances. "Boys on that side. Girls on the other. After you bathe, you will find nourishment for your body within that room. You may sleep in one of those beds. To nourish your mind, read as many of these books as you possibly can. Take notes. Within the pages of these books, between lines of thousands of paragraphs and sentences, you will discover the truth. Hidden in plain sight."

"How many am I supposed to read?" I asked staring at the hundreds of books. "It'll take me years to finish!"

"Listen to your inner voice. It will guide you." He waved his hand over a sensor on the wall. "I must leave you now."

"What about The Teacher? When will I see him again?" I asked.

"The Teacher will appear when you are ready."

"One more question before you leave…"

He paused at the doorway to listen.

"How long am I going to be here?"

"That is entirely up to you. Master your abilities quickly and you will progress to Level 5."

"Level 5?" What happens at that level? Will I be moved somewhere else?" When he didn't respond, I asked, "Can you at least tell me if this entire dome is Level 4?"

"You said one more question and I have answered it." Before he disappeared, he advised, "Study well, my sistah. You are closer than you think."

Chapter Thirteen

Soon after the brother left, I found much nicer clothing than the ones provided by the other guards. The private bathroom offered a freestanding soaking tub, where I took the most relaxing salt baths ever. I immersed my tired stressed muscles in the fragrant warm water and soaked for at least an hour, listening to soft meditative music playing over the loudspeakers, looking at snow laden trees through the panes of a frosty window.

An array of healthy food was available in the dining area for the taking. There I helped myself to a healthy salad comprised of at least a dozen fresh ingredients conveniently cut into bite sized pieces. I tossed all the veggies into a huge bowl, found a fork in one of the drawers, and dug in. Either I was extremely famished, the fruit and vegetables were surprisingly delicious and full of flavor, or perhaps both.

As I was finishing up, Samaria and two other young girls entered the shared room. I noted I was much older than the others by at least five years. Or so I thought.

"Sistah Kenya?!" she asked with surprise and delight in her voice. "Is it really you?!"

"Hi Samaria," I replied. "I mean... sistah."

"It's okay. You can call me Samaria." We embraced as if we were dear friends who had not seen one another in a long while. She then joined me at the table. "I am surprised to see you here so soon."

Upon realizing they were identical twins I couldn't help staring. Their skin tone was the color of toasted almonds which projected a warm healthy glow that originated from within. An abundance of loosely coiled dark brown hair framed their pretty faces, but what really caught my attention was their eyes. The twins' eyes were the color of 22 carat gold! I didn't want to look away because I was immediately overwhelmed with a sense of peace and eternal love seemingly emanating from those eyes, the windows to their souls. The twins were ethereal; as if they were angels, capable of flying away at any moment.

"These are our sistahs. They are very old souls helping me in my journey back home."

"Hi," I said.

Neither spoke, just smiled warmly in my direction.

I heard, *'Welcome to the journey, sistah.'* forming in my mind. Yet, it was not spoken words, but a vibrational sound, sinewy and delicate like the threads formed by a spider spinning an early morning web. Strong and fragile at the same time. Like the gentle breeze of a thought you're not quite sure is your own.

"Did you hear that?" I asked Samaria.

"Yes, my sistah. I heard."

I watched as Samaria communicated telepathically with the girls, but I did not hear that part of their conversation. The two girls left us.

"How did you learn telepathy in one day?"

She furrowed her brow and replied, "A day? I have been here for at least two months."

"That's impossible! We were taken just a couple days ago. It was only yesterday I arrived to this dome."

"Sistah Kenya, consider all you have gone through. It is possible for only two days to have passed?"

I thought about the awful day Samaria and I were snatched. The long scary trip to the encampment site. Meeting the girls in Section D and the conversation with the redhaired woman in her office. The morning after breakfast when I first spotted The Teacher in the green flight suit. Getting tossed around the backseat of a jeep as we ascended through the forest on our way to the dome. Sleeping on palm tree fronds inside the dome's entrance. Feeling awed when I met the Magnificent Queen—I mean Auntie Sistah—and everything that had transpired since.

"Do you actually believe you could have done all that in just two days?" She wasn't trying to be nasty or condescending, just stating the facts. "I have learned that time is irrelevant as it relates to reality. A conundrum. What you believe was two days was actually much longer."

"It's not possible for two months to have passed!" I blinked numerous times, trying to maintain hold of the delicate thread loosely tethered to my reality. "How did I lose track of so much time?"

"Let it go," Samaria advised. "Clear your mind. Hours in a day, the days of the week, the months of the year… those are merely a means to track your current reality. Look to the sun and the moon and the change in seasons. That is how the ancestors lived."

"This isn't happening…"

"Until you learn to let go of your old beliefs, you will continue to believe in a world that is not of your making. Open your eyes. Open your heart. Open your mind."

I dropped down to a chair and rested my head on the table for several minutes. When I opened my eyes, Samaria was there waiting.

"Come with me. I want to show you something," she said.

"Where are we going?"

"Walk with me." She reached her small hand out towards mine.

I accepted her tiny grip. We left the confines of the room and strolled through the interior of the dome. She led me to a great door, but I was hesitant from the brothah's warning about freezing to death on the outside. But, I trusted Samaria and followed her through the portal. We pushed our way through a tangle of vines and underneath massive mangrove trees I imagined should not be possible of growing in these conditions. If I didn't know we were on a mountaintop, I would have sworn we were on an island in the tropics.

"What makes you think we aren't on an island?"

"Ugh… Not you too," I replied exasperated. "Can you do me a favor and not read my thoughts?"

"Fine. After I show you this, I promise I won't read your thoughts without your permission."

We must have walked a mile through a jungle that materialized out of nowhere. The high humidity left my once clean clothes drenched in perspiration. I stepped over lush vegetation and pushed low hanging vines out of our way, before breaking through the trees.

"Close your eyes," she instructed.

I did as requested. I held her hand, walking with my eyes tightly shut.

"You can open your eyes now."

"Where are we?" I gasped in amazement at the spectacular panoramic scene laid out before us. "How is this possible?"

"I have brought you to a very special place that allows you to glimpse the world you want to live in. You created this beach scene within your mind. When the twins first brought me here, I found I had created an intimate art gallery filled with many wonderful paintings and works of art."

"I did all this?" I recalled my earlier conversation with the brothah.

She nodded.

"But if this is all in my mind, how are you able to see it?"

"Because this is collective consciousness. You are sharing your reality with me." She smiled. "Similar to how we created the greenhouse for your arrival."

We stood with our toes resting in warm fine sand at the edge of an ocean that went as far as the eyes could see. Fluffy clouds danced on the wind in the blue skies above. Tall graceful, coconut laden palm trees swayed as gentle breezes passed through its fronds. The air was perfumed by coconut and fragrant with the scent of tropical flowers. I watched in awe as dozens of baby turtles crawled through waves pushing them back towards the beach.

"This cannot be real." I walked towards the water and scooped up a handful. I tasted the saltiness with my tongue. "How is this possible? We're inside a dome on top of a mountain covered by snow."

"When you close your eyes, you see the world you want. If you desire to see your family or even travel to another country, you can. Just place images of what you desire in your mind and it will come to you."

"This feels like the lucid dreams I used to have. Only I'm not asleep. I am wide awake."

Samaria waded into a shallow tide pool. She traced one small foot along the sand, leaving a small imprint of her foot and watched a baby turtle settle inside.

"Sistah Kenya, I learned that within our dreams, we have an ability to create the world we want to live in. But this ability to create is not limited to while we are asleep. It is possible while fully awake! When you stop allowing others to create your reality, you begin to create your own."

"You are so smart, Samaria."

"Only because I know who I am and from whom I come."

I whispered quietly in case anyone else was within range, "Do you know about Nigiro?"

"Yes. But I have only seen Nigiro in my spirit. Not yet with my body. Sistah, it is absolutely beautiful there. The most fantastical, amazing, absolutely breathtaking place I have ever seen! So much better than Disney World and Wakanda combined. All the people look like us. There are no guns. Nobody is concerned with being shot and killed. The vibration from everyone is purely love."

"What do you mean you have only gone in your spirit? You can travel to Nigiro without your body?!"

"It is possible to travel there in spirit as well as the physical body. You shall learn this also. In time."

"That is awesome!" I replied, jumping up and down in excitement. I couldn't believe I might actually get the chance to travel through outer space. To view the earth from the vantage point of the heaven above would really be a dream come true. I could barely contain my enthusiasm.

Samaria abruptly stopped speaking and closed her eyes. When she slowly reopened them, we watched a storm forming on the horizon. She retreated from the water and said, "Sistah Kenya, I am afraid that I might have shared too much with you. We must return so you can study."

"Wait! Did I say something wrong?"

"We have to go." She led me back through the thick tangle of vegetation as if she'd done this dozens of times before. Though I pushed aside solid vines, stepped through streams of water teaming with fish, and ducked under low hanging tree limbs on our way back, I still found it difficult to comprehend how we had walked for miles through a jungle, ended up on a tropical beach, yet still remained within the confines of the dome surrounded by ice and snow. We returned from the portal by means of the door. Just like that, we were back inside the king-dome. I followed Samaria back to the cozy shared space. The twins patiently awaited our arrival, motioning for my young friend to join them.

"I don't understand. Why did we have to leave so soon?" I thought it was much better hanging out on the beach than it was in a room full of books.

She offered no explanation, other than pointing towards the bookshelf filled with all those amazing authors. "No more questions, my sistah. Please read. Study."

"Fine," I replied, noting the silliness of my response. After all, I was older and supposed to be the more mature of us two.

"Until we see each other again, safe travels," she responded via thought, leaving the room with the ethereal twins at her side.

Before I proceeded to undertake the tremendous challenge of reading more books than I'd read in my entire lifetime, and to make sure I hadn't totally lost my mind, I returned to the bathroom where I had bathed earlier. I peered through the frosty window at a blanket of snow covering the ground. Long thick icicles hung from low lying pine tree branches. Nothing had changed. I was exactly where I thought I was, safe inside the confines of the king-dome.

I plopped down on the bathroom floor and closed my eyes. If what Samaria said was true, I could use my mind to conjure up a new reality. Travel to distant lands at will. Never having meditated before, I wasn't sure of the process. I sat with my legs crossed, my hands resting on my thighs, palms turned upwards with my thumb and middle fingers pinched together like I'd seen folks do when practicing yoga. I cleared my mind and thought about home.

Focusing only on my family took some effort because random thoughts of events from the last few days continued to dribble in. But Samaria said to clear my mind so that is what I continued to do. After several minutes passed, all stray thoughts finally ceased and I was in the zone.

I found myself in my bedroom, 'feeling' my mother's emotion as she fretted over my whereabouts and safety. I was there, but not there; as I was now pure energy. My spirit form descended the staircase and into the kitchen. Mom sat at the kitchen table rocking back and forth, wringing her hands; head bent over a cup of coffee warmed up at least three times in the microwave. My heart broke seeing her like that. I needed to do something to let her know I was alive and well so I willed my energy to gather the air and focused on a picture of us taken last summer. In the picture, I made a funny face while she looked on lovingly. The photo broke free from the refrigerator magnet and fluttered to the kitchen floor. She leaned over and picked it up, looked around and called out my name. She felt my presence all right because I caused a shift in her reality when I brushed against her cheek. But I don't think it was welcomed. Before I realized what was happening, I heard her release an audible gasp followed by a horrific scream that frightened me back into myself.

"Oh no!" I whispered loudly, standing up to face the mirror. "What did I just do?"

"For starters, you broke the first rule of astral projection..." replied Auntie Sistah.

"I didn't see you there," I replied, startled by her reflection as she stood in the doorway behind me. It would take some getting used to not referring to her as queen because I had never met anyone who was anywhere close to this level of wisdom. "Astral projection? Is that what you call it?"

"Sistah, though I am not pleased with you contacting your mother without understanding how your spiritual presence would impact her, I am impressed by how quickly you learned on your own!"

"I didn't mean to scare Mom. I just wanted to let her know I was okay."

"For future reference when you are spirit, never initiate physical contact with a hue-man. They do not understand the dynamics behind spiritual astral projection. To the unbelievers, it is unfathomable that a mind can release its spirit for travel to distant places only reached in the physical world. They do believe in ghosts for some reason." She laughed for the first time.

"Until today, I had no idea of the concept or that it's actually possible." I replied feeling amazed. "Ghosts are real, aren't they?"

"Ghosts are images that linger between the two dimensions like wisps of smoke from a fire that no longer burns. Shadows of what once was. Spirits, on the other hand, are those who have lived in the physical world but have transitioned to another realm. The spiritual realm," she explained. "In the spirit, there are no physical boundaries."

"That's cool and all, but I have a question. If you start playing around in the spiritual realm, do you also encounter evil spirits just as easily as the good ones? Is there the chance of one attaching itself to you?"

"That is a very good question, sistah." She was even more pleased and showed it by instructing the brothahs to bring her two cool banana drinks made from ripened bananas and fragrant vanilla beans that grew wild within the geodome. "One must be just as cautious while operating in the spiritual realm as you are in the physical. Discernment of spirit is one of the greatest abilities one can possess."

"I'm glad to hear it. I wouldn't want to accidently invite an evil spirit into my world, or my families."

"Evil attracts evil, as like attracts like. What you place into the world is what you receive. If ever an evil spirit tries to attach itself to you, do not engage with it on your own for those spirits are powerful, especially when your light is newly visible. Call on your ancestors for help and they will come."

I filed that tidbit of information to the back of my mind for safe-keeping, not that I ever imagined I would need it.

"Do not worry about your mother. She will be fine, as she instinctively knows you are alive as a result of a visceral connection which exists between a mother and child."

"I hope you're right," I replied, before changing the subject. "Can I ask you another question?"

"You may."

"What's the deal with Samaria? She told me about extraordinary things that I can do with my mind. Am I going to be like her?"

"The young sistah is extremely gifted, as are you... Except in different ways. She arrived to us virtually untouched with an almost pure soul; a rarity nowadays. She is still learning her capability and will soon progress to a place not of this Earth."

"Nigiro?"

She nodded.

"Wow!" Was all I could utter.

"I believe you are ready." The billowy fabric of her dress made a soft whooshing sound against the clay floor tiles when she turned from the mirror. "Follow me."

I followed her to a small bedroom. A narrow bed, nightstand, lamp, and an overstuffed chair were the only furnishings.

"Please, lie down. Relax."

Her manner of speaking was so comforting, I did as I was told without hesitation. Not to mention I needed a nap after that unexpected excursion.

"Remember how I told you I was rescued as a young girl?"

I nodded.

"Well, I didn't know it at the time, but Watchers— spiritual beings from whom we descended—have kept an eye on me from the moment I was born. Just as I do now for my family. And as you shall for those who will come after you."

"I don't have children and at this rate with my being here, I probably never will." I looked at her skeptically. "You say you're a Watcher? How does that work?"

"We watch over our family members. Parents, siblings, nieces, nephews, cousins, and so forth. That way, no one is ever left behind."

"I see..."

"During the phase of the moon when it is at its fullest, I visit those in my direct bloodline in the spirit form. I reach out to the receptive ones with gentle nudges to awaken. I contact them through snippets of dreams, or visions when it is critical to warn of impending tragedy. Sometimes I am successful, other times not so much."

"Did it work with your parents?" I asked with hopes for my own.

She released a weary sigh. "My family was very poor. This was during the depression and often there were days we barely had enough food to eat. My mother and father raised eleven children on the scraps of the land."

With all I had learned so far on my journey, Auntie Sistah was far from poor. Those black people looked out for each other back then, not like today where people lived under the mentality of 'every man for himself'.

"I was too late to awaken my father before he transitioned. Before he passed, he became embittered by unfair life bent on his destruction. He succumbed to inadequate health care at a very young age and died from an entirely preventable illness. My mother was so distraught that any contact from myself in a spiritual form would have sent her over the edge. She was left to raise my brothers and sisters. Unfortunately, there were many horrible things she had to do for money. I watched. And it broke my heart."

"What happened to your brothers and sisters?" I asked, surprised that her life experience was more similar to my family's, than not.

"Of my ten siblings, I was successful in reaching all but two. My oldest sister never got over my abduction. She felt responsible and started drinking heavily when she was but a child. The damage she did to her mind and body was irreparable. And my younger brother was murdered by white men who thought he was being 'too uppity' when he refused to walk through a puddle of muddy water to allow them to pass. He was hung from a tree, and then shot when he didn't immediately expire from the hanging. Afterwards, his body was burned and dismembered. He had been home visiting from college at the time. The only one of my siblings who pursued higher education. He had just turned twenty years old when it happened," she explained.

"I am so sorry to hear about your sister and brother. I can't imagine how your parents must have felt."

"Unfortunately, that was a way of life back in those days. The killings became a normal occurrence for the majority of our people."

"What happens to the descendants who don't wake up? Are they forever lost?"

"Not forever lost, but their souls continue to return in physical form to this Earth until they remember who they are. A physical death does not provide an awakening of the spiritual self. One must know thyself; the soul must know the truth of The Almighty." Her eyes temporarily misted over as memories from a long-ago childhood resurfaced. "As for my sister, her soul has recently returned in the form of a child and I have already contacted her. Whether she retains the knowledge of herself remains to be seen, as much will depend who her parents are and how she is raised."

"My cousin RayRay, that's what we used to call him, was believed to have an 'old soul'. My uncle used to tell us that our cousin was an old man who had returned in a baby's body and he knew that because he could see it in RayRay's eyes. He thought RayRay had been here before because of his mannerisms, strange expressions, and interest in fixing old cars all before he turned ten. I never understood what my uncle meant until now."

"That is a good example of what I mean," she remarked. "My brother's soul has returned many times, yet he remains tortured. He is bent on taking revenge not only on the men who took his life, but also the children of those men. He has returned twice already in his quest for vengeance but both times his life was cut short."

"What has he done?"

"In the physical form, he always found a way to get close to those men and their family members by fostering close relationships—personal and professional. But because The Almighty sees the hatred in my brother's heart, he is not permitted to remain on earth. Consequently, he has died at a young age; first from a tragic auto accident and then, cancer."

"Wow!" was my reaction.

"In the spiritual realm, he tortured the murderer's souls by placing horrific images of his dismembered body within their minds and dreams, never allowing them to find peace. As a result, one man drank himself to death and another committed suicide. But his revenge didn't stop with those men because he also sought revenge on their children by inflicting them with diseases of the mind and body. Those people never understood their families were cursed as a result of the sins of their fathers. However, the third man repented, made amends to our family and then dedicated his life to ending hatred and stopping the violence inflicted on our people."

"That sounds like a generational curse..."

"Yes, it was. But I shall continue to reach out to my brother as many times at it takes so his soul is able to rest."

"Were you reincarnated, too?"

"Of course! When life is eternal, one goes through many lifetimes. Personally, I have been here many, many times before. I have lived as other races on various continents, during every known time period. I've been rich, poor, and everything in between."

"That may explain my feelings of deja vu. I have dreamt of foreign lands, cities and countries I have never visited. I used to think it was due to foreign movies I've watched and books I have read. Never ever considered the images were memories from different lives."

"You have been here before. That is most certain." She rested, leaning her head back against the headrest. "From the beginning, when the Elders became aware of the conditions our people were suffering under, a concerted effort was made to bring the children home. But first they had to awaken the Nigiro from their slumber. They tried rescuing adults, but due to the degree of indoctrination embedded within their minds they discovered their efforts were futile. After generations of systematic racism, adults over a certain age simply would not accept our story. They chose to embrace the Trickster's Eurocentric version. The focus was then shifted towards waking up the youth."

"What happens to the grownups since you only want the children?"

"That is a good question," she paused. "We have other methods of awakening older Nigiro. Sometimes it takes decades before the seed of truth takes root and begins to grow. That is what is happening now, courtesy of the world wide web. Old video footage of what the mainstream has termed 'Afrocentric', to discredit the great works of influential men and women sent here to shake things up, are now resurfacing. An entirely new generation is seeing what their forefathers once learned and what they have subsequently forgotten."

"Why not just reach the children while they are living at home with their family?"

"Too many distractions exist in this materialistic world that undermine our efforts. These distractions prove much too attractive to a young impressionable mind," Auntie Sistah explained.

"You're absolutely right! We now have twenty-four-hour television with thousands of programs on just as many stations to watch. Then there is the internet, video games, and virtual reality to distract us."

She closed her eyes with intense concentration. "At a very young age, when I first noticed the disparity in how we lived compared to the dominant society, I asked my parents about the white Jesus we worshiped. I was abruptly punished. Questioning the authenticity of a god who resembled the very people who treated us worse than animals was considered blasphemy. Therefore, I never questioned them again, but it didn't stop me from thinking about what I was being taught. My parents chose to embrace a man-made religion rather than focus on the spiritual teachings of the ancestors."

I allowed her words to take hold.

"What you have been taught in school are lies." She laughed out loud. "Spaniards and Portuguese explorers did not discover America because this land was already inhabited. They mistakenly believed they had landed in

India when copper colored people greeted them upon arrival. That is why they started referring to the indigenous as 'Indians'."

"Christopher Columbus didn't discover America in 1492?"

"The man never stepped a foot on this land they now call America!" She scoffed.

"But that's what we were taught in school." I narrowed my eyes trying to determine if what she said was true. "How do you know?"

"I know because the Nigiro lived peacefully alongside other native tribes for thousands upon thousands of years on this land. All was harmonious until European settlers landed. They brought with them disease, misery, war, and then stole the land after killing and displacing millions. History wants us to believe those early explorers were heroes, but actually they were bloodthirsty opportunists determined to colonize the land and enslave the indigenous people in order to increase their own fortunes."

"That's incredible.... I'm never going to celebrate Columbus Day again!"

"The Nigiro thrived in this country. We lived in modern cities. Our people were doctors, architects, engineers. We were farmers and carpenters. We created art that has lasted eons. We knew how to live off the land in harmony with nature. We respected the other tribes and they respected us."

"How were our people enslaved if they were so intelligent? Why didn't they fight back?"

"From the time they landed on this continent, the Tricksters studied and plotted ways to eliminate the indigenous tribes. The tribes were unaccustomed to the ways of the Tricksters, who were well-versed in exploitation, lying, and making promises they had no intention of keeping. The colonizers brought blankets filled with the small pox virus, of which the natives had no immunity, and also plied them with whiskey and other useless items valued in their cold countries, in exchange for their land. Those English colonizers then brought weapons and guns with them, which was eventually used to force the native indigenous population, including the Nigiro, into total submission."

I listened to this history lesson laden with extraordinary morsels of uncovered truths. Nothing my sistah explained, had I ever heard before. I was absolutely enthralled.

"These colonizers used those same tactics to enslave Africans in their own land and then brought them to this continent to build the country in what they referred to as, 'The New World'. The slave masters and overseers hired to keep the enslaved Africans in line continually raped the women just as they did the bountiful earth. Those heathens planted their seeds within our mothers' wombs to increase their bottom-line profits. When those babies conceived out of rape were born, they had fairer skin than other slaves, yet those poor children were still considered as property. And do you think they freed their own flesh and blood?" she asked, not waiting for a response. "That wasn't even considered! The wives of plantation owners got together, implemented a color caste system for the children of their husbands, brothers, and sons, and classified those offspring as Colored, Mulatto, Quadroon, and Octaroon, which resulted in the fairer skinned slaves to falsely believe themselves superior to their darker brethren. The closer one's skin color was to the slave masters, the easier one's life was, but despite their new classifications, they all remained enslaved."

"I remember overhearing my grandfather say, 'If you're white, you're alright; if you're brown, stick around; if you're black, get back'." I exhaled slowly, "I'm sad to say that same colorism is still alive and kickin'."

She nodded in agreement. "Once the mind is controlled, getting the body to follow is fairly easy. That is how Britain managed to enslave an entire people on their own land."

"That's awful how one group of people can treat others so badly."

"They destroyed families. Women were raped. Men were murdered in the most heinous fashion. Children were routinely sold off to other plantations throughout the colonies. By dispersing tribes across the land, they also destroyed the ability to communicate in the native language which is troubling because our people relied on oral tradition to pass on our culture. Accurate or not, European history is written down in books, and then taught to our children as the gospel. Due to this, it was a simple process to erase our history and replace it with their own."

I felt waves of anger rising within but I continued to listen. This was not the history I had learned in school. I never knew that my ancestors were doctors, nurses, engineers, mathematicians, inventors, architects, teachers, and skilled tradesmen. I didn't even learn about the Tulsa Race Massacre of 1921 until last year when I happened upon an online video. The massacre of hundreds of successful black people, living their best lives in a successfully run all black town, was intentionally left out of the history books. No teacher ever taught me that NASA employed black women as mathematicians and engineers in the 1950's and 1960's. Or explained how their involvement was critical in launching the first mission to the moon. As far as we knew, the only black people who worked at NASA during that time in history was the janitorial staff.

On the other hand, just like clockwork every February during Black history month, we heard the same old tired ass narrative focusing on The Trans-Atlantic Slave Trade, about millions of Africans being enslaved and then shipped to America in 1619. I heard over-and-over that slaves suffered a miserable existence picking cotton on plantations only to be beaten, lynched or tortured as a part of daily life. We learned that after Lincoln "freed" the slaves in 1862, white southerners immediately began lynching freed Negroes who in their words, 'got too uppity'. I couldn't count how many times I heard Rosa Parks' feet were tired so she didn't want to give up her seat to a white man. And I cringed watching the old news reels showing black people with fire hoses turned on them, running from police and their bloodthirsty dogs. Those heartbreaking images were seared into my memory.

Now I understood why American history wants us to believe our story began with slavery. The propaganda served to keep our minds enslaved with this annual ritual of reliving that time. There was never any mention of the accomplishments so many African-Americans made to build this country. The civil rights movement was not for the privilege of sitting at lunch counter with whites, or to live in their neighborhoods, or be allowed to sit in the front of the bus. My ancestors suffered those indignities for the simple fact of wanting to be treated like everyone else in this country. To be treated like a human being. A citizen of this country with all its associated rights and privileges.

"You must first understand our people originated on the planet of Nigiro. Hundreds of thousands of Earth years earlier, our Elders arrived to this planet and inhabited many continents, making wherever they resided, home. This includes the entire landmasses of North, Central and South America, Africa, and Asia before those continents came to be named as such. We are wanderers. Explorers in every sense of the word. Always have been."

"I did a report on aboriginals for world history. Millions of black aboriginals are living in Central and South America and the Caribbean islands. I was surprised when I learned about Afro-Mexicans. I studied Aborigines in Australia, the black people of India, Asia, and what they now call the Middle East. Black people originated everywhere. So what makes us think we weren't also here before the 'Divided States' came into existence?"

"Those known as the present day Native American Indians arrived much later than we did to the Americas. They settled primarily in the Northern and Southwestern states. Unfortunately for those Indians, as you can see, their tribes are almost at the point of extinction. They too believed the Trickster's lies and fell for the deception," explained Auntie Sistah.

"I wish every American had learned this history. If my sisters and brothers growing up believed we could become more than athletes and entertainers our lives would turn out so different."

Auntie Sistah nodded, pleased she was getting through.

I shook my head in disgust.

"With the swipe of a pen, a new race of people was created. The American Negro. And as a result, the Nigiro were eliminated through a paper genocide."

As she spoke, my thoughts settled on St. Louis. My parents often reminisced with stories told to them by their parents about how different St. Louis is now as compared to the past. The suburban counties that used to thrive in the late 1970's and early 1980's, with a majority white population, deteriorated once they moved out and took their wealth with them. You could see the gradual decline occur when high end retailers followed the wealth exodus, leaving vacant spacing for pawn shops, liquor stores, fast food joints and nail salons to take over. Very rarely were the owners of these businesses black. They were Asian, Arab, white, even some Africans, but never black Americans.

"The Tricksters used their twenty-four-hour news cycle and connections in Hollywood to bombard the world with programs dominated by negative images, false history, and criminalized blacks, disguised under the umbrella of news and 'entertainment'."

"I know this world isn't Heaven, but I'm starting to believe we're living straight up in hell."

"Beloved, the world in which you live is not hell. But your existence in this world is."

Auntie Sistah's patience was infinite as she communicated her explanation of how things operated. Discovering that not only you've been lied to all your life, but also your parents, their parents, and generations of ancestors who came prior, was a huge pill to swallow.

"One day I asked my parents why we stopped going to church like most of my extended family. My dad said he noticed how well pastors lived compared to parishioners. Said it wasn't fair to have us poor people struggling to pay our bills, trying to make ends meet every month, but faithfully tithe to the church. At the end of the day, we got nothing in return except a feel-good message. When he found out the pastor had bought a multi-million-dollar home, he told my mother he would never give that man, or any other fake religious man, another nickel of his hard-earned money. While he wondered where all that money went, I wondered why God and none of the angels in that Bible looked like us..."

"Is that all you have wondered?"

"What do you mean?"

"Think, my beloved." She opened her eyes and leaned closer. "What is the one burning question always on your mind? What is the one question that everyone asks, but no one seems to have the answer?"

I closed my eyes again. 'Why is the sky blue?' 'How is it possible that airplanes can fly or ships sail on the ocean without sinking?' 'What happens when we die?' 'Why do we have five fingers instead of four or six?' 'Is there really a God?' 'If so, why does He allow so much suffering in this world?'"

"Those are all certainly wonderful questions," she said, reading my thoughts. "Go deeper. Think about the one question that has haunted you every single day of your life."

I closed my eyes again, thinking of my parents, my family, my friends. When I was a child, I hated the feeling of desperation hanging in the air when my parents struggled to cover any expense out of the ordinary. Having to ride the bus for over an hour just to get to school never seemed right, especially when the one within walking distance was shut down. And listening to my youngest brother and of his friends discuss dreams of making it to the NBA so they'd never have to worry about money, caused me to question why sports was more important than education

My community was overburdened with single mothers who relied on government assistance for housing, food stamps for survival, Medicaid for health care; many became totally dependent upon welfare to raise their children. Over the past year, at least a dozen people in my neighborhood had died from drug overdoses or gunfire, and at sixteen I had attended more home goings than some folks did their entire lives. It seemed like hardly anyone I knew could catch a break. Those who did, never looked back.

I thought about a police force tasked 'to protect and serve'; whose rank and file was filled with officers who harassed young black men, including my brothers, just for being black. I wondered why almost every young black man I knew had gone to prison, was on probation, or was burdened by years of never-ending parole. Yet all across America, thousands of innocent melanated citizens were killed annually by those same police who were supposed to protect them, yet used the excuse that they were 'in fear of their lives' as justification. I felt sick to my stomach thinking about my mother's constant fear for her children being murdered in the street for sport.

I reflected upon my Uncle Ricky and the conspiracy theories he spouted over the years. He was always complaining about how the white man kept his foot on the black man's neck to keep him from progressing and passing him by. And finally, I questioned why was there so much distrust within our community amongst ourselves?

"You are on the right track." She released a weary sigh and uttered, "There is an unseen system that was instilled long before the inception of this country to keep its citizens, especially black people, trapped in a web of deceit. It exists in education, religion, the food and drug industry, the media. It is everywhere and has almost completely taken over the minds of our people."

"I know things are bad, but it's getting better. Black people are beginning to awaken and a new consciousness movement is growing. People are using the internet to post videos about the injustices we face in this country with homelessness, lack of health care and such. The Black Lives Matter movement made this country aware that our lives are just as valuable as anyone else's. It's not all doom and gloom. Is it?"

"All is not lost, however, many of our people have lost touch with the inner spirit; having sunk to such low vibrational frequencies they are unreachable. Look at how they behave! How they speak! They eat trash they think is food! The clothes they wear and the garbage they place on top of their heads are ridiculous!"

"I think people are just trying to assert themselves by standing out from the crowd to make a statement. Everyone just wants to be a famous."

She sucked her teeth loudly, seething with disdain for the proliferation of ignorant behavior, and proclaimed, "Most entertainers today are clowns hiding behind costumes and make-up! They rely upon smoke and mirrors because they have no talent. They are only out to make a quick dollar! They should not be emulated!"

"Not all are like that. Some entertainers are very talented."

Auntie Sistah replied, pursing her lips tightly. She had heard similar assertions from others while bringing them to the truth. "We have sent so many great people to help you rise up from this condition, but they were foiled each and every time. Deported by government. Characters destroyed. Assassinated. Not only by the Tricksters, but also the hands of their own misguided people."

"Are you referring to activists such as Malcolm X, Martin Luther King Jr., Elijah Muhammad, Medgar Evers, and more recently Francis Cress Welsing, Louis Farrakhan, Dr. Ben-Jochannan and Dr. John Clarke?"

"Yes, those men and women were all great Nigiro, but there are many more teachers whose names will never be known. They are in the streets of the communities doing the day-to-day work and getting no credit for their sacrifices."

I took a deep breath allowing the history lesson to continue to sink in. I don't know if anything different could have been done. A very clear message was sent after the Civil War. Any attempt to help black people overcome their poor condition, could result in you or your family members being harassed, tortured or murdered in the process.

"We hoped our message would get across through music and inspirational songs to increase awareness. This music crossed all genres—jazz, the blues, rock n' roll, soul, R&B, hip-hop. For example, songs from the 1960's included messages filled with black empowerment and offered hope for a brighter day. Songs of the 1970's brought forth messages of love and peace. And finally, when hip-hop came about in the1980's and 90's, it was the voice of a new generation of artists who put a mirror up to America and showed everyone who she really is." She wore the disgust on her face like a frightening Halloween mask. "After stealing our music, they used it to make their own musicians famous on the backs of Nigiro, never attributing credit to the true artists."

Once my tears started flowing, they would not cease. The horrible conditions of everyone I knew seemed to land within my young brain at the same time. I was overwhelmed with grief.

"The music was forever changed, but the old school music is still relevant today. Listen to great musicians and artists like Stevie Wonder, Marvin Gaye, Prince, Michael Jackson in his last years.... There are messages within their songs that will help guide you. For example, listen to the song by Maurice White of Earth, Wind & Fire's *'Keep Your Head to the Sky'*. She began to recite the lyrics,

> Master told me one day
> I'd fine peace in every way
> But in search for the clue
> Wrong things I was bound to do
>
> Keep my head to the sky
> For the clouds to tell me why
> As I grew with strength
> Master kept me as I repent
>
> Keep your head to the sky...

With tears still streaming down my face and listening to her recite the spiritual uplifting words, I turned to the beautiful Auntie Sistah and whispered, "The question I have always wanted to ask, but never knew how is, Why are black people so hated?"

"Yes!" she exclaimed, displaying a perfect smile on her glowing face. "Why indeed?! I'll tell you why!" She said, standing to her feet.

"I don't get it! Everyone loves our contributions to society, yet we are treated like crap no matter where we live. Why is that?!"

"The Tricksters have sold us nothing but lies! Great big white lies! The Elders gave us the Book of Life so we would always remember our stories through the ages. But when these people discovered the true magnificence of our people... first they banned, then burned all books, especially those chronicling our achievements from ancient civilizations. Even banned *The Book of Life!*"

"Why would they do something like that when most of us don't even read The Bible?"

"The modern reader requires a key to decipher the original intent of scripture. The ancient texts were translated and given contemporary English meanings that are not wholly accurate. Tricksters have manipulated the Bible, inserted themselves into our story, gave it back to us, then told us we were the lowest of the low. Less than human! That we were born to be enslaved and to obey them. Made themselves out to be our masters! Gave our people a fake god who did not resemble us in the least. Removed the Nigiro as The Chosen Ones and then had the gall to make our story into theirs. These liars will do anything to keep the world from discovering the truth. Ha!"

I shook my head not because I didn't believe her, but because I *did not want to believe her.* My world was slowly turning unraveling.

"Those masters of deception appropriated our culture, stole our land, our history. Annihilated our past in order to destroy our future. These people now believe we are redundant. We're considered as disposable, useless drains on society. Something they no longer have a need for so they are finding ways to entirely replace us with another lower class of people. Brown has become the new black."

"I know what you say is true, but it doesn't make much of a difference because black people don't seem to care."

Auntie Sistah laughed, but not because she was amused; on the contrary, she was extremely dismayed. "The descendants of Nigiro have not only bought the lie, they have wholeheartedly embraced it! If it were not so diabolical, I would be impressed with the strategic implementation of a plan that only took hundreds of years to dismantle the future of an entire 'race' of people they re-labeled as black."

My eyes overflowed with salty tears. Everything she said resonated within my soul. There was no other answer that made sense. We had to be extraordinary! Otherwise, why did it feel like a war was being raged on us for generations?

"My beloved, do not be dismayed. When the Nigiro discover who they truly are and what they are capable of doing, the world the Tricksters now know, will cease to exist. This is why we must rescue and liberate the children. We are trying to wake up an entire nation of sleeping Nigiro because very powerful men are doing everything within their power to exterminate our people."

"Since this has been going on for centuries, why do you come for me now?" I asked, perplexed.

"The world as you know it, is coming to an end. Those in power are intent upon destroying this world and taking out most of the population, especially Nigiro. We have come to awaken the children and you are going to help us do that."

"Why me?" I asked, feeling more confused than ever. "Who am I to change anything?"

"Why you?!" she raised her head high and proudly proclaimed, "You are Nigiro! Of the original hue-mans. A child of Yahweh! The Most High God! The Almighty! The eternal Source! The Great I Am! The Alpha and the Omega! The Creator of All that exists! We are the Chosen, blessed with unlimited gifts, abilities, and talents. Nigiro have built great civilizations on every continent of this Earth. The ancestors constructed massive pyramids without lifting a finger! We can cure diseases with only the plants provided by our Creator. We make beautiful music from instruments carved from wood, stone and precious metals gleaned from nature. We possess the ability to communicate telepathically! There is nothing we cannot do when we put our collective minds together!"

"I think I'm starting to understand, but there is still so much I do not know." I pressed the palms of my hands against my throbbing temples.

"Our people have lived in bondage for long enough."

"I'm thinking about the millions of enslaved Africans—I mean Nigiro. And when you consider how many have died at the hands of not only white people, but our own mentally enslaved since this country began... The number is mind-boggling! The degree of hatred inflicted on us is unimaginable!"

"My purpose is not to instill hatred in your heart for anyone. It is not white people who have done this to you. They too, are very lost. Many are also victims of the Trickster's deception and have come under the spell of believing they are superior."

With the redhaired woman's words still fresh in my mind about how the social construct of white people came about, I responded, "This is all so confusing. White people are the ones who have done all these horrible things to us, and yet, I don't hate them as a group. I can't! I have white family members whose hearts are so filled with love and kindness, that I don't consider them as 'white'. My aunt is married to a white man and he is awesome! And so are my biracial cousins. I've known many who have gone out of their way to help my family. And my parents are friends with a white couple and they visit each other's homes all the time. So, while I understand that all white people aren't the same, I also know they're not all evil."

She smiled as if she were sharing a secret when she said, "I must tell you that many of the people who consider themselves 'white' are also descendants of Nigiro. They just do not know it. Or they won't admit it."

"I do remember my Great Nana explaining that back in the day, light skinned Negroes chose to pass because it was much easier to be considered white. I thought they were cowards for giving up their heritage just to gain privileges. And in this country, you can be certain the majority will deny their black roots 'til the day they die.

But I also know there are whites who are now beginning to acknowledge their African ancestry."

Auntie Sistah looked away forlornly and whispered, "The people will perish for the lack of knowledge."

"If only they knew about the Nigiro, they'd be proud instead of ashamed."

"We are the aboriginal people also known as Negro, Moreno, Taino, Latino, Hispanic. Though we were originally copper colored, our people are now a range of skin tones from the palest of beige to the deepest purple-black. We can be found on every continent and island."

"How can you tell who is who if not by color of skin?"

"The blood is how we identify who is truly Nigiro. It's in the DNA."

"I remember reading about DNA. Scientists have discovered that some humans have extra strands than the two they originally knew about. They call it junk DNA." I recalled how excited my cousins were to have traced their ancestry back to West Africa by submitting samples of spit through the mail.

"DNA results can be manipulated by statistics to justify anything the Tricksters want." She shook her head, releasing a weary sigh. "Besides, those samples provided by millions of hapless Nigiro are only helping the Tricksters to conduct research on how best to destroy you."

"I thought those ancestry tests were blind to a person's race. The test results can't be manipulated that easily. Can they?"

I remembered TV commercials touting how everyone should purchase an ancestry DNA kit, the way mattress companies advertised the need for a new bed. I knew dozens of people who scrambled to purchase a kit, sent in a sample, and eagerly awaited results of their heritage. Then they'd post videos with the reveal of their DNA results as if announcing the sex of their unborn child.

Her expression relayed the weariness she felt inside. "Disregard what you have learned from contemporary science books. The truth has been twisted to the degree it is unreliable. Read the books written by the descendants of the Elders. Study what was written prior to the 1600's, before North America was colonized. Familiarize yourself to the ways of the Tricksters and learn who the oppressors truly are. And when you read, pay close attention to the words. Because words do matter."

"I will do as you say, Auntie Sistah."

"Keep this in the back of your mind, beloved. There will come a time when the Nigiro, the so-called blacks, African-Americans, the niggers of this nation..." She didn't roll her eyes but came very close to it, "...will once again rise up to claim their righteous place in this world!"

"We will finally be recognized as Nigiro!" I responded, hopefully.

She sighed when she explained, "When that day arrives, just know those who now condemn our blackness will lust after it with a fierce passion. Many will proclaim themselves as your supporters and try to win you over with declarations they are the same as you. They are not. Listen carefully to what I say, if the descendants of Nigiro once again allow others to steal what remains of our heritage, all will be lost."

"We used to have a saying back home, 'All skin, ain't kin', so I understand what you mean. All Nigiro have melanin, but not all people with melanin are Nigiro."

Auntie Sistah's nostrils flared in anger as she explained, "There was a time when these heathens paraded around in mockery of us. Even passed around pictures of themselves all blackened up as a sick joke. But were you aware that scientists have discovered means to temporarily alter pale skin to drastically increase the amount of melanin in the body? And an unexpected side effect also alters physical features?!"

"Blackface, huh?" I figured that must be some real deep-seated hatred to alter your body to resemble something you despise.

She did not respond.

"I remember a story from China a few years back. A so-called doctor supposedly treated two men who were dying from a 'virus'. The news reported his patients were horrified when they awoke because their skin had turned dark and their hair napped up. I didn't believe it. I thought it was made up."

"Experimentation to resemble Nigiro is not unheard of. So the truth is stranger than fiction," she replied. "Listen to me! Until the descendants of Nigiro proudly rise up and withdraw from this capitalistic American system, we are doomed to perish. Our people will become extinct on this Earth as many other species have. Mark my words."

"Do you really think we could go extinct? I mean, there are still millions of us in America."

"Look no further than to what happened to the modern-day Native American... the so-called aboriginal people."

"Hold up... the Indians—Native Americans, aren't the aboriginal people of America?"

"Yet another lie! As I indicated earlier, not all black people are descendants of enslaved Africans. According to *their* history, the first dozen or so Africans arrived in Virginia in 1619, brought here by the English. Then for another two centuries, the Spanish, Portuguese, and Brits claim to have successfully transported over ten million African people to the Americas. And that estimated number of enslaved people isn't even counting the ten million or so estimated to have died during the crossing. Do you actually believe those lazy men made tens of thousands of voyages across the ocean from the 1500's to the mid 1800's transporting tens of millions of Africans?"

"If that actually occurred and those numbers are correct, why doesn't the world recognize that an African Holocaust also happened? That an African genocide is no less important than a holocaust that killed 6 million

Jews. But the holocaust is an event they will never allow us to forget what happened. As a matter-of-fact, even to this day, the United States and other European countries are paying reparations to those descendants." I frowned and uttered, "That doesn't make sense for American taxpayers to be paying for something this country had no hands in. Does it? Unless they did..."

"That is an interesting comparison. And I like the fact that you are now starting to look critically at what you are seeing." Auntie Sistah smiled as she was now getting through. "Consider this for a moment, there are no actual slave ships to be found in their museums. Just a few shackles and chains from an old ship wreck is supposed to be the only evidence? That doesn't make sense when you consider several Viking ships from the 1000 AD were recovered and are currently stored away in a Norwegian museum."

"I never really thought about why there are no slave ships in museums, especially the way Europeans love to display relics from our ancient past."

"The Native Americans you recognize today are the descendants of Mongoloid-Asians who migrated much later from the cold climate in the north. The Nigiro taught them how to survive on the land and a peaceful coexistence was formed. The early tribes agreed to share the land and its resources as The Most High intended."

My head felt as if it would explode; my mind vacillating between disbelief and trying to wake up from a nightmare.

"All this time, African-Americans who swore they had Indian blood, I thought were delusional. We didn't look anything like the red-skin Indians. Now I know why. It never occurred to me that history lied and had reclassified all the dark copper colored aboriginals of this land as Negro or Colored."

"Yes, my beloved. As we discussed earlier, the white man is a master of trickery and manipulation. After understanding that the origin-al hue-mans and Nigiro are one in the same, they intentionally misspelled Nigiro as Negro, creating a new race in the process. Because they truly abhorred the originals, the word 'aboriginal' was coined for our melanin rich brothahs and sistahs in Australia and other indigenous cultures."

"Dang! I'll bet most people have no clue how often Europeans tinkered with the language to cover their evil tracks. I wish I could find a dictionary to see when new words are introduced and how they changed the meanings of those words over a period of time."

"During colonial times, in exchange for the natives' trust and loyalty, they were rewarded with disease, introduced to whiskey to anaesthetize them, and then slaughtered while their land was stolen from beneath their feet. Survivors were eventually pushed to designated land reservations for their descendants to live a life without jobs or hope. What remained of their culture was hijacked by others who have all but pushed aside the very ones they now pretend to be. Ask yourself, who today benefits from being an Indian?"

"Well, from what I've learned about the native tribes in Missouri, they look more European than indigenous." I shook my head at how deeply the lie went. "All this time, I believed the native people had died out from disease and alcoholism. I had no idea that millions of black Americans, the descendants of Nigiro, had been reclassified as black or Negro. We never learned they were indigenous to American long before others arrived."

I stared at the bookshelf, trying to keep my eyes from glossing over at all the titles before me. I sighed loudly. Although I loved reading, my preferred subject was science fiction. And though my parents proclaimed to be Afro-centric, we had no books by these great authors in our home and I could count the number of books I'd read by black writers on one hand.

"When a people no longer know their history, have no culture, no common language, are indoctrinated by a false religion for generations, their minds eventually belong to the captor. Once that happens, they practically enslave themselves."

"Auntie Sistah, you have given me an awful lot to think over." I sighed wearily. "What happens next?"

Before she left the room, she turned and softly said, "As the others before me have told you, The Teacher will arrive when you are ready. He will assist you on your journey. Until then, learn as much as you can on your own."

I sat on the bed with my feet firmly planted on the floor. All my senses were heightened. Mesmerized by the words dancing in the playground of my mind, I wondered, *Why me? I wasn't special. I had done nothing in my short life to prepare me for a life of greatness.* In fact, in my mind I wasn't worthy of the monumental task I was being prepared for. My heart swelled with the knowledge that so many had faith in my abilities! I was amazingly proud, yet at the same time, extremely terrified of being me.

Chapter Fourteen

My first few days after the visit with Auntie Sistah were spent primarily within the shared confines of the dormitory. On occasion, I ventured into the dome to read. I had very few interactions with the other students as they were also consumed with studying.

One morning, as I sat with my back pressed against the transparent exterior wall watching the snow fall, my thoughts went to the children, wondering what they were learning. I had tried to mingle with several after their lessons were completed, but I discovered I didn't fit in. Though much younger than myself, these children were different from the rambunctious boys and talkative girls I was familiar with back home. These kids, gifted with supernatural abilities and off the chart talents, behaved like miniature mature adults.

My time had been short time with the girls from Section D, but I missed them already. At least they were closer in age. We talked about things I could relate to, like our shitty home lives and aspirations for the future. But now, with all this infinite time to myself, trying to get into these books everyone suggested I read, I felt the first inklings of loneliness.

In spite of everything Auntie Sistah and the brothah had taught me about the condition of the Nigiro, I wanted to return to my old familiar comfortable life in St. Louis, no matter how awful it could be at times. I know misery loves company, but at least I would be around others as miserable as myself; instead of feeling alone among the hundreds of children. I wandered back to my area.

I was surprised yet happy to find that Samaria was in the quarters. However, I was then taken aback to see that she was removing the bedding from the bed and placing her meager belongings inside a reusable cotton bag. Her head was bent in deep thought when I entered.

"Are you going somewhere?" I asked.

"*Sistah, I will not be here when you return. I will be taking a very long journey to visit our home planet, Nigiro,*" she explained, telepathically.

"You haven't even been here that long. Why are you leaving now?"

"*The children here bridges between the Nigiro on the planet, and the humans on earth. I have work to do on Nigiro which is why I am leaving now.*"

I responded verbally as I had not yet mastered my mental abilities. "Are you afraid?"

"*There is nothing to fear. On the contrary, I am extremely excited because I have never even been on an airplane. Besides, the melanin throughout my body is activated to withstand space travel.*"

"Melanin can do that?" I stared at my own cinnamon toned skin, comparing it to the rich coffee of hers. "Do I have enough?"

"*Of course! You have plenty!*" She replied telepathically, "*Did you know that melanin is more precious and more valuable than any other substance on this planet? What we were naturally given by The Creator is priceless! Melanin exists in our skin, organs, and every single cell of our body. This dark matter is not only beautiful to look at, but is extremely functional as well. Melanin protects us from radiation and the damaging rays of the sun. Without melanin, none of us would be able to make this journey.*"

I recalled my conversation with Auntie Sistah with regards to melanated Nigiro.

Samaria explained, "*You are correct, not all humans with melanin are Nigiro. Therefore, just because one's skin contains some melanin, that is no indication they are able to make this journey to our planet. They must be activated first.*"

"That sounds so exciting! Tell me, what is the planet Nigiro like?"

Her face lit up with excitement when she asked aloud, "Have you ever heard the song, 'Saturn' by our dear brother, Steveland Morris?"

"Who?"

"*He's better known as, Stevie Wonder,*" Samaria explained. "*My parents loved playing his old albums.*"

"No, I haven't. He must be old school. Way before my time."

"*Listen to the words of that song, 'Saturn'. Then you will have an idea of how life is on Nigiro. Stevie Wonder has chosen to remain on this planet. Though born blind—without visual sight, his assignment is to open as many eyes as possible.*"

"He sounds interesting. I'll have to check out his music one day."

"*Although he mentions the planet Saturn, I believe that song expresses his memories of visiting Nigiro.*" Her high cheeks almost touched her eyes when she laughed and said, "*I can't wait to get there!*"

I asked wide-eyed, "Will you be flying in a spaceship?

"*Yes, I will be traveling in a spacecraft of some sort.*"

"Really?! How long does it take to get there?"

"*The journey is equivalent to approximately a thousand light years. But in the spacecraft, and for my body, it will actually feel like just a few weeks travel from here to there. Which is nothing when you consider time is infinite.*"

From what I knew about the universe and the recent knowledge I gained regarding the limitations of our technology, one light year was equivalent to a distance of trillions of miles from Earth. And if I understood Samaria correctly, Nigiro was thousands of light years away which meant it was located in an undiscovered galaxy. Not within the vast Milky Way solar system where Earth is located.

"That's an incredibly long time to travel through outer space. How can you be sure you will survive?"

"The Nigiro do not travel space by primitive methods used by earthlings. We have the ability to navigate via wormholes. Much like taking a shortcut from one galaxy to another." She paused, then pushed another thought from her mind, *"Consider this... The current space program launches men into space in a flimsy little space shuttle, strapped to a rocket with a ton of jet fuel and explosives underneath. That is insane! As advanced as these people claim to be, they have yet to discover a method of breaking through the filament."*

"Private companies are now pursing space travel instead of waiting on NASA which says they haven't been to the moon since 1969. NASA also reported the data used for the lunar landings had been destroyed and couldn't be duplicated." I spied a book on the bookshelf relating to conspiracies of the 20th century. I picked it up and flipped through the pages. "I don't believe that NASA hasn't gone back. My uncle told me he read a previously classified report that a colony of evolved humanoids from previous civilizations are already living on the moon. And when the astronauts landed up there, they discovered they weren't the first men to walk on the its surface. That's why astronauts don't talk about what they actually saw up there. He also believes the government is secretly sending imprisoned young black men to the moon to build a lunar colony."

"Using our brothers for slave labor because their melanin allows them to withstand extended time in outer space?" She ceased packing her things, placed her finger on her chin, and nodded her head. *"Hmmm... That is an interesting theory to discuss with your Teacher."*

"I guess..." I replied, wondering when and if the battle to regain basic human rights would ever end.

She continued, *"As for how I will travel, my physical body will be immobilized using Nigiro methods for preservation and sustainment. However, my spirit will remain fully conscious in a state fluctuating between the physical and the spiritual realm. Not fully awake, but not asleep either. The sensation is similar to what one experiences during night terrors, but without the terror involved."*

If we were in the outside world and one were to walk by, they would wonder why I was having a one-sided conversation with a little girl. I spoke out loud and she responded telepathically. I said, "I've had night terrors before and it was the most frightening thing I ever experienced."

"Sistah, there is nothing to fear. I am in total control of my mind and spirit."

"But what if something goes wrong with the flight?" I asked, nervously biting my fingers, wondering what was in store for me.

"Nothing to worry about. The Nigiro have transported hundreds of thousands of descendants to our planet since the beginning of time," she communicated matter-of-fact.

"If we are given the option of leaving or remaining on Earth, I don't understand why anyone would want to stay here." I thought of my parents and my brothers in St. Louis, probably worried to death about me. "Well, I guess I do know why some choose to stay..."

"Many of the sistahs and brothahs elect to remain on planet Earth, like Auntie Sistah. They use their special gifts to awaken others rather than return to Nigiro. However, the majority must remain on this planet until their souls are summoned home for their final journey."

"So that's why we celebrate our loved ones homegoing, instead of calling it a funeral. It makes perfect sense to rejoice when a loved one becomes free of this crazy world."

Samaria paused to reflect. *"Only the original ancient Nigiros and their offspring possess abilities to travel the spiritual astral plane. They can cross physical dimensions and materialize at will. They are shape shifters. But because I am a fairly new soul and born of the humans and not of the original Nigiro, I do not have the ability to do those things."*

"That sounds really cool!" I imagined before asking, "Do you think we have come across these elders and didn't know it?"

"Chances are highly probable we have. The Elders have always walked in our midst. They make contact long before a child is rescued and may appear in the form of a relative, a friend, or a teacher. I discovered one of my teachers at school was an elder Nigiro who had kept tabs on me since I was born."

"Wow! The planet Nigiro sounds like the promised land. Kind of like Heaven."

She responded with a smile.

"Won't you miss your family? Your mothers?" I asked, hating to see her leave so soon before we could reconnect and become good friends.

"I have made contact with my biological mother and father and was successful with planting seeds of doubt in regards to their current existence. They will begin to study the true history of America, which in turn will lead to more questions. I have already contacted my adopted mothers in the spiritual realm."

"That's cool," I said, suddenly feeling out of my element speaking to this young child as if she were an adult. "Um, do you have any advice for me? Especially since I skipped a few levels?"

"Meditate frequently, my sistah. Learn how to free your mind from the physical realm and the illusions of the world controlling you."

An image of sitting in a lotus position with my fingers pinched together, came to mind was. I had no clue how to mediate.

"Be still. Locate a serene place, close your eyes, search deep inside yourself. Rid your mind from all manner of thoughts tied to your life before. Then, when you encounter your Teacher, your questions will be answered. Any remaining doubt or uncertainty will fall away. All will be revealed, in time."

"Thank you," I replied, feeling relieved for the first time since my arrival.

She smiled warmly. Holding my hand gently in her smaller one, she whispered aloud, "Sistah, we are forever connected. Always remember... You are me. I am You. We are One."

Though she gave no indication of wanting or needing it, I embraced her petite body with a hug for good luck. Or more probably, I needed to immerse myself in her beautiful spirit. This eight-year-old little girl, who was so terrified when I first met her, had matured in a short time by leaps and bounds in extraordinary ways.

I searched Samaria's eyes. What I observed staring back at me from this young child's face was startling. The windows of her soul reflected an ancient wisdom one could gain only from experiencing an unlimited number of interesting lives. Auntie Sistah explained that a soul returns to Earth continuously until the lesson is learned. From the look of things, hers had finally gotten it right.

Chapter Fifteen

After my illuminating conversation with Samaria, I dove into my studies with a vengeance. I wanted—no, I needed—what she had. To experience an undeniable sense of calmness and serenity was an intoxicating possibility. To be so young, she possessed a true knowledge of self, gained only by searching deeply within.

I re-shifted my focus from searching for answers in the external world, and began looking inwards. I wanted to be the narrator of my own story and discover an exciting new world where mysteries and possibilities would emerge. I realized that I was not just a poor black girl from the hood whose best talent was running. I was so much more!

As newly sparked neurons in my brain disconnected from an old way of thinking took over, I literally became a new person. Areas of my former life I once considered crucial, like making sure I purchased the right designer clothing, how to style my hair just right, choosing a career to maximize personal wealth, suddenly became unimportant. I had a whole new attitude. An entirely different mission.

I spent more time alone, away from others inside the king-dome, but I was no longer lonely. By reading those books, I traveled across time and space with these incredible people to witness the best and worst of humanity. I cried. Got angry. Became hopeful. The authors of the books, revealed incredible stories of their existence one word at a time. In those instances when I wanted to share an interesting tidbit that I'd read, I imagined my great-grandmother, Nana, standing over me with approval. Instead of holding in my excitement, I'd just blurt my thoughts out loud and imagined she was there to listen.

Funny thing that I noticed from reading... Afterwards, I would wander the confines of the dome for literally hours, but I never reached the outer limits of the enclosure. What I came to discover was, as the knowledge of myself expanded, so did the area within the king dome.

When I wasn't reading, I wrote. Filling up journal after journal with stories of my old life, as well as chronicling the journey I was now experiencing. Up until now, I never knew how much I enjoyed writing, but an entire new world opened up as I explored and pushed the boundaries of my imagination. Surprising tales about my ancestors flowed from my thoughts into the pen and unto the paper as if I were transcribing stories of their lives. I often re-read what I'd written, perplexed by how I managed to capture the essence of people, places, and events of which I had no knowledge.

One day while out taking a walk, I noticed something unusual. I spied birds flying inside the dome for the very first time. As I watched a beautiful red cardinal fluttering about, I glanced up at the ceiling. It had mysteriously transformed from the transparent plexiglass tiles to reveal a majestic blue sky. Was I still inside the king-dome? I had no idea.

As Samaria suggested, I tried to meditate, but quickly discovered how difficult it was to quiet my mind from the distracting internal chatter that never seemed to end. But with each passing day, the more I practiced, the easier it became. On the fifth day, I found a quiet place where I laid flat on my back, closed my eyes, controlled my breathing, listened to the sounds of nature, and closed the doors of my conscious mind to all stray thoughts trying to push their way in. I felt the sensation of sinking into darkness, but it was not an uncomfortable feeling. When an inkling of panic began to creep in, I pushed away the fear, re-calmed my mind and went deeper. The first wave of vibrations was barely noticeable—sort of a very pleasant tingling sensation. As I sank deeper and deeper, the vibrations became so strong I actually wondered if an earthquake was underway. The vibrations ceased only to be replaced by an immensely bright light.

That is when I felt my spirit break free! I was outside of my physical body but totally conscious in the spirit. The sensation was unlike any I had ever experienced.

My spirit soared over the exterior of the dome allowing me to gaze down upon the massive structure. I was high above the trees, part of the clouds, inside minute particles of the wind. It was incredible and I wanted to go further! And to see more!

Yet without warning, the unexpected sensation of being yanked back to my body took me out of the meditative state. When I sat up, that is when the realization hit me! I was ecstatic! I am a spiritual being having a physical experience on this planet. I am not my body! I am so much more! I knew with every fiber of my being that a physical death of the body is not the end. When our bodies die, our spirits and souls return to The Almighty. After this mind-blowing revelation, I was forever changed.

My mind, powered by imagination and fueled by the words of those incredible authors, allowed me to astral-travel the world. I literally wandered through great valleys and forests, pressing my toes in the water of pristine beaches, viewing amazing flowers growing in tropical rainforests, and traversed ruins of ancient cities. I never became hungry nor thirsty during my excursions. I ate only when my physical body craved food. Drank when my body needed water. My body became leaner, though my mind expanded with a knowledge I never considered possible. Whether or not I remained inside the physical confines of the king-dome was a mystery. And at this point, I no longer cared. My mind was free!

The more books I read, the more I learned, and the more I learned, the more I questioned all the years of formal education I had received. What I learned from those books contradicted most everything I had been taught, the research papers I'd written, and the tests I'd taken. I craved this new knowledge of my people, devouring as much of it as possible.

The running joke in the black community even to this day is, if you want to hide something from our people, put it in a book. I learned that the sentiment behind reading being an undesirable trait had originated during slavery as a method of keeping the enslaved in bondage— physically and intellectually. Any slave possessing the ability to read meant punishment or certain death. Through time, the characteristic of being intelligent soon became associated with 'acting white' and sadly became embedded within our DNA. Upon this realization that this was how reading became 'demonized' in the black community, I became infuriated all over again.

I soon discovered my reading speed increased with each book read. And after the first few days, I was reading a book or two a day. I began with an unfamiliar version of the *Holy Bible*, translated from an original Hebrew version into olde world English language full of thee's, thou's, doeth's and shant's. When the translation became too difficult, or the stories' literal translations took me away from what I thought was the true intent, I switched to a modern-day translation of *The Emerald Tablet*. This book was thought to be one of the many tracts of the Hermetic text discovered around 330 BCE. And due to my difficulty understanding the ancient concepts, it which took numerous days to get through. Upon completion of that book, I then undertook reading the complete *Autobiography of Frederick Douglass* to return me to the harsh reality of what my people were currently facing.

My studies introduced me to a 'recently' discovered ancient civilization in Central American. Archaeologists excavated remains from a society of people they named the 'Olmec'. This ancient tribe was found to have occupied the land centuries before the more known, Mayans. Great statues resembling myself and every melanated human I have ever known were unearthed from forested areas near the coastal city of Veracruz, Mexico.

Massive heads of great men with strong features wearing helmets carved from volcanic stone, and life-sized statues of women dressed like royalty, provided proof of an ancient existence, stumping archaeologists who seemed more focus on disproving a relationship to the citizens they now call African than researching their similarities. I found it interesting that these supposedly intelligent well-heeled scholars were stumped by the prospect that people with African ancestry had lived in Central America and possessed the knowledge and skills to build a great civilization long before *they* believed it was possible.

Every theory under the sun was considered for the origins of the Olmec statutes, including ridiculous assertions the faces were carved with thick features because it was easier than making them delicate. And they did not resemble the actual people but were modeled after African tribal leaders encountered during travels abroad. Other theories on why the heads were carved wearing helmets included the possibility that these men were athletes, warriors, or perhaps gladiators. Seems any reason was plausible with the exception of an acknowledgement these were hue-mans who had created a civilization long before the Brits and Spaniards arrived and colonized the land.

Scholars were bewildered as to why no descendants of these great people remained in existence today. They were perplexed as to how an entire race of people could have disappeared without a trace? I know why! The Olmecs had not traveled from Africa. These people were not Africans because the landmass of Africa was not named that until thousands of years later. These people had originated on the landmass of the Americas simultaneously as those civilizations began in Africa. The Olmec hue-mans were Nigiro, the original people who migrated throughout the land of the Americas. And many remain in Mexico to this day.

From the moment I opened my eyes, my nose was stuck inside the pages of a book. Sometimes I had two going at the same time, soaking up the knowledge of those who came before me.

After I had gone through all the other books, there was one book remaining on the shelf. I saved it for last because it was massive in size. And it was also written in a strange language I had no idea existed. But I knew that if it were placed along with the others, there had to be a reason. I removed everything from my backpack, shoved the big book inside, along with several blank journals, pencils and ink pens, and a six-pack of water. I took one last look at the dormitory before heading out on what would be my longest journey yet.

Chapter Sixteen

My eyes scanned over the horizon. The valley laid out before me displayed miles upon miles of lovely springtime flowers bursting in vibrant shades of yellow, blue, purple and red blanketing the ground. From up this high, it reminded me of a painting. I surmised I must have astral-traveled to the scraggly, precarious outcropping of boulders because I had no memory of scaling the treacherous mountain to reach the summit. I carefully peeked over the ledge. I found myself standing in a dangerous position, a spot where I never should have been; feeling more akin to an eagle perched high in its nest rather than a sixteen-year-old girl on a journey of self-discovery.

The air temperature began to lower significantly with the coming of a strong wind. I estimated at this altitude, the wind must be barely above freezing. Yet, I somehow remained completely comfortable. Situated at that altitude high on a mountaintop, with no other people in sight, with no idea how I got there or how I would return to the safety of the king-dome, you may think I would be terrified. On the contrary, I was totally in my element as I accepted my position and became one with nature.

I pulled the massive book from the backpack and studied it. The oversized leather-bound volume was filled with hundreds of fragile yellowed goatskin pages containing handwritten symbols in an obscure language of which I should not have been able to read, nor comprehend.

As if somehow by osmosis, I slowly began to understand the symbols and could translate so they made sense. The book was titled, *The Book of Life*. Hours, days, or possibly weeks may have passed as I engrossed my mind deciphering the difficult text. I did not eat, nor did I sleep. My body craved only the wisdom offered by ingesting the knowledge gained from reading the entire book. From sunup to sundown, I read. And at night, I dreamt of what I read. Vivid and realistic dreams of alien spacecraft soaring through the air, only becoming visible in the wee hours of the night, crept into my subconscious. Interestingly enough, none of my dream aliens ever resembled the terrifying small gray beings with huge black eyes portrayed in movies and television. The extraterrestrial aliens in my dreams resembled relatives who were taller and had taken much better care of themselves than those I actually knew.

Only after I completed the very last sentence on the very last page, did I stop reading. I slowly closed the ancient book, tracing my hand over the unfamiliar symbols etched on the cover in gold leaf. And then I exhaled.

Something deep within my soul shifted upon reading text centered around an ancient civilization of people I recognized as my ancestors. I became ecstatic reading about tribes of beautiful people who possessed unimaginable supernatural abilities in a time period when they were truly gods and goddesses, destined to experience abundant lives as God's Chosen Ones. I read how their descendants branched out to cover the world, spreading the fruit of The Most High's kingdom all over this planet.

I rejoiced to discover my ancestors had built successful civilizations on all seven continents using the tools and technology given to them from the Elders. I later cried uncontrollably when I read of their downfall as they began to believe all that was created was of their own making and came under the spell of strange beings who deceived them into a worshiping false gods and idols, leading them astray from The Creator. The people soon forgot who they were, but most importantly they forgot who created them. They instead elected to worship power, money and false idols.

Devastation settled in my heart when I equated how the events of the past that resulted in the fall were also happening now. History repeating itself... Nothing new under the sun... All that was old is new again...

As my hands lovingly caressed the weathered leather, I felt a question developing inside. Was this account scripture? Did this book contain the Word of God? Or was it a historical account of the Nigiro? Or was it both? Was this truly *The Book of Life*, the precursor to what would later be known as *The Holy Bible*? Regardless of what one may call the book, my amazement was not only due to the nature of the stories, but also from my ability to comprehend the foreign language.

I removed a blank journal from the backpack and furiously scribbled down my thoughts upon reading the ancient text. I did not want to forget anything concerning my new discoveries. For reasons unknown, it felt like it was extremely important to write down everything. I was not weary. I was energized!

Not once did the frigid temperature cause discomfort or distract me. Only when I noticed the waning daylight did I pause in writing. I turned towards the western horizon where the sun slowly began to sink lower in the sky. The brightest of blue skies gave way to a sunset full of pink, lilac and orange tinted cirrus clouds. Breathing in that fresh air, I took it as a beautiful sign from The Most High that I was on the right path.

Innumerable days had passed since venturing from the safety of the dome. Of that, I was certain. But I wasn't exactly sure how I had gotten to the top of a mountain, nor how to climb down from that ledge. I decided to settle in for the night and figure out a strategy for the descent in the morning.

I rested my head on the book, using the soft leather as a cushion against the hard, unforgiving ground. My gaze was fixed on the brightest star while my heart remained transfixed on the stories in the book. The night sky was truly a magnificent sight from my vantage point! An ocean of infinite stars shone brightly as twinkling points of light in an eternal darkness of which seemed to go on forever. Dozens of meteors streaked across the horizon so quickly, at times I wasn't sure if I'd seen them or not.

I promised myself when the sun arose the next day, I would find my way down. A large bird floated effortlessly on the wind, leaving its shadow behind to cross my vision. I sat up quickly with a new revelation! Every day the sun rose and each night it set in a predictable cycle. From the beginning of time with the sun's rise, a new day would begin. A chance to start anew! That's when it hit me! The rising of the sun was a promise of The Most High's everlasting love for His children! It provided us warmth, food, light. All the things we needed to survive on this planet. Without frequent kisses from the sunshine, every living thing in this world would all surely die.

Watching the heavenly celestial bodies gradually appear in the darkening sky, I thought of the first time I realized how different I was from others.

~ ~ ~

My dad managed to snag an inexpensive vacation package to a ritzy resort in the Dominican Republic, thanks to a coworker not having vacation time to use his family's time-share. The all-inclusive package included air travel, accommodations, and food for our family of five. The four-bedroom, two story villa was outfitted with an outdoor kitchen, inground swimming pool and a detached game room. The newly built house was modern, tastefully decorated, and absolutely beautiful! My parents took the master bedroom on the lower level while my brothers and each had our own master bedroom complete with private baths on the upper floor.

While my parents remained inside the house making dinner arrangements, my brothers and I stripped into our swimming suits and headed to the pool. They both dove in without hesitation, splashing one another, and having a great time. I stuck one foot in the water and almost changed my mind. It was cold!

"C'mon in, chicken!" taunted Stokely.

Well, I couldn't be outdone by my younger brother so I took a deep breath and jumped in feet first. The water was so cold it took my breath away. After several long seconds of jumping up and down to get my blood flowing, I got used to the temperature.

The valet soon arrived with our luggage. My mom called for my brothers to help move the suitcases inside. Both brothers gave every imaginable excuse to avoid having to get out of the pool, but all it took was one look from my dad to get their butts in gear. Since I am a girl, he let me slide and told me to have fun in the water.

Within the first few moments after my brothers went inside the villa, I experienced an unexpected shudder course throughout my body. I initially believed the chill in the air was due to clouds crossing over the sun and lowering the temperature of the water, thus I swam several laps to warm up. But even after the clouds had lifted, the coolness in the air remained. That is when I saw a shadow forming on the bottom of the pool. Because I was still alone, I convinced myself it was only a reflection of more clouds passing over the sun. I turned over and floated on my back, trying to absorb warmth from the sun, but it did nothing to alleviate the drop in temperature. I stopped swimming and then stood on my feet, now fully mesmerized by the dark shadow creeping towards underneath the clear water. Not knowing what this thing was, I decided to get out of the pool. But the shadow was faster, managing to reach my feet before I could exit the water. At that moment, I experienced a chill so indescribable, it seemed to touch my very soul. The hairs on the back of my neck stood up and I rushed out of the pool to wait for my brothers to return.

Both Stokely and Malcolm burst through the door eager to return to the swimming pool.

"Do you guys see that?" I asked pointing to the shadow, still visible on the floor of the pool.

"See what?" they asked simultaneously.

"There's something down there."

They both shrugged and jumped into the water, totally oblivious and unaffected by what I experienced. But I did not get back into water, instead I rushed inside to retreat to my room.

"Kenya, are you okay?" my mother asked, noting something was off.

"I'm cold. That's all," I answered before going upstairs to my room. I shut the door, plopped on the floor, and quietly wept. My heart became heavy with a level of unimaginable sorrow I had no right to experience at my young age. And yet, sorrow was the only way to describe how I felt.

Later that night, I was awakened by the sound of voices whispering in what sounded like gibberish. I sat up in bed, listening for my brothers to break out in laughter at the joke they were playing on me. I left my bedroom, ready to let them have it. But when I checked their respective bedrooms, both were sound asleep. I returned to my room even more frightened because the whispering had not ceased. Finally, the weariness of getting up early to catch the flight, combined with the stresses of traveling in today's environment, had caught up with me and I drifted off to a fitful sleep.

Within my dream state, I returned to the swimming pool to witness a humbling sight. Hundreds of melanated men, women, and children's whitewashed faces were deeply embedded within the floor tiles of the swimming pool. My heart skipped a beat upon watching the opening of their sad eyes. The confusion within those faces pleaded for me to listen to their forlorn woes. After a horrible existence of being enslaved, their wasted bodies were callously tossed into unmarked mass graves, where they had been forgotten for centuries, and then those graves were plowed over by real estate developers. They relayed to me how their souls were unable to rest because their people had all but forgotten them. Rather than embracing a rich legacy, many of their descendants had shamefully erased them from history as if they never existed. I told them I was sorry. I didn't know about their plight but I would do my best to tell the world about them. I would share the tale of the forgotten people I would later discover were also Nigiro.

The next day, when everyone else was in the pool enjoying the refreshing water, I sat on the side dangling my feet in. I watched my brothers having a great time, unburdened by what I'd seen or heard. When my parents encouraged me to join them, I would not.

"What's wrong, honey?" my mother asked concerned.

I hesitantly shared my experience with both parents. But only after my mother pulled it out of me.

"You're a highly sensitive young lady," she explained. "When spirits need to relay a message, they are drawn to empathetic people. You happen to have this. Do not be afraid. They will not harm you."

"How do you know that?" I asked naively. "Why did they contact me?"

"Why do *you* think you were contacted?" my daddy asked.

"All those hundreds of faces were sending me a message. I believe they want us to know about them. That both sides of this fractured island, Haiti and the Dominican Republic, were once joined in solidarity against their oppressors, just as in the states. The Haitians and Dominicans are brothers and sisters who have completely forgotten who they are. Their ancestors' spirits and even their bodies, are still here. Forever tied to this land, maybe buried underneath all these new resorts being built. They don't want to be forgotten or have their very existence continue to be denied. Those lost souls have become weary trying to reach a people who are filled with shame and self-hatred."

She smiled, hugged me closely, and offered some of the best advice a parent can give, "Then don't let them be forgotten."

"I won't," I replied feeling much better. I was surprised how easily they both accepted what should have been an unbelievable experience. "Someday, somehow I'll make certain I tell the world of their existence. Maybe I will even find out their names."

"Kenya, you can do anything you put your mind to," my father replied.

Later that day, I dangled my feet at the poolside while my family was on an excursion I decided to skip. This time when I looked in the pool, I did not see shadows lurking on the bottom. What I did see was delightful! Hundreds of interlocked circles, the connecting spaces filled with every imaginable color of the rainbow, reflected up from the pool's floor. Some may believe this was just an optical illusion resulting from rays of sunlight hitting the water, but I know it was much more significant. I had witnessed what true joy looks like when it appears in a physical form.

For the remainder of our vacation, no further mention was made of my spiritual experience. Whether my family believed me or not was of no consequence because I knew what I saw and heard. And I vowed to keep my promise to those restless souls.

~ ~ ~

As I closed my eyes to welcome much needed sleep, I felt a wave of vibration come at me like a soft whisper in the night. The gentle rumbling began in my chest and spread throughout my body in tiny ripples. Through my closed eyelids, millions of brilliant stars suddenly appeared like tiny pinpoints in the night sky. Different shapes and angles sped towards me in varying colors interspersed with historical images of faces of which I knew not. I had no idea what was happening; only that I was still awake. I felt myself sinking into a strange place. I inhaled sharply to calm my wildly beating heart.

Seconds later, I felt a second wave of vibration hit. This time it was much stronger. And louder. The effect was unlike any I'd experienced before whether asleep or when awake. My entire body shuddered as wave after wave of stronger vibrations passed through head to toe until my spirit was loosed from my physical body and to the other side. A light as bright as the sun appeared in my vision. And then there was absolutely nothing but total darkness. A space vacuum void of all sound. I felt no physical sensations at all. But I was fully conscious. Free of form in a vast expanse of nothingness.

Chapter Seventeen

"Kenya," came the faint voice through the thin veil dividing sleep and wakefulness. "Kenya... Wake up, my love."

"Nana?" I responded, confused by the familiar sounding voice of my deceased great-grandmother. I tried focusing on the blurred images in my line of sight, like I was seeing through layers of thin gauze. Or a delicately crocheted veil.

"Sweetie, it is time to open your eye."

I recalled falling asleep on the mountain ledge, clutching the heavy book in my hands. Dreaming or awake, astral projection or stark reality, I did not want to tempt fate by falling over. I slowly turned in the direction of the voice, raising my hand to see five fingers composed entirely from tendrils of steam curling upon itself.

"Nana?" I blinked what should have been my eyes several times. A form materialized from the void of darkness. "Is that really you?"

"Come with me, Kenya. Times a wastin'!"

I stared into my great-Nana's much younger looking face, free of all wrinkles and those tiny dark moles that once crisscrossed the bridge of her nose. She wore a beautiful purple dress that made fluttery movements when she approached. It gave the impression she was floating underwater. Her snowy white hair was a massive unruly halo atop her head, cascading past her shoulders in beautiful locs. Years ago, when I questioned my great-grandmother on why she stopped combing her hair, she replied that if the Good Lord had intended for her hair to grow any other way, he would have created it that way. My mom thought her grandmother had entered the early stages of dementia when in spite of everyone's pleadings, she refused to style her thick hair. But I knew otherwise. Nana had embraced her natural hair when she allowed it to do what it pleased.

As a child, I loved climbing up on her lap, playing with those thick tangles matted together in an intricate web that took us both back to our roots. It was a delicious pleasure to rest my head against her ample bosom. Like soft pillows of love. Her voice was soft and melodious as she spoke in the lilting accent of southerners from generations passed. She had a contagious laugh that infected all within earshot. And the stories she shared about her days growing up in Mississippi would stay with me forever. I was six when she passed but missed her more each day.

"Is this a lucid dream, Nana?" I relayed, staring past her face at dozens of unfamiliar men and woman gathered closely nearby. "I-I-I don't feel like myself."

"This ain't no dream, sweetie."

"Where am I?"

"Come with me," Nana instructed. "I got lots to show you 'bout your 'ssignment but I cain't keep you here for long."

"What assignment?"

"From The Almighty God, of course. Ya made it this far which means you's now ready ta receive it."

I did not question her or why God would give me an assignment. I placed what I imagined were my feet on the floor and tried to stand. But there were no floors, or ceilings, or walls. Nor did I have feet, hands, or even a body. Nothing was solid in the sense of familiarity. I was formed, but without form. Like a mist or steam. Similar to delicate smoke curling upwards from a cone of incense. I was fully conscious, yet floating in an indescribable darkness. I was not afraid. I was fascinated!

"Are you real?" I relayed, trying to reach out and touch her face. My hand was water vapor trying to connect with itself. "This doesn't feel like a dream."

"Like I said, this ain't no dream. You's in the spiritual realm, the ancestral plane. A dimension outside of what you's used to livin' in." She motioned towards an army of light forms clustered nearby, that seemed to go on forever. "Them's there is the spirits of our ancestors; an infinite number like grains of sands, generations that go all the way back to the very beginnin'."

"Really?!" Is what I wanted to say, but the sentiment of incredulous did not translate here. Instead I projected a loving respect to the Elders who shifted in and out of my vision.

"Yes, indeed! They's all here watchin' us! Praisin' The Almighty that ya finally here! Ya cain't tell, but they is filled with joy cause ya fin'lly knows they is with ya."

"Why aren't they trying to communicate with me?"

"They's spirits is too far gone from that old livin' world ya came here from. All that remains is that essence ya see appearin' like smoke tryin' ta take shape. In this here spiritual realm, most folks spirits can only communicate with ancestral spirits when they's is gone an no longer dwellin' in the earthly plane. You's still gots ya phys'cal body, but they can contact ya cause of ya gift ta see. And you can calls on 'em when ya need ta. I can communicate with 'em cuz my earthly body is long gone."

"So the dead do not speak to the living?"

"They's not dead honey! Not in the way you thinkin'. They's bodies done returned to dust, an they's spirits done transitioned long ago. They's souls is up in Heaven an beyond."

"Is it possible for spirits to contact me since I can now 'see' them?"

"Some recently passed souls gonna try ta hold on to the livin'. They's spirits wanna make contact with they's loved ones who gots the gift; the 'bility to communicate with 'em in they's spirit form. They might try an reach out ta ya. But I'm tellin' ya not to do it."

"Why not, Nana?" I felt my image begin to shimmer. "It may help them understand what happened."

"Communicatin' with the recently deceased is gonna prevent they's soul from crossin' over. When ya keep holdin' on too tight ta yo loved one, they's cain't fully transition to the spiritual realm or go on up ta the Heavenly realm. They's souls remain in a confusin' space that keeps 'em in a state 'tween phys'cal death an eternal spir'tual life. Some calls it limbo. Not til they completely let go will they's be free ta move on."

"I am communicating with you. How is this possible?"

"I's ya Watcher. I'm the most directly linked ancestor here ta guide ya through this earthly life existence."

"Why me?"

"Most of the women—an' even somes of the mens—in ya mama's and ya daddy's bloodlines gots the gift. The ones who cain't see ain't never tried to embrace they's. Or they's so enamored with livin' in the world they cain't no longer tell up from down. But you's different. You's always had ya inside eye open to see the truth. Now ya just gotta nurture it. Embrace it an its gonna get even stronger."

"Both mommy and daddy's sides of the family have special gifts?"

"That's right. You's been blessed by both sides of the fam'ly so yo gift must be sumthin' else!"

"Sounds like I might have many more than five senses." I focused my thoughts to solidify my form, yet continued to fade in and out. "Do you know what my gift is?"

"That's for you's ta discover on ya journey. And you's got many mo' senses than five, baby. Many mo' than ya mama or even me. You's is really special," relayed Nana.

"What do you mean?"

"The Almighty made the 'riginal bein's b'fore creatin' the resta us. You's one of The Almighty's orig'nal," she explained.

I don't understand, Nana. Isn't mama my mother, and your daughter? Aren't you two also special?"

"Ya mama is yo mama and she is my daughter by flesh n' blood. An just like I used ta tell ya when you's was just a baby. Yes, ever'body is special in some kinda way. But you's really special cuz you's an old ancient soul from the 'riginal ones. Y'all the only ones who gots the gift ta communicate with the ancestral spirits in the astral realm when ya's still livin'."

As much as I know Nana wanted me to understand her explanation, I remained clueless.

"You's can be in ya earthly phys'cal body an with only ya mind, ya can travel the astral plane, visit the ancestral plane, an sees inta other earthly dimensions. Ya gots what we call, perfect divine 20/20 vision."

"Does this mean I will die a physical death soon?"

"Not anytime soon, sweetie. Ya's gots lots mo' work ta do. We needs visionaries like ya ta continue doin' The Almighty's work by spreadin' Tha Word."

I didn't respond as there was no need to.

"Not ta worry none if ya don't know what I'm talkin' 'bout richt now. You's gonna learn what I means when ya continue on ya journey."

I accepted this explanation for I knew there was so much I had to learn. "How long will you be with me?"

"For as long as I'm needed, I'm gonna remain in this here ancestral realm, watchin' over you on ya journey 'til the 'ppointed time for me to transition over."

"Where are we going?" I relayed, noting Nana seemed pleased at my understanding.

"This way."

Nana did not speak in the literal sense. For that matter, neither did I. We communicated not through words, because we had no mouths or vocal cords from which those sounds would come. The best way to describe our communications was through vibrations. Or sound waves. Changes in pitch. Her familiar speech pattern hit my senses like a southern symphony filled with beautiful musical notes drifting freely on a summer breeze.

I followed her formless essence sometimes disappearing entirely; similar to how one loses a radio station's reception the further away you travel from the broadcasting satellite. But in the very next moment, she reappeared as if she were solid, wearing a long purple robe, seemingly floating through the ether.

My sightless vision took it all in. At one point, we emerged from the dark void and became part of cotton-candy clouds, lazily floating high above the ground below. I had an unobstructed birds' eye view of the landscape, surprised by how parcels of land were naturally separated by bodies of water or clusters of trees, much like I'd seen from the only airplane flight I'd taken. We returned to the ether to the type of darkness that exists only in your mind.

From my perspective high above the stratosphere, what I once thought were merely stars in the sky were not that at all. Infinite points of light—playful fireflies on a humid summer night—zoomed by my formless body as if they were escaping capture from the hands of bored little children who would place them first in jars and then pull their florescent tails off for their own amusement. The points of light were souls traversing through the universe downwards to the physical plane below. The scene was reminiscent of embers from a massive bonfire floating to the sky.

Truth be told, it was not an unpleasant sensation being free of my body. I experienced no pain, no fatigue, no hunger, and no emotion. I became part of the totality of the universe. Part of The All. I was everything, yet I was nothing.

"Does ya know who ya is?" Nana asked.

"Yes, Nana. Just like you told me a long time ago. I am a beautiful child of The Almighty God. A spiritual being experiencing a physical human experience on Earth."

"You's almost there!" She again transmitted her pleasure. "C'mon. I's gotta show ya some more."

I watched as an all-encompassing darkness morphed into a series of snapshots from my entire life. A whirlwind of images surrounded us like a top spinning out of control. Scenes of my parents bringing me home from the hospital; taking my first steps at seven months and falling down over and over again until I finally got it right; trailing behind my oldest brother as we walked to school; a tearful, victorious grin after I lost my first tooth; holding my dad's hand as he took me to the library for the first time; gardening with my grandmother, eavesdropping as she explained the differences between sweet potatoes and yams to my mother; an awkward first kiss; my excitement driving alone for the first time; disappointment losing my first track meet. And then I watched as those awful men pushed me into that van and sped off. I thought the images would cease there, yet they continued on.

An older version of myself stood next to a handsome man professing vows of marriage in a ceremony fit for royalty. Over the years, we raised seven children who blessed us with dozens of grands. Another scene had me on a stage eloquently speaking to large audiences, they being mesmerized by fascinating topics I brilliantly presented. My husband and I aged gracefully into an elderly couple perched comfortably on the front porch of a large home, sipping glasses of sweet tea while our grandchildren happily climbed an ancient oak tree, chasing one another on fertile land we would later will to them as inheritance.

With heartbreak and sorrow, scenes of placing both my parents to rest within six months of one another came into my view. What gave me comfort was both had lived long fruitful lives and their home-going services were well attended by several generations of family and hundreds of dear friends.

Images of unfamiliar women, dressed in clothing from various historical periods, appeared within those visions. Some were dark skinned, while others were lighter and paler versions of myself.

"Nana, why are you showing me all this?"

"Chile', just that fact that you's here means ya gots the 'bility to see life in ways others cain't." She disappeared and then reappeared. "There's many unseen thangs in this here world happenin' not only right 'fore ya eyes, but in other dimensions."

"I know that saying... There is more to life than meets the eye," I replied. "Why do the scenes continue to loop?"

"You had ta keep repeatin' life 'til ya got it right. Only then will ya be set free."

I continued watching the images loop back upon themselves. "Who are all those women?

"Them's women is all you... in diffr'ent human bodies."

"I am reincarnated?"

"I prefehs ta say, 'Rebirthed'. But as ya can see, you's has taken a whole lotta paths over many lifetimes tryin' to fulfill ya destiny an' get home. I prays this time ya finally makes it there."

I was transfixed watching myself transform into various other bodies across the ages. In one ancient lifetime, I was a queen, regal in appearance with many peasants bowed at my feet, ruling over an impressive dynasty. I lived a bountiful life in a mansion by the sea. I read about the remarkable Queen Nzinga, ruler of the Ndongo and Matambaki kingdoms during the 16th and 17th century. She was a fearless woman who liberated the country later named Angola, from European influence. I wondered how my previous life stacked up against hers.

Disturbing images of myself as a child of slaves, naked with feet shackled together, huddled up with dozens of other slaves for warmth, on a cold desolate night brought back long forgotten memories. Several men on horseback continually cracked their whips with threats to keep moving. I saw myself holding back tears while watching an older man hanged from a tree, punished for requesting rest for the women and children. My heart was filled with anger as I watched a young version of myself being raped by evil white men who took extreme pleasure in my suffering. I could see how hatred for those men who enslaved my family would prevent my learning the ultimate lesson. There was certainly more hatred in my heart than love.

At one point, I lived an interesting life as a woman with skin so pale, I passed as 'white', and was married to a horrid man who was incapable of loving me. We farmed fruits and vegetables in the valleys of California. Though the farm was extremely successful, my existence had not been happy because my womb was barren. My aged eyes held many years of sadness and my mouth was set in a permanent scowl at the end. It was easy to see I had not learned the lesson as I had not yet learned to love myself.

Various other lifetimes flashed across my vision. I was dressed in unfamiliar clothing, living in strange and unrecognizable lands with unknown people flashing in quick succession before my sight. The images never ended, but continued in an infinite loop.

"Ya seein' yo'self in diff'rent forms 'cause the existential soul selects the human form it wants ta experience its life on Earth. Phys'cal appearance don't matter to the soul."

"I can choose how I want to return?"

"Um huh. What's most impo'tant is to pick the best body ta help ya learn the lesson."

"The lesson? What is that?"

"The ultimate lesson is learnin' how ta love one 'nother unconditional. The commandants was given in the beginnin'. One; Love The Almighty with all ya heart an soul. Two; Love others as ya loves yo'self."

"Nana, if love is the most important lesson, why is the world in the shape it's in? Why are we so hung up on race and skin color?"

"I learnt long ago that ain't no sucha thing as race. Some ig'nant folks made up all that mess havin' to do with the color of theys skin was s'posed to make 'em better than e'rbody else. We's all made in the image of The Almighty, baby. Just that most of dem don't wanna admit it cuz they's hell bent on rulin' over others."

"A friend told me that not all children are from God? That some are born without souls?" I recalled a conversation with Auntie Sistah.

"The Almighty don't like ugly, but it sho nuff is a whole lotta ugly goin' on down there. What yo friend told ya is right. Men in all they's arrogance done tampered wif nature an created soulless creatures who done grown inta some evil mens an womens. Us who got discernment can easily spot dem monsters 'cause they's diff'rent than the rest of the chil'ren. They's sometime very pretty on the outside but nasty as heck on the inside. But ya an' I knows, The Almighty's chil'ren all recognize each other. That's why we was taught to speak ta one 'nother."

I recognized what Nana said used to be true back in the day before I was born. There was a time when all black people used to greet one another as sistah and brothah, even though the blood running through our veins was not biologically related. But somewhere along the way that familiarity became lost as we integrated within the American society.

"I don't want to bring bad news Nana, but the people ruling, and also *ruining* the world have lost their minds and souls... or maybe they never had one to begin with."

"You's might be right. Some of dem empty vessels done learnt how ta shape-shift inta black skin to fool e'rbody that they's kinfolk."

"That explains why once some black people elected to powerful positions have forgotten who helped get them there. White people in black bodies... that's a new trick."

"The body ya pick when you's rebirthed is very impo'tant. I sometimes whisper to dem new souls ta be careful in they's choices. I say if ya was orig'nally created ta have a womb, I don't see why they would wanna pick a man's form. An vice versa. That only causes confusion in the long run. Now I can unne'stand why some folks choose diff'rent skin colors so they knows how it feels to walk in 'nother's shoes. That's diff'rent." Her image flickered momentarily before she continued, "Does ya 'member how ya usta love playin' dress up when ya was a little gurl?"

If I were solid form, I probably would have nodded my response. Despite not having that capability, Nana understood perfectly.

"When you's was younger, ya loved playin' dress up. You'd be wearin' a partic'lar outfit ta emphasis who ya wanted to po'tray in this world. Nurse. Pilot. Scientist. School teacher... The same goes for when a heavenly spirit picks a human form for they's physical 'xperience. The ultimate goal ista learn the lesson so ya don't ever hafta return to this Earth. If you fail to 'chieve the lesson, you gonna hafta continue the cycle of life 'til you do. An each time folks return, they tend ta forget all lessons learnt from they's previous life."

What I quickly realized seeing all the versions of myself in all those lifetimes is I must have been a horrible student because I had failed miserably with each new opportunity. I had returned too many times to count.

"Kenya, my dear. Don't worry 'bout all dem times ya been down there an back. They's was unlimited chances ya had ta go through b'fore ya could get it right."

"Loving unconditionally sounds simple, but putting it into practice must be extremely difficult." I watched a flurry of bright lights zip across the vast sky. I imagined those were new souls returning for another assignment. "From all those lifetimes I've had so far, apparently I have not learned my lesson."

"In time you will." Her image faded then became brighter.

"Nana..." I felt my own aura shift in intensity when I asked, "Why am I here? With you? In the astral dimension?"

"You is on a very difficult journey in an interestin' time. I'm here ta guide ya. Ta offer encour'gement to keep ya movin' fo'ward when times get tough. Me an yo ancestors been sendin' ya little signs when ya started ta doubt yo path. Tryin' ta get ya ta pay attention. It took a quites a few tries but ya took notice."

"I thought my life was going fine up until I was abducted by those men. But now I know those people in the king-dome say they want to help me. To help us. The Nigiro people. And the children. They want to wake us up from our slumber, but I don't know what I'm supposed to be doing." I faded momentarily with my musings.

"I'm aware of all ya been through an' I'm sorry it's been so diff'cult for ya since I passed."

It made me feel good to know Nana was on my side. This was true when she was still alive as it is now.

"Dem Nigiro folks is real and we's is they's descendants. They live ina whole 'nother dimension than what ya sees with ya two eyes. I didn't know nothin' 'bout the Nigiro when I was still livin' in the phys'cal plane. They's didn't reveal demselves to me likes they's has ta you."

"I have so many questions."

"Go on..."

"My first question is, because I was snatched off the street myself, why are so many children being abducted?"

"Men who ain't got no souls is stealin' the chil'rens'! They's do many bad things to dem kids." Her image grew brighter in intensity. "Dontcha fret... Those devils mighten be able ta do ugly thangs to dem babies' bodies, but they's cain't touch them chil'rens souls. The Almighty done sent Nigiro, the ones ya workin' wif, to help put an end to all that foolishness goin' on!"

I thought about Auntie Sistah, as well as The Teacher. They must be included as my helpers.

"My next question is, for the last several hundred years our people have been treated so badly, not just in the United States, but all over the world. Why do you think we're being slaughtered in the streets by men who treat their animals more humanely than they treat us?"

"Your curiosity is 'xpected." Nana sometimes appeared as she were fighting against a great wind trying to scatter her about. "How evah', I think ya already knows. Tell me whatcha believes to be true, chile'. What does ya see when ya close ya eyes an search within?"

As I watched the scenes continuing to unfold, I started to see a repeating pattern. "Although the faces and time periods change, the events remain the same. What is occurring in the world today has happened many times in the past. The world is speeding up towards a destination where time and space intersect. Pretty soon, we won't be able to distinguish what happened in the past with what is happening now."

"But that don't answer ya question now, do it?"

"Well... I think that whoever—or whatever—runs this world doesn't want us to know we are the original hue-mans. The Chosen Ones. And the ones who do know the truth, won't tell. For the ignorant and weak-minded, it's easier to kill than try to understand what you don't know. They don't understand the peaceful ways of Nigiro, so the only way they know how to deal with us is to hate us. Keep us at the bottom. Imprison us. Murder us."

"Baby, our elders tried ta warn us when they's wrote that there Bible an presented it to the world. We was too bullheaded an ig'nant ta sees the truth 'cause we done followed all dem other made up religions. We been misled from the very start."

"I understand."

"The ancestors gave us a true 'ccount of what was an what will be. Told us the world moves in infinite cycles and ta look ta the past to see what was comin' back 'round next time. Like that infinity symbol."

"You're referring to the symbol that looks like the number eight turned on its side? Doesn't it symbolize something that never ends?"

"That's right. The loop is gonna continue on 'til all y'all finally wakes up."

"Nana, I read many people in ancient civilizations turned their backs on The Most High. Is that true?"

"The chil'ren did allow others ta turn their heads away from The Almighty, that is true."

"Instead of worshiping God, our society worships money, power, and manmade technology. Cell phones, computers, internet, video games. Nowadays, you don't even have to leave your house! You can purchase everything online. Whenever a company rolls out a new phone or laptop, we stand in line to buy it. Some of my friends would die if their parents took those items away from them."

Her eyes blazed with a golden glow as if lit with fire from within.

"That bein' said, dontcha unnerstand what's happenin'?! The Almighty is sendin' folks ta help free y'all from the madness overtakin' this ungodly world. He gonna wake up all His children ta deys true knowledge of self 'fore it's ta late."

"Is this where I come in? I'm supposed to use my gift to help awaken others?"

"That's right child!" She raised her glorious transparent hand and pointed towards the expanse. "Look upon The Almighty's glorious creation. Heaven an' Earth an ever'thang in between! He created The All for us!"

I gazed in the direction of the brightest star in the solar system.

"The sun is burnin' brighter an gettin' hotter again! I can sees the planet is warmin' up by the number of souls travelin' to an fro. With a quickness, its gonna seem like you's standin' alone on a battlefield wif soldiers dyin' all around ya. The ones who ain't got they's souls right is gonna burn up like somethin' fierce. Can'tcha feel it changin' down there?"

"Winter is warmer and the days of summer are getting longer."

"I don't understand. Why is the sun growing hotter?" I pushed the vibration of my thoughts into the universe for Nana to receive. "Great-grandfather told me a long time ago, that when he was a little boy, the sun used to be pretty yellow-orange color. But now, it looks white most of the time."

"Er'body knows that white fire burns hotter than yella. The earth is fixin' ta cleanse herself of that ugly virus unleashed upon the world that's suckin' the life outta the chil'ren. The Almighty's blessed chil'ren is returnin' in mass numbers at a quick pace 'cause of that virus called 'mankind'. All dem points of light ya see ain't no stars. Dem is souls returnin' to The Source 'til they's next appointed time in the phys'cal dimension. The brighter the light is, the shorter the 'mount of time the soul done spent in the phys'cal world."

If I had a head to shake, I would have. "The government officials told us the Earth was warming due to climate change. Global warming."

"Don't let cha heart be burdened. The Almighty is gonna place the Earth back in balance. All dem pandemics that's goin' now in the phys'cal dimension ain't no coincidence. Those is the plagues mentioned in The Bible."

The redhaired woman believed big pharma was responsible for developing the viruses that created the pandemic. Though well-intentioned, she was ill-informed and had only seen the tip of the iceberg.

"He done chose folks to do His Will on Earth. You's is one of The Chosen."

"You're not the first person who has told me that. Why do you believe I am one of The Chosen?"

"Err'time ya was reborn, ya retained some of whatcha learnt in a prev'ous life. You took dem 'periences an' continued ta grow in spirit with knowledge 'bout the truth of who ya is. Not all folks have this 'bility to 'member. Or to see clearly in this realm. But ya does. You's was born with the 'bility to see the truth behind the veil that was created by those mankind beings. And yo 'ssignment while ya is on the Earth is to 'waken otha's minds ta the truth."

"That's it?"

I saw a smile grace her lovely sun-kissed face.

"If I am one of The Chosen, why is it taking so long for me to get it right? It looks like I've been here many times before doing the same thing."

"Like I said 'bout that infinity symbol, there ain't no beginnin' an no endin'. The All is happenin' at once." The features on Nana's face blurred momentarily as she explained, "Whiles ya in human form, a lifetime is less than one hunnit Earth years. In actual'ty, a hunnit years is only a blip in time. A fraction of a second. In etern'ty, a lifetime passes ina blink of an eye. If'n The Almighty had the notion, He could snap His spiritual fingers an' one million years would pass just like that without any of us knowin' it."

"What happens when we die?" I asked.

"Most folks souls transitions ovah ta the spir'tual realm b'fore they goes on ta Heaven."

"The spiritual realm is where the soul resides if it hasn't fully learned its lesson? It return backs to the physical realm on Earth until it does?" I added, to make sure I understood.

"That's right. Once they's souls makes it ta Heaven, then they's transitions to the ancestral realm where ya is now. You is gonna have a diff'rent 'xperienc cuzza who ya is, but unnerstand death of the phys'cal body ain't the end. It's a transition ta the eternal life cuz energy don't end, it just transfers to someplace else. Ain't no reason to fear dyin' ifn ya soul is connected ta The Almighty."

"Nana, did you learn the lesson before you passed?"

"Baby, ya don't know this but I use ta be some kinda mean when I was young! Ooo wee! I had a mouth on me that would make a grown lion run away with his tail tucked 'tween his legs! Never had a kind word to say 'bout nothin' or nobody."

"That's unbelievable! You were the sweetest and most lovable woman I knew!"

"That's cuz by the time ya came along, I'd already changed. Didcha know that yo momma useta be so scair't of me she refused ta speak in my presence, lest I would smack her right 'cross the face wif my bare hands? She called me Mean-maw b'hind my back. But once you's was born an' started crawlin' up on my lap cooin' an such, she got terrified, 'spectin' me to start yellin' an screamin' at ya too. I surprised her an myself by hows much I loved ya."

"I can never imagine you being like that."

"Baby, when I was a child, 'twas a dang'rous time in the world for colored folks. Much more dang'rous than it is now... Us colored chil'ren was disciplined ta remain quiet 'round grown folks. 'Specially dem *white* folk. Ta be loud an' boisterous, or smart-mouthed could getcha killt. So just like err'body else I knew, I learnt ta keep that pent-up anger I gathered from the outside world, inside. I only let it out when it was safe. Unfortunately, it was safer ta 'spress my anger towards those closest to me than it was ta who I was truly angry with."

"What happened to change you?"

"I received a prophetic vision from an ancestor, My Watcher, who turnt me right 'round. I took what she told me in that dream ta heart. Started readin' the Bible for what it was an' not some allegorical text. Dem words softened my heart ta love. I learnt it was easier to 'spress love over hatred. I also learnt my gift was encouragin' others ta rise up in themselfes. Ta stop bein' so scared of every thang."

I tried to get a glimpse from the visions of how my life would positively impact the world, but it was no use. "You say I have a gift of vision, but I don't know how that will help anyone. I guess I have to discover how to use it."

Nana pulsated her response in a myriad of vibrant colors.

"What happens when I finally learn the ultimate lesson?"

"When it is ya propah time an only The Almighty knows when that is, ya gonna receive you's final reward. Ya precious soul is gonna return to its eternal existence within the infinite universe."

"To Heaven? With The Almighty God?"

The brilliant aura surrounding Nana's form shifted brighter. It was as if a star had come to life right before my non-existent eyes.

"I have a question about my family because I always felt like I didn't belong. Does one have a choice when it comes to selecting which family I get? Or my parents?"

"Don't nobody get ta choose they's parents or fam'ly members. The Almighty blesses a child ta a family best 'quipped ta help 'em move forward. Sometimes a child's only purpose in life is ta move they's parents towards knowin' how to love. Unconditional love."

"My parents gave life to me and my brothers. Even though we are related biologically, we are not the same spiritually. Our purpose in life is dependent upon the gift we received and how we use it to help others. Right?"

"Yes, sweetie. You's seein' it the propah way now."

"Yes, Nana. I believe I am."

The bright aura surrounding her essence faded from blue to purple, to bright yellow as we continued to travel the expanse.

"I do not doubt the existence of The Most High God. But I do wonder why He allows so much misery to exist in this world."

"Sometimes it may appear that there ain't nothin' but sadness in the world. But what you chil'ren gotta learn an' unnerstand is, ya create yo own reality. Good an' bad. That's why ya got to get all those folks always messin' in ya business aways from ya!"

"I think I understand... Free will allows us to make a choice on how we live. And the goal of life is not about accumulating things. Or gaining wealth. Or becoming famous. It is all about loving one another."

"That's right. And ole Satan been real busy during his brief reign on the Earth. His followers done changed what was once right, inta wrong. Made what was once up, down. Caused worldly confusion ta turn the children's eyes away from goodness. Evil knows it ain't gonna never win, yet that don't prevent dem from tryin' ta destroy this world and err'thang with it. But evils time is 'bout up. Hallelujah!"

Subtle waves of vibration coursed through what must have been my spirit as my understanding continued to grow. Pulsating and vibrating as if I were actual musical notes within a somber song of sorrow.

Nana's image fizzled out and then solidly re-materialized. "I'ma tell ya somethin' else, Kenya. All children is born with imagination. I likes to call it 'eye-magi-nation'. The 'eye' represents the The Almighty, Who keeps watch over All He created. 'Magi' is the wisdom originatin' from knowin' The All. And the 'nation' is the children who s'posed to receive His wisdom. That is you! Yo gift is a 'present'! An' the present is the bridge b'tween the past an' the future!"

"I know what you say is true. Tapping into my imagination connects me to the Universal All," I replied, now extremely comfortable with this astral experience in the ancestral realm.

"We's all connected. We's all one, sweetie. The problem is most of that chil'ren done forgot how ta use they's imagination to connect wif one 'nother."

As if I were looking in on myself, I observed my own aura become a brighter version of yellow and then intensely white. The positive vibrations emanating from Nana at her tremendous pleasure of my knowing lit up her aura in shades of brilliant blue and dazzling purple.

"Spread the message of Love ta all who got eyes to see an ears to listen. Tell 'em The Almighty God is real. He is Love! He will never leave them, nor will He forsake them. It's time for these chil'ren to wake up!"

"That seems so simple."

"The earthly world is in deep trouble. Folks is now divided in ways never imagined possible. Y'all needs to start prayin' for the truth to be revealed."

"I'll do what I can to help make things better. I just wish I knew what I could do."

"This generation is the ones we been waitin' for. The Spirit of The Almighty done gone down an' blessed these young ones with somethin' 'xtra special. This generation is the super-natural chil'ren who is standin' on the shoulders of the ancestors." She shimmered as a wave of energy flowed downwards from the tips of her fluffy white hair to the bottom of her caramel colored feet.

"I just have one more question." I watched her fade in and out sensing my time on the astral plane was coming to an end. Her form seemed to have difficulty holding itself together as it became more blurred around the edges. "Is the world going to end?"

"For the Almighty's chil'ren, it is the end of the world as they know it. But don't be dismayed. Where there is an endin', there is also a beginnin'. A brighter day is on the other side of this madness!" Her face glowed with the approaching of the sun. "The cycle of life is gonna continue. This is cause for rejoicin' not sadness."

"I see clearly now." I felt a delightful wave of positive energy flow within and throughout my form. "This is evil's last stand. It's throwing everything at hue-manity to create as much chaos, confusion, and destruction before it all comes to an end. All we have to do is stand strong together. Love one another no matter our race, religion, ethnicity, or nationality. Together, we are one in this fight against evil."

We continued on with no more communication until reaching an area of the expanse, closer to the sun than I ever imagined possible. In front of us appeared two massive golden gates. Nothing was solid, but still maintained a form. The gate posts of the structure were comprised of iridescent pearls, shimmery with hues of blue, purple, and gold. It was surrounded by an endless field of different shades of purple flowers as far as the spiritual eye could see. Within my spirit, I gazed at the powerful sight wanting with everything in my soul to get nearer for a closer look.

"Is this Heaven?" My essence hovered outside the massive gates watching glowing bursts of light forms, soul-filled lights, pour through.

"My love, I done told ya thangs ta help ya unnerstand who ya is, an what ya mission in life is s'pposed ta be. How ya get there can be reached by many ways. Just listen to ya heart."

I listened to the wisdom of my elder, grateful for all she had shared.

"This here is the entrance to the eternal resting place. Those who complete they's mission is gonna spend out eternity here."

"The pearly gates of Heaven are real?!" is what I would have exclaimed had I a physical body. But I knew that if I were in my physical body, "seeing" the gates of Heaven would not be possible. "Every soul ends up here?"

"Heaven ain't a phys'cal place built outta mortah an' bricks. It's an idea that exists in de hearts an' minds of all those who believes. Ya sees Heaven as havin' pearly gates cuz that's what the collective believes, but ya can change it ta what suits ya. I don't wantcha to get what I'm sayin' wrong. All souls don't make it here. Some of 'em believes theys Heaven is on earth."

"I don't see how Heaven can ever be on earth, especially with how we've been treated down there. But if this is what its really like: I can't wait to get here!"

"Don't be in no hurry ta get ta Heaven. Ya got lots mo' life ta live b'fore it's yo time." A vibration of infinite love emanated from Nana's aura and projected tiny ripples through the ether into my immediate surrounding space. I felt my own vibration become stronger with her spiritual hug.

Nana raised her robed arm. "Wait here, my love. Ya Teacher is gonna arrive here soon enuf."

"My Teacher?"

"From that Nigiro place ya talked 'bout. Yo Teacher is gonna show you thangs, an give ya answers ta questions, I cain't. He's gonna take ya to phys'cal worlds an dimensions I cain't travel ta no more."

I willed millions of stardust particles to gather together to form a densely packed shape. I reached out to touch my great-grandmother, pleasantly surprised when my solid hand connected. My heart soared as I sensed her love.

"Will I ever see you again?"

"The Almighty has blessed me ta be ya Watcher. Ya won't see me again in the ancestral realm 'til it is yo time, but I will stay with ya to the end. Guidin' an gently nudgin' ya in the right direction usin' yo intuition. The love I haves for ya is timeless. I won't leave ya till ya reach the end of ya journey. Keep watchin' for the signs sent by the ancestors. We is always with ya!"

"I love you, Nana." I transmitted before feeling my spiritual body once again dissipate to vapor.

After watching Nana's beautiful aura fade into a bright ball of brilliance and zip off in the direction opposite the Pearly Gates, I felt my spiritual body drawn backwards as if pulled by a powerful magnet away from the massive otherworldly structure. Nana had not gone through the gates because she had chosen to stay behind. She was my Watcher and was here to help me navigate through this confusing thing called Life.

Chapter Eighteen

I awoke with a start, discovering I remained on the mountain, precariously perched on the ledge where I fell asleep the previous night. My heart pounded frantically within my chest as if I'd just run a marathon. I took several calming breaths to push away the urge to flee. My heartbeat gradually slowed to a normal pace with the delightful recollection of a beautiful dream tugging on the outskirts of my mind.

The warm rays from the rising sun lovingly caressed my cheeks with a good morning kiss. Both my feet were pushed against a large rock, wedging me securely in the narrow space, preventing me from slipping into the deep crevices below. I glanced around, touched my face, my body, and the cool ground to quell any lingering fear that I was no longer alive. All seemed normal, except now I sported a sparkly gold-colored flight suit and matching pair of golden boots. I quickly sat up, allowing the large Bible to rest in my lap as I ran my hands over the strange outfit. In my waking moment, I questioned whether the entire spiritual encounter with Nana had been merely a dream.

A slight whooshing sound, like the parting of air, caught my attention. When I turned to locate the source, the silhouette of a mighty man standing over me took me by complete surprise. I shielded my eyes from the brightness of the sun, instantly recognizing the man dressed in an emerald green flight suit and holding that strange object in his right hand.

"Greetings, Braveheart." The Teacher spoke not in words, but relayed his greeting telepathically.

"Teacher! You're really here?!" I responded, totally elated by his presence.

He nodded.

His beautiful dark skin glistened almost purple as if lit from within by an old-fashioned 'blacklight' bulb made popular in the 70's; the ones that changed ordinary velvet pictures of sisters and brothers sporting magnificent afro's and dancing to mystical music, into funky shades of florescent colors when the bulb was switched on. I glanced at my hands and briefly wished my cinnamon colored skin could magically darken to become as deeply rich as his. My second thought was to wonder if he had also arrived on the ledge by means other than his own two feet. My eyes then trailed to the metallic object in his hand, noting the similarity to the strange symbols etched on the Bible.

"I am here because you are now ready," he responded in a powerfully authoritative voice, booming deeply from within the confines of his barreled chest cavity.

Remnants of last night's vision—I won't say dream because I discerned that isn't what I had experienced—provided my understanding of the importance of what I must learn.

"Follow me," he instructed. "And I caution you to not look down."

This time, without question I eagerly did as I was told. I found my bearing on the uneven ground, stuffed all my journals inside my backpack, and dropped everything else except the old Bible, which I clutched securely under my arm. The Teacher began the descent down the side of the mountain like an expert hiker, making an easy path for me to follow. With only one free hand to steady myself, I stumbled along, following his footsteps as we navigated away from the treacherous ledge.

While The Teacher effortlessly descended the steep mountain crest, I gingerly maneuvered around boulders large enough to be houses. We inched along a treacherously narrow footpath that was barely the width of my two feet. I honestly started to question The Teacher's confidence in my ability to safely perform this descent and not kill myself in the process.

I continued on, grasping every bit of vegetation springing forth from the rocks to prevent me from tumbling over the side. With one hand still clutching the book and the other groping for random tree branches for dear life, I slowly ambled forward.

The Teacher did not slow down, nor did he show pity at my plight. He continued forward as if I were as surefooted as he.

After I had lost my footing for about the fifth time, I stopped to catch my breath. Glancing up from where we had come, and then the trail that laid ahead, I tried to gauge the distance of how much further we had to go before we reached the bottom. I did not want to sound as if I were complaining, but the tone of my voice said otherwise, "Man, I sure hope we're almost there. I could use a break." And when I received no response, I added, "Are we going back to the dome?"

"Yes."

Hearing his curt telepathic response, I decided it was in my best interest to remain quiet for the remainder of the descent, no matter how long it would take. I vowed to hold my tongue, follow The Teacher, and carefully watch my step. I was the pupil. Therefore, it was not up to me to question the one who knew more than I.

The fourth time I lost my footing, I barely caught my balance, thanks to a sturdy tree branch that snagged unto my backpack. For several brief moments, I imagined my mangled body bouncing off dozens of trees before finally resting on the forest floor.

"Would your journey be less difficult if you were not burdened by such a heavy load?" he relayed telepathically.

He was too far ahead on the trail to be seen. But I heard his voice in my head as if he were standing right beside me.

I relayed, *"Teacher, I am carrying one of the original Bibles. I believe this could be the only true Book of Life in existence! I can't just leave it up here to rot."*

"Braveheart, you have learned all you can about the outside world, not only from reading many books, but from

speaking to the ancestors. It is now time for you to learn from the world within."

I glanced down at the cumbersome book I refused to put down, despite my arms feeling like warm jelly from its hefty weight. This ancient script within the weathered covers had opened my eyes to the world as it once was. When life for Nigiro was the way it was intended. This book was important. Sacred. But I had to admit, my journey would be much less difficult without carrying such a heavy load.

"Why do you hesitate?"

"I feel strange about leaving it. This is an authentic Bible to be shared with others so they also know the truth," I said, aloud.

"You deciphered the strange text? Memorized the stories?"

"Yes."

"Then the book has fulfilled its purpose. It is of no use to anyone if you give up your life to protect it. Verily, the value does not reside within the pages, but in the one who has read and understood."

The ingrained connections in my brain about the sanctity of religion were very powerful. The Bible was to be respected, as it shared a special place in the homes of most black Americans. I knelt to the ground, tracing my fingers over the ancient writings, and carefully stowed the book in an alcove away from the elements. The Teacher was right; it had served its purpose. I must let it go or risk dying in an effort to save it. The freedom from laying my burden down energized me to quickly move forward. I regained my footing and hurried on until I caught a glimpse of the brilliant green flight suit ahead. With each successive, sure-footed, quick step, I narrowed the distance between us in no time at all.

The Teacher continued along the path, nary missing a beat. The manner in which he approached our treacherous journey was not with a fear of falling, but with certainty the rocky trail would rise up to meet his feet. Each raising and lowering of his foot was a lesson I was quickly learning. I stopped creeping along the side of the mountain as if my next step would result in certain death and focused on the Teacher. He didn't trouble himself looking down. Only ahead. I took note and mimicked his gait, approaching each step with the expectation of the ground shifting just enough to keep me upright.

"Better?" he asked, his powerful voice reverberating through the thick branches of trees.

"Much better," I replied, now easily keeping up with his quick pace.

~ ~ ~

In no time at all, the transparent geometric shapes of the dome's covering came into view. I spied armed guards patrolling the perimeter to ensure my newly discovered family remained safe from harm. My eyes scanned the massive structure situated high on that mountaintop, hundreds of miles away from the nearest city.

"That is so weird... I don't know how I ended up outside. In fact, I had no idea it was possible for me to be out here without freezing to death."

"*Your mind is very powerful to not accept the confines imposed by a false reality. You were free to leave at any point, but only when you recognized you were never imprisoned in the first place were you able to truly break free.*"

"That is cool! I had no idea how powerful the mind is."

"*We returned to this location because my vessel is near.*"

"Are we going back inside?" I asked, referencing the dome.

"There is no longer a need for your return to the king-dome. Under your own tutelage, you have quickly mastered all we could have taught you." He glanced down at the structure and continued, "...however, there remains much more for me to teach you about Nigiro."

We stood in a field under a moonless sky blanketed by millions of stars. With no humidity and at that altitude, a view of the heavenly bodies was almost perfect. I side-glanced The Teacher, my heart swelling with a feeling of gratitude. He represented the knowledge and wisdom of all the men in my life who never had the opportunity to fully develop theirs due to the oppressive system they suffered under in this country. Had they been allowed to develop to their full potential, the Elder standing before me was a representation of what they would have become.

As my heart swelled with love and appreciation, the appearance of several strange objects moving across the sky at high rates of speed caught my attention. If I didn't know better, I'd think a line of stars were moving in tight formation. I pointed and whispered, "Teacher, what is that?"

He looked to where I pointed in the sky. "The children are practicing their aviation skills."

"Are those spaceships?" I asked incredulously, watching various spectacles of light appear in the night sky. Some were evenly spaced, trailing single-file in groups of six to ten. Others appeared to be bright stars streaking across the sky like meteors that never fizzled.

"Some are spacecraft. Others are manmade satellites they are polluting the sky with, in their quest for world domination."

"How is it possible for me to see the spaceships? Don't they want to remain out of sight?"

"The spacecraft absorb solar energy and uses it to power the vessels, but pilots do not require lights to navigate. Sometimes we allow our ships to be seen during the day. And at night, we often use colorful lights to communicate with other Nigiro who are on the ground. While our spacecraft are visible to the naked eye, we remain stealth to mankind's radar technology. Ultimately, we want the entire world's population to know of our existence even if your governments do not.

Especially the Nigiro need to believe that life exists outside the world they know."

"Will I also learn how to pilot a spaceship?"

"Perhaps you will. If that is what helps in the completion of your mission," he replied, cryptically.

"That's so cool!" I replied watching several more orbs of light zip across the atmosphere. "If it's not me flying one, at least I hope one of the girls I met when I first arrived at the camp ends up piloting one."

"That is a very noble thought, Braveheart."

"I didn't get that much time with those girls, but if they have a Teacher like you on their side, I think they all have the potential to become great people."

He remained quietly humble, though accepting my praise.

"Speaking of the camp, I have a question about that white lady. The one with the green eyes and red hair. If you're focused on helping Nigiro, why is she involved with this?"

The Teacher directed my focus back to the king-dome. "We recruit non-melanated Nigiro, the ones who possess the most power in this warped system, to assist with our building of king-dome structures all over the planet."

"The redhaired woman is Nigiro?" This tidbit of information actually did surprise me because I thought she was as white as white could be.

"She is a distant relative of Nigiro, but because of the excessive degree of dilution within the structure of her DNA, she may never come to the full realization of who she is. Not in this lifetime. But that miniscule degree of melanin does allow her to empathize with the plight of the people."

"What about those awful white men she uses for guards? Or those mean white ladies who help run the place. Are they also Nigiro?"

He looked down and me and allowed a slight smile to erupt on his face as he uttered a simple, "No, of course not. They are merely the help."

I turned my attention to the structure and asked, "So how is it possible this facility has remained in almost complete secrecy?"

"What you see is courtesy of the Nigiro to assist in our mission. The Elders created the king-dome with a protective covering to shield the children from both natural, as well as unnatural elements. It provides a climate-controlled environment designed to restrict inhabitants from harmful electromagnetic low frequencies projected from thousands of artificial satellites orbiting the earth. Your government is unaware of our existence as we employ methods to remain hidden in plain sight. As far as they are concerned, there is nothing on the mountain other than trees, boulders, and various forms of wildlife."

"I read about the controversy surrounding EMFs being used for mind control. Cell phone companies supposedly put up those towers to push low frequencies to every corner of the planet. But the government says cell phone towers place no risk to humans."

"Your government is not the most reliable source to determine what is safe for hue-mans. We continue to monitor the advances in their technology. Mankind has come very far in a short time."

"Teacher, I have to give props to the men who discovered all those great inventions. We've been in a technological revolution ever since the turn of the 21st century."

His eyes appeared to blaze with fire as he replied aloud, "A Nigiro book of technology was stolen by thieves who have made mankind very powerful using their ill-gotten knowledge. Fortunately, the majority of the book has not been decoded, despite their incessant attempts at cracking the code. What they were successful in deciphering changed the modern world. Take for instance, the world wide web..."

"That was Nigiro?!" I remarked in amazement.

"Our Elders are responsible for developing the 'magic' used in the world wide internet communication system, of

which this country claims to have invented. Did you know the current version of your internet was our initial failed system for communication between various planets? The technology behind it is archaic at best. Instead of using it to bring mankind together, unscrupulous men stole it and first used it for military purposes. To control the masses."

"All this time I thought those people from Silicon Valley were brilliant. We were led to believe they were geniuses."

"Mankind is not as intelligent as they want you to believe. They are merely the recipients of stolen ancient Nigiro knowledge. All of man's technological advances of the past century are a result of reverse engineering interplanetary space ships."

"I don't understand... If it belonged to the Nigiro, how did those men get their hands on it?"

"Upon seeding the children on the planet, we deposited the knowledge of our existence deep within the Earth's surface. This knowledge was intended for the Nigiro children to discover, but only after their hue-man brains expanded to a level to interpret it. But it was discovered by others first. Now many nations are researching methods on how to uncover more of our technology and to unlock the secrets.

"Teacher, this sounds like something from a science fiction movie," I thought.

"Yes, it does." He was not upset, only resigned to how things had turned out. "Science fiction is the manner in which mankind disguises the truth of his stolen technology. This allows him to operate freely in plain sight."

"Hollywood releases movies about aliens, space travel, and artificial intelligence—robots—all the time. I had no idea those movies are based on actual science that exists." Many movies came to mind, *ET, Star Wars*, Marvel comic superhero movies, *Men in Black*, *Prometheus*, *War of The Worlds*, and any movie about traveling to Mars. In all honesty, too many movies to count had been produced since the 1950's that were centered around science fiction and extraterrestrial life forms. But my favorite movie was *The Matrix* because it planted the first seed of doubt in my mind that something was not quite right in this world.

"Mankind is very crafty. He gradually presents fragments of advanced technology to the general public through movies and television. When that particular technology is introduced to consumers for consumption, they easily accept it because they've seen it before. Then it quickly becomes embraced. And, finally consumers will demand the technology and then pay a premium to keep it. For mankind, money is their power."

"Like computers and cell phones... At first, both were so expensive only the wealthy could afford it. I remember the first time I saw a cell phone or computer in a movie. They made it look so cool! And if you didn't have one, you were a loser. Now, practically every family on the planet has several devices. Which means after they created the demand, they made more money by lowering the prices and making it affordable for everyone. No wonder the heads of these companies became trillionaires."

"That's right. In the hands of evil men, even the most highly advanced technology can be used for destruction. The pursuit of riches has led to the downfall of many ancient civilizations. As it will also destroy America and many other nations with her."

Images of cavemen discovering fire, rejoicing around the warmth as they carelessly danced about, but then later becoming terrified when someone got burned came to mind.

"Nigiro technology is thousands of years ahead of mankind's. They have no idea what they are about to unleash with the development of their artificial intelligence."

"What do you mean, Teacher. Isn't AI supposed to make our lives easier?"

He took a deep breath because even he had a difficult time with this concept. "For over 6,000 Earth years, an intelligent ancient reptilian species, unlike anything you can imagine, has lived deep within the interior of the planet. These creatures are intolerant of heat and sunlight and only come out in the extreme cold and darkness of night. This is the environment of which this species was intended to inhabit."

I gasped my surprise and horror. "You mean like the 'Creature from the black lagoon'? Or the Sleestaks from that 1970's television show, 'Land of the Lost'?"

"Something like that, but not the terrifying monsters mankind would have you believe." He nodded, relaying, *"A handful of powerful families govern the entire planet. But these people are not what they appear to be. They present themselves as humans, but are actually advanced artificial intelligence lifeforms. Scientists working for the reptilians used AI to create these beings. What you recognize now is what evolved. The reptilians employ these mankind creations to do their bidding, in an effort to reclaim the earth and return it to the ice age that existed eons ago."*

My mind went to the very few, ridiculously rich, and increasingly powerful owners of a handful of technology companies. Lately, their focus was not so much on making life better for the billions of humans living on the planet, but in cooperation with the U.S. government, were wasting trillions of dollars on a space program for travel to Mars and other planets in the solar system, while worldwide levels of poverty, homelessness, water shortages, and starvation increased.

"Incredibly, the reptilians have gradually inserted artificially created, mankind-like beings into all positions of power. Like a deadly virus, these intelligent humanoids took control of Europe, then spread to the newly created United States, and then throughout every continent. They are Heads of states. Presidents. Owners of powerful

companies... These creatures are found at the highest levels of all governments, wreaking havoc at every turn."

"They really don't care about us," I thought with despair. *"How are we supposed to fight what we can't see?"*

"The Nigiro are peace-loving, soulful, warm-blooded hue-mans, who live on the surface and draw energy from the sun. Reptilians are a coldblooded, soulless species that dwell underneath the icy layers of the planet and draw their energy from human strife, chaos, and war. For eons, both species battled to rule the planet Earth. It was impossible for Nigiro and reptilians to live simultaneously on Earth. Thus, an agreement was made. The reptilian would rule for a certain period, then the Nigiro."

"Our ancestors had an agreement with reptiles?" In my mind, I pictured beautiful blue-black, intelligent and powerful people speaking to snakes, lizards, and other cold-blooded reptiles. Only not the reptiles we recognize today, but man-sized reptiles standing on two feet. "Why did the Nigiro allow them to do this for all these years?"

"Braveheart, you must remember what appears to be millennia in earth years is, in the big picture, actually just a blip of infinite time."

"The reptilians understand their time on Earth is rapidly coming to an end. The evolved AI beings have chosen to not honor the reptilian agreement made with the Nigiro. Thus, they implemented measures to totally annihilate the Nigiro, first when they infiltrated and then colonized not only Africa, but also the Americas. Genocide, slavery, followed by Jim Crow laws, segregation, institutionalized racism, intentional poverty by means of welfare, drugs, abortion, AIDS.... Police forces, which are just more advanced forms of plantation overseers, have consistently terrorized the Nigiro under the guise proclaiming 'to protect and serve'. There is nothing these creatures won't do to annihilate the Nigiro. You should also understand that when man lies only with man and woman lies only with woman, the hue-man species will quickly go

extinct. No procreation, no babies, no more children, no more people. Total Extinction is the end result."

"I never thought about it like that," I whispered.

"The mankind humanoids began to procreate with the Nigiro, initially believing they could get rid of the Nigiro with each successive generation. That too was in vain because the blood of the Nigiro is powerful and not easily destroyed. Just one drop of the Nigiro blood overtakes all others."

"Ah... So that's where the one drop rule came from." I frowned in bewilderment. "All this time, I thought people were being racist when they said one drop of black blood makes you colored, or Negro. I didn't know our blood was so powerful that just one drop changes a person's entire genetic makeup."

"The power *is* in the blood!" he explained, sounding like a St. Louis Baptist pastor giving an Easter sermon to a standing-room only congregation.

"Teacher, from what I know of the world, it really seems like the reptilians are getting what they want. So many innocent people have perished on this Earthly plane. I often ponder what the world's population would look like black and brown people didn't abort their children to the degree they do. I know there is a movement that makes one choose to be either 'pro-choice' or 'pro-life', but even that is tied to the ills of this awful societal structure. And where I came from, getting raped might seem like a valid reason to abort a baby. But I know many girls my age who are using abortion as birth control. Getting an abortion is as easy as making an appointment, visiting a clinic, paying the fee for the procedure, and thirty minutes later, you're done. It takes more effort to adopt an animal than it does to kill a child. What nobody tells those girls is how messed their minds will end up after it's over, when they have time to consider what they've done."

He listened intently to what I had to say, giving full credence to my opinion. For though I lived in this world, he lived vastly above it.

"If there were no such thing as war. Or murder. Had Europeans, with their colonizer mindset, just left us to everyone to our own devices and stayed where they were, this world would be so much different."

"Braveheart, you must understand. Those humanoids would have quickly gone extinct had they not taken diabolical measures to ensure their survival on this planet. Our numbers would have quickly overrun theirs if left unchecked. Earth is all these ungodly beings will ever have. Unlike the Nigiro, *this* is their heaven." He explained, not as a means of agreement with their methods, but merely to offer a factual explanation.

I dropped my head in disbelief at the enormity of this revelation. Tried to wrap my mind around the unimaginable numbers of innocent lives lost, all resulting from the evil deeds of a few.

"Their time is almost over." He pointed his long spindly finger towards the horizon. "Look at the magnificent sun. The earth is warming in preparation for the great awakening of our people!"

"My Nana in spiritual form told me the same thing. The sun is growing hotter and brighter with each passing day."

"Your scientists tell you the earth is getting warmer due to the actions of men. Do not believe it. The Earth has been in existence millions of years before mankind and will continue long after the last man takes his final breath. This planet is more powerful than to allow mere mortals to destroy it. She will find a way to rid Herself of this virus known as mankind. Droughts across the planet will end with melting of the polar ice caps. Fires will scorch the land to cleanse the soil of chemicals. The desire to ruin this planet before it is handed over to the Nigiro will be thwarted."

"This is some pure evil..."

"I wish no harm to any of the non-melanated hue-mans, but they must prepare themselves. The entire planet will soon become inhospitable to all except the people of the sun. Those who are unable to live and thrive in the sunshine will take flight in search of other worlds, or go underground to avoid what's coming. The Nigiro children will make rightful claim to their place in this world. No longer will they be hated or scorned, but instead will be loved for the gifts and treasures they bring to this planet."

"From your lips to The Almighty's ears," I replied, repeating a phrase my Nana often said upon hearing something deeply profound.

"I have something for you." He unzipped a side pocket. *"A small gift."*

Pushing down my excitement of receiving a present from The Teacher, I waited patiently as he reached inside his flight suit and brought forth an object similar to what he carried, though slightly smaller.

He offered it to me.

"That's the symbol etched on the Book of Life," I replied, examining the metallic object in my hand, experiencing a slight tingling sensation, as if it were charged with electricity. "What is it?"

"Through the use of this teleportation key, the Nigiro can travel to other realms. You have the ability to transport your physical body anywhere you wish in the spiritual and physical realm."

"Thank you, Teacher," I replied, holding the key up to the sky, allowing the sun to sprinkle its rays upon it, activating the etched symbols to action. "Do you think mankind has gotten their hands on this?"

"Yes, they have uncovered many in their archaeological digs. Each teleportation key is individualized and activated only by the Nigiro to whom it is given. For the uninitiated, this item is nothing more than a useless piece of metal or an ancient artifact. When in all actuality, it is composed entirely of an organic matter resembling what you recognize as metal." He motioned to the key and explained, "This one belongs to you. It will only become activated with your unique vibrational signal."

Holding onto the key, staring at the etchings seemingly lit from within, a strong sense of deja vu came upon. A moment of complete clarity hit me like a ton of bricks. Nothing of what I was going through at this moment was new. Not getting abducted and tossed into that detention camp, not comforting Samaria, or meeting Auntie Sistah, nor was this my first encounter with The Teacher. I had experienced similar events before! Many, many times before. Nana said I would continue repeating my life until I finally relearned the lesson of love. This realization was jolting!

"Your question is...?"

I turned to The Teacher and asked, "How many times have we done this before? You and I? How many lifetimes have I gotten this far and still failed?"

"The number of attempts it takes to fully awaken to the power of your gifts is of no consequence. What does matter is completely mastering it. And as the concept of time does not truly exist, you have all the time in the world. I am here to help you reach the point where you become totally aware of who you truly are."

There was nothing left to do except press forward. Maybe this would be the life in which I fully awakened to myself and actually made a difference in the world. Maybe in the body of a sixteen-year-old Black teenager in America, I would finally be successful in warning others about what was coming if they remained asleep. I could help others to get out of the "matrix". Many others were now questioning all they've been told and have taken to the internet to spread the message. I wasn't the only one chosen to awaken others.

"Braveheart, when you awaken one million souls, the millionth is no more important than the first. The point is to do what you can."

"I understand," I replied.

He touched my shoulder for confirmation that I was ready. He raised the mysterious object an arm's length before us. I repeated his motion. Once again, I heard that strange whooshing sound. Before I realized what was happening, we were in an immense space, void of light and sound.

"Where are we?" I whispered.

"Pay close attention," his booming voice reverberated within my mind. *"As I previously attempted to explain— before your young mind was ready to accept the truth— our people did not originate on the planet you know as Earth. We, the original hue-mans, are from the planet Nigiro."*

"Teacher, I must humbly apologize for my disbelief when you first introduced me to the concept of Nigiro. That was before my mind was expanded."

He acknowledged my apology. No need for further discussion.

"You said we originated on a planet called Nigiro. Did we colonize Earth?"

"Not in the manner you have come to know. The Earth was created for the Nigiro children to experience a human existence. This was to be a Garden of Eden. A Paradise. As it is on many other planets."

"The Book of Life referred to the garden as something other than the Garden of Eden. And Earth wasn't even called *earth*. I wish I could pronounce the names, but there are no words to describe it. I only felt the vibration and the feeling it gave me when I read the symbols."

"You are correct, Braveheart. The names and titles you are most familiar with are used only to communicate to your level of comprehension. In time, you will regain the capability to communicate as it was intended."

As he spoke, I studied his physical appearance. The Teacher fit the definition of statuesque as his very presence commanded attention. Without effort, he truly did appear otherworldly. I silently wondered his actual age because the condition of his skin appeared to be ageless. The whites of his eyes were pretty much non-existent, rather gold-tinged black irises contrasted sharply against the dark skin. Dozens of intricately tangled locs of coarse black hair extended down to his shoulders. I guessed he was between nine and ten feet, much taller than any person I had ever seen up close, including all the basketball players at my school and the pro ballers lectured at last year's assembly. His build was athletic. Tall and lean without any visible signs of fat. In his strong hands, I imagined a basketball would appear to be the size of a grapefruit. However, it wasn't his physical appearance that struck me as fascinating, but his entire demeanor emanated a power and strength. I felt honored to be in the presence of a Nigiro elder.

The immense dark void instantaneously came to life with an infinite number of solar systems filling the space in every direction. Enormous systems of planets, moons and vibrantly dazzling stars in every color of the spectrum expanded and contracted seemingly at will. Standing next to the Teacher, once again I teetered on the precipice of the universe, as if I were a child getting ready to play a captivating game of marbles.

"That is what you know as Earth." He pointed to an unremarkable blueish sphere orbiting the sun. I recognized Saturn, Mars, Jupiter, and several other planets within the same orbit. *"The Creator encompassed it with a protective barrier to keep stray celestial objects from destroying the garden."*

"A protective barrier? Sounds just like the king-dome." From my vantage point, it was hard to comprehend why we couldn't get along down there. If everyone had the chance to see Earth was but a tiny grain of sand in the universe, we'd forget about hating each other and realize that we are all in this together.

"Our planet, Nigiro, is located in a galaxy far away from Earth. Many light years away."

I watched in awe as he swiped through a series of undiscovered galaxies, simultaneously zooming further and further out. After the first few iterations of galaxy expanded outwards, I could no longer identify the tiny speck of light as our solar system. Finally, he zeroed in on a planet so astronomic in size, I could only compare it to Jupiter. Two large moons orbited on opposite sides, while twenty or so smaller planets maintained a tight orbit around a colossal sun. The fiery sphere appeared to spew forth a cascade of substances resembling hot lava in colors ranging from brilliant red, to dull orange and pale yellows. The Sun permeated a sense of warmth even within this virtual existence.

"That's a whole lot of space between our two galaxies, Teacher. How did the Nigiro find Earth in the first place?"

"Gazing at the stars provided the first astronomers with hidden knowledge of the universe. Based on what was uncovered, our explorers searched the expanse for planets with similar climates; locating several in the process."

"That's an amazing ability to be able to read the stars." I considered my curiosity of celestial bodies, wondering if it were related to my gift. *"That must have taken forever to get from one side of the universe to another! I don't see how anybody survived the journey!"*

"I will try to temper my explanation to your level of comprehension," he relayed.

I watched as he located an area of the expanse with no planetary systems. Streaks of scattered light from tails of shooting stars was all that remained visible from celestial objects that had been sucked inside that vacuum of space.

"Have you ever taken a shortcut through your neighborhood as you made your way home? Especially when you were in a hurry?"

"Yes, I used to cut through the neighbors' yards all the time. It was faster jumping fences than taking surface streets. And in my neighborhood, far less dangerous."

"Traveling the outer space is similar. We take advantage of portals to reach other galaxies is less time. Your scientists have deemed these gateways as 'worm holes'. However, with no idea of what these spaces consisted of, or if they could return to Nigiro afterwards, our explorers paved the way and charted courses for others to follow. A 'black hole' is a void in space where no light exists. Within the expanse of one of those voids, is the planet Nigiro."

"That must have been terrifying being the first ones to travel through a wormhole without knowing what was on the other side. They had no way of knowing if they would be killed instantly or if they would ever make it back home."

"Thank The Creator! The explorers returned with news that entire worlds existed outside our own. Whereas we ultimately became aware of those planets, they were always in existence. The Creator blessed Nigiro with gifts of intense curiosity and high intelligence, so we were destined to go forth and populate the universe."

"This is incredible! I come from Nigiro who were amazing people! Engineers, mathematicians and space travelers! Our people—my people—discovered how to get off the planet and travel across the universe! They not only build the space vessels, but were the pilots navigating through those mysterious wormholes!" Considering the heights our intelligence had once reached, it was almost unfathomable how far we had fallen.

"From my study of hue-mans, very few of you are living up to your fullest potential." He stopped what he was working on and placed his focus on me and said aloud, "When the Europeans began to steal and then enslave Africans from the continent, they selected only the ones whom they believed would survive the horrific journey to

the Americas. Thus, Nigiro in the Americas are the most powerful and intelligent hue-mans in the world. Not only did your ancestors survivor the genocide inflicted on the indigenous tribes who were already on the land, you also descended from the strongest and most intelligent Africans brought to the land. Your Nigiro African DNA is extremely powerful and is encoded for survival."

"That explains why no matter what they do to us, we always survive. And even thrive under the worst of circumstances," I replied, feeling pride for all who came before me.

"*However, even though you are the most powerful Nigiro, I estimate the average hue-man uses less than ten percent of their brain capacity at any given moment. And I estimate you utilize around fifteen.*"

"Only fifteen percent?" I uttered, screwing my face up at the unintentional reference to my low intelligence. "I've been told I'm pretty smart for my age. So, if I'm not using the remaining eighty-five percent of my brain, that would mean I might have superpowers if I did!"

"*Many of you do, but none of you know it.*"

I imagined what a person operating at full brain capacity would look like. We'd all be considered as geniuses! But that concept was so far outside my realm of comprehension, I set the notion aside.

He shifted his focus back to the screens and zoomed in closer to the planet's atmosphere. "*The Nigiro utilize several methods for transportation. To relocate our physical bodies, we use star ships to travel through the expanse. When a star ship is within range, it is possible to conduct an atomization transfer between two coordinated points using the position tracker.*" The Teacher referred to the object that was always in his grasp. "*Which is why we returned to the king-dome. My space vessel is near.*"

"*Now I understand what caused the ruckus in the forest when I was in that detention camp. The guards must have been reacting to the arrival of your space ship! It also explains how I was the only one with the ability to see you when none of the other girls could."*

"Your gifts have made you very perceptive." He turned his focus away from the screen, leaving the planet of Nigiro within view. *"We prefer to maintain a low profile as to not cause a panic. Our space vessels will sometimes arrive in what appears to be a burst of wind from the clear blue sky. If there are many vessels descending upon one location, we disguise our arrival within the midst of a mighty storm, as the surrounding air becomes displaced with extreme amounts of solar energy."*

"Is that what causes all that thunder and lightning?"

"Sometimes." He offered a hint of a smile as he explained. *"Although our vessels are undetectable to the eye, it is impossible to avoid disturbances in the air. Our vessels are what causes what you believe to be cloud-to-cloud lightning strikes."*

"I knew there was something strange about those strong electrical storms that produced no rain or thunder! I remember powerful bolts of lightning crossing from one cloud to another, wondering why there was no thunder associated with them. Sometimes during a night storm, there would be so many strikes of lightning at the same time, the sky would be lit up like day!" I grinned at The Teacher. "Never in a million years would I have thought space ships were the cause."

"The average man is unable to witness our arrival because Nigiro travel in a dimension of which their eyes cannot see. What man does not understand becomes explained away with a theory. They may report our arrival as an unexpected storm or tropical depression. Our vessels remain hidden in plain sight which allows us to freely walk amongst you. We transport our bodies at will."

I relayed to The Teacher, *"I've seen something similar to atomization on television. Star Trek is the television series where they first showed people being beamed up from other locations. Called it teleportation. I thought it was just make believe."*

"Men became aware of this knowledge from the ancient stolen texts, but are unable to duplicate it. Thus, it has been portrayed as science fiction while they pursue means of perfection. But they will never be successful because they are lacking one essential element. A soul."

The Teacher gazed off into the distance, in deep thought contemplating the foolish and immature nature of mankind. His dealings with men over the years had left him filled with disdain by how they intentionally chose to embrace ignorance over knowledge.

He regained his composure and continued to explain. *"The advanced elder Nigiro possess the ability to project their astral form to multiple dimensions, anywhere in the universe using only the power of the mind. Time and space hold no limitations. However, whenever we travel with humans, we must use vessels because it is much safer on your fragile bodies."*

"Teacher, do you have the ability to mind travel?" I relayed, wanting to know if he was one of the elders.

"You pose an interesting question." He tipped his head in approval. *"Yes, I have conquered my mind to make full use of my cerebral abilities. As to your wonderment, I do not count years of my existence. I am one of the originals, thus time is of no concern to me. Nor shall it be for you."*

I stared at the ancient man before me who was apparently older than anyone or anything I had ever encountered. One of the firsts. An original. The Nigiro hue-man.

During my brief lifetime on earth, surrounding myself in nature was of the utmost importance. Our house was filled with houseplants, but my favorite place was the backyard, especially in the springtime when dormant trees began to sprout leaves and colorful flowers blossomed. Spring was also the season when me and my mother planted our annual vegetable garden for a summer harvest of tomatoes, cucumbers, green beans, watermelon and strawberries. Placing my hands in the rich soil just somehow felt right. And I loved the feeling of a warm gentle rain on my face as spring storms arrived to prepare the vegetation to grow.

Every once in a while, powerful thunderstorms rolled in bringing dark and ominous clouds that sometimes dropped a tornado or two on the city. I'd take a seat in my hammock that was attached to the pergola, getting rocked like that baby in the nursery rhyme, until my mother yelled at me to get my butt inside. I marveled at how easily strong gusts of wind caused those mighty oak trees to sway back and forth, as it blew through its leaves like currents of turbulent white-water coursing down river streams. Though the wind was unseen, I learned it could be extremely deadly, and the only way you knew it was present was to hear or see it passing over an object. Observing what those trees went through, I often felt connected to them. They communicated with me. Teaching me that no matter how bad things were at a particular moment, as long as I held firm to my principles, I would get through the storm. Don't get me wrong; those trees got beat up and even lost a few branches during really bad storms, but in the end, they most always remained standing.

"Let me explain in terms you may understand. The Creator created the universe and all that is present, which included the planet Nigiro. Thus, there is but One Universal Soul. However, it is also infinite. The Creator desired for Her Universal Soul to have a physical experience, so from the star dust of Nigiro the original children were formed. She breathed life into each and every form and instilled within them a soul. This allowed Her children a direct connection to The Oneness of the Universe and also to one another. The children were spiritual beings created to have a physical experience. When those original children descended upon Nigiro, She placed a sun in the sky so they would always have food to eat. A moon to regulate the planet's orbit..."

"The book of Genesis says God placed a firmament between the waters above and the waters below. Was that to prevent celestial objects from entering in the orbit and possibly destroying the Earth?"

"Unfortunately, what you truly know about the Universe would fit through the eye of a needle. And what you have read in your Bible, without addressing the complete books that are missing, it is extremely difficult to provide an accurate interpretation of something tampered with by men."

I nodded my understanding. "So how did we get to Earth?"

"While the children of the Nigiro multiplied across the planet, they also grew restless. For millennia, they had used their creative minds to experience life to the fullest while on Nigiro. Creating and inventing to their heart's content. In time, that restlessness led to discovering the means to travel off the planet. The early travelers learned not all planets were hospitable to our lifeform..."

"Does that mean there are other lifeforms on other planets?"

"Of course! The Creator not only made hue-mans, but also created other lifeforms which reside on other planetary systems. Each species was given its own special place to enjoy life as it was meant to be lived. Harmoniously with others."

"I guess that makes sense..."

"The Nigiro arrived on the earth, found it to be similar in climate to our home, and began to populate each continent. For millions of years, our people lived in harmony with the earth. Never taking more than what was needed to survive. The early Nigiro did not know where there were also animalistic creatures living deep within the earth. The cold dark caves was their natural habitat and where they were supposed to remain had they followed The Creator's plan. Had that occurred, all hue-man people would be living together harmoniously."

"And that's how it all began...." I inhaled sharply. "The beginning of the end for us."

"I want to show you something you may find quite interesting." He changed the view to show the moon orbiting the Earth. *"Look closely. The Nigiro discovered another purpose for the moon. We have always used it as a way station when traveling to other planets within this galaxy. But with our stolen technology, mankind was able to decipher enough code to build spacecraft. They built a lunar habitat on the far side of the moon's surface."*

"I thought NASA had shut down the moon program. They told the public they no longer had the technology to get there. They said the focus was on reaching Mars."

The Teacher relayed, *"That is not entirely true. Mankind of many nations joined forces and used our technology to build a colony on the moon. They have continued to travel there to this day."*

"Why would they lie about living on the moon?" I relayed, *"It's not like anyone would know the truth one way or the other."*

"From a distance, we observed their arrival; curious to see what they were up to. Their vessel was positively archaic, yet ironically they named it, Apollo! We watched their astronaut's, Neil Armstrong, first attempt to walk on the lunar surface and then the others. The men were clumsy, childlike, and inappropriately dressed for space travel, but only remaining outside for a short time. When it was time for them to leave, we saw they were having difficulty with the space capsule. It had malfunctioned and would not lift. After some discussion, we offered our assistance."

"Why did the Nigiro decide to help them?"

"As I indicated earlier, the moon is regularly used as a waypoint when we traverse the universe. The Nigiro explorers helped those astronauts because it is in our nature to assist lesser intelligent creatures when they are in distress. However, upon their return to the moon only fifty earth years later, our explorers were disappointed to

find mankind had actually began the colonization of the moon. The exploration team were even more disgusted to learn the United States and several other nations were using incarcerated Nigiro. These young men were being involuntarily transported to the moon to construct a lunar colony."

He zoomed out to refocus on the dark side. I gazed down at what appeared to be a series of interconnected greenhouses with separate 'wings' jutting out in three different directions. From my view above, the structure resembled one of those 'fidget spinners' my little brother used to play with.

"That's impossible!" I stated with a conviction I no longer felt because apparently nothing was too ridiculous or off-limits when it came to what this government would do to its black citizens.

"In the miniscule expanse of time it took for the Nigiro to travel the universe and then return to the lunar outpost, we discovered mankind had built their own lunar base. They were very industrious and reverse engineered the technology we provided them to return to Earth. They are now trying to perfect the technology to conduct long-distance space travel. The moon was just the beginning of their plans to colonize hospitable planets within the solar system."

"Please tell me that they are not sending our incarcerated brothers to the moon," I said, feeling like my heart had dropped to the pit of my stomach.

"The lunar colony built on the dark side of the moon was a test case. It was constructed to determine if it were possible to live in outer space." He appeared to peer right through me when he uttered, *"The labor from modern-day Nigiro, enslaved workers, was used to build the base. And they were also tested to determine the effects of a space atmosphere on the human body."*

I shook my head in pure disgust. I felt like crying. "How and when did that happen?"

"Through extensive research of the hue-mans' DNA, mankind discovered that highly melanated are capable of surviving in outer space for an extended amount of time with no ill effects. And similar to how Nigiros from the African continent were taken and enslaved, they did the same with American Nigiros. Instead of sailing across the ocean in ships, they transported the enslaved Nigiro to the moon in spaceships."

"Where did they find the men? And how was it done without the families' knowledge?" I relayed.

"Not just men. Young women, too," he explained in that authoritative voice that sent shivers down my spine, "It was a fairly simple process that began with the industrial prison complex. After the government located the strongest most virile young men, they separated them from the general population, and then stored them away in solitary confinement where they supposedly 'died'. When families asked for the bodies of their loved ones, they were informed they had already been cremated. The government then commissioned unscrupulous black men to gain the trust of residents, and used them to peruse small towns, villages, and the streets of larger cities to capture and enslave Nigiro women of child-bearing age. Every four months or so, they loaded up the young people in spaceships and launched them to the moon under the guise of placing satellites in orbit."

"Why am I not surprised to hear that this government participated in an interstellar slave trade?!"

I recalled another conversation with my Uncle Ricky who insisted the entire purpose of private prisons was to provide free labor. But, like every other law written to keep the Nigiro at the lowest levels, the United States Constitution abolished slavery in 1865 for all its citizens, except for those imprisoned. Consequently, the U.S. has only 5% of the world's population, but over 25% of its prisoners. And the vast majority of the imprisoned are African-American and Hispanics.

"In the years since we first learned about the existence of the lunar colony, thousands of hue-man children have been born. The governments were breeding Nigiro children in that atmosphere, much like they did when they enslaved the so-called Africans. The offspring were being separated from their parents and told very little about the existence of their ancestors, only that they originally migrated from Earth. Just as you knew nothing about our people on Nigiro, they know nothing of you."

"I-I-I don't know what to say," I relayed, staring down at the climate-controlled buildings, wondering how many of my people had been used to colonize the moon. Imagined most were discarded like trash after they were no longer needed. I suddenly felt foolish for the many nights I spent staring up at the moon now that I knew there was someone up there staring back at the Earth.

"Do not despair, Braveheart. We returned and rescued all the Nigiro from the horrors being inflicted on them by mankind. For eons, The Creator has witnessed Her children's mistreatment at the hands of the cave dwellers. And like a good mother, She is not pleased with how her children are treated."

"What did the government leaders do when they learned 'aliens' had rescued the workers?" I asked.

"Actually, we rescued our brothahs and sistahs without the awareness of government leaders. It was a clandestine operation with inside assistance. The people operating the lunar base had no idea what had actually occurred. Only that all the workers had mysteriously disappeared. Of course, they could not make this event public, lest they expose themselves and provide confirmation that a lunar colony was actually operational. The U.S. government would have to acknowledge their role in the abduction and enslavement of American citizens, and also admit that trillions of dollars were being funneled into a space program that was supposed to be dormant," The Teacher explained. *"With the total labor force*

removed, the lunar base was permanently disabled and the men returned to Earth."

"I can see why The Creator is angry. Most of us have lost our minds because of how we've been forced to live." I thought about the state of the world. "What's going to happen now?"

"The Creator will reset the world to how She originally intended it to be. The children will be liberated and mankind has no say about when, where, or how this reset will occur. All Her children will be made to sit still and reflect on their behavior. If they do not learn from their mistakes and take the necessary steps to correct the errors of their ways, She will do it for them. And it will not be to their liking."

"The Most High—The Creator, is going to place everyone in a time out?"

"Precisely." He returned to the previous view of Nigiro and zeroed in on the planet's atmosphere. A thick layering of clouds came into view. *"Those who do not listen, who choose to disobey Her punishment, will suffer greatly."*

"I cannot imagine how She can make the entire world sit still for any significant amount of time."

"Close your eyes," he instructed, aloud. "Clutch the teleportation object tightly and do not let go. We are going on a journey of the mind."

I did as I was told and held the tool, what I would refer to as my 'tob', firmly in my clenched hand.

"What do you see?"

"Nothing. Total darkness."

"Take your time, Braveheart. Search deeply within yourself."

I focused on my breathing and concentrated. The weight of the metal felt reassuring in my hand as it reminded me that I was still conscious. Slow breaths in through my nose, followed by extended exhaling through my mouth. I did this over and over again; for how long, I don't know. The Teacher remained quiet, allowing my mind to take over on its own. Ever so gradually, the darkness gave way to colorful triangular shapes zipping by at quick paces. I began to experience the sensation of weightlessness, as if I were drifting away on a soft bed of fluffy clouds, or floating lazily on my back on a calm river stream. All manners of stress disappeared from my physical body. Then I felt the vibration begin like the buzzing of a million bees. It continued to grow stronger and stronger until my entire body was overcome with waves of powerful vibration. My spirit freed itself from the body; from its protective earth vessel. As quickly as it started, it ended. Freedom! I was once again total consciousness existing only on the astral plane. A bright glow emanating from the dark, pulsated with an energetic vibration.

"Teacher? Is that you?"

"Yes, I am with you."

"I sense your presence. It's beautiful!"

"As is yours, Braveheart."

"Wow! This is amazing!"

"Indeed. Now I want you to astral project."

In spirit form, we descended through the clouds, existing as one with The All. I observed what I thought was the earth below, but the terrain appeared slightly different from what I remembered. We zoomed over a vast ocean of blue, teaming with strange aquatic creatures I thought were dolphins but weren't, skimming the surface, jumping over and beneath the gentle waves. I heard their screams, or maybe it was cries of glee. I surmised the animals were merely chasing each other the way children played.

I took in a luscious landscape that went on as far as the eyes could see. Gentle waves lapped against a sandy shore, gracious palm trees laden heavy with coconut-like fruit swayed in the ocean breeze, and young children played in the shallow shore with their parents looking on. In the distance, peaks of great pyramids were scattered as far as the eye could see amidst the tropical forestry.

"Where are we, Teacher?" I relayed in awe.

"Welcome to Nigiro." He had easily transcended from spiritual essence into physical form and advised me to do the same.

"I don't know if I can."

"Focus on every part of your body. Imagine each cell connecting with the others. Gather your thoughts and all else will follow. You are the master of your own universe."

"I am the master of my universe," I repeated the phrase over and over again until I finally believed it. *"Mind over matter."*

"Precisely."

I was formless, yet totally aware, but just as well could have been a breeze upon the wind. My spirit form possessed the ability to 'see' everything. Yet, from a totally different perspective than what was visible in the physical realm. I observed many other spiritual beings surrounding us, encouraging me—their essence welcoming me home.

"You are almost there..." he encouraged.

I fully focused my consciousness on each cell of my body to bring matter into existence. My body underwent a transformation from nothingness to solid matter in a matter of moments! I successfully projected not only my mind to the astral plan, but with the guidance of The Teacher, I had projected my entire body down to the planet of Nigiro!

Chapter Nineteen

To be physically standing on an otherworldly planet I had only imagined in my dreams was beyond words! It felt as if I had emerged from a cruel world dominated by shades of grey, and had finally awoken to the real world, beautifully and vibrantly colored in every shade of the rainbow. My eyes rejoiced upon seeing the bluest of blues, and all shades of red, orange, yellow, and green painted houses. Flower of purple, indigo, ocher, and crimson abounded in patches of wildflowers growing freely! The rich green grass blanketing the ground looked nothing like the pale artificial color of what grew in my neighborhood back home. It was all I could do to contain myself from wallowing in it.

The sky was clear with a bright sun blazing down upon the ancient city, raising the temperature to an almost unbearable level of heat. If I had to guess, the temperature was well over 120 degrees! And that was in the shade of towering trees that resembled the mighty palms that grew in the desert! Ever so often, a gentle breeze provided a brief respite from the oppressive humidity. However, in my wondrous fascination with the planet Nigiro, I dared not complain.

A flock of large colorful birds burdened with oversized beaks and large wingspans, that reminded me of the pretty toucans I'd seen in zoos back home, vigorously flapped their massive wings to remain in-flight. The birds swooped down closer to where we stood and eventually landed nearby in the shore. The sight was so unexpected, I was completely caught up in the moment.

As I looked over the land, taking in all the glorious sights, I tossed my head back in gratitude, lifted my arms to the sky in praise and gleefully shouted out, "Hallelujah!" The joy I felt deep down in my soul came not only from myself, but from all those who came before.

Upon my arrival to Nigiro, every last one of my ancestors had finally returned home.

The Teacher was unfazed by my reaction, as he had frequently witnessed similar emotions from those first experiencing a return to Nigiro. It was impossible to contain my excitement, nor did I try. His over-the-shoulder glance instructed me to securely tuck the tob into my flightsuit pocket for safekeeping.

We approached the ancient city, proper, but it was difficult describing the images my sight took in. The only comparison I came up with was ancient Egyptian or Kemet ruins I had read about in history books. But here, there were no ruins. The buildings were well-maintained with several covered in what looked to be, sheets of 24k gold. Several structures were also painted in vibrantly eye-catching colors, not the weathered beige that I was used to. Magnificent statues of Nigiro warriors—what I was previously taught were Egyptian figures—graced the entrances of buildings. Far off in the distance, dozens of larger pyramids towered over hundreds of smaller ones.

The joyous sound of laughing coming from an open market brimming with activity drew my attention. Groups of strikingly attractive, highly melanated statuesque women, beautifully dressed in styles reminiscent of various African garb from many nations mingled with one another. The men were also very tall, extremely dark-skinned and exceedingly handsome—a few wore what appeared to be crowns atop their heads. Several younger males were rearranging heavy containers, under the direction of the older women. Many men also sported flightsuits similar to The Teacher's, but none were the same shade of emerald green. I glimpsed at what the ladies were selling. An array of tropical fruits, vegetables, and grains overflowed from stalls staffed by children offering up their assistance. I saw no money being exchanged. The customers took only what they needed and nothing more. Music that reminded me of my parent's favorite old school groups played softly in the background.

"Where are we going?" I asked, timidly while trying not to stand out amongst the very tall and beautiful people. But it was in vain. I blended in about as much as an old possum surrounded by graceful gazelles.

The Teacher's simple reply was, "Patience."

As we perused the streets, I studied the people who looked like highly evolved versions of myself and family members. They were all at least two feet taller than me and appeared very healthy. I noticed no one was overweight, not even by a little. They were fit and sported cheerful dispositions. Their glowing skin ranged in tones from purplish-black, to coffee, pecan, through café au lait.

A loud whooshing sound from overhead drew my attention upward. I shielded my eyes from the sun to see what appeared to be humongous birds in flight. But they were not birds! My mouth dropped open in astonishment watching four young Nigiro women dressed in dazzling blue flightsuits with wings protruding from behind, swoop through the air! I watched in disbelief as another young sistah dressed in purple prepared to take off. She knelt down and released an eight-foot wingspan from wherever one would keep wings stored. And with one powerful push off from the ground using only her bare feet, she was airborne, swooping higher and further away until she caught up with the group.

"Wow!" I exclaimed watching them gracefully perform a sky dance.

"Many of the youth are very gifted in aerodynamics."

"That is amazing!" I marveled at how normal this seemed to everyone but me. I must have been the only person walking around with my eyes gaped open as wide as my mouth.

Every single person we passed on the street greeted The Teacher with affection and offered a heartfelt greeting towards me. Some spoke to me using the English language I understood, while others communicated their welcomes telepathically. I quickly came to prefer using telepathy because the spoken language did not fit this beautiful planet. Within minutes, my self-conscious feelings of inadequacy were replaced with loving acceptance. And I didn't have to do anything except be me. I had nothing to prove and no reason to pretend I was something I was not. Tears of joy spilt forth with the realization of this was how I was *always* supposed to feel. Safe in body and happy within my melanin rich skin.

"This way. I will now show you where we bring the children upon their arrival."

I kept slow pace with the Teacher who gratefully allowed space for sorrow to release its lifelong hold from my soul. I tried to wipe the tears away with the back of my hand, but with each swipe they continued to flow. It wasn't my intention to be overcome by emotion, but upon witnessing the glory of black achievement without restraint was almost too much to bear. How far we must have fallen from where the Nigiro began. In another world, on a different planet, black people thrived and had successfully created a cultured civilization unrivaled by any I had known. Or expected to ever know had I remained in the Divided States of America.

"Why do you weep?" relayed the Teacher.

"I am so proud to finally know that I, and those on earth, have ascended from these great people. We really do have greatness and brilliance in our genes! Deep down we may have known it, but somehow it never truly resonated because of the conditions we were made to suffer through. I am heartbroken because we were never allowed to fulfill our maximum potential. We never truly got to realize how great we could be."

Upon noticing my despair, a mature elder stopped to provide comfort and encouragement. Telepathically, she whispered, *"Beloved, do not let your heart be troubled. Trust and believe in The Creator. In time, all will be made true again. Welcome home, my sistah. There will always be a place for you here."*

"*Thank you, sistah,*" I relayed, allowing all remnants of sorrow to move on. My soul was set free. I fully understood who I am because now I know from whom I come. My ancestors *are* magnificent beings! They are not only kings and queens, but gods and goddesses created in The Divine's image and filled with the Spirit of The Almighty God. Which means, so am I. My eyes took in the bluest sky imaginable before I closed them. I sighed happily and released a heartfelt, "Thank you" into the universe, praying this sentiment would find its way home.

"What you are experiencing in this moment, I admit I can never know. Only those who have lost everything and then have it restored, can. Braveheart, though I will never entirely grasp how you feel, I empathize with you and our earthly brothers and sisters, which is why I have dedicated my life to being a Teacher."

I acknowledged his admission with an appreciative smile. We stopped at an open-air building with a grand entrance. It appeared to be a temple. Massive marble columns, flanked by statues of majestic lions perched on either side, similar to ones unearthed in Egypt, greeted our arrival. We stepped inside where the temperature must have dropped at least thirty degrees from the heat of the day.

"This way," he indicated, gliding down the long corridor.

"Who are they?" I asked in reference to detailed carvings of men and women dressed in what appeared to be space gear. Flightsuits, helmets, and all carrying a unique device used for teleportation.

"These are the early explorers who traveled the galaxies in search of other worlds. They are now ancestors and abide with the Elders on the astral plane."

Taking in the images of hundreds of ancestors who came before me, who might have shaped my world differently had circumstances on earth played out according to God's plan, left me feeling some kind of way. Regardless of what I previously experienced, I now understood I'd been blessed with their DNA. Knowing that it was their blood running through my veins caused my heart to swell to the point I thought it might burst. The intelligence of these people would be impossible for some to fathom, considering all our lives we had been told how dumb black people are. I shook my head in disgust. How foolishly jealous mankind on earth must have been of the Nigiro to steal our birthright and then replace it with one built on pure ignorance and stupidity.

We paused outside a room where more chatter resided. Only this time, the laughter came from children. I looked in. Several dozen youngsters were huddled together in groups as they each worked to design different projects. One worked on a water filtration system to bring fresh water to a dry planet. A second group focused on building pyramid structures using only their minds and the materials at hand. And the last group was designing a miniature version of a space vessel with properties of enhanced invisibility.

Within the third group, a familiar figure came into view. "No way!" I whispered to the Teacher. "That is my young friend, Samaria!"

"Braveheart, be not disappointed if her response to your arrival is not what you expect. The child you remember is no longer. Her mind has expanded to a level of intelligence unknown to the average hue-man."

"That's okay. I just want to see how she is."

"Go. I will await your return."

I cautiously approached the group of children who no longer behaved like the kids I was used to. Though they freely laughed together, it was not over a silly childish matter, but an unfortunate mistake one had made with the design.

"Samaria?" I came closer. "Hey... It's me, Kenya."

She turned towards me. The scared little girl I first met in the van on that fateful day was no longer. The eyes that regarded me were without recognition, yet belonged to an ancient soul who had found her way back home. But then she did recognize me and greeted me warmly.

"Greetings, my sistah," she uttered in a voice better suited coming from an adult.

"How are you?" I asked, foolishly making small talk.

"I am well," she replied.

"I see you're working on a space ship." I glanced over her shoulder to the others, who continued on as if she had never stepped away.

"This is our project." She nodded towards her group. "From the time I arrived, after I became acclimated to the intense heat from having a super sun..."

"Super sun?!"

"Planet Nigiro orbits around a sun the size of which100 earthly suns can fit inside. The planet has ten times the circumference compared to Earth and thus, requires a substantially larger sun for adequate light and warmth. Where we are now is closest to the planet's equator; the sunlight is much more intense. There are also three moons orbiting Nigiro. And if I were to compare a year on Nigiro to the 365 orbital days on Earth, it would be four times as long. And the length of a day is accordingly longer."

"Remarkable..." I uttered, feeling more stupid with each additional sentence I spoke.

"As I was saying, I have been in instruction from almost the moment I arrived home. Our project involves designing a space traveling vessel using the old stealth technology, but adding a new process for transparency from all light spectrum available to human sight. We're also outfitting it with safe travel pods. This vessel will to be used to help retrieve our people from earth and bring them home safely."

"That's awesome, Samaria!"

She smiled appreciatively.

"This planet is like nothing I could have imagined! Did you notice all the people look like us? And they can fly!"

"They are Nigiro, after all. So, of course we look like them. This planet... These super intelligent people... All the hidden knowledge I have untapped inside my own brain! I would have gone through anything to get here!" She stared down at her own two feet. "I have not mastered flying or even levitation yet, but both are on my list of areas to study."

"You mean you have the ability to fly?"

She nodded. "We all do. Even you. We just have to tap into that part of our brain to instruct our bodies what to do."

"Incredible!" I exclaimed, recalling the many dreams I'd had about levitating and soaring high above the clouds. Maybe those weren't dreams after all. Perhaps, they were a memories from another lifetime. "Do you miss being home at all?"

"If you mean Earth, not really. This is my home now. I have made lots of good friends here. They are my family. I am safe. I don't have to be concerned about any of the things I used to worry about. And I often communicate with my earthly mother through our means."

"That's great to hear you've adjusted so well. I was worried about you."

Her gestures belied her patience. She was itching to get back to work. "Would you like to see what we are working on?"

"Yeah. It sounds fascinating."

Samaria returned to the group with me closely trailing behind. Watching those children communicate telepathically as they solved complicated formulas for space travel was truly a sight to behold. This child—these children—were truly gifted. And to think had she remained in St. Louis, she most certainly would have continued to live an unremarkable life, or suffer a worse fate at the hands of people who meant her harm. If she noticed the hopeful expression displayed across my face, she made no mention of it.

A young boy with dark curly hair continually pushed locs of thick hair from his eyes. Although the studied expression on his face was that of an adult, he was probably all of seven. He rotated the space vessel to gain a different perspective using only his mind, and then made adjustments to the circuits causing the model to shimmy into operation. The boy cheered, revealing several missing upper and lower teeth. He reminded me of my toothless little cousin who we called, "the boy genius".

"How long have you been here?" I asked.

"The length of time I have been on the planet Nigiro is not important. The question you should have asked is, why am I here?"

Had I still been in my old state of mind, I might have replied back with some ignorant smart-assed comment. Instead, I asked the question he posed to me, "Why are you here?"

He explained, "We are all children born of the Earth in a place called 'America'. We are the blessed children of the ancient ones, unlike the unfortunate children who fell victim to the ills of society including child molesters, murderers, and human traffickers. We were returned to Nigiro. To our rightful home. It is my sacred privilege to assist in helping others escape not only the prison of their minds, but also of their bodies."

I did not reply, but acknowledged his keen mastery of the situation at hand. To be so young, he was very perceptive.

"That is correct, brothah," Samaria cosigned. "Let us demonstrate to our dear sistah, who has only arrived today, how our vessel operates."

"We think it may be a few additional days before it is fully operational. Then we will submit our design to the engineers for refining before it is fully assembled. After completion, it will be taken for a test flight," he added. "If you like, we can take you on a practice run."

"That would be great!" I replied.

And as I listened to the children explain complicated principles of time, space, and multi-dimensional travel, I was inspired. Not only by their high intelligence, but their enthusiasm and determination to make this project work. It was important to them. And to all of humanity. I was no longer concerned for Samaria. She was safe and had found her home in all ways that mattered. Now I understood what happens when all limitations imposed by a sick society are taken off children and they are allowed to expand their creative minds. The possibilities are endless! I gave a quick wave as I left the children immersed in their project.

"Back so soon?" The Teacher remarked, uncharacteristically amused.

"You were right. She found her tribe and I'm not part of it, but that's okay because she's home. And more importantly, she is happy."

"There is much more to show you, Braveheart. I will introduce you to the origins of yourself and our planet. The situation on Earth becomes more dire with each passing day so we have no time to waste." He stretched his arm forward. The transporter fob came alive, vibrating in his hand. "Are you ready?"

"Yes, Teacher. I am."

"Take my arm. Our journey and your lesson shall continue…"

We moved through time and space. Crossing through dimensions as effortlessly as swimming in the calmest of seas. As Nana had indicated to me in the ancestral realm, because I have the ability to recall my previous lives, deeply embedded memories from those lives began to resurface like flashes of light.

Sailing across a vast ocean on a mighty vessel and inhaling the scent of saltwater, triggered a recollection that the first time I had traveled by water had not been in the annals of a slave ship. Next I caught whiffs of freshly cut grass as I watched a man (I instinctively knew was a close relative) tending to the summer lawn charming cottage. I recalled being a mother, marveling at the softness of my newborn baby's cheek pressed up against my breast. I saw myself as a child holding a hail stone for the first time and examining the intricate details embedded within. And in another lifetime, I was a free spirit soaring high on currents of an unseen wind, witnessing infinite numbers of sunrises and sunsets.

Those were the grand images flashing through my mind as I felt my entire body scatter into trillions of atoms. In this form, The Teacher and I then soared through the ether far into outer space. Before I knew it, we had arrived to a Nigiro space vessel orbiting high above the planet earth.

Chapter Twenty

"Teacher..." I unconsciously patted down my body, confirming that I had indeed arrived in one piece. My clothing and backpack also managed to survive the atomization. Through clenched teeth, I whispered, "...I don't feel like myself. Maybe some parts of me didn't make it through."

"What you are experiencing is normal. After a number of teleportations, you will no longer feel that strange sensation." He removed the tob from my tightly clenched fist and placed both in a holder for optimization.

"Are we on a space ship?" I asked, taking my surroundings in slowly. This was nothing like spaceships I'd seen in movies where everything was dirty, dark, and resembled a bucket of bolts pulled together from scraps in a junkyard. The vessel in which we stood was sleek, modern, and built from a stainless-steel type material. Superior technology was evident in the hidden operating panels and entrances that seemed to mysteriously appear based on The Teacher's request. I watched dozens of young men and women, all dressed in flightsuits, walking to and fro. No one spoke aloud, thus it was quiet except for soft music playing quietly in the background. Yet the overall atmosphere buzzed with purposeful activity.

With The Teacher by my side, I regained my bearings and tried to maintain my composure despite having the knowledge we were probably flying a million miles a minute. One young woman in particular caught my attention: The short neck, the broad pug nose, and gentle slanted eyes were all too familiar.

"Teacher, I know her." I pointed towards the young woman. "We were together in the camp."

"She is very busy with her duties. Be brief."

"I can't believe she finally made it out." I thought, while approaching her. *"I guess she had special abilities after all."*

Within my mind's voice, I called out to her so as to not disturb any of the others. *"CraCra?"*

She turned slowly, smiled and telepathically replied, *"Wow! It has been years since anyone called me that. Do I know you?"*

"It's me! Kenya... from the detention camp."

"Sistah? It really is you!" She stepped back for a complete view. *"We all wondered what happened after that day you walked off. We thought the guards did something awful to you when you didn't return."*

"I have been on an amazing journey..." I searched her face and noticed she seemed more mature. Wiser. Far less crazy than when we first met.

"Follow me," she said, motioning towards a closed door. *"We can go in that room. I don't want to disturb the others by speaking this crude language out loud."*

Listening to the gentle strains of music that flowed throughout the space, I understood why she didn't want to introduce the sound of the ugly English language into it. She passed her hand over the glossy surface of the wall. An entrance to a small room appeared and we walked through.

"How are you?" I asked. "You look wonderful, by the way..."

"Sistah, I am no longer the girl you remember from the cell. Ever since I can remember, I thought something was wrong with me. The girls in that camp weren't the first ones to call me crazy. Even my family thought I was mentally challenged, not only because of my appearance but also because I thought differently. I spoke about things they had no concept of so they labeled me as a slow learner."

"I am sorry that I went along with what the girls told me. I was just getting to the camp and didn't know anything different."

"What they didn't know, and what I didn't believe until much later was I actually *can* move things with my mind. I can also foresee the future. No one except the redhaired woman at that camp believed in me. She was the only one who told me I was gifted." Her eyes temporarily misted over. "I know who I am now. I first had to believe in myself before I could progress."

"That's great, sistah. I am so happy for you." I no longer wanted to refer to her as CraCra because she was never crazy to begin with.

She first stared at me, and then nodded appreciatively at my no longer referring to her as that awful nickname. "If you prefer a name outside of using my vibrational frequency, you may call me Sistah Oya."

"What's an *Oya*?"

"Oya is an Orisha warrior. To give you a fairly simple explanation, she is a force of nature who controls the wind and lightning. She can be quite fierce when needed."

"I like that. Sistah Oya, it is."

"So, Sistah Oya, what is your specific role in this spaceship?"

"This isn't just any ordinary spacecraft! This is the Exodus!"

"The Exodus?! What a cool name!" I exclaimed.

"The Nigiro warriors are making final preparations for the liberation of our people. I know our species is supposed to be loving and all, but I am more than willing to kick some butt if we have to. Especially since they're killing our brothahs and sistahs in droves."

"What's your role in this?" I asked, surprised by how different Sistah Oya's attitude was from the old CraCra.

"Well, since I have mastered using my mind's ability to move objects, I will help to cloak our arrival by using the weather as a distraction. Whip up a few thunderstorms, maybe even a tornado or two to cause a distraction. It just depends on how many ships need to be hidden."

"You can cause a tornado?" I asked in amazement.

"It's not difficult. All I have to do is grab the wind, add lots of moisture from the ocean and begin rotating the clouds. Nature takes over and does the rest. Once we no longer need the storm, I move drier air to stop it."

"That is fascinating!" I stated.

"It is, isn't it?" she remarked, giggling like the teenager I remembered.

"So how long have you been up here on the spaceship?"

"In reference to Earth time, several years have passed since the day you departed."

"What?! I thought it was only a few months."

"I am most certain your Teacher has taught you that time does not exist in the way we were taught. We are accustomed to twenty-four hours in a day... Hours are but a measurement used to track the rotation of the planet around the sun," she replied unemotionally, which was in contrast to her friendly smile.

"He did teach me about time." We had both changed in so many ways, it was difficult finding the right words. She was not rude, nor was she unfriendly. I guess the best way to explain her demeanor was, no nonsense. She had no more time for foolishness. "Guess what? I saw Samaria on Nigiro."

"Oh yeah? How is she?"

"She's great! In fact, she is working with a group of other children on a special project. I gotta say, I think Samaria is an absolute genius!"

"We are all genius on some level. Each person just needs to discover where their specific genius lies." She turned her wrist inward and tapped a wristband to check status of her next job. "I've been extremely busy learning all about mine."

I was pretty sure I didn't have a single genius bone in my body and was starting to feel like they had made a huge mistake choosing me for this. I was no closer to discovering my gift than when I started.

"Don't be so hard on yourself. If you had finished the entire process of Levels 2 and 3 like the rest of us, uncovering your gift may have been much simpler."

"Speaking of the detention camp, whatever happened to everyone after I left?" I asked.

"About a year after you left, the project was shut down... Shortly after I was freed, the government discovered the camp wasn't performing the actions of deporting illegal immigrants. But because I foresaw what was coming, I was able to warn the woman in charge and they were able to move all the children out before the military poured in. Only thing the government found when they raided the camp were empty buildings that could have been used for any purpose."

"The site was supposed to be secure. What happened?"

"That I do not know. We suspect one of the guards caught on to what was really happening; that they were actually rescuing children instead of jailing them, and probably started talking about it outside work."

"Do you know what happened to the other girls in our group?"

"The one you called KC discovered her gift and true calling was to be a nurturer. After the camp was disbanded, she joined with another camp and continued the mission as the protector of small children. She is now serving in a position to help move rescued children upwards to another level... Like what the redhaired woman did for us. She also located her son and he's currently one of the children under her protective watch."

"That's fantastic!" I recalled our conversation and how despondent she was over leaving her baby behind to be raised by her mother. "Any news on the Jamaican?"

"She returned to her community in Los Angeles after discovering she is gifted with communication. That sistah is a master of speaking the truth!" She laughed before continuing. "She partnered with a brothah who was well versed in mass communication. They are using the internet as a platform to reach out and awaken as many as possible to the lies we've been told. So far her message has reached millions."

"What about all the other children from the camp... Are they safe?"

"They are, but not the millions of others who remain on Earth. It has gotten really bad down there. A plague of epic proportions is said to be killing off so many of us now...."

"Another pandemic?!" I recalled my first conversation with the redhaired woman. "That woman told me about companies developing deadly viruses to unleash on the world. There are forces at work trying to totally annihilate the Nigiro."

"Well, they've almost done it. That virus out now is killing black and brown people all over the world by the thousands," uttered Sistah Oya.

"When are we going to catch a break? I'm sick and tired of us always being on the bottom. All my life we've been the doormat of the world," I complained.

"Indeed! Did you know that some non-melanated people thought they were immune to the pandemic? But they're finding out they were wrong cuz' it's also killing everybody. Poor dumb suckers!" A bit of the old CraCra I remembered came out as she continued, "Now why you think that is, Ms. Kenya from St. Louis?"

"I guess they also need to wake up to realize the powerful ones don't care about them either."

"People not dying from the virus are slowly starving to death." She dropped her head, not in defeat, but resignation. "Sistah, the sun has gotten so hot it has raised the temperature all over the planet. All the manmade lakes and rivers in the heartland of America have dried up. Nothing grows there anymore. Farmers can't raise livestock without water. And the ones who have access to water don't have enough workers to work in the slaughterhouses because they're the ones who are dying from the virus. It's a nationwide food shortage."

I hadn't realized how long I'd been gone. What felt like days for me were actually years in real time. "Now I understand why The Nigiro started showing up now. My people are so messed up in the heads, we don't even know what's going on right under our noses."

"Sistah, we *are* running out of time, but it's never too late to make a change." CraCra, I mean Sistah Oya had resigned herself to hold on to a small sliver of hope.

My mind drifted to my family still in St. Louis, wondering how they were faring in a world spinning out of control. Food was scarce. I prayed my mother had maintained the small garden we planted in the backyard because my Nana instilled in us the importance of growing our own food. She used to warn my dad that one day the stores would run out, and if we didn't prepare for that day, we would starve to death. Because black people are always the last people anyone ever helps.

"Before I left for the final time, one of the guards told me that those yahoos are trying to start an actual civil war."

"Really?!" I didn't know if I were more surprised or heartbroken. "A civil war like what was fought in the 1800's?"

She nodded. "They've been stockpiling guns since the 1980's when Reagan was President. That guard told me 'if they simply killed a nigger in the streets, they might get arrested and come across the wrong judge and get imprisoned. And since the prisons are filled with niggers, that is the last place they want to be'."

"He actually said that to you?"

"Sure did." She twisted her face in disgust. "That's why they had to find another way to kill African-Americans with impunity. Racists are doing the next best thing in their little diabolical brains and joining the police force. Hiding behind a badge allows them to legally murder us. That man said the new initiation for many cops is to kill their first nigger."

I thought back to my years growing up in St. Louis. "A civil war between whites and blacks is an interesting concept, but I believe a war is already underway— mentally, economically, physically, and spiritually—

- 280 -

picking up where slavery and Jim Crow left off. Unfortunately, most of us are so battle-fatigued, we refuse to recognize war was declared on us a long, long, time ago. Like Malcolm X once proclaimed,' we have been hood-winked and bamboozled'. It's much easier to deal with a beautiful lie than it is the ugly truth."

"Facts," she replied.

"You can see the future. Tell me... What will happen next?"

"The world will not end in total destruction. America will fall because the United States was built upon a foundation of horrible lies. And we all know when a foundation is weak, the walls of the house built upon it will crumble and fall. The mighty Earth will rid itself of the plague called mankind and punish those who have hurt so many others. She will unleash a fury so powerful those people will not know what hit them. No one has the power to stop it. And their feeble attempts to block out the sun are all in vain for they are like tiny ants fighting against a mighty giant."

"What will become of us? Our friends and families?"

"Many will perish. Others will survive and come out much stronger once the Earth cleanses itself. The people will come together to defeat the powerful elite and their plan to destroy civilization."

I stepped back for a better look at the young woman who now stood so confidently before me. The gold flight suit made her appear futuristic, like someone straight out of a sci-fi movie. Her natural hair was braided in cornrows with the ends hanging loosely to frame her face. Her slanted brown eyes sparkled with the newfound knowledge of self. She was right. She had changed.

"Very soon the Nigiro will descend upon the Earth. We are preparing our vessels to arrive across all lands in a massive wave of thousands. We will locate our people and help them ascend from the clutches of those who continue to do harm. Many will accompany us back to our planet. Others shall remain on Earth to prepare it for a brand-new beginning."

I explained, "The U.S. military is very powerful. They've created a space force and have poured trillions of dollars into research and development of space weaponry. I'm afraid they may know we're coming. And thanks to Hollywood propaganda with all those alien movies they've already prepared the public to shoot to kill anything extraterrestrial. Especially black ETs."

"Nigiro leaders are well aware of mankind's shenanigans. We have hue-man agents who have infiltrated the highest echelons of government to learn their pitiful plans. Our hands and minds are all over this. Do not be concerned. We are well-informed. And very well prepared to deal with whatever comes our way."

The first time I gazed through the lens of a telescope and spotted the International Space Station orbiting high above the earth, I was thrilled. Just the thought of men living in outer space blew my young mind. I had no idea seventy years of space exploration was part of a plan to totally leave this planet to colonize others. "Before I was rescued, I was very interested in NASA and space exploration. There are men whose wealth has made them very powerful; they are building spaceships with the intent of leaving Earth. These men have so much money, they are researching ways to colonize the moon, Mars, and every other planet in our galaxy."

She poo-pooed my observation. "Mankind's feeble attempts to colonize space will all be in vain. And they will be so surprised when they find out we already inhabit the very planets they intend to explore. They are spending all this money on their space program. Wait until they find out we're already inhabiting several planets in this solar system, including Mars!" She laughed out loud. "I'd love to see their reaction when they land and see melanated people!"

"Wow!"

"The Nigiro are super awesome beings! When I found out it was our ancestors who built all those mighty pyramids...! And not only on the earth, but also erected pyramids on other planets! And they used the power of the mind to do it all! Girl! When I tell you that we come from brilliant people, you'd better believe it!"

A surge of pride unexpectedly filled my gut with hope for my brothers and sisters back home.

"When will the Nigiro arrive on earth?"

"The elders began planning the liberation when the heinous crimes against humanity were first revealed. It may appear that the exodus is taking forever to happen, but it will occur when the alignment is right. You, I, and others like us are the final pieces."

"That's great that there's a plan in place. But our people have suffered for centuries at the hands of a few evil beings. I don't understand how things got so bad and why our people didn't try to stop it when it first began."

"Do you know the story about the frog and the water?"

"Yeah, I learned it from my grandfather. He was a huge fan of fried frog legs, but I could never understand why..." I turned my nose up in disgust at the very thought of eating those poor, but very slimy creatures. "Anyway, the story goes, a frog finds itself in a big pot of water. It's not concerned because the temperature of the water is comfortable. Not too cold; not too hot. Everything's fine at the beginning, but gradually, the fire is turned up. The frog squirms a little but still isn't worried. It quickly gets used to the warmer water. However, the temperature of the water slowly increases. But the frog doesn't try to escape because it continues to adjust to the heat. The poor thing doesn't understand the danger it's in until it's too late. In the end the frog boils to death."

"That describes the state of our brothers and sisters in every city in America. And on every continent of the world. The sad thing is, most of us still don't know we are the frog."

"That's messed up, but so true." I glanced at the familiar object hanging from a belt loop of her flightsuit. It was similar to the one The Teacher had given me, but hers was smaller.

She took a step back and touched the cool metal object. "Aren't these things cool?"

"Yeah," I replied, recalling that The Teacher had placed mine in what I believed to be a solar charger, upon our arrival on the ship.

"I first saw one in a world history book. Then again in a museum exhibit. I was taught this was an Egyptian artifact, but they really had no clue what it was or it's true purpose."

"In my sophomore year, I took a field trip to The St. Louis Art museum to see an exhibit of Egyptian artifacts removed from the tombs of the pharaohs. We were each assigned a particular topic to write a paper on. I chose to write about the pictograph that showed the ancients weighing the heart of a human against that of a feather on a scale. It was used to determine whether that person would proceed to the afterworld. If the heart was heavier than a feather, they could not go on."

"I saw that too! That hieroglyph showed a drawing of a man with the head of a bird." She giggled. "I cannot believe they actually got it right when they said the figure represented MA 'at, the goddess of Truth, Order and Justice."

I joined in her laughter because usually the interpretations were one hundred percent inaccurate. "The museum removed, or more likely stole, most of the ancient hieroglyphic stones from synagogues and pyramids in ancient Egypt, Kemet, Sumaria or whatever the region was called at the time. If I remember correctly, they said the device we used for teleportation is called an *ankh*."

"Whatever they named that region... Africa, Egypt, Ethiopia, or Kemet, the original humans were Nigiro." She unhooked the tob from her beltloop and placed it in my hand. "Look at those inscriptions and tell me if it speaks to you."

I held the heavy object in my hand. The symbols were familiar, yet unfamiliar at the same time.

"The truth is, it works by synching up with our thoughts. This key can tele-transport us to different dimensions and realms. The crossed shape represents all the different directions the Nigiro can travel the universe and the oval represents our infinite connection to universe. It also functions as a planetary compass. When you orient it towards the sun it activates the embedded directional codes."

"That is so cool," I replied, studying the apparatus. "Did you know technology companies are now developing microchip implants to use instead of cash? I wonder of the Nigiro ever considered using implants instead of carrying this heavy thing around?"

She shook her head from side to side. "No, no, no, sistah. It is forbidden. The Nigiro would never implant foreign objects into our bodies because it interferes with our reception—the natural antennae—which picks up vibrations from the universe."

"I just thought a microchip would be more convenient. I mean, it would eliminate the possibility of accidently leaving this thing behind." I felt the tob begin to vibrate as if it were alive.

"You notice that too, huh?" She said studying the inquisitive look on my face. "It automatically synchs with the mind of the owner. Its only vibrating because I'm nearby, but nothing can happen unless it's in my possession."

"I'll bet those chips can't do that," I stated, returning the tob to Sistah Oya.

"And that is a bet you would win. Besides, those manmade tracking devices—which is what they really are being used for—are dangerous. They are being used to manipulate the minds of ignorant people who have no idea of what they've agreed to have inserted in their bodies."

"I hadn't thought of that. But you're right! They can use microchips to keep track of us. And like what's in Revelations, that would literally be the mark of the beast!"

"Indeed!" Sistah Oya replied.

An explosion of knowledge erupted inside my brain. Back then, it never occurred to me that what those archaeologists told us could be totally wrong. Knowing now what I did not know then, those mostly European researchers had made up stories to intentionally erase darker-skinned people, our people, from the history books.

She looked at me quizzingly. "Sistah, do you know what your gift is yet?"

I shook my head. "Not yet. I'm still on my journey."

"I see..." She motioned her hand to open the door. Strains of the comforting music made its way inside. "Like everyone told me when I was still searching, your journey begins with the first step. Look where you are now. You're well on your way."

"I'll feel a whole lot better once I know what I'm supposed to be doing." I studied the face of the teen I once thought was mentally disabled. Her eyes no longer randomly shifted focus, giving her the appearance of being lost. On the contrary, she now radiated a level of self-confidence I did not possess.

"When you discover your gift, and you will very soon, be sure you relay this to parents of young children: Encourage and nurture the child's creative side. Listen to what they have to say, no matter how insignificant you think their thoughts are. Limit their use of technology because it stifles creativity. Introduce your children to all varieties of music. Encourage playing a musical instrument; piano, horns, woodwinds, drums, guitar... it doesn't matter what type, because reading music—the only true universal language—develops vital connections in the brain critical for problem solving. The children are truly the future of all humanity, but their young minds are in danger of being poisoned by toxic chemicals in vaccines and food, and by the internet and social media. They are being miseducated by a white-washed history. Young people are bombarded with images of unbridled sexuality, rampant racism, and extreme violence without consequences, on a daily basis. Then those same children watch adults brutalize each other and think this is the way things are supposed to be. Young adults, and even some children, are now committing suicide to escape the horrors of the world rather than face them alone."

"Is that what you foresee happening in the future?"

"No. This is what I see in the now." She shook her head in disgust. "For the immediate future, hopelessness and despair will become the norm. Humans will stop procreating because they no longer desire to bring children into a world such as this. America will no longer be the world's leader and the countries in Africa will be stripped of resources by the usual suspects. And on all continents, fresh water will become even more scarce, causing more suffering not only to the Nigiro, but to all planet dwellers."

I sighed wearily at the prospects of a very bleak future. Although the founders of this country and their offspring who continue to exploit others for profit and gain, would soon get what they deserved, knowing that the country my ancestors built with their blood, sweat, and tears would soon be destroyed was a bittersweet victory.

"Don't be dismayed. Whatever happens going forward, it will be Allah's Will," she responded, confidently.

"With all that you've learned about yourself and the situation of our people, it must be really hard not to be discouraged. How do you remain inspired to continue moving forward?"

"If *we* don't push forward, who else will liberate our people?"

I paused momentarily for Sistah Oya's words to sink in and allowed them to take root in my spirit. She was right! If not us, then who would come forth to stop the insanity?

I lovingly embraced my spiritual sister because I discerned we would never see one another again. Our paths had crossed for the final time as we were both embarking on dangerous endeavors with no certainty of where either of our journeys would take us.

"Be well, sistah. This is the last time I'll see you until we get together on the other side. But just know... *We* are the ones we've been waiting for. You, I, and all the other chosen ones. This is the time for *our* lights to shine, like the beautiful sons and daughters of Allah we know we are."

She exited the room using her tob. I watched her dissipate before waving my hand across the sensor to open the door. I was comforted to know The Teacher had patiently waited for me in the corridor, standing near the entrance with his arms folded behind his back as if he had nothing else in the world to do. Other Nigiro strolled by, silently greeting him with affection. My Teacher was not only well respected, but sincerely loved by his people. Our people.

"Thank you for giving me a few minutes to see my friend." I watched the girl I once knew as CraCra catch up with a group of her cohorts. Taking in the events of the last days, I was physically exhausted, yet spiritually fired up. I turned to The Teacher and asked telepathically, *"When does my official training begin?"*

"Braveheart, from the very first moment you stepped foot into the King-dome, you have been under my tutelage." He was amused because he knew the most effective method of teaching resulted from the pupil being unaware that they were being taught. *"Follow me."*

I laughed out loud because in hindsight, what he said was true. Ever since being snatched off the street, my life had been filled with nothing but life lessons.

I followed The Teacher to an elevator that rotated in a circular fashion instead of the normal directions of up or down. He selected the appropriate room in the vessel and we effortlessly rotated over to the location.

"Why aren't we using the tob instead of the elevator?" I asked.

"Traveling to the Exodus required your body to utilize an extreme amount of energy. Until your cells become more accustomed to undergoing atomization, using an elevator is a much safer method for you physically."

"I understand."

The elevator stopped and we stepped into another corridor. He motioned my attention towards a closed door that materialized upon his waving his hand over it.

"Is this where I'll be staying?"

"Yes. Now use your mind to open the door."

"How do I do that?" I asked.

"You and only you have control over your mind. Once you control your thoughts, they will no longer control you. I want you to know when you use the mind given to you by The Creator, everything is possible."

I faced the door and focused all my efforts on opening it. *Open!* I commanded. Nothing happened. *Door open!* I shouted in my mind. *Open says me!* Still nothing. In my mind, I visualized opening the door, yet it remained closed.

"This isn't working," I uttered after several failed attempts.

"It is not working because you are focusing on the wrong thought. You do not merely want the door to open, you desire to enter the room. Now focus on removing the obstacle that prevents you from doing so."

I nodded my understanding of The Teacher's instruction. *I don't want the door to open, I desire to be inside the room.* I closed my eyes tightly and visualized myself on the other side of the door, standing inside the room. In my mind's eye, the door was no longer there. And when I opened my eyes, I discovered to my delight the door was open. The obstacle had been removed using only my mind. My thoughts!

"Excellent!" The Teacher expressed his pleasure. "Now make yourself comfortable as you shall be here for several more days of instruction."

The room was sparse; furnished with a desk, chair, and a built-in nook with padding inside for a bed. I casually tossed my backpack on the floor and took a seat in the chair, luxuriating in its comfort, allowing the weariness I felt deep inside my bones to momentarily seep away. I hadn't realized how tired I was. Sleep threatened to overtake me and I was going to be its willing participant. I changed my mind about the chair, instead opting to sit on the bed.

"Everything you need is at your command. Ask for it and it shall be provided." The Teacher motioned his hand over the room.

"You're telling me that no matter what I need, I can have?! Just by thinking on it?"

"Within reason..."

"You mean like, if I wanted a million dollars, a Lamborghini, a beachfront home, or a gallon of chocolate-chip ice cream, all those items would magically appear if I just asked for them?"

"Yes, but why would you?"

"Hmmm.... I see your point. I don't need, nor do I actually want any of those things," I replied, allowing a huge yawn to escape. "I'm sorry, I didn't realize how tired I am."

"I want you to relax. Lie down. Close your eyes and tell me what you see. Let the voices inside guide you towards the truth of who you are."

I did as instructed. I closed my eyes and opened my heart to fully experience gratitude and love. Initially experiencing total darkness. Gradually the dark lessened until I was surrounded by light.

Images began to flutter by like fragments from a dream. The scene shifted as I found myself on a small rowboat drifting in a vast ocean with no land in sight. I glanced upwards to see a thick marine layer blanketing the sky. *Where am I?* I asked myself. Holding on to the side of the boat, I peered into the water. The water was crystal clear, revealing hundreds of wrecked ships settled on an ocean floor. Sharks, whales, and other large sea creatures maneuvered in, around, and through the submersed vessels. The boat slowly slipped below the surface. Believing I was now protected by the confines of a submarine, I watched schools of fish lazily swam past me, changing directions as if they were one body. A sense of calm overcame me; I felt hypnotized, wanting to let go and slip under the coolness of the water.

Pull up! I screamed to myself. *Don't fall asleep!* I resisted the urge to succumb to the tranquility of the ocean and frantically gripped the boat's oars. The rowboat sliced upwards through the water, past all the fish, and finally broke through and returned to the surface. I did not wish to remain in the ocean, so I pulled the oars back and morphed into a glider instead of the boat. I rose higher and higher, breaking through the cloud cover until the sunshine was visible once again. Next thing I knew, I was soaring high above the surface. Free in my spirit.

The next vision I found myself in a busy mall. People were shopping, running mindlessly from store to store buying everything in sight, spending money on items they neither wanted nor needed. I remained motionless watching shoppers taking escalators up to the second level to access more stores. I began walking slowly, but then stopped when I noticed the mall had begun to deteriorate right before my eyes into abandonment. Banners previously draped across the front of stores, advertising deep discounts, now haphazardly drooping to the floor. Thick layers of grime crept over surfaces.

And then right before my eyes, the storefronts gradually disappeared, leaving only the skeletal wall structures behind. But my vision did not cease there, as layers of paint right down to the concrete sheeting also disappeared. I understood what was occurring. I was literally experiencing the de-construction of the mall. Slabs of concrete blocks disappeared, one by one allowing natural light to enter. Building cranes moved in reverse, rearranging heavy pieces of roofing from the rooftop to the ground below. Finally, the building's metal frame was visible. Once all manmade materials were gone, I stood in an open field of wheat grass. Within the span of moments, I observed a shopping mall go from its hedonistic heyday, only to succumb to its certain demise.

I next found myself in an unfamiliar neighborhood standing in the middle of the street at a crossroads. It was nighttime and all was eerily quiet. I surmised there must have been a power outage because the houses were silhouetted by only the moon. I noticed not even the solar-powered street lights were illuminated. It was the type of darkness one only finds in the deepest backcountry, far away from city lights. Something was definitely wrong. There was no electricity. Anywhere. Then I heard faint voices. People, including families with small children, were out walking being guided by only the light of the moon and stars.

The last vision I recalled was the sensation of soaring high in a night sky past an infinite number of points of light. From the ground these lights would have appeared to be stars, but from my viewpoint, the 'stars' were actually individual masses of brilliant illumination. Orbs of light. Triangular patterns in every color of the rainbow emerged from the darkness zipping past me at high rates of speed. I could not say for certain if I were stationary or traveling at the same rate of speed as the objects. Then something wonderful happened. As I realized I was part of the fullness of the universe, I discerned that I was not merely a casual observer. I was actually one of the illuminated orbs.

I jolted up, reaching for the solid surface of the bed. I needed something to let me know I was safely back inside my own body.

"W-W-What just happened? What was I seeing?"

"Braveheart, you are gifted with prophetic visions which are projected to you from the Elders," he whispered. "While some visions are easily defined, others include messages you must learn to discern."

I rested my head back on the chair. I could barely keep my eyes open from the exhaustion. "Teacher, do I have any control over when or how I receive the visions? Because this time, all I did was relax like you told me."

"If you're wondering if you'll receive visions each time you close your eyes..." He smiled, "...don't worry. That is not how this works. The Elders projected those visions at this particular moment to allow you to ask me questions while you are under my tutelage."

"What am I supposed to after I receive these visions?"

"You will know what to do," he responded.

The Teacher reached down to the floor and grabbed the handle of my backpack. He held the heavy bag up with two fingers as if he were studying some kind of science project. In his large hands, the sturdy burlap fabric appeared ancient against his ultramodern clothing and the futuristic setting. He unzipped the zipper, flipped the backpack above the desk, and dumped the contents out. Dozens of dirty and worn journals spilt forth.

"What is this?" he asked, eyeing the dirtied books.

I glanced over at The Teacher. Another loud yawn escaped my mouth before I could answer. "Excuse me," I said before continuing. "Those are my journals. I've been writing down all my experiences going back to before I was abducted."

"Why do you feel the need to write down memories you will never forget?"

"Huh?" was the only response I could muster. I had no answer to a question that on the surface seemed ridiculous.

"The mind does not easily forget traumatic memories. The events from the very moment you were abducted, to teleporting unto this space vessel where you find yourself now... seeing your great-Nana on the ancestral plane... Those memories will never be forgotten. Those moments are forever seared into your memory as being incredulous. You will forget nothing that you have seen, heard, or experienced since your awakening." He took two steps towards the bed, holding up a journal. "I ask you again, why do you write down thoughts you will never forget?"

"I guess I want to have a documented record of everything I'm going through. In case I wake up one day and have unintentionally forgotten everything because it was too much to handle. I want to know I'm not crazy. I can always pick it up and re-read my journals when I begin to question my sanity."

"Are those the only reasons?" The Teacher took a step back to give me space, and then leaned over and whispered, "Search deep within."

I thought about my response before answering. I glanced at the dozens of journals haphazardly tossed across the desk, not realizing the number that were completely filled. I rose from the chair and removed the book from his outstretched hand. I flipped through the pages of notes detailing my journey, written in a prose that could not have originated with me. I took a deep breath, then exhaled. And as if a light bulb had finally been switched on, I blurted out, "I keep written journals because I need to share my experience with others. To tell anyone who will listen that we come from great people because we are the original people! The Nigiro! Children of The Most High God! I must share the stories, *ourstory*, received from the ancestors given to me in dreams and prophetic visions. I must awaken as many as possible to the truth that we have been lied to our entire lives! I must offer encouragement to continue moving forward and not give up!"

"Excellent," he whispered, returning to his normal stance. "You are much closer to knowledge of self. Very soon your gift will appear."

The fatigue began to dissipate. I needed to see my face. Consequently, a mirror materialized on the wall. As I searched my reflection, I noted nothing on the outside had changed, but everything inside had exploded. Every single cell of my body harmoniously joined together to reveal tiny details of my existence. All five of my senses— sight, hearing, smell, taste, touch—became heightened with the knowledge that so many more supernatural senses were possible. My old mind was shattered and then blown away.

He slowly backed towards the door. "Try to rest. I will return for you later."

I was hyped! More like, invigorated! There was no more time for sleep! With this latest revelation, I recognized I had finally uncovered my gift! The Creator has gifted me with a supernatural ability to see into the ancestral realm, to view multidimensional worlds, and astral travel to distant planets, as very few others are able to do. I am blessed with a supernatural spiritual gift which allows me to connect with ancestral spirits and otherworldly Elders, to write down their stories and spread the truth about the Nigiro to the world. I use my eye-magi-nation to recreate their stories from bits and pieces of information retrieved from the ether, plucked like ripened fruit from a bountiful tree of wisdom.

First and foremost, I am a beautiful child of The Creator. I am also a storyteller. An author. A writer. A scribe.

~ ~ ~

The Teacher explained the walls of the room were designed to change scenery based on the characteristics of its occupant, as it did in the king-dome. The intent was to induce a sense of relaxation. The grey walls morphed into a tropical beach scene complete with the sounds of a light breeze pushing the water gently against the shore. Lively seagulls called out to one another as they played in the surf. I went to the desk, pulling out every single drawer in search of a computer, a laptop, tablet or even pen and paper. The desk was empty, as was every other surface.

How are books written in the future? I placed my finger against my forehead and fell deeply into thought.

"I will transcribe my journals in an appropriate manner to spread the ancestors' messages to the world," I thought. Instantly, a small device the size of a computer mouse materialized. I picked it up, turned it over in my hand, and frowned. This thing had no buttons, no openings, no keys or instructions. "What am I supposed to do with a paperweight?"

Because the thing had 'magically' appeared to solve my problem, I figured it must work. I selected the very first journal which documented my abduction and plopped down in the chair and began to read aloud. The mouse came to life projecting a screen about the size of a large monitor directly in front of my face. Every single word I read was displayed grammatically correct with no misspellings or punctuation errors. And when I mispronounced a word due to minor voice inflections resulting from my St. Louis accent, the words autocorrected to show my true intent without any prompting. It was as if this thing were synched with my thoughts. This was so much more efficient than writing or typing where I would have to go back and make revisions. I was even able to add notes to previous sections when they came to mind. I only had to think about what I meant to say and the new text was automatically added.

~ ~ ~

As I recounted visions I had received from the Elders, there was one important encounter I simply could not overlook. All my other visions had come to me while asleep, through dreams. The only occasion, thus far, that spirits had attempted to make actual contact while I was awake was during that family vacation in the Dominican Republic. Those ancestors had first reached out to me while I was in that swimming pool. Later that night, their whitewashed faces appeared in my dream. And after I experienced that prophetic vision, I was then awakened from my slumber by the whispers of sorrowful voices.

From the wisdom gained by my journey, I discerned the vision of those whitewashed faces was a representation of how the African ancestors were literally 'whitewashed' from the Caribbean island's history, and their existence was subsequently hidden behind a wall of shame in Dominican Republic museums. The melanated islanders did not come about as result of only their European heritage, but the vast majority possess the DNA of enslaved indigenous Taino, and also Africans; those unfortunate souls who were enslaved in African and then transported across the ocean to work the sugar cane fields.

The colonization of the land and subsequently of the people's minds resulted in a strange system of racism implemented by means of colorism. The embracement of racism on the small island previously known as Hispaniola after it was supposedly 'discovered' by Christopher Columbus, would be shameful even by American standards. Many of the islands elders blame the former president and dictator, Rafael Trujillo, who ruled the island throughout the 1930's and 1960's, for the implementation of a caste system built upon colorism. He all but demonized darker skinned Haitians and Dominicans to the point they began to deny their ancestry. As a result, knowledge of the enslaved Africans was delegated as a minor footnote in the history of the island, if at all.

As young Dominicans flocked in droves to the shores of the United States in search for better lives, they refused to acknowledge their African—the Nigiro—heritage of those ancestors. Opting instead to proudly identify with their oppressors, the French and the Spaniards.

A minor known historical fact in the island's history was the DR was occupied by the United States military for 8 years from 1916 – 1924, which would pretty much sums it up. And a visit to the island today would reveal the continued source of racism and colorism is due to an influx of foreign developers who consistently state preferences for lighter complexioned employees over the more melanated to work their resorts. While the unmarked gravesites of Africans (Nigiro) and Taino continue to be bulldozed over to make room for larger real estate developments, I made a vow that I would tell the world of their existence. Their lives mattered then, and they should matter now.

~ ~ ~

It was fun using the advanced technology. If only my brothers could see this they would go absolutely nuts! But this was not playtime. I had dozens of journals to read out loud, adding information and details to make sure I spread the message accurately. Ultimately, upon completion of the story of the Nigiro—Ourstory—I would ensure the text would be permanently 'locked' to prevent additional edits and revisions. The book would be similar to being written in stone, but without the bulky tables.

The Teacher remained on the other side of the door, breathing a great sigh of content and relief. He wanted to be there when Braveheart received the MA 'at. Upon the realization and discovery of her gift, his job was almost done. Again. For perhaps the thousandth iteration. Only this time, he knew something was different because this child's soul possessed a greater sense of perception. Her supernatural abilities are more insightful than ever before. Maybe this time she would be successful cutting through eons of mental torture imposed on the Nigiro and finally awaken them to reclaim all that is rightfully theirs. He believed with all his heart that Sistah Kenya, using her prophetic gifts and insightful writing, would be successful in spreading the message of the Nigiro to the entire world. And when that finally happens, the Nigiro across all the lands will throw away the shackles on their minds and come into the full knowledge and truth about the greatness of who they are.

Chapter Twenty-One

(Three Years Later... Present Day)

After Carmen's daughter went missing, the family remained in St. Louis for almost a year praying Kenya would find her way back home. But when that did not happen, living in that house and seeing her empty room on a daily basis became unbearable. If she wanted to retain what was left of her marriage and family, they had to leave the city she loved. Her husband, Gerald, found a job 500 miles away in Oklahoma City and they'd been there ever since. Over three difficult years had passed, yet there wasn't a day gone by her baby wasn't in her thoughts.

The weatherman on the local evening news explained a meteor shower could be observed in the western sky shortly after sunset. This once-in-a-century occurrence was predicted to be phenomenal; on the same scale as the 2017 solar eclipse, and best viewed over the northern part of the states. It was times such as these when she really missed Kenya. Her child was the one who used to drag her outside to witness any heavenly event. Sunsets, a full moon, meteor showers, and occasionally she woke her up early to watch the sun rise. Kenya used to spend countless hours staring up at the sky, always trying to get her mom to join in. Today, she would trade anything to have that time back with her daughter. So, in solidarity with her daughter, Carmen took up watching the sky, praying there still was a sky for her to see... wherever she was. There was always something about the infinite sky that terrified her, but totally intrigued her daughter.

Even for an early spring day in Oklahoma, twenty-degrees was cold by any one's standard. But she wasn't going to allow the cold air to keep her from watching—just in case Kenya was doing the same. Carmen bundled up in a blanket and headed to the backyard. Her husband Gerald usually joined her, but he was out of town at yet another training conference. During these quiet days alone, she took advantage of the time to sketch a few pictures which was a great diversion from her career as an accountant.

Carmen's oldest son Malcolm, his wife Drena and their baby lived in the next town over, twenty miles away. He too had planned on observing the celestial show. Kenya's obsession with astronomy had rubbed off on her oldest child because he was just as excited about the meteor shower as she would have been.

She prepared a cup of hot tea and went outside, all the while gazing westward towards the horizon. It was eerily quiet for a Thursday night; the familiar sounds were absent. No cars on the neighborhood streets, or airplanes flying overhead, nor did she hear any barking dogs, chirping crickets, or the croaking of the occasional bullfrog. It was as if she were inside a sound vacuum.

She tried calling Malcolm, but it would not go through. After several more attempts, she gave up and texted instead, reminding him 'The show is about to begin'.

The last remnants of the sunset remained, lighting up the vast darkness of the sky with pastel shades of pale pink and burnt orange. Placing her Adirondack chair squarely in the middle of the yard to avoid having the rooftops of surrounding homes block the view of the sky, she waited patiently for the first 'shooting star'. The phone beeped with an incoming message. It was from Malcolm. He too was outside taking in the magic of the evening sky through a telescope to enhance viewing.

The sun slipped completely below the horizon giving space for the moonless sky to grow dark. Gradually, tiny specks of light twinkled in the atmosphere one-by-one. She spotted several shooting stars streaking across the sky in a race to determine which one would burn out first. The meteor shower went on for several minutes; her excitement of witnessing the celestial phenomena intensified with each quick flash of light. As far as she could tell, none of her neighbors were outside watching.

She tried calling Malcolm again, but the call didn't go through, nor did the subsequent texts sent to Stokely or Gerald. Each text was rejected and returned as unsent. Carmen shook it off and surmised that the meteor shower must be interfering with the cell phone signals.

Her now tepid tea did nothing to take the chill from her bones. It needed refreshing. As she stood to go inside, the appearance of an unexpected burst of bright colors in the western sky stopped her dead in her tracks. A loud rumbling noise—like that of an out of control freight train—rode in on the reigns of a developing storm with clouds violently blossoming in colors of pink, orange, and grey similar to what she witnessed in the earlier sunset. She had no idea what she was now seeing or hearing, only that it felt ominous.

She pulled the blanket taut around her body, now shivering more from fright than low temperature. She surveyed the neighbor's homes for other witnesses to this unusual weather event, imaging the earsplitting sound would bring them out from their houses. And yet, she remained alone in her private viewing party.

"What in the world is going on?" Carmen asked into the cold night.

Seemingly from out of nowhere, an orb of light so bright it could have come directly from the sun itself, appeared in the yard less than three feet from where she stood. The terror she expected to experience upon seeing her first UFO, changed to fascination. She briefly shielded her eyes before realizing the light did not hurt her vision. The cup of tea fell from her hand to the ground. No longer afraid, she reached out to touch it. When her fingers connected with the orb, a feeling of warmth reverberated in her midsection and spread throughout her body. Love. Happiness. A sense of overwhelming joy. Whatever this thing was, it was not here to impart harm.

Chapter Twenty-Two

"Carmen, wake up, my love," Gerald whispered softly.

She moaned softly as she turned to her side. Every muscle in her entire body ached.

"C'mon sleepyhead," her husband said again, gently caressing her back. "It's time to wake up."

"I am so tired," she yawned, stretching out every muscle the way a lioness would upon waking.

"Baby, it's almost noon. Why are you still sleeping?"

She grumbled, rubbing her eyes in an attempt to wipe away the sleepiness. When she pulled the covers back and gingerly sat up, she was quite surprised to be wearing the same clothes as the day before.

"You must have really been out to get in bed without undressing," he joked. "I hope you at least took off your shoes."

Carmen stared blankly at her husband. Her reaction was how one would feel if they woke up in a house that didn't belong to them. Something was off. Her mind was all jumbled up tightly in a ball of confusion, trying desperately to return back to a perverted reality she instinctively knew she could no longer believe in. Her mouth was horribly dry. She reached for the bottle of water on the nightstand and sucked it down in one gulp.

"Thirsty?"

"Yeah, I guess I was..."

"I was worried last night when none of my calls went through, to you or the boys."

"I think something was going on with the cell phone service during the meteor shower. I wasn't able to receive or make any calls either." Carmen pushed her body to an upright position. And stuffed a pillow behind her back to keep from slipping.

"I'm sorry I wasn't here to see it with you, love." He knew his wife's recent interest in astronomy was mostly a way to stay connected to their missing child. So, if that was her way keeping hope for their daughter alive, who was he to say anything.

"Don't worry about it, Gerald. Most people couldn't care less about meteors. Unless it's a trending, it's a non-event. These days, unless a story has a million followers or just as many 'likes', it barely gets mentioned in the news."

He remained skeptical that his wife was fine, though he did admit she didn't look like anything was wrong. At least, physically.

"... and a meteor show definitely wasn't going to be the event that changed their minds. Hardly any of the neighbors comes outside anymore."

"Well, we do live in a police state since that latest pandemic. Besides, I don't blame the neighbors for not leaving their homes unless it's an emergency. After all, who wants to get randomly stopped and frisked every time they go out for a run or to the grocery store?"

Carmen remained still, watching him continue to rant.

"Nobody wants that germy thermometer rolled across their forehead before entering a place of business," Gerald vented. "And if I didn't have to travel for work, I wouldn't have bothered leaving the house at all, either."

"Well, the country is taking this pandemic much more seriously since all those people died during the last one," Carmen remarked. "Anyway, I'm glad you're home."

"Me too," he responded before further explaining, "actually, since it was raining in Dallas on Thursday night, I couldn't have seen that meteor shower even had I tried."

"I thought you weren't coming home until Sunday," Carmen replied, gradually feeling her senses return to a semblance of normalcy.

"When I couldn't get through to anyone yesterday, I was worried, especially in this climate. So I switched my flight to leave first thing this morning."

"Wait. What?" She leaned her head back against the headboard trying to get a grip on things.

Gerald took a break from unpacking his suitcase and sat on the edge of the bed. He rested his hand on her forearm. "My love, today is Saturday. High noon, to be more specific."

"No, it's not. Today is Friday which means..." she retorted. "Oh shoot! I'm late for work!"

"Sweetheart, calm down and listen. Today is Saturday and tomorrow is Sunday. I caught an early flight this morning."

"That's not possible... It is Friday."

"Trust me. I was still in the conference for most of Friday."

"The meteor shower was last night. So yesterday was Thursday," she insisted, mentally counting off the days. Trying to make sense of the feeling like something had changed.

"I'll prove it to you. Where is your cell phone?"

"If it's not on the nightstand, I probably left it on the kitchen counter."

"Stay here," he said. "I'll be right back."

Carmen threw back the covers and was relieved to discover she had enough sense to remove her shoes before getting to bed. Pieces of a strange dream involving Kenya's whereabouts, tugged at her heart. She pulled her foot close for a better look and plucked blades of grass from between her toes. "How in the world did my feet get this dirty?"

Gerald returned to the bedroom quite alarmed. "I checked the kitchen counter where you usually charge your phone. It wasn't there. But what I did notice was all the lights in the house are still on. And the back door was wide open!"

"Wait a minute..." she furrowed her brow trying hard to remember the events of Thursday night. "You're telling me I went to bed without locking the door? I also left it open?"

"Well, I did a complete walk-thru to make sure we're good. There are no signs of a break-in."

"That's so unlike me."

"I checked the backyard and found your phone on the chair in the middle of the yard." He rested the back of his hand against his wife's forehead. "You don't feel warm."

"That's good. The last thing I want is to bring the 'temperature police' to our front door." Carmen shook her head as a shiver went down her spine. "I don't want to end up like our neighbor, that woman at the end of the block. She was sent to a quarantine camp because she had developed a fever. Once that monitor tripped and didn't shut off, the paramedics were at her house picking her up within minutes. I heard it's been months since her family last heard anything about her condition."

"Well, like I said. You don't have a fever so that damn monitor won't be notifying any officials," he replied with relief in his voice. As a result of the pandemic that killed millions of Americans several years earlier, the government mandated temperature monitors be placed in every single home. If any member of the household's temperature spiked above normal and remained high for several hours, they could expect a prompt visit from a special team of paramedics they now referred to as 'temperature police'.

"I always make certain the house is secure before setting the alarm. Check the locks and set the alarm. This is what I do every night. It's routine. Especially when you're away." She took the phone from her husband and checked the contents. There were several missed calls from Gerald, Malcolm, and her supervisor. "I don't understand... my phone says today is Saturday."

He nodded.

"This can't be right."

"That's what I've been trying to tell you."

"Something isn't right." Carmen massaged her temples with the intent of increasing the blood flow to her brain to stimulate her memory bank. She felt like she did after having a significant dream that immediately dissipated upon awakening. The sensation would not go away. There was something extremely important that she was supposed to do!

Gerald became extremely concerned about his wife's state of mind. They were approaching another anniversary of their daughter's disappearance. Even though they had moved out of state, they still maintained contact with the detective assigned to the case. Unfortunately, the police had no clues and for all intent and purposes, had given up searching for Kenya less than a year into her abduction. Because the case remained unsolved, it was turned over to the FBI's division of missing and exploited children. Common knowledge was once a child's picture was posted to the FBI site, chances of ever seeing them again was one in a million.

"I'm trying to remember what happened yesterday. How could I have lost a day?" Carmen swung the covers away and plopped her dirty feet on the bedside rug. She was slightly disgusted that she'd actually gone to bed this way.

"When I checked the backyard, I saw your cup beside the chair. But that's not the weirdest thing," he replied, standing there wild-eyed with his arms crossed.

"Last thing I remember was having a cup of tea while I was waiting for the meteor shower." She scrolled through the missed calls and texts. "What else did you see?"

"Well..." he cleared his throat, struggling to contain the emotions tightening his throat when he uttered, "There's very large circular patch of bright green grass that sprouted up around the chair. But the grass in the rest of the backyard is still brown."

"That's impossible!" she scoffed, peering through the blinds of the bedroom window shaking her head. "The grass in the front yard is dormant. Just like it should be in the backyard!"

"I'm just telling you what I saw with my own two eyes." The expression on Gerald's face changed to display the uncertainty of his mind. "Carmen, what is going on?"

"I really don't know."

"Get dressed. I'm taking you to the emergency room."

"I don't need to go to the ER with all those sickly people. I feel fine. A bit tired, but I'm okay."

"No, you're not! You slept through an entire day and a half!"

"I need to take a shower. Clear my thoughts and try to figure out what has happened to me."

"That's fine. Go on take your shower. But I'm watching you closely and I want you to tell me if you start feeling strange."

Carmen plodded to the bathroom leaving dirty footprints in her wake. She turned her head, coolly tossing her response across her right shoulder, "I promise. Now go call your sons. You haven't spoken to either one in a week."

She turned on the shower creating billowing puffs of steam to remove the chill from the bathroom before getting undressed. Gerald closed the bathroom door to allow her privacy.

Meanwhile, he selected Malcolm's profile and then waited for him to answer. When he finally picked up, he quietly spoke into the phone, "Hi son..."

Carmen stood in the shower allowing streams of hot pulsating water to caress her aching muscles. A tender patch of skin between her shoulder blades caught her attention. She stepped out of the shower, staring at her own reflection. And using a hand-held mirror, she maneuvered her body just so by using the larger vanity mirror to get a better angle of her back. She spotted two bright red markings, each about the size of a quarter, between her shoulder blades on either side of her spine.

"What in the world? How did that get there?" She questioned her reflection. "I must be losing my mind."

She returned to the shower and desperately hoped the ordinary task of cleansing her body would rid her of the otherworldly images that kept appearing inside her thoughts. More than anything, she desired a return to some semblance of normalcy.

Gerald entered the bathroom with an even more worried expression on his face. He handed his wife a fluffy blue bath towel when she stepped from the shower stall.

"What's wrong?" she asked, as soon as she noticed the usual cheerful disposition her husband maintained after he spoke with either son was not present. "Are the boys okay?"

"You're not going to believe this." He stood with a dumbfound expression covering not only his face, but it somehow managed to trickle down into his entire body. With one foot pointed in one direction, the other was pointed in another; his hands didn't know what to do with themselves... He rearranged items on the vanity that hadn't been moved in months.

"What's wrong?!" She wrapped the towel around her damp body, barely containing the urge to shake the news out of him. "Will you just tell me?!"

He blurted out, "Stokely is fine. He's in the dorm studying for finals and hasn't spoken to his brother in days. But Malcolm told me he also slept through Friday."

"That's impossible! Drena and the baby wouldn't have let him sleep like that."

"They weren't home. She and the baby spent the last few nights at her mother's. Apparently, she fell ill and asked Drena to drive down. She took the baby with her because Malcolm had to work. His supervisor called her when he didn't show up for work on Friday, but she also couldn't get any calls through to him. She wasn't concerned because we all know he is notorious for forgetting to charge his phone. He says when he woke up this morning, he realized it was Saturday."

"How is he?"

"The same as you. He says he is extremely fatigued."

"Did you tell him about me?"

"Yes, and he's on his way over."

"Good. I need to place my eyes on my child even if it's just for a few minutes," Carmen hugged herself tightly to quell her nerves. Since martial law had been implemented, maintaining a grip on sanity had become more precious than developing immunity to the latest virus threatening to overtake humanity.

Carmen rested her head on Gerald's shoulder. His mere presence made her feel safe. Whatever happened during that missing day, or was about to occur now as a result, she knew beyond a shadow of doubt she could not get through this without her husband. He was her rock.

Chapter Twenty-Three

"What do you remember about that night, Mom?" Malcolm asked, adding a shot of Bailey's Irish Cream into his first cup of coffee for the day. He too was shaken up more than he cared to admit.

"I remember going outside. It was very cold and extremely quiet. You remember how much your sister used to love watching those shooting stars..." Her old friend sorrow visited so frequently now, she no longer waited for an invitation before coming in. "I remember getting excited because I had just spotted several shooting stars and wanted to share the experience with someone."

"Well Mom, those were actually meteorites. Nothing more than tiny pieces of ice that have broken off comets falling through the earth's atmosphere at very high rates of speeds. But I do understand your fascination."

"It doesn't sound as fascinating when you explain it like that." Carmen sipped the hot liquid, eager for the caffeine to take hold. "I was probably the only one in this entire neighborhood standing in that cold, staring up at the sky."

"Don't get me wrong. I was looking forward to this particular meteor storm because it only comes around every 100 years. I guess most people don't pay attention anymore because there's so much manmade space materials orbiting the earth that from our perspective, it's very difficult to tell the difference between a celestial object and a satellite."

Malcolm absentmindedly stared at a picture of his family frozen in time less than a month before his sister went missing. He and his brother referred to that time in their lives as B.K. and A.K. B.K. was the period of life before Kenya went missing and it was for the most part, pretty wonderful. But after Kenya was gone, none of their lives were ever the same. As time continued to move forward, both brothers accepted they were forever destined to reside in the shadow of their missing sister's disappearance.

"Okay, enough of all this chit-chat about star-gazing. I want to know how in the hell both of you managed to miss an entire day!" Gerald exclaimed.

"Well," Malcolm explained, "I was setting up the telescope on the upstairs balcony to get an unobstructed view of the sky when I received a text from Mom. I stopped when I heard this noise, as loud as thunder, approaching. I remember thinking that was strange because the sky was clear. The source of this sound came closer and was even louder. Whatever it was felt like it had stopped over the house."

"Did you happen to see a bright light?" Carmen blurted out, as glimpses of memories similar to a forgotten dream tried to resurface.

"A light?" Malcolm paused. His memory was fuzzy as well.

"Yes. As bright as the sun. But it wasn't the sun. It was something else entirely."

Gerald guffawed loudly. "I think watching all those movies about aliens and outer space has finally caught up with the both of you."

"I did not imagine this, honey. I also remember hearing something that sounded as loud as a freight train." She shut her eyes tightly, coaxing those recessed memories to surface. "I remember seeing a bright glowing light appear out of nowhere."

"Mom, now that you mention it, I did see something! I was looking through the telescope lens when I saw a light so bright, it almost blinded me."

"Carmen, my love, please don't be angry, but..."

"Whatever you're about to say, I know it's gonna piss me off. But go for it," she replied to her husband.

"Is it possible you might have hit your head on something? A mild concussion would explain the hallucination and your oversleeping."

"If I was so clumsy that I fell down without knowing it or I somehow managed to knock myself out, don't you think I would have noticed it by now? Where is the lump on my head, Gerald?!" Carmen neglected to mention the markings on her back. Her husband was already having a hard-enough time taking this in, so she'd spare him that detail until later. "And what about Malcolm. Did he hit his head too?"

Malcolm's story suddenly took a turn when he blurted out, "Mom! Dad! I think I know what it was!"

Carmen's eyes grew twice their normal size in anticipation of what her son had to say. She hoped his memory would trigger hers.

"It was a helicopter. It was probably doing some low-level maneuvers which took it directly over my house. The bright lights must have come from it."

"Well, that certainly explains it. You both saw and heard a helicopter. Mystery solved," Gerald tossed his hands up in relief.

"Don't you think I know what a helicopter sounds like! We grew up in St. Louis hearing those damn things flying in the hood every weekend! And ever since we moved to Oklahoma City, I can't begin to count the number of times the police have flown over this house with searchlights passing over our yard. That was no damn helicopter! Besides, why in the world would a helicopter hover over *our* backyard?"

Malcolm remained silent as he scrolled through texts on his phone. The troubled expression on his face said he wanted to agree with his mother, yet to do so out loud would mean he too had experienced the unexplained. If there was one thing his short career as astronomer taught him, it was if science couldn't prove a theory using facts, then there was probably no solution to be found.

"I don't know what that thing was, but it was definitely not a helicopter," she mumbled, pouring herself another cup of coffee, beginning to second guess herself.

Gerald focused all his attention on his wife and son, now thoroughly concerned about their mental states. He shoved his hands inside his pockets trying to come to terms with what was destined to remain a mystery. "As much as I want to believe there is a simple explanation for the lights and the noise, it still doesn't explain the matter of you both losing a day."

Malcolm said, "I may not remember everything clearly at this very moment, but I will in time. My memory is still fuzzy... Like I'm remembering bits and pieces of a dream."

"Since you both refuse to go to the ER, I just want you to relax. Until we figure out what we're dealing with, I don't want either of you under any more stress." His eyes went to the required temperature monitor installed at the front door by the local government. Intermittent flashes of red lights confirmed it was still operational.

"Mom, Dad... I'd better get going. Drena and the baby are on their way back home. Its family day since our lottery number came up at the movie theater. She's excited about finally getting to see that latest 4D movie about AI humanoids taking over the planet after the apocalypse."

Carmen shook her head and replied, "I don't know why anybody would want to see a movie about the end of the world. Especially since the last two pandemics seem to be moving us towards it."

Gerald wrapped his arm around Malcolm's shoulder and escorted him to the door. "I understand you don't want to miss out on that. No telling when the next chance your names will come up again for a movie."

She hugged her oldest son tightly, not caring if her husband scolded her for spoiling him. She had already lost one child and would do everything in her power to not lose the other two. Even if it meant hovering over grown men as if they were still children. "If you think of anything else, call me."

Malcolm was halfway down the driveway before he turned on his heel and returned to the door. Gerald was on the phone placing an order for food delivery.

"Did you forget something?" his mother asked.

"Mom, until we find out for sure what happened to you... To us... it's probably best to not mention this to anyone else. Not even to Grandma or your sisters, especially when you're talking over the phone."

"Why would you say that? Is there something I should know?"

He pushed both hands deep into the pockets of his jeans, sighed wearily, and looked around to make sure no one was eavesdropping on their conversation. "I didn't want to say anything with Dad in the room, but after he called and told me what happened with you, I called Drena. She just texted that there were lots of reports of strange occurrences during Thursday's meteor shower. It's all over the internet. Also, people are posting stories about getting strange visits from government officials asking questions."

"What? Come back inside and tell me what's going on."

"I don't know what's going on, yet. That's the problem because I don't remember anything. Drena's going to try to find out more when she goes back to work on Monday. For now, promise me you won't tell anyone else about this."

"That's a good idea. I won't talk to anyone except you and your father." Her eyes went to the picture on the mantel of their family.

"I don't mind you and Dad talking about this, but remember he's got that government job. He might be obligated to notify the authorities about any change in the family's medical history. And you know him, he'll be all over the internet, researching different types of ailments and using combinations of words on the 'hot list' trying to find out what happened to us. We want to avoid a visit from the police, not invite one."

"I promise I'll keep this just between us three for now. And I'll remind him to stay off the internet."

Carmen glanced past Malcolm's shoulder. Her neighbor on the opposite side of the street, appeared to be blatantly monitoring their every move. Had he always watched them so closely, she now wondered. Suddenly, the neighborhood populated primarily by whites, who for the most part left her family alone over the years, had recently began to look at her family suspiciously. To keep up appearances, she raised her hand and released a friendly neighborly wave to let all her pale-face neighbors know her family wasn't going to be starting no mess.

A civil war, between whites and every other so-called black and brown minority, had been averted by a fragile truce. A peaceful coexistence was being held together by school children's colorful shoestrings and bubble gum being distributed to adults with messages of hope and peace. Unfortunately, as a truce required grownups agreeing not to fight, the peace threatened to fall apart at least once a day.

The younger generation's response to break the cycle of ignorance, stupidity and unbridled racism, rampant in their parents' generation, was a refusal to participate in their call for a civil war. They recognized previous generations had bought into the lies sold to them by the government and had succumbed to the media's fanning the racial flames touting white supremacy. To mitigate police brutality and the effects of institutionalized racism, the youth of all colors got together and began selling shoestrings and bubble gum to bring awareness to the injustices black and brown people faced on a daily basis. The children understood that if nothing was done, it would be they who ultimately inherited the fallout from a tragic war. So far, the peace held. But one small spark would ignite the racially charged powder keg, fueled by hatred and ready to erupt at a moment's notice in a violent war that would destroy half of this country.

"I love you, Mom."

"I love you right back, Malcolm. To infinity...."

"...and beyond!" he finished their private greeting, established when he first learned how to talk.

Gerald returned to the door. "What was that about?"

"I'm not sure. But Malcolm said to not talk about this with anyone else."

"I agree because I don't want nobody besides me thinking that my wife and son have both lost their ever-loving minds."

She playfully punched his arm. "That is not funny."

~ ~ ~

Later that evening, Gerald and Carmen sat at their dining room table enjoying homemade pizza, sharing a bottle of Pinot Grigio, and listening to a new jazz artist they'd recently discovered. As they continued their conversation from earlier, going over different scenarios about the origins of the mysterious light, a forceful knock at the front door interrupted their meal.

"Who do you think that is?" she asked. "We're not expecting anyone."

"Probably Malcolm. Maybe he forgot something."

"You know good and well that is not our son. Malcolm and Stokely know not to knock on our front door like the police." She filled her plate with a second helping of stir-fried vegetables while her husband went to answer the door. The voice of an unfamiliar man who seemed intent on filling their small foyer with loud multi-syllable words sprinkled with a large helping of governmental doublespeak, did most of the talking. When several minutes passed, she went to the foyer to find out what was keeping him.

Gerald explained, "These men are from the National Security Agency. They say they're conducting random visits in the subdivision. They want to know if we've had any visits from anyone claiming to be from their agency?"

"Are you Gerald and Carmen Williams?" the younger one asked her directly.

Carmen glanced at Gerald skeptically.

"Um, can I see some ID?" Gerald asked.

The older man with the large vocabulary pulled out his official government credentials, motioning for his partner to do the same. He handed both ID cards to Gerald who passed them on to Carmen.

"Yes, I'm Mrs. Williams and this is my husband," she replied alarmed, returning the IDs to the younger man. "What do you want with us? And how do you know my name if you're conducting random visits?"

"It's our job, Ma'am." The older man stated before adding, "...as we were saying, have either of you had any strange visitors or experienced any unusual activity within the past few days?"

Gerald was much more careful with his response. Sharing too little information was almost as bad as sharing too much. He decided to state the basic truth, something the men could verify and leave it at that. "I was out of town last week, until this morning. On official government business..."

She searched her husband's eyes for clues on how to respond to these two Caucasian men who were dressed in business casual clothing.

The couple was married for almost twenty-five years and possessed that special connection most couples developed after many years of being together. Both understood that these men already knew Gerald had been out of town. The person they were actually interested in was her.

"With the exception of you two droids, I haven't had any unusual visitors," she replied, annoyed at the interruption. And the interrogation.

"Are you sure, ma'am? We've had recent reports of possible criminal activity in this neighborhood." The NSA man removed his hat and tried to force his face into a smile. If you've ever seen a smile that exists only at the corners of the mouth; never reaching the cheeks, the nose, the eyes, the ears or even the eyebrows, you know it's not a genuine smile. A smile using only lips is just a controlled muscle spasm. This man's attempt at portraying warmth only made him appear more demonic. He glanced past the couple into their living room, trying to catch a glimpse of how they lived. "Please. Understand. We intend to keep you and your neighbors safe."

"Nope. Nothing unusual happening here." She looked past the men to her neighbor who had taken up surveillance of their home from a chair positioned inside his garage. A small cooler filled with bottles of a local craft beer rested at his feet. "Have you checked with the neighbor across the street. He seems to be spending a lot of time outside lately. Maybe he's seen something."

The younger man turned towards her neighbor and informally waved as if they knew one another. The fine hairs on the back of her neck stood up when she observed the greeting of familiarity that was often shared only between close friends.

"If you guys don't have any other questions, my wife and I would like to return to our dinner. It's getting cold."

"Certainly." The shorter man gave Carmen his card. "If you see or hear anything, please do not hesitate to call."

She held the card gingerly with two fingers, fighting the urge to flick it towards his face. "Hold on... I've got one question. How many other families in this neighborhood have you spoken with today?"

"Just yours." The younger man blurted out, but then quickly realized his mistake when the older man glanced his way. "Uh... But our intent is to visit several more of your neighbors before the evening is over."

"Well, if we see anything unusual, you'll be the first person we call," Gerald stated, shuffling them outside and then promptly locking the door.

"What was that about?" she asked.

Gerald dropped his head in anger and disgust. "I knew we shouldn't have moved in this damn neighborhood with all these cracka's. Should have stayed in the city where we don't stand out like a couple of peppercorns in the sugar bowl. Criminal activity, my ass! We are the only melanated people on this damn block and only a few in the entire subdivision. And I'll bet money that we're the only family in this entire neighborhood who received a personal visit from the goddamn NSA!"

"My love, I don't think those men's visit had anything to do with us being the only black family in this neighborhood. This is about what happened the other night. They're searching for something. Or someone."

"What makes you say that?"

"It's what Malcolm told me earlier about this possibly being something more. Apparently, he and I aren't the only ones with an unexplained loss of time. The internet is filled with accounts similar to ours. Yet, he advised me to not talk about our experience with anyone. And we shouldn't be searching for similar stories on the internet. Then we get a visit from the NSA?!" She leaned her head against her husband's chest and sank into his embrace. "Baby, I don't know about you, but I am really scared."

~ ~ ~

Later that night, after they made certain their home was secure, Carmen laid in bed unable to sleep. This night, an actual helicopter patrolled overhead as if they were searching the neighborhood for someone. Though insomnia kept her awake, she was comforted by her husband's soft snoring; his peaceful sleep reassured her that everything was going to be all right. She cleared her mind of this evening's events to focus on Thursday night. Like pieces of a puzzle, the memories started to slowly click into place. The last thing she remembered was how she felt when she touched the orb of light. The love emanating from that orb was unlike any she had ever experienced coming from anyone, including her husband, parents, and children. With the resurfacing of this particular memory, her subconscious mind gradually began to release the hidden mysteries from that night. Tears of gratitude sprang from her eyes.

"Gerald, wake up," she whispered, gently shaking his arm.

"Huh, what's wrong? You okay?" he responded, still half asleep.

He heard her rifling around, trying to locate the box of tissues she kept on the nightstand. She pulled one free and gently blew her nose.

"Honey, what's wrong?"

"My memory is still fuzzy, but I think I'm starting to remember!"

His eyes snapped wide open. Upon hearing her declaration, he reached over to the lamp and turned on the switch.

"Tell me now! Before you forget!"

Carmen took a deep breath as if she were summoning all her strength to continue. She sat upright in the bed and began to speak, "The sun had just set and I was getting ready for the meteor shower. I settled in my chair and watched the sky grow dark. It was so cold, even with the blanket wrapped around me. Seemed like all the stars in the galaxy were visible that night. It was absolutely beautiful. My cup of tea had gone warm so I was just about to go in the kitchen for more hot water. Then the strangest thing happened."

"Should I be writing this down?" he asked.

"The sky grew lighter like it does right before sunrise when dawn gives way to morning." She continued as if he hadn't uttered a word. "But that's impossible, right? The sun had already set and the stars were out. I'm absolutely positive about that. I waited there for a minute, wondering if the sunset I saw earlier was some kind of optical illusion. Thought I'd somehow lost track of time... I tried calling Malcolm and Stokely. Tried calling you too."

"I think I should be writing this down." Gerald pulled a pad of paper from his nightstand and began to scribble at a feverish pace. His eyes went to their cell phones resting on the dresser, both plugged in to chargers. He briefly considered using the phone's recording function, but ever since learning that smart phones were being used for surveillance and tracking, he changed his mind. As much as did not want to disrupt his wife's flow, he couldn't risk having this conversation surveilled. So, he jumped from bed and tossed both phones in the contraband lead-lined box, what we used to block all random incoming or outgoing transmissions.

She continued on as if in a trance, "I heard a really weird noise. Sounded like rolling thunder. But I didn't see anything in the sky. Not an approaching storm. No airplanes. No helicopters. Nothing was flying in the air. It wasn't a car or a truck. I just heard that really loud noise coming from above. In fact, it was so loud I thought the neighbors would come running out from their houses just to see what it was. But no one did."

Gerald listened as if his life depended upon every word coming from his wife's mouth.

She exhaled and continued. "I jumped from my chair because I was scared and I was going to run into the house. But that's when I saw this brilliant ball of light. Floating. Or levitating. It was right above the house. I swear to goodness that thing lit up the entire yard to daytime. It was so bright! I knew for sure *this* would bring people outside. I shielded my eyes because I thought I would go blind if I stared at it for too long. But the light didn't hurt my eyes."

"What was it?"

She took a long sip of water before responding, "I think... I believe... No, I know it must have been a UFO!"

"A UFO? As in extraterrestrial?"

"It couldn't have been anything else." Carmen's eyes glazed over and she continually shook her head from side to side. "I know this all sounds unbelievable, but I am not crazy. I know what I saw."

He stopped writing and placed the pencil to the side. He gripped his wife's shoulders and asked, "Sweetheart, were you smoking your medicinal weed that night?"

She exhaled deeply and took a breath to calm herself before responding, "No, I was not smoking or drinking. I know what I saw! It was a UFO!"

"I'm sorry, love. I had to ask." He didn't want to chance messing up her story with more interruptions, but so many questions swirled inside his head.

"Standing there underneath that glowing thing, I was too scared to move. I tried to scream but nothing came out. Then I watched it descend down to my level."

"You must have been terrified!"

"I was, but then I wasn't." Her eyes misted over again. "It was so close that I reached my hand out to touch it. When I did, I began to cry. This light generated warmth and infinite love."

"My God..."

"My body... The yard... the house... The physical world as I know it was no longer important. After I placed my hand on the orb, I was no longer cold. And I didn't hear a sound. I became part of this 'thing'. Connected to it. I felt the love of my Nana, my grandfather, and all my long-lost relatives who passed away decades ago. I didn't see any of their faces, nor did I hear actual voices, but I knew they were there. I felt their presence! All at once!"

Gerald stared at his wife as if she had truly lost touch with reality, but his skepticism did not stop her from continuing.

"Now this is really going to blow your mind."

"You mean, what's left of my mind..." he laughed nervously, but continued to take notes.

"I became engulfed by the orb. I ascended up to a light-filled space with no walls. But it wasn't a blinding light like you'd imagine. I looked outside and could see the ground below and the stars in the sky above. Before I realized it, I was high above the earth looking down."

"Above earth?" he asked incredulously.

"I told you this was going to blow your mind. Once I saw the horizon of the Earth, I was terrified and thought I made a huge mistake not trying to escape! That light orb began projecting images of relatives from my childhood days. I thought it was a trick! That this thing had stolen my memories and was using them to create an illusion."

Gerald dropped his pen and stared at his wife, dumbfounded. He waited for her to break out in laughter like she usually did when she pulled his leg or told a bad joke. But she did not laugh. In fact, he had never seen her as serious about anything as she was now.

She jumped from the bed and shouted, "Oh my God! I just remembered! You're really not going to believe this..."

"What?!," he replied, figuring he had nothing more to lose.

"I haven't told you the best part!" Her eyes grew wide as her most exciting memory returned. "I saw Kenya that night!"

"What?!"

"Our daughter Kenya was inside the light orb!"

"You mean you hallucinated her image... from your memory?"

"No! It was not a figment of my imagination. I actually saw and spoke with our daughter!"

"Sweetheart... That isn't possible for you to have seen Kenya." Gerald set the pad and pen aside as his concern for his wife's mental health overshadowed the need to transcribe her account. He rested his hand against her forehead, once again checking for signs of a temperature.

She pushed his hand away. "I am not sick! And I did not hallucinate any of this. I spoke to Kenya. Our baby girl is alive!"

"Get dressed. We're going to the hospital..." he said, tossing the bed covers aside.

"Wait!" she shouted, now appearing more like a lunatic than his wife. "My God! I remember everything now!"

He whispered in a calm soothing voice trying to not upset her more, "Take it easy, my love. Let's just have the doctors check you out." Although he had never questioned the sanity of his wife before, this time was different. Something happened to her that night to push her over the edge.

"I said I'm not sick and I for sure am not going to any hospital so they can admit me to some loony bin." Carmen grabbed her robe and headed to their shared office.

"Where are you going?" he asked, trailing after her.

"I have something to show you!" She riffled through her desk drawer and pulled out a shiny object.

"What is that?"

"Kenya gave it to me." She examined the small black object in her hands. It was the size of a wireless mouse, but heavier as it was made from a metallic material. "But I have no idea what it is."

"Let me see that," Gerald said, reaching for the thing. He turned it over in his hands, running his fingers over the smooth surface trying to find a button to activate it. "You say Kenya gave this to you?"

"Yeah. I remember. She told me it was very important that I share this with every person we know. She said she also tried to contact Malcolm but his mind wasn't ready yet to accept the truth." Her eyes danced around gleefully as her memories returned. "She said I am the only one who can get this out. And I have to do it now before it's too late!"

"What is that supposed to mean? What truth?" He gingerly placed the object on the desk, wondering from where or whom his wife had gotten this thing. He considered it may be contaminated with the virus. She wasn't feverish, but had obviously lost her mind.

"I believe that *thing* holds secrets Kenya wants us to share." Carmen sank into her chair to encourage the conversation with her daughter that felt more like a dream to fully return.

"You want me to believe that our missing child showed up in a ball of light and gave you something she wants shared with the world?"

"Not with the entire world... Just God's children." She held the object in her hands, giggling like a little girl.

Gerald crossed his arms across his chest and stared at his wife who proclaimed at the time Kenya went missing that there was no God. He had no idea what was happening, but he instinctively knew it was not good.

"She showed me how to operate it. Said there was nothing to it," she said, absentmindedly tapping her forehead with her fingers. A gesture her grandmother did when she was trying to remember something important. "Now what did she tell me?"

"Stay here. I'm calling Malcolm."

Carmen studied the object. She held it to her chest and closed her eyes tightly. In the darkness, she whispered, "Kenya... Honey, if you're still around I need your help. What am I supposed to do with this thing? How do I make it work?"

Gerald retreated to the bedroom and plucked his cell phone from the lead-lined box. Despite the late hour, he called his son because he and his mother shared a special bond. If anyone could talk some sense into her, he could.

He whispered into the phone, "Sorry to wake you son, but I'm worried about your mom. Can you come over?"

"Kenya, honey, tell me what to do.... I can't remember how to work this thing," she whispered into the quiet space of the office.

As Gerald became more worried about his wife, he also understood there was something more going on beyond his comprehension because his faith in God never wavered. And if this was a spiritual and divine intervention, who was he to question it. He picked up the pad and jotted down the conversation that took place in the office. "Great son, I'll see you soon."

Carmen took several deep breaths to calm her rapidly beating heart. She felt the adrenaline rushing through her body and realized if she wanted to receive a message, she needed to be still. And listen...

"Hey, I just talked to Malcolm. He's on his way..." Gerald said, but stopped dead in his tracks when he entered his office and saw his wife holding the object in her hand. Like how a movie projector emits streams of light into images on a screen, this thing projected hundreds of pages of text on the wall, using the space as a six-foot monitor. "What in the world is that?!"

Carmen sat back in the chair feeling two types of relief. One is that she hadn't lost her mind. Two, and most importantly, her child was still alive. With a huge smile on her face, she moved slowly to avoid any sudden movements or making any loud noise that might cause the thing to shut off. To her husband she whispered quietly, "Look honey, I got it to work."

Chapter Twenty-Four

Time as I once knew it ceased to matter. But relative
to Earth, three and a half years had elapsed since I first
went missing. Within my new awareness, the *All* was
happening at once. Past, present, and future became
intermingled to the point I could slip in and out of
differing points in my lifetime at will. I absolutely loved
everything about Nigiro! There was so much to learn and
experience in my newly reclaimed home that each day
proved to be another adventure.

What I was learning under the tutelage of The Teacher
revealed mind altering truths I never thought were
possible. He made me believe in myself to understand
how my gifts and abilities would provide a unique means
to awaken others. I knew without reservation that if every
Nigiro embraced their higher spiritual selves, the world
will become a much more loving space in the universe.

After my encounter with Sistah Oya on the spacecraft
Exodus, The Teacher and I took many tours of Nigiro.
Though we could have teleported to anywhere on the
planet or used the power of our minds to travel, he
preferred that I have a physical experience. We piled in a
solar-powered vehicle that transported us from one
location to another. When we ascended to a height just
below the clouds, I filled my lungs with fresh clean air,
heavily scented by tropical vegetation and rich fertile soil.
In all directions, I spied different species of strange-
looking animals that grazed freely on plants and trees
growing wild in the spectacular savannahs.

We trailed along a coastline where the ocean was vast
and the blueish-green water, amazingly clear. An
occasional cloudburst of rain gently crossed over the
lands, providing fresh water for all manners of life to
subsist on. The Teacher proudly pointed out small villas,
large family compounds, and the towns that sprang up

around them, all the while providing interesting historical background on the families who lived in them.

But what was most fascinating to me were the cities! The sun and wind powered the many modes of transportation. Magnificent and efficiently built structures that used only naturally occurring materials in their construction, housed homes and businesses. We buzzed over several large fountains scattered through the city, spouting lively streams of clean water into the air before returning the liquid to its base. Vibrantly dressed Nigiro in all shades of black and brown, buzzed about freely as they shopped or just mingled. With music blasting over loudspeakers and sounds of joyful laughter reverberating through the crowd, from the air it looked like a party scene. But in actuality, the activity was surprising orderly. Point is, these cities rivaled any futuristic models that were created in movie studios using their popular technique of CGI.

On one particular outing, The Teacher and I visited a beautiful family compound, comprised of many mansions scattered across a hilltop. One is particular caught my eye as it was situated to overlook the ocean. Graceful palm trees and various other fruit-bearing trees seemed to grow wild in the rich soil. When I expressed my familiarity with that specific mansion, he was not surprised. The compound belonged to my family and had been our ancestral home since the very beginning. I recall my surprise that the structures had not degraded with time like so many ruins scattered throughout the Earth. My ancestral home remained as sturdy as the day it was first constructed.

During that particular visit, I encountered many ancestors whose features I recognized from staring at my own face in the mirror. The wide faces and high cheekbones I had once incorrectly attributed to a 'Native American' ancestry were evident on most everyone I encountered. My slanted eyes were considered 'exotic' within the black community; but the women's large, soulful slanted eyes were the norm here. The women were beautiful, tall, and elegant. The men standing even taller, were all handsome and proud. All were poised, yet humble and very mild-mannered. The clothing they wore reminded me of colorful African garb.

Everything was familiar because the love my ancestors had for me had transcended through the annals of time and space. I learned it was they who invited me home as often as possible, trying to awaken my soul to the truth of where I belonged. When asking how old they were, I was shocked to discover these blue-black beings had been in existence for so long, they felt no need to count the years.

One Elder, a distinguished looking gentleman who walked with his arms crossed behind his back in the manner similar to that of The Teacher, addressed me telepathically, *"I have observed you on numerous occasions wandering along the beach, kicking up sand and playing in the surf like a youngster. Though you always appeared to be happy, I noted you also wore the heavy cape of a lost child. I knew it was only a matter of time before you discovered your true origins because of your more frequent visits. Welcome home, my sistah."*

"Thank you, my brothah."

Looking down at my cinnamon colored skin, now considered to be utterly pale in comparison to theirs, I questioned the Teacher on how I had ascended from these beautiful Nigiro.

He explained, "The Nigiro you see are the Elders, gods and goddesses, who have resided on this planet since the beginning of time. They are not carbon-based human beings in the sense you have become familiar with. Because they are the original soulful beings created by The Creator, they possess supernatural powers and may 'live' thousands of earthly years. The ethereal Nigiro are more spiritual than physical manifestations. As a rite of passage, when the Nigiro children reached a certain level of maturity, they descend from Nigiro to experience an earthly existence.

"Why?" I asked.

"The children must learn the meaning of love. The best way to do that is to place them in challenging situations so they understand what it truly means to experience love in the face of adversity."

The expression on my face told The Teacher I still did not understand, for he continued to explain.

"All the original Nigiro children, when they first come into the world, are like the purest forms of carbon—diamonds in the rough. The elders know the only way to make a diamond is to put the carbon under intense pressure. But once the diamond is revealed, it becomes one of the hardest substances in the world. Nothing can destroy it. That is what they wish for the souls of their children."

"But aren't the children already created to be pure love?"

"Yes, in spirit form they know only love. However, in the physical form—which the children are, the flesh is weak. Thus, they must travel to another realm where their souls await their appointed time to go into the earth in the form of a hue-man infant. Although all Nigiro children must undergo the rite of passage, they were also given eternal life of which no man can ever take."

I replied, "The points of light that my Nana showed me in the astral plane... Those are Nigiro souls?"

"Yes. They may not return to Nigiro until that lesson is mastered."

"Teacher, I have another question..."

He patiently waited for me to process the information. Comprehending the idea of simultaneously existing within two worlds—physical and spiritual—was a difficult concept to understand.

"How many children were created in the beginning?" I asked, keeping in mind that at my level of awareness, I hadn't even scratched the surface of truly understanding the number of Nigiro who lived on this humongous planet.

"The Creator's original Nigiro? The exact number is unknown because no one has ever attempted to count the Elders. But for the Nigiro children who populate the universe, they are as infinite in number as the grains of sand."

"I see..." I thought about the girls I met in the camp. "There was one girl I arrived with, Samaria, she was much more advanced than the others. Why was that?"

"She is a firstborn child of the Nigiro Elders. Samaria and the brothahs and sistahs you met, are all very unique. Though they are biological children of the hue-man, they may return to Nigiro to live out the remainder of their hue-man lives before their souls will transition to begin the lengthy process of becoming an Elders. But you are not like them. You are origin." He laughed wholeheartedly for the first time since our initial introduction.

"So, there are different levels of Nigiro? Origin, firstborn, hue-man, and so forth?"

"You must remember, in addition to Nigiro and the Earth, our people inhabit planets throughout the entire universe."

The story of my existence came together like placing the last piece in a puzzle. I thought about what he said and allowed my soul to breathe, which was extremely easy to do in this familial land. I stared at the Elders patiently watching on, inhaling the sweet fragrance permeating the prana, and wafting over the ocean. I closed my eyes to see inside myself for the fullness of the truth.

With a newfound confidence I answered, "I know who I am, Teacher! Not only have I ascended from generations of Nigiro while on earth, but I am one of the original children sent there for the rite of passage you spoke of. I have gone through this cycle thousands of times learning the lesson and also trying to remember the truth of who I am! And I have finally awakened! I am home!"

"Well done." He gazed down to find a plethora of flowers blossoming at my feet. "My time with you has been well spent. Now it is time for you to use your gift to help others awaken."

The sunshine felt wonderful beaming down on my face. With my chin held just a little higher and my heart feeling much lighter, I nodded my acknowledgement of the task ahead of me. I understood that not until all our people were released from the bondage of mind and body, would we all truly be free. If one of the children remained enslaved, we all remained enslaved.

An Elder woman materialized by my side. She was so beautiful my eyes began to tear. Shiny long ropes of tightly coiled silver hair were piled atop her head; she smelled like fresh coconuts. Her slanted eyes—black like the night with no signs of white—were larger than what I was accustomed to, but totally normal for them. Multiple gold bracelets that tinkled when she moved, decorated each arm. She placed a necklace made of fragrant flowers over my head, and then bent down slightly to gather me in a loving embrace.

She whispered in an unknown language that I somehow immediately recognized, "This is the land provided to us by The Great I Am. Our Father. The Almighty Creator. On it are many mansions. We have awaited your return. Welcome home, my sistah."

Her throaty voice was ethereal, whispering melodious words that caressed my ears as if her vocal cords were strings of a well-tuned instrument. I wanted to hear more from the goddess of whom I resembled.

"This is your ancestral home," she gestured to a hilltop mansion located near the water. "Sistah, you have gone through infinite rebirths whilst on your journey. We are so very grateful for your return to the land."

My eyes followed the sistah's gaze to my family's mansion. The one I had visited so many times before, not realizing it existed anywhere other than in my dreams. I was so happy to finally have returned to my place of origin that I began to levitate. This totally shocked me! The Teacher gently put his hand on my shoulder to lower me back to the ground.

She continued, "The Creator established twelve disciplines, or what we call 'tribes', for the children to follow. Each tribe has its own unique purpose: Agriculturists, Teachers, Healers, Engineers, Scientists, Philosophers, Architects, Mathematicians, Carpenters, Technologists, and Great Warriors. Our discipline is Art. We are a tribe of Artists; Musicians. Painters. Sculptors. Poets, Writers and Storytellers. Our creations are how we demonstrate Love. Artistry is our contribution to the universe."

"Sistah, I have found my tribe. I am and always was destined to be a scribe. It is in my blood. It always has been and it always will be." The revelation continued to sink in, forcing me to review the ordered steps from previous lives which ultimately lead me home.

"Yes, my sistah. With each new physical experience, you pursued creative arts in one fashion or the other. The Elders have watched as you experimented playing a musical instrument, photography, painting, dancing, and even acting in school plays, but you never truly understood your true calling. It was important for you to experiment with different facets of fine arts in order to understand what is and what is not for you.

You have finally discovered you are a writer, a gifted storyteller with the ability to share the ourstory of the Nigiro with the world. During this life, not only have learned to love, but you are loved tremendously. This is why you are allowed to return home to be with the tribe. Your place in Nigiro is assured."

I truly had ascended from the original people who were endowed with supernatural talents, gifts, and abilities. I must tell you; all chains were broken from my mind when I finally came into the realization and knowledge of who I Am.

~ ~ ~

Now that I had received the truth, my mission became even more urgent to complete. There was no sense in waiting any longer to deliver my very important message. So, with the blessings of the Elders, The Teacher and I headed back to the Earth for my final mission.

"Teacher, it's been several years since I was back there. How will I locate my family?" I asked, now expertly maneuvering the light vessel away from the Nigiro mothership, which was the size of a small city. "I'm not sure what to tell my family when I finally do see them again, especially my mom. I don't want to break her mind."

"Locating your family is fairly simple..." he replied, keeping watch to make sure the departure from the airlock went smoothly. He'd seen too many pupils in their eagerness to get going, misjudge the tiny space connecting the light orb and the behemoth vessel when making their first trip back to earth. "...search the universe for your familial vibration. Just think of them. Your mother, your father, your brothers... feel the love they have for you and the orb will direct you to where they are."

I did as I was instructed and flooded my mind with memories from my childhood. I sifted through the collective consciousness to locate my father's unique way of laughing when he heard a funny joke. I remembered how my mother used to quietly sing her favorite songs as she cooked our meals. I thought about the hibiscus bush that grew wild in the backyard and how my mother always brought a small bouquet of gorgeous red and pink blooms inside during the summer. I searched the universe for vibratory signals from both brothers' longing to see me again. Recalling how proud I was watching Malcolm struggle playing a tune on his guitar, and how

Stokely scarfed down everything in sight to bulk up for his football games.

"Found them!" I told The Teacher.

"Well done!"

The orb's sensors let me 'feel' everyone except Stokely who remained in St. Louis. The rest of the family had relocated to Oklahoma City. I didn't know exactly why they would want to move to Oklahoma, but I suspected it had to do with my father. His family had settled in Tulsa shortly after slavery ended. And with each and every visit, my old aunts and uncles brought stories with them about the rich history of the area and how successful black families lived before the Tulsa Massacre of 1921, when devilish white men destroyed the entire community. For over a hundred years, my dad's father had been fighting with the U.S. government to regain title to land that was stolen from the family. So far, the state had only rewarded the descendants with the runaround; intent on bogging them down in a mountain of bureaucratic red tape meant only to discourage.

Our tiny light vessel broke free from the mothership. As I used the stars to navigate towards the Earth, I gazed back through the transparent walls of the orb. The Nigiro were making final preparations for their mission and thousands upon thousands of spacecraft, similar to the one I had just detached from, had gathered together in formation. Had I not been privy to the overall plan of the Nigiro, I would be scared out of my mind. All those menacing looking motherships positioned at the edge of the universe, waiting for the moment to descend upon the planet, might be misconstrued as taking an attack posture instead of the real purpose: the rescue mission.

In the meantime, as the plan for the mass liberation was in final preparation, I and others like me were taking advantage of the lull in activity to contact our loved ones with a final warning of what was about to take place. To tell them not to be frightened. That all would be well in the end.

I imagined most earthlings would be scared witless when they spotted massive extraterrestrial spacecraft hovering above their cities. The size alone was frightening; not to mention the defense mechanisms each vessel was equipped with for protection, ensured their invincibility. The arrival would probably resemble a scene from the movie, *Independence Day*, when all the people exiting their homes, staring up at the sky in wonderment. Ultimately, the question centered on my mind was, *would we fight against and destroy aliens who resembled us?* The answer would be learned soon enough.

We soared in and out of wormholes to arrive at the destination of Earth. I stared at the 'blue marble' as it came into view, noting it looked nothing like the artists renderings I'd always seen in the science books. In stealth mode, I maneuvered around way too many satellites and hundreds of pieces of obsolete space junk. We passed over the continent of Africa. It was much larger in land mass than I originally thought, but on the other hand, the states were so much smaller than what I had been led to believe.

"Teacher, what about the spirits trapped on earth. Will we rescue them as well?"

He looked at me as a father would gaze upon his child. With absolute love and affection. I suppose in some ways, that is what our relationship had evolved into during our time together. The feeling was mutual.

"Yes, all Nigiro will be rescued. And the spirits which have remained in-between, will be released to complete the transition."

"I see," I replied with relief. "Well, we'd better get going. No telling how long it's going to take for me to ease back into my family's lives and convince them I am who I say I am."

"You are doing very well controlling the orb. Much better than I expected."

"Thank you. I thought it was going to be much more difficult learning how to pilot the spacecraft, but considering how advanced the technology is, it really doesn't take much effort to fly." I cycled through several screens to confirm the coordinates of my parent's new home.

"Which family member will you make contact with first?" asked the Teacher.

"I considered my brother Stokely, but I think he will accept my story much quicker than the others because of his age. I won't need much time with him so he'll be last. My older brother moved to Oklahoma to be near my parents. He has a job and a family which means he's more embedded in the system. I don't know how persuadable he will be."

"That leaves the most challenging ones... your parents," he replied, studying the stars. "How will you make contact?"

"Not sure yet. I know I don't just want to show up at the door one day. It has to be planned to allow me to reach my mother first. She was always more receptive to embracing the unknown than my dad."

"As you wish," he replied. "Your mother, it shall be."

"What are you doing?" I asked, trusting in The Teacher, though expressing concern for my mother's safety.

"I am manipulating events so as to provide you with an opportunity to interact with your mother on a one-to-one basis."

"You can do that?!"

The Teacher did not reply. He simply smiled and began rearranging the screens until the order he intended was reached. "You recall that present time is pliable. It is a fairly simple matter to restructure events to best meet our needs."

"What do you suggest?"

"Because you were an avid star-gazer, your mother will have wanted to participate in this celestial event as a means to remain close to you. Within the next few days, the earth is projected to be in the path of a massive meteor shower with millions of space particles entering its atmosphere."

"That's perfect. I used to love watching those events!"

"Exactly... I will position your mother in a time and place where she is alone. Then you will be able to make contact with no interruption."

"We should wait until dusk. Hopefully no one else will be around to see me arrive."

"No one will see you."

I had no reason to doubt The Teacher. I understood the depth of his ancient supernatural abilities would never be known to me. If he told me I had nothing to worry about, that proclamation might as well have been etched in stone.

"We are here."

In about the time it took for us to finish our conversation, the house in which my parents had moved, to ease the loss of losing me, came into view. It was a modest home on large acreage and far enough away from the city to avoid light pollution interfering with the sky. The view from above revealed hundreds of homes in the large subdivision were covered by rooftops resembling miniature pyramids. In the center of the neighborhood was a clubhouse, a place for the residents to gather for special occasions. The layout reminded me of the villages we'd flown over in Nigiro. I wondered if my mother had subconsciously selected this subdivision because deep in her psyche, it reminded her of an ancient past. My parent's backyard was unobstructed from trees and perfect for stargazing. In one corner was a small plot filled with the remnants of old plants. Seeing this brought a smile to my face because my mom had continued her gardening. I positioned the orb high above the house and patiently waited for the sun to set.

Chapter Twenty-Five

When the first glimpse of my mother came into view, my heart lurched inside my chest. Her hair was closely cropped with more strands of gray than black springing forth. The lively eyes that used to greet me first thing in the morning with a smile, now appeared tired and listless. Only a few years had passed, yet she had aged considerably. The enthusiasm she used to have for life must have disappeared the same day as I. The Teacher gripped my arm cautiously.

"Give her a moment to get situated," he advised. "We have time."

Fighting back the urge to descend quickly, exit the safety of the light, and go wrap my arms around my mom, I remained in the orb, watching her drag a heavy chair from underneath the pergola and into the yard. It must have been a chilly night, as she was wrapped under a blanket. I gasped in surprise and delight. It was the old ratty blanket I used to keep at the foot of my bed... the one my Nana gave me with the sun, moon, and stars printed all over. She went inside the house and came back out with a cup of hot liquid, probably tea, clutched in her hands for warmth. I watched her attempt to use her phone, becoming frustrated, courtesy of The Teacher's interference, when no calls or texts would go through. Finally, after what felt like an eternity, she sank down in the chair to watch the sunset.

"Now?" I asked.

He nodded.

I began my descent slowly causing her to look upwards in confusion.

"Can she see us?" I asked, my eyes scanning the surrounding houses for any neighbors who might appear.

"She can see the light, but no one else can. And with our descent, she also hears the displacement of air which causes a tremendous roar."

I watched my mom push herself out of the chair to her feet. She stood motionless, clutching the blanket tightly around her body, staring at the bright light. I took a deep breath, afraid of how she'd react to my unexpected arrival and futuristic appearance. Even I was surprised by my "otherworldly" look the first time I saw a reflection of myself dressed in the extravagant gold flightsuit and boots. As a side note, the reason it sparkled had to do more with energy conductivity than appearance.

"Go to your mother. I shall wait here." He then added, "Remember, while you are outside the orb, your presence is no longer shrouded by the cloaking system. Your signature can be picked up so do not linger."

I gathered my thoughts and projected myself downwards in a ray of light until I was mere inches from my mother's face. The cup she held in her hand dropped to the ground. I remained shrouded in the light, protected from the various forms of disease and poisons dispersed in the surrounding air unbeknownst to any of them. When she reached out to touch the light, I projected the love I had gathered from all the ancestors, into her. Tried to touch the depths of her soul so she would not be afraid.

"Kenya?" she asked, cautiously. "Is that you?"

"Hi Mom," I replied with tears streaming down my face.

"Oh my God!" she exclaimed, stumbling backwards, clutching her chest.

I became frightened because the last thing I wanted was for my mother to have a heart attack. I reached for her hand and engulfed her into the light, cleansing away all traces of a toxic environment that would cause harm to me. And eradicated those within her.

"It's okay," I reassured her upon seeing the terror registered on her face.

"You can't be my child!" she shouted, with eyes widened by fright. "Who are you?!"

"It's me, Mom. I am your daughter... Kenya," I said, no longer recognizing that name in connection to myself.

"You look like my child, but you don't sound like her." She took a step backwards for a full view and then reached out to touch my face. Her fingers searched their way over my eyes, my nose, my mouth. She gripped my shoulders tightly before wrapping her arms around me, in an embrace that relayed all the hurt and anguish she'd suffered over the years.

"Baby, is it really you?" she whispered, streaming down happy tears.

"Yes, its me." I replied, receiving an incoming telepathic message from The Teacher.

"Where have you been? Are you alright?" Her eyes trailed over every inch of visible skin.

"Mom, I have so much to tell you, but we can't stay here."

"I'm scared," she stated outright as she stared into my eyes. Still full of skepticism, she murmured, "How do I know it's really you?"

"Trust me, I am your child. And there is nothing to be afraid of. I've been on a very long journey that has changed me in many ways, but none that are bad." I pulled back from her embrace and asked, "Will you come with me?"

Every fiber of her being screamed 'no!', but something deeper inside told her otherwise. "Yes, baby. I'll go with you."

I clutched her arms and we both ascended upward into the orb. The Teacher awaited my return, showing no surprise to see that I was not alone.

"W-w-who is that?" my mother asked, slowly backing away from us both.

I had to admit The Teacher was an imposing figure. I reminded myself that my mother had not undergone my intense journey of self-discovery, so she had every right to be frightened. She knew no more about the world than she did the day I left. Other than it had become more heartless when the police gave up on searching for her child in less than four months. Her authentic mind was virtually destroyed from living under a system of total oppression. So the very consideration of a ten-foot tall blue-black alien accompanying her long-lost daughter home had to be unsettling.

"Mom, this is The Teacher. He has come to help us."

"Help us to do what?" she replied, feeling less afraid.

"He wants to help black people get from under this system of lies and oppression. He rescued me."

"Is… is he… is he some kind of an… a-a-alien?" she stuttered.

"Not in the way you think."

"Where did he come from?" she asked studying his choice of clothing, his beautiful black unblemished skin, and the refined manner in which he carried himself.

"The Teacher is from Nigiro."

"Did you say Negro?" she asked, appearing to be offended by the term.

"No, mom. *Nee-JHEE-row*," I replied.

"I never heard of any city with that name. What state is that in?" she asked.

"It is a very long way from here."

"Is that where you were all this time?"

"Yes, that is one of the places I've been on my journey," I replied pulling her closer and offered a comforting thought to ease her mind.

"Oh…" she responded, still unsure of what she was experiencing as her thoughts now rested on her grandmother, my Nana.

"Mom, you're wearing my blanket! The one I used to keep on my bed for those cold mornings when daddy didn't want to turn up the heat. If I said I was cold, he'd tell me to put more clothes on." I laughed.

She glanced down at the blanket still wrapped tightly around her shoulders and smiled. "Your daddy was always concerned about the heating bill."

"That's right. But daddy didn't know Malcolm and Stokely used to turn up the temperature after he went to work. They'd always blame it on me when he found out."

"...Wait, you ARE my daughter!" she shouted. "Oooh, I'm going to get those two!" With that revelation revealed, she laughed and visibly relaxed enough to take in her surroundings. "Kenya, where are we?"

"This is an orb. A small space vessel used for short trips from the mothership," I explained.

She nodded, taking it all in, but remained wary of the alien operating the orb using technology she'd only seen in science fiction movies.

"Braveheart, we must go now." The Teacher had just picked up signals that someone was trying to track them.

"Who is 'Braveheart'?" she asked, keeping an eye on the strange being. He was certainly different! She'd never met anyone that tall or that dark skinned. And his eyes were very odd as there were no white showing. Though her daughter trusted him, she had no reason to. She then studied Kenya who hadn't aged in appearance, but seemed to have definitely matured into a different version of herself. Her heart went out to her child, wondering what horrors she had experienced in those three years of disappearance.

"That's what he calls me, on account of me never being afraid to try new things," I replied, nodding towards The Teacher. *"We may go now."*

"Where are we going?" she asked, bracing herself for the ascension.

"Mom, I need to make contact with Malcolm. And Stokely, if we have time."

"Wait until I tell your daddy! He is not going to believe any of this!" she whispered shaking her head.

I strapped my mother securely in a seat and then made the floorspace below her feet transparent, which allowed an unobstructed view of the ascent.

"Whoa! We sure are up high!" she exclaimed, tightly clutching the armrests. She was now more excited than afraid as we zipped over the familiar neighborhoods she'd driven by on a daily basis.

"This is nothing." I took over the controls and easily navigated to Malcolm's apartment building. "Wait 'til we get so high you can see the curvature of the earth."

Within minutes, my mother and I spotted Malcolm at the same time. He was alone on the balcony setting up his telescope. I hovered the orb over his building and began making preparations to descend in the light stream, just as I did with my mom. The bright light drew his attention directly in our direction.

"There he is!" shouted my mother, pointing wildly. "We were supposed to be watching the meteor shower tonight, but I couldn't get through to make sure he was ready." As an afterthought she added, "Of all the celestial events we had to choose from over the past few years, we picked tonight to dedicate this one to you. In your memory..."

"That's so sweet of you both..."

Before I realized what was happening, The Teacher overrode my controls, stopped the descent, and shut down the light stream.

"What's wrong?" I asked, my sight on my big brother. He was so close, yet still so far.

"There," The Teacher said, pointing in the distance. "We have company."

"It's a helicopter. They must have tracked us when we were at my mother's house."

He quickly guided the orb up and away from the apartment building. In the blink of an eye, we were once again in the stratosphere, soaring at an altitude I guessed was over 37,000 feet due to the passenger airplane in the distance.

"Wait! You're not going to stop by to visit your brother?" shouted my mother, pressed back in her seat by the unexpected acceleration.

"As much as I want to see Malcolm and Stokely... We can't, Mom," I replied sadly. "I don't want to chance the possibility of attracting unnecessary attention. I'll just have to contact them both another way."

"Well then... What now?" asked my mother.

I looked to The Teacher for guidance.

"Braveheart," he addressed me directly. "I will briefly leave you with your mother. Allow you the space to properly fill her in on your absence. This will be good for you both," he responded. The Teacher raised the tob and did what he does.

"Um... okay..." replied my mother dumbfounded, watching The Teacher dematerialize from our view.

"Mom, I have so much to tell you. But you have to promise to keep an open mind." I searched my mother's expression for any sign of cracks in her mind. The fragile borders of her universe had expanded with knowledge that no one would believe had she told them. And if she did, she would surely be carted off to the psychiatric ward. I had to know that she knew she was all right.

She pinched her forearm to make sure she wasn't dreaming. With wild eyes, she gazed upon every surface inside the light orb, staring through a section of transparent wall at celestial bodies that stretched to infinity. She reached for my hand. Strong fingers traced over a healed scar on my wrist, one I'd gotten after a bad fall on my bike when I was just seven. The action was to convince my mother that I was indeed solid.

This wasn't how I intended this visit to go. There was so much to share and so little time. Unfortunately, the experience of flying through outer space with a daughter who mysteriously turned up in a ball of light that descended from the sky, would overshadow anything I had to say from this point forward. I considered my mother's well-being before I said anything more. All those times when I got angry with her, the many times I wished I could get as far away as possible from St. Louis and my family, became awash with regret. How I missed this woman and all she'd done for me. She turned to face me. The love coming from her eyes was so endearing, my soul shifted to freely receive her affection.

With tears in her eyes, she whispered, "Am I dead?"

"No, mom. You are very much alive. And so am I. And so is The Teacher."

"But he just disappeared. A ten-foot-tall black alien went poof! Right in front of my eyes. He was here. And then he wasn't."

I knelt down to my mother to wrap her in a loving embrace. I would not break her brain. I'd go easy. "You are very much alive. This is not a dream. You and I are in a space vessel built by our ancestors."

"Kenya Mali Zambia Williams! What in the world are you talking about?!" That snapped her back to her reality. "You know good and well that is not true!"

"Listen, Mom. We are not who they've been telling us we are. We came from greatness!" I struggled to find the right words to express how I felt without being disrespectful. "They lied to you, your parents, their parents, and all the other ancestors who came before them to keep us from learning the truth of who we are."

"They? Who in the world is 'they'?"

"*They* are our government. *They* are our schools and our churches. *They* is every institution that told us— black people, African-Americans, indigenous natives— that we are less than. This inferiority complex was drilled in our minds from the very moment we had our first thought. Everything you've been taught is a lie!"

She frowned. "You know, you sound just like your uncle. He thinks everything is a conspiracy against blacks to keep us down."

"He's not crazy, Mom. Uncle Ricky was right in all he used to say." I placed the metallic object that resembled a mouse in her hand. "We are so much more than anyone has ever told us. We are the original people, blessed by The Almighty God. We are the Nigiro. God's children, which makes us gods and goddesses. Our people were meant to thrive on this earthly plane."

"You know your great-Nana would call you out if she heard you speaking like that. Only one God in this world and it ain't us." She looked at me as if I was the one who had lost my mind.

"Nana is watching over me. She is helping me along my journey." I closed my eyes briefly and inhaled. "Matter-of-fact, she is with us now."

My mother pursed her lips tightly together as she had no way of disproving that great-Nana was with us. After all, when she passed, my mother was the one who told me that Nana was in Heaven watching over me.

"What is this?" she asked turning the object over in her hands.

"It is my story. Ourstory. I want you to read it, publish it, and then share it with the world. You will discover why I was taken and what is happening with all those children who have gone missing. You will realize why our government has done everything within their power to keep us oppressed."

She opened her mouth to speak but thought better of it. For many years, she and her husband often complained about the unfair treatment of blacks and how it had intensified under the new president. In some ways, black and brown people were worse off now than they were in the 1960's. At least then, they were united.

"I finally know why the world hates us..."

"Kenya, there is nothing anybody can do to change the world from the way it is now. Look what happens to those who have tried."

"I know, Mom. But that doesn't mean we just give up and die. Our lives are too important." *Plus, this will never end if we fail to get it right*, is what I wanted to add, but she'd learn about that later.

"How do I turn this thing on?"

"Hold it near your heart and think about me. Pray for the truth to be revealed."

"That's it?"

"Pretty simple, huh? All you have to do is think about what you want and it will be given. In this case, you want the truth about what happened to me to come out. I've written it down for you. Everything."

"What about your daddy? Or your brothers..." She tucked the mouse into her bra. "Is it alright to tell them?"

"Yes, Mom. You can tell them. After you read my story, you will understand how important it is to share it with as many as you can. Our people need to know that they are more than what they've been told."

"Okay, Kenya. If that's what you want, I'll do it." She gripped my hand. "I will share your story with the world. And if I have to, I will travel to the four corners of the earth to make sure not one more mother suffers over the loss of her child by the hands of others."

"Are we ready?" came The Teacher's voice before he reappeared.

"Yes, we can go now," I replied.

"Hold up a minute! Were you there all the while listening to us? Spying on me and my daughter's private conversation?!" Mother asked in indignant anger.

He did not address my mother directly. As he considered my level of comprehension was that of a newborn, comparatively speaking, he considered hers was that of a zygote. Alternatively, he began making preparation for a descent.

"Mom, its fine. The Teacher knows everything about everything. He has no need to spy on us." I glanced admiringly in his direction.

"If you say so...."

"One more thing." I rested my hand on my mom's shoulder. "Because we're in the upper atmosphere, you're breathing a different mixture of oxygen and hydrogen. Your body isn't used to this so you're going to be really tired for the next few days. And it'll probably take just as long for you to remember details of my visit."

"I'm going to have amnesia?"

"Only temporarily." I glanced outside and saw we were approaching her house. "Try to get some sleep. Your memory will return a little at a time, but it will return."

"We are here," said The Teacher, gently lowering the orb above the yard.

I unbuckled her chair and helped her stand. We descended within the light to return where I had arrived two hours earlier. We stood in the grass of a house I had never stepped foot in, but would be considered home if I did.

I hugged my mother good-bye for perhaps what would be the final time. "It's been so good seeing you again, Mom. I missed you so much."

She looked me over and asked, "You're not staying?"

"I can't, Mom. I don't belong here."

"Where are you going?"

"It's all in the book. After you read it, you'll understand why I can never return to my old life."

A frown tugged the corners of her mouth slightly before she quickly replaced it with a smile. "I guess I understand. I wouldn't want to be here either the way things are now in this world."

"I wish I could take you with me. You and Daddy. But your bodies... This way of life you've lived... they're too many toxins are in your blood and your minds. Neither of you would survive the trip to Nigiro."

"So we're from the planet *Nigger-o*?" she asked, laughing. "That sure is ironic that we're niggers after all, huh?"

"Not Nigger-o. It's pronounced, *Nee-JHEE-row*. They bastardized the name of the original people, and our planet, and then changed it into that offensive curse word nigger."

"Nee-JHEE-row... Nigiro," she repeated slowly, yet correctly this time. "That's all right..."

"I'm sorry I cannot stay longer. I would have loved to see daddy, too."

She nodded her resignation. "What about your little brother Stokely? Trying to carve out a life in St. Louis is harder than ever for a young black man. Since life is so great where you are, will you consider taking him with you?"

"I'll try…" In fact, Stokely was the next stop after dropping her off.

"*We must be leaving soon*," warned The Teacher.

My mother enveloped me with a loving embrace and kissed my cheek. "I'm so happy you're still with us. And I'm proud of you for pursuing your dream."

It was not my intent to ignore The Teacher, but I felt I had to clear up one misconception before leaving. "Mom, my dream wasn't to be abducted."

"Not getting stolen," she corrected, shaking her head. "You realized your dream of traveling through outer space. All you ever wanted when you were a child was to be up there. High above the clouds, soaring through the air like a bird on the wind. Traveling the universe and discovering new planets. Now look at you! You are an astronaut!"

"Mom, I am not an astronaut. But I have always wanted to know where I came from. Now, I do."

"Well, I'm still proud of you anyway." She stepped outside the stream of light. "My goodness! I cannot wait to tell your daddy about you! And I can't wait to read your book."

"I love you, Mommy," I said as she stepped back into her reality and away from mine. "Thank you for being my mother. And thank Daddy for being such a good father to me."

"I love you, baby." She tossed a kiss. "I'll tell him."

I gave a brief wave and forced a smile as I held my emotions in check. Last thing I wanted was a tearful good-bye.

"You'd better keep my child safe!" mother shouted at the orb, warning The Teacher, who paid her about as much attention as a genius would an imbecile. "She might be 'Braveheart' to you, but she is still my baby girl!"

With a heavy heart, I watched my mom return to her new home through the back door. Only this time she walked with her back straighter and held her head a little higher.

As much as I wanted to scoop up my entire family from the rat race of this evil society, they were not prepared for the journey. What gave me hope was my mother understood the monumental task she was charged with. Chances of her making it out of this physical realm unscathed were not good. However, I now understood that both she and my father would have another go at this thing called "life" if neither fully learned the lesson.

The Teacher retracted the light beam. I regained my position at the controls and slowly ascended to the heavens. I watched my parent's home for as long as I could before the house disappeared into the landscape thousands of feet below.

With my free hand, thinking of my mother, father, two earthly brothers, and all my family and friends who remained, I wiped away tears that continued to fall, as we made our way back to the mothership.

Epilogue

Nigiro is Paradise. This is a magnificent space where I can finally breathe freely. And love abounds within every soul I encounter. There is no such thing as Fear. Or Anger. Or Hatred. Or Strife. Life is now bliss.

In my compound, I am considered to be no more than a baby who has opened its eyes for the first time. I have so much to learn from my Elders, but thankfully, I now have a lifetime of which to learn it all. During my time here, I have met many incredibly talented Artists; some which I had a difficult time believing I was actually related. I had truly found a heaven I could believe in! I see The Teacher on occasion, but he is now charged with awakening another lost soul.

As for my parents, they both read my account and as anticipated, were skeptical. However, after some deliberation, they reached the conclusion my story was credible and should be distributed to as many family and friends as possible. They published the novel and subsequently handed it out. Some who received the book casually tossed it aside with a claim they did not read fiction. A few were turned off because of the similarity to religious bible stories, thus, considering it 'blasphemous'. Others placed the book in a pile to be read later, as did many who downloaded it from the internet, but never got around to reading it. They even gifted it to curious strangers who were drawn in only by the interesting title, *Out of Nigiro*. But there were a precious few who heeded the warnings of what was coming and acted accordingly.

At the end of the day, the Nigiro did as promised.

To Be Continued...

Made in United States
Orlando, FL
07 July 2022

19524246R00214